CODE OF CONDUCT

CIPHER SECURITY SERIES #1

APRIL WHITE

WWW.SMARTYPANTSROMANCE.COM

COPYRIGHT

DEDICATION

"There is boring. There is sensational. There is mediocre. There is lazy. There is good. There is evil. People do implausible things all the time, and they run the gamut of moderately weird to truly extraordinary. But there is no normal. The world is an unbelievable place full of unbelievable people doing unbelievable things."

- PENNY REID, *LOVE HACKED*

[1]

SHANE

"If you think they're cheating, they probably are. Or you are, and you're just trying to wipe your conscience." – Shane, P.I.

I intimidate people. It's one of my superpowers.

I learned the benefits of intimidation early. When I was thirteen, I was five feet-nine inches tall and could wield a well-timed glare like a weapon. Now in my late twenties and six-one, I had bravado, athletic ability, and superior survival skills to add to my arsenal of intimidating glares.

I also had a pretty badass array of prosthetic legs with cool functions and Swiss Army-type gadgets at my disposal, but most of my clients didn't realize they were getting Black Widow with an Iron Man leg when they hired me. And monogamy-impaired Chicagoans certainly had no idea who was coming for them.

Another superpower, my private investigator's license, added a little extra steel to my spine, which also helped disguise the limp that no amount of carefully-weighted titanium could erase.

The limp and the height were the reasons I'd arrived early to the little, out-of-the-way north side restaurant for my eharmony date with Chicago businessman Dane Quimby.

I say "date" because that's what he thought it was. To me it was a job with a high probability of being mostly unpleasant, but also served with a side dish of smug satisfaction.

I use the Black Widow analogy because of my Iron Man leg, but I grew up on a steady diet of Charlie's Angels reruns. Even though I'd been compared to Jaclyn Smith, the glamorous P.I., I was way more Kate Jackson, the athletic one. My own P.I. license had taken six thousand hours and a test to earn, and as far as I was concerned, the fact that it was only legal in California, where I'd lived until the previous year, was a technicality. To get a license in Illinois required a twenty-hour training course and forty hours of firearms training, neither of which I'd done. I wasn't a fan of guns, and I didn't really want my fingerprints on file with the State of Illinois, because … reasons.

So, there I was, waiting for a married guy to buy me dinner before he tried to get into my pants. They happened to be my favorite skinny jeans, with enough Lycra to make sitting possible without blood-flow constriction, and they were tucked into my super-favorite tall riding boots. The boots were flat and therefore comfortable. They also did a great job of hiding my prosthetic lower leg from casual judgment and stale notions of "handicaps." Someone would have to get me naked to know I was a below-the-knee amputee, and no one but my dog ever saw me naked.

Dane chose the location for our date, which was notable for its lack of pretension, a curvy waitress, and a cheap menu. I had nothing but respect for large-busted women, since I could only imagine the back pain and underwire bras they endured. I was just as happy with the two-dimes-and-a-piece-of-tape version of lingerie which kept my nipples from becoming a distraction that diminished my powers of intimidation.

The waitress greeted Dane with an enthusiastic kiss on the cheek when he came in, and I smirked at the difference between his internet dating profile picture and the truth of him.

My date for the evening was somewhat vertically challenged and sported blond from a bottle. He had the athletic build of a man who did his treadmill miles with the Nasdaq scrolling under his news, and the smile of a shark who negotiated deals for a living.

His eyes found me with just the slightest double-take, and I watched him take stock of all my visible body parts with a vertical visual sweep as he approached the table.

"Sophie?" he asked, wearing his attempt at a rakish grin. I didn't bother to point out the bit of something green stuck in his teeth. Sophie wasn't my real name, of course. I am far too paranoid to use verifiable information on the internet, and a name came with a degree of identifiability that was outside my comfort zone – my comfort zone encompassing all four U.S. time zones.

I held my hand out to shake his. "Hello, Dane. It's nice to finally meet you." Dane was obviously not paranoid enough, or just exceptionally cocky, as that actually was his real name. His wife hired me to discover if he'd been cheating on her, and it had only taken three internet searches and fifteen minutes to determine that he was on four dating websites and was practically a platinum member of Tinder.

He sat down across from me and shook his head with a chuckle. "You look exactly like your picture. I guess that means everything else in your profile is true?"

It had taken me twenty minutes to hack into the website and data-mine his search histories, and another ten to build a profile to match his wish list. "Yes, I really am a tantric yoga instructor. Doesn't everyone tell the truth online?" I said with nary a blink.

He licked his lips, and I felt queasy. "I can't really talk about my time in Special Forces, so I guess you could say my profile is true-ish."

It had taken thirty minutes of background checks using mostly public databases to determine he'd left the military in disgrace. "Oh, wow. Were you, like, a spy or something?"

He chuckled. "You're from California, aren't you?"

Smile. Blink. "I basically grew up on the beach." I'd grown up backpacking in the Sierras, but I threw the guy a bone and added a bikini to his mental image of me.

"I always thought I should live in Cali," he said. "I'd work out on

3

the strand like those guys in Venice Beach, and be friends with movie stars."

The effort not to laugh out loud was costing me. "I've seen those guys in Venice. You'd fit right in," I simpered. My first job as an insurance investigator had been in Venice, and I'd had to navigate sneering gangbangers and strung-out homeless guys every day. Also, no one in California *ever* called it Cali.

He held up a finger and did the "I'll have what she's having" thing to order a drink like mine. I smirked at the waitress's raised eyebrow. Wouldn't he be surprised when he got sparkling water with lime instead of the vodka tonic he thought I had?

"You must wonder what attracted me to you," Dane said with a knowing smile.

Actually, I was mentally calculating my billable hours and hoping to be done here in less than thirty minutes because ... round numbers. "You read my mind," I said with a low, breathy voice. To my own ears I sounded asthmatic, but experience had taught me that horny guys dug breathless women.

Dane set his cell phone on the table next to him, screen up, so I'd see how very important he was when he got all those calls and texts he was expecting. A call from a number I recognized as his wife's flashed on the screen as the phone buzzed, and he quickly declined it.

"Your profile says you're looking for uncomplicated with a side of kinky," Dane said, leaning forward to trace the path of ice sweat down the side of my glass. His meaningful glance was all *imagine me doing this to you*, and I barely suppressed a shudder as I forced a languid smile.

"I guess that's one way to interpret my profile," I said. *The other way is to actually read the words, dumbass, which said I like simple pleasures and I'm open to trying new things.* I pushed my drink away because he'd touched it and now his cooties coated it like crap smears on a public toilet. Dane took the gesture as an invitation to share, because he was presumptuous like that. He slid his hand down the outside of the sweaty glass with a suggestive wink. This guy had *all* the moves.

4

"So, tell me about tantric yoga." His hand fisted up and down the glass before he took a big gulp. To his credit, he hid his shock at the bubbly lime-water well, but I shot the waitress a grateful smile when she set the fresh drink down in front of me.

"Are you ready to order?" she asked. Dane was about to answer, but I quickly interrupted.

"Could I have a minute?"

"Sure, take your time," said Tiffani, with an "i" dotted by a smiley face sticker. She walked away with the self-assured hip-sway of a woman who knows her own appeal.

I turned my gaze back to Dane and answered his question with a slow, seductive smile. "Imagine the possibilities of a person who can hold her leg behind her head."

I conveniently forgot to mention that said leg wouldn't actually be attached to the rest of me at the time. I pictured my peg leg prosthetic resting on my shoulder like a wooden bat. Of course I had a peg leg prosthetic, because who wouldn't?

Dane thought my low chuckle was for him, and I could just imagine the mental images with which he was torturing himself. And because the thought of giving him even a moment of pleasure was approximately as appealing as sucking all the snot out of a dog's nose, I changed the subject.

"Tell me about yourself, Dane. What do you do? I mean now that you're out of Special Forces, there must be something you do besides work out."

He actually preened. "Oh, you know, I dabble in web development, mostly for social media."

This guy was awesome! What he really did, according to my background check and an hour's worth of research on his company, was sell digital ad space. It explained his confidence in the ex-Special Forces cover, because if you could sell the promise of eyeballs – not the actual eyeballs themselves, mind you, just the possibility that x-amount of people *might* look at your thing for the two seconds it takes to scroll past it – you could probably sell birth control pills to your Great-Aunt Fanny.

"You must be really good at computers," I purred. Actually, I was trying not to giggle and had to drop my voice to keep from choking.

"Oh yeah, baby. I'm the best."

Seriously, how had this guy ever gotten laid? *Ever.*

"Are you on Tinder?" I thought about batting my eyelashes, but decided I'd probably blink out a contact lens.

"Of course I am. Aren't you?"

I shook my head and bit my bottom lip. I'd practiced the move in a mirror once and thought it made me look dim, but apparently dim was like catnip to men who lied to get laid. I looked at his phone. "Can I see your profile? I've been trying to decide if I want to join."

His grin went wide, and he quickly unlocked his phone for me. "Sure," he said, as he scooted closer and showed me the app. "You get in like this, and see, here's my profile."

"That's a great picture," I said. "You look super fit." *In the ten-year-old photo.*

"I know, right? I get a lot of matches with that pic."

"Do you mind if I scroll around for a minute, just to look?" I asked sweetly.

He waved his hand at me. "Go ahead. Just don't swipe right on any ugly chicks."

Just for that I'd be swiping right on the biggest, most redneck, *Deliverance*-looking guy I could find.

Tiffani approached the table again. "What can I get you, Dane?"

I silently blessed her for her timing, and after my right-swipe on Junior No-Teeth, I navigated to Dane's Notes app, and about a second later air-dropped the whole file to my own phone. He had three banking apps in his office folder, and I clicked on one randomly. The account name was ADDATA, which was his business, so I switched to the next one. Dane was ordering something off-menu with a whole bunch of substitutions, so I took a minute to look back through his notes.

I had been counting on Dane's arrogance and the simple statistics of probability, and neither one disappointed. The Notes app from his phone included a page of account information and passwords, which listed, among other vital things, his social security number and all his banking passwords. It took only a few more seconds to find Dane's private bank account – the one which his wife suspected paid for his "entertainment" – and another minute to transfer half of the rather large sum of money into an account she'd already set up in her name. The wife had wanted to take it all, but I convinced her that a cornered dog was likely to bite, and she'd have a better chance of getting away with it if she left him some operating cash.

"Hey," Dane said suddenly. I cursed myself for jumping as I pasted a smile on my face. "Since you have my phone, you should just put your number in my contacts."

"Oh, sure. Do you want me to put it under my first or my last name?" I was pretty sure the answer would be neither, and he confirmed my suspicions.

"Just leave it open to that page, and I'll add your name."

I typed in the number to my favorite bankruptcy specialist as he finished up his elaborate, high-maintenance order with Tiffani, and then I slid the phone across the table to him.

Tiffani stood patiently, waiting for me to order. "I just need another minute. Go ahead and put his order in, okay?"

She shrugged charmingly. "Sure. I'll get his appetizer started."

"So, what do you think about Tinder?" Dane asked with a slow wink.

I bit my lip again and realized I'd chewed off all my lip balm in my attempts to appear unthreatening. Dry lips were my kryptonite, so I re-applied and took enough time so it seemed like a tease. "I've heard it can be hacked, and that makes me nervous. You seem pretty confident about putting your information online, though."

He shrugged. "Oh yeah, my company has the best private security money can buy. No one can touch me without setting off alarms all over the place."

I was about to ask about such mythical security, but just then Dane's phone rang. *Cipher Security Systems* flashed on the screen as he picked it up.

"Speak of the devil," he said with a grin. "I'll just be a minute." He answered the phone with a deep voice. "This is Dane," he said importantly.

I looked up at Tiffani and said quietly, "I don't think I can eat anything, thanks." I'd heard about Cipher Security Systems, and they actually were pretty mythical. They were the kind of company banks used to check for hacking vulnerabilities. I hadn't thought Dane's business was big enough to rate that kind of protection.

Someone spoke briefly, and Dane answered. "At the Northside Cafe, why?"

My gut clenched in a way that usually signaled lactose intolerance or an attack of the flu. I didn't like any association between Dane Quimby and Cipher Security Systems, much less one that placed me in Dane's proximity.

I stood up to pull a twenty out of my back pocket, and Dane's eyes widened as they followed me up and up and up. He scowled and covered the phone again. "Where are you going?"

I nodded toward the phone in his hand. "You're busy, and I have to prep for a colonoscopy tomorrow."

He made a face and spoke into the phone again. "Hang on," he snarled. Then he covered the mouthpiece again. "When can I see you?"

I brightened. "Why don't I find you on Tinder and we can look for men to share."

He frowned. "To share? But I'm not gay."

I put on my saddest face. "You're not? Oh, that's too bad, because I am."

Before he could untangle that ridiculous parting shot, I handed Tiffani the twenty as I headed for the door. "Thanks, Tiffani," I said brightly. "Keep the change."

"What happened to your leg?" she asked. "You okay?"

She must have seen my limp, and she looked sweetly concerned. Dane was still on his phone, and I could hear his voice rising angrily in the background. "What do you mean you'll be right here? Why?"

"Oh yeah, it's nothing. Just a shark bite," I said with a quick glance back at Dane before I stepped outside into the evening twilight.

I'd taken about five strides down the sidewalk when a big, black

SUV barreled around the corner and screeched to a stop in front of the restaurant. The passenger shot out of his seat and stalked into the building so fast I barely caught a glimpse of a good suit and neck tattoos. The driver was still in his seat, and I could see his eyes on me in the side view mirror.

Something in those eyes locked my knees in place and forbade my legs to move.

Then the driver opened the car door and was out on the sidewalk facing me before I could exhale. I catalogued my options. Bond? Bond Girl? Or Bond Villain? I knew I looked good, and I could charm my way out of most situations, so Bond Girl was on the table. I'd worn a special knife holster on the titanium shaft of my prosthetic leg, invisible inside my boot, which gave me Bond powers of attack and defense. But I'd just emptied Dane's private cootchie fund of half-a-million dollars and transferred it to his wife as payment for fifteen years of services rendered. So Bond Villain seemed appropriate too.

Then I took a breath and actually *looked* at the man on the sidewalk in front of me.

He wasn't much taller or older than me, which made him about six-two or -three and put him in his early thirties. He wore a sharp, black suit tailored to make his shoulder-to-hip ratio look like an inverted triangle, which made me think quarterback instead of linebacker. He stood like a cop and dressed like a CEO, which made me think private security. If this was Cipher, I was in trouble.

An aura of power radiated from the man like wavy heat above a desert road. It didn't help my temperature that the guy's Idris Elba smolder threatened to set my skin and various articles of clothing on fire. For one insanity-filled moment, I imagined casually walking over and introducing myself.

I must have flinched, because his hand twitched toward a holster he wasn't actually wearing. Then reality intruded on the fantasy. I was a Caucasian female alone in a predominantly Puerto Rican neighborhood in Logan Square, having just committed something akin to a felony, albeit justly deserved, standing in front of a guy who probably used to be in some form of law enforcement.

And perhaps because I must have truly gone insane, I smiled at him. It was pure reflex, like the sigh at a spectacular sunset or the grin at a child's laughter. He very nearly took a step toward me, then seemed to come to his senses and halted in place. It was at this point that I compounded my idiocy by accidentally waving to him as I turned to hurry away down the street.

Who waves at the guy who could probably bust her butt ten ways from Tuesday?

Finally, cold logic, survival skills, and James Bond took over control of my hands. I powered down my phone, took out the battery, and tucked both into my back pockets as I walked. I also ducked down an alley and circled back on myself twice. I never carried a purse if I could help it – my phone, keys, a credit card, my Ventra card for the CTA, lip balm, and two twenties were all I ever had on me.

I half expected squealing tires and slamming doors to find me before I got to Fullerton, but remarkably, I made it onto my bus unimpeded. My heart still pounded uncomfortably in my chest as I dropped into a seat, and it annoyed me that I had reacted so strongly. Was it because the philandering asshat I'd just relieved of five hundred grand had connections to Cipher Security, or was it the Man in Black who had made my stomach clench in a way that was decidedly *not* like lactose intolerance or the flu? I was almost grateful for the two young hoods who sat down across from me and leered suggestively.

Seriously boys? That's all you've got? I front-loaded disdain into my pointed glare until they got up and slid down the bus, leaving me alone with my slamming heart.

I'd just hijacked Dane Quimby's phone and moved half his money into his wife's account. How long until someone connected the dots between my "date" with Dane and the missing money?

I absently rubbed the skin above my leg socket and let my head fall against the window. I might have even tapped my head against the glass a couple of times to drown out the whooshing sound of impending doom that filled my ears.

[2]
GABRIEL

"You have to be smarter than them, talk softer, smile bigger, and let all the words roll off your back. It'll be hard, son, but someday you'll find someone who wants to see your light, and when you do, you're going to shine." – Miri Eze

---

Who the bloody hell was that?

I took another step forward, but she was already walking away – fast, as though she had a place to be. She had on tall riding boots and had a slight hitch in her gait, and I almost got back in the car to offer her a ride. But that was madness stemming from an overactive protective gene I seemed to have developed along with a penchant for self-destructive behavior, so I ignored the instinct. It didn't matter how nice the suit was, a black man in an SUV did not offer a ride to a beautiful white girl he didn't know, not even when the man in question had a British accent and an Oxford education. At a minimum, she'd call the police, and I did not need to explain my misguided chivalrous instincts to Chicago's finest tonight.

"You alright, man? Why'd you stay outside?" O'Malley asked as he stepped out of the restaurant. Dan O'Malley had the Boston accent and tattoos of a thug, but the generosity of a gentleman. He'd been showing me the ropes at Cipher since I'd come on board, and he was one of those people who made the new bloke feel welcome without doing anything in particular to show it.

His voice broke the spell I was under, and I tore my eyes away from the excellent view disappearing around the corner. "I'm fine. What's your opinion of Quimby?"

"Well, Quinn's been phasing out private clients, and this one's definitely on the block. Alex is taking a look at the numbers, but my gut says the guy's a fucking mess. His company's hemorrhaging stockholders like rats from a sinking ship, and guys who cheat on their wives lie like shag rugs. The liability's too high for us to keep untrustworthy clients."

"How do we know he cheats?" I hadn't read the file yet and wondered if fidelity was a usual part of Cipher's client profiles.

O'Malley gestured inside the restaurant. "The waitress said he brings a different woman in about once a week. Last one just left, actually."

I tried to shrug off the unaccountable feeling of disappointment at the thought that the lovely bird with the spectacular rear-view had already been claimed.

"The account breech that called us here is going to jack this up, since he's still technically our client and he's got one of the old insurance policies, which means we pay if we can't protect. Hopefully we can wade through the shit and figure it out. Come on, you should meet him, get a feel for his rating on the dickhead scale."

I followed O'Malley inside and wondered how any man, much less a married one, thought he could shag a girl after a date here. The waitress was Caucasian, in her early twenties, and wore a practiced pout. The bloke I assumed was Quimby sat at a table in the corner, scrolling manically through his phone. He was probably about my age, also Caucasian, and handsome enough to make up for being short in a tall man's world. His date had looked to be over six feet tall, and this bloke didn't seem like he had the confidence to pull that off. A mystery to ponder some other time, perhaps.

We approached the table, and Quimby looked up with a wide-eyed expression that had shades of panic in it. His quick glance dismissed me and landed on O'Malley.

"It's gone!" He sounded as though someone had his stones in a vice.

O'Malley didn't say a word, just arched an eyebrow and waited. A good tactic, and one I'd used often during my tenure with the Royal MPs. I wondered idly if he'd ever been with the police.

Quimby nearly shrieked. "My money! It's gone!"

The waitress looked over at us from the salt shakers she was refilling, and I gave her an easy smile. She looked away quickly and went back into the kitchen.

"Calm down, Mr. Quimby," said O'Malley as he pulled out his phone. "Why don't you tell Mr. Eze the details while I get our tech person on the line." O'Malley pronounced my name with the proper "Ayzay" inflection that told me he had a good ear for language.

Quimby continued talking to him as though I wasn't in the room. It was a standard attempt to establish hierarchy that I routinely ignored. "I have an account at National. It's been emptied," he said.

"How much is missing, Mr. Quimby?" I asked.

He seemed startled by my accent, then glared and spoke to O'Malley again. "There was a million dollars in that account!"

O'Malley turned his back and walked away a few steps to speak on the phone. I knew he was doing it on purpose, and it seemed to infuriate Quimby.

"So, how much is actually missing?" My voice was deep, and I usually spoke quietly enough that people had to lean closer to hear me – a useful tool for gathering information about everything from unfortunate personal hygiene to lipstick or blood splatter on a collar.

Quimby glared at me. "Who are you?"

"Gabriel Eze with Cipher Security."

"I don't know you. I'm going to wait until he's off the phone so I don't have to repeat myself."

I shrugged. "As you wish."

I adopted an at-ease posture and studied the table Quimby had shared with … someone. I had no proof it was the lovely bird, but it was she I pictured sitting across from him. A barely-touched glass of sparkling water with a wedge of lime sat in a small puddle of ice-sweat on the table. She'd had at least one sip, but the sides of the glass were wet enough to make fingerprints unusable. She wore some sort of lip balm rather than lipstick, which, for some reason, made me think of pretty young girls and athletes instead of mistresses.

The chair had been pushed a significant distance back from the table, as though a tall person had been seated there. I studied the chair-back and saw a few strands of long brown hair caught in a crack in the wood. Again, totally circumstantial – the hair could have been there for months – but the bird outside was a brunette, with thick hair she'd worn down past her shoulders. I pictured it up in a sloppy ponytail, or long and loose, spread across a pillow, and I had to shake myself sharply to concentrate on Quimby again.

Why him? Why would she choose him? Unless …

"May I see your phone, Mr. Quimby?" I asked just as O'Malley returned to the table.

"I'm not giving you my phone!" he spat.

"Give him the fucking phone, Quimby. We have to talk." O'Malley sounded tired and disgusted, which was no mean feat for a man whom, despite his colorful vocabulary, I'd only ever seen behave like a professional.

O'Malley's tone startled Quimby, and he shoved the phone across the table at me through puddles left behind by wet glasses. I didn't pick it up. It would be a cold day in hell before I wiped the water off on a tailored suit.

The phone was unlocked and on the home screen, so I navigated to the call icon. The screen opened to a blank contact containing a phone number but no name. I memorized the number and then searched the recent call list. There were three missed calls from "home," then about ten minutes after the last one, O'Malley's call. I took a screenshot of

14

his call list, air-dropped it to myself, and then navigated back to the home screen and slid the phone back across the table.

O'Malley was just barely keeping his temper in check, if the jaw muscle flexing with every clench of his teeth was any indication. "Exactly how much is left in the account that you claim no one knew about?"

Quimby's voice was back up to glass-shattering levels. "Five hundred thou."

I started chuckling as I dialed the number I'd memorized from his contact list. "Half," I said under my breath.

"You think it's funny to have half a mil stolen from an account I worked damn hard to fill, Easy?" Quimby squeaked angrily. Calling me Easy rather than correctly pronouncing Eze with long "a" sounds was another tactic I'd come to expect from men with dominance issues. I also noted that he said fill, not earn, but I ignored him as the ringing phone in my ear was picked up by an answering machine.

"You've reached Cheatham and Howe, *the* divorce and bankruptcy specialists of the greater Chicago area. Please leave a message—"

I hung up and my chuckle turned into full-on laughter as I jerked my head at O'Malley, indicating we should leave.

"We'll be in touch, Quimby," he said to the cocky bastard as he followed me out of the restaurant.

"What's so funny?" O'Malley asked as I climbed behind the wheel of the SUV.

"It was the wife, and she must have used the girlfriend to do it." I told him about the phone number, the wife's calls, and the fact that exactly half of the money was gone.

O'Malley looked impressed by my assessment, and he chuckled as I drove away from the curb. "Serves him fucking right for bangin' someone else's bongo."

[3]
SHANE

*"*P*ay attention to how he treats waiters and animals. How he treats waiters is how he'll eventually treat you. How he treats animals is the way he'll treat your kids."* – Shane, P.I.

Oscar was the world's most dominant dog. I inherited the Bernese mountain dog from my neighbor in L.A. who couldn't train him because the dog believed he was the boss of her. Oscar and I had settled on a fairly comfortable roommate situation, rather than master/beast, and sharing my apartment with him had made me a much better housekeeper – and shot – than I used to be. It was either hit the laundry basket with the socks and underwear every time, or find them in his poop the next day.

He greeted me with his usual dangerous exuberance, and I braced myself for impact as all one hundred pounds of him leapt straight up in the air like a bouncy puppy. I pushed past him to drop my keys and phone in the kitchen, then made my way to the bedroom to pull off my boots, jeans, and leg. Oscar waited until I flung myself back on the pillow before he jumped up, licked my face, then stretched out next to me for properly worshipful scratches.

I hadn't been able to shut my brain off since I left the restaurant. Cipher Security had called Dane exactly three minutes after I'd transferred the money out of his account, and they were at the restaurant five minutes later. That was scary effectiveness.

I sat up and pulled my laptop off the nightstand. I did my work in bed, mostly because it was easier for Oscar to sit next to me there, and the bulk of it was internet research anyway. Cipher Security Systems had a simple, straightforward website, which wasn't a surprise. They specialized in designing custom security systems for financial institutions, universities, hospitals, and any large corporation with significant assets. It seemed to me that Dane's mid-sized internet advertising company was on the small side of Cipher's business model.

There were no photos of Cipher employees – also not a surprise – so there was no way to confirm that the guy I couldn't stop thinking about actually worked there. There was, however, a photo of Cipher's owner, Quinn Sullivan, standing next to a dangerous-looking guy with neck tattoos who looked familiar. Since a very simple search on their part would show that the time of the bank transfer coincided with my "date" with Dane Quimby, I thought I should know who I might be up against.

Cipher had several mentions in the news, but all of the articles just confirmed what I already knew – I didn't want them on my tail.

I disabled the internal wireless router on the laptop, then plugged in the external hard drive on which I kept my client files. I would admit to having a high degree of paranoia, but I knew what kind of unauthorized entries and data extractions *I* could affect, and my hacking skills were fair-to-middling at best.

I extracted the Quimby file from the external drive, then made my private notes about the encounter with Dane. I pulled Dane's Notes file off my phone via thumb drive and added it to the Quimby file, scrolling through quickly to see if there were any other financial sources that his wife might not know about.

Mostly, the notes contained numbers – gym memberships, airline miles clubs, pin codes, passwords, his passport number, and, I kid you not, his mother's maiden name. I was honestly shocked that he had any money left at all.

I shrugged, and Oscar grunted at the disturbance of his very important nap. I absently scratched his belly as I navigated to the Denise Quimby billing sheet, added the hour and forty minutes door-to-door that my rendezvous with Dane had taken, subtracted ten minutes for the sake of the round number, and created her final invoice, minus her deposit, payable by check to S. HANE Information Services. I then saved the invoice in my billing file, moved the case file back onto the password protected external drive, disconnected that, and then reconnected the laptop's wireless router so I could e-mail Denise Quimby her final bill.

Shane wasn't actually my real name any more than Sophie, but it was what everyone called me. Not that *everyone* was a lot of people, or more than ten actually, not counting clients. My list of friends could safely be counted on two hands and did not, for example, include the Vietnamese food delivery boy, who knew me as Miss Hane, or the Armenian family who ran the market and deli where I shopped every other day.

Shane was who I'd been since I left home. It wasn't on my high school diploma, my college transcripts, my passport, or my P.I. license, but it was who I'd chosen to be. I wasn't searchable, identifiable, or easily found as Shane, so when I answered to it, the person asking was always someone I trusted.

I shifted Oscar off my thigh, and he grumbled but cracked an eyelid open to watch me. I hopped across to the dresser and grabbed a pair of tights that I'd modified for my prosthetic leg, and by modified I meant cut off. They fit just over the silicone liner that rolled onto my residual limb like a giant condom and attached to the leg socket with a pin locking mechanism. The modified cheetah leg I wore for running was one of my favorite prosthetics, not counting the fake nose I sometimes used when I needed a disguise for work.

A black hoodie went on over my head, and I laced up my left running shoe. Once a year I sent a box of right men's size nines to Wounded Warrior Project, and last year I got a letter back from a

19

twenty-year-old kid thanking me for the great shoe. It inspired him to try running again, he said, which made me smile for a whole month.

Oscar's head had perked up when he saw the cheetah leg, but the shoe going on was his cue to race me to the door.

I liked to run by the lake after dark, the closer to midnight the better. Street traffic had slowed to almost nothing by that point, and even the homeless were mostly asleep. I stuck to bike paths for the smooth surface, and wasn't worried about things that went bump in the night because physical therapy had made me strong and fast, and because Oscar was a deterrent for most predators. To me, a five-mile run by streetlight was like releasing the steam from a pressure cooker. It was always the most peaceful part of my day.

The early spring night was clear, and a breeze came in off the lake. I went south on the Lakefront Trail toward Waveland Park, and I let the wind push me into a nearly six-minute-mile pace. Oscar kept up with me easily enough, and we both reveled in the feeling of flying down the paved trail.

I spent the first mile clearing my head of noise – not so hard to do at nearly midnight on a Tuesday. I listened to the step-slap of my running shoe and the blade of my cheetah leg, heard my breath punctuate Oscar's panting, and was dimly aware of the distant sound of nighttime traffic. When the scope of my world had narrowed to the sounds in it, I expanded it to include the shapes of trees, of streetlights, and in the distance, the skyscrapers of the Loop. Anything that moved caught my attention – car headlights on Lake Shore Drive, a rabbit scampering away from the sounds of the dog, and in the distance, down the trail, someone on a bicycle heading toward me.

I saw midnight cyclists occasionally, but they were rare, and I tightened my grip on Oscar's leash. Bicycles and skateboards were approximately as welcome in his world as lice and misogynists were in mine.

This offender was a racing bike, with the clip-in pedal system that always made me slightly tense when I imagined stoplights and pedestrians. The rider had no headlamp or light of any kind, just a few strips of reflective tape on the forks of the bike. To be fair, I was dressed in head-to-toe black too, but I was attached to an unmistakably large black and white dog, and there was enough silver on my cheetah leg to catch headlights as needed.

When our encounter became inevitable, I hugged the far right of the path to keep Oscar's lunge out of range. I should have stopped and pulled him off the path entirely, but I was at mile three and had just hit the sweet spot in my run. It was a perfect storm – I hit a hole in the grass with my blade and stumbled, which loosened my grip on the leash just as Oscar lunged to demand that the bike yield to his superior size. He traveled farther than he meant to, and the cyclist swerved to avoid the impact of a hundred pounds of indignant dog. And, because the cyclist's feet were clipped into those damn racing pedals, he couldn't drop them for balance and had nowhere to go but down.

So down he went in a spectacular crash of man over handlebars and bicycle over man. His feet did finally unclip from the pedals somewhere in the cartwheel of man and machine, but it was a brutal thing to witness, and a giant cavern of dread took up residence in my chest.

I yanked hard on Oscar's leash and barked at him, "STAY!" The rider was curled on one side, facing away from me, and the bike had landed a few yards beyond him. One wheel was bent and the other was spinning like a bad cartoon.

"Are you okay?" I gasped as I knelt beside him and put a hand out to his shoulder. He was wearing a helmet, thank God, but in the dark I couldn't tell where his black clothes ended and blood might begin.

The guy moved slowly, tentatively, as though testing for pain before straightening his joints. It took a few agonizing seconds before he finally rolled onto his back.

"Oh!" I stumbled backward, lost my balance, and my butt hit the ground. Oscar came to my side immediately, giving the vanquished bicycle a wide berth. I grabbed his leash before he could investigate the man on the ground, as I attempted to regain coherent thought.

The man I'd just caused bodily harm to was the possible Cipher Security agent from outside the restaurant where I'd had my "date" with Dane Quimby. He would undoubtedly recognize me – unless he was concussed and/or would die without speaking.

"What the hell are *you* doing here?" he growled in a deep voice laced with a British accent I could've listened to for days. I guessed a mute death had been too much to hope for. That he recognized me was oddly comforting, because maybe he'd been thinking about me like I'd been thinking about him, but it wasn't good, particularly as my prosthetic leg was currently parked about three feet from his face, making me far too identifiable for someone with a reason to find me.

"Causing you injury, clearly." There was too much sass in my tone for the circumstances, but he'd scared me, and I got defensive when I felt cornered. I took a breath and tried again. "Are you as badly hurt as you should be?"

"As I should be? You were *trying* to take me out?" His voice was too quiet for the depth of it, and even with the edge in his clipped accent, I wanted to lean in to catch his words. I shook myself out of the thrall.

"If I'd tried to take you out, you'd be in the lake." I was proud of my matter-of-fact tone, even if I sounded like a twelve-year-old. *I know you are, but what am I?*

His eyes flashed dangerously, and I scooted backwards out of his reach. It was an automatic reaction to a perceived threat, but it drew his attention, and his gaze darted to my prosthetic leg.

"What happened?" he asked, probably before he could stop himself. Most people did that – asked reflexive questions without really wanting to know the actual story.

"Crushed in a thresher," I answered automatically.

His eyebrows furrowed, and then his mouth twitched as if he were trying not to smile. Who smiled at an amputation story? Granted, it wasn't my story, but still – who smiled at that?

"Right. Well …" He pulled himself to a sitting position, wincing as he did. "We'll see if I need one of those after this." He winced again and held his breath as he tried, and failed, to stand.

"Hang on," I said, scrambling to my feet. I held out a hand and braced myself.

He hesitated too long before he reached for my hand, and I was oddly insulted. Because I was female? Or white? Or "disabled?" Why hesitate to accept my help?

When he did finally take my hand, I had to resist the urge to snatch it away again. His hand was too big, too warm, too male, just ... *too*. I pulled harder than I needed to, and he rose easily, if a little gingerly, to his feet.

He let go of me the moment he was upright, and I automatically wiped my palm on my tights to erase the memory of *too much*. It didn't work, except that he noticed, and the line of his mouth tightened. Was it from pain, or did he imagine I wouldn't want his touch?

I almost reached for him again, but then I stepped back and nearly stumbled over Oscar, who had completed the grass-sniffing task on his to-do list and sat down behind me. "Oscar was protecting me from your bike," I said inanely.

The man picked his bicycle up off the path. "How noble of him." There was a bite of well-deserved sarcasm in his tone, and I clamped a metaphorical hand over my mouth to keep from answering in kind.

He was moving slowly, but I was amazed he moved at all. "What hurts?" I asked.

"My pride. Everything else will hurt tomorrow." He hefted the bike to his shoulder and started to walk south. He went about ten steps, then stopped and looked back at me.

"Are you coming?"

I stared at him. "What? Why?"

"So you can tell me about Dane Quimby." His voice had dropped so far down in volume I almost jogged up to him just to make sure I didn't miss any words. I resisted, but just barely.

"I don't know a Dane Quimby." I resorted to belligerence to cover up the feeling of being cornered again.

His eyes narrowed, and he studied me with a full up-and-down gaze that made my heart beat faster and my palms sweat. I rubbed my right hand absently against my tights, which brought his gaze back to my cheetah leg.

"He didn't know about the leg, did he?" His voice thrummed deeply, and I felt it in my chest.

"I don't know what you're talking about." I did know, I just couldn't admit to any of it, because once I did, I'd admit all of it.

23

"Quimby's too shallow. Even a stunner like you couldn't get past his idea of perfection with that."

I couldn't decide whether I should be insulted or flattered, so I was both – and neither. And I waited. Even Oscar stood silently at my side while I debated my next move.

He didn't seem to need an answer and nodded to himself as he spoke out loud. "You're also too tall for him, so you didn't meet him in person. A blind date? Unlikely. Quimby doesn't do blind. Online, then. That's it. You found him, made him think you were his type so he'd meet you, and then you got in and moved his money."

I felt my insides flutter in an idiotic reaction to his deductive skills, and I crossed my arms in front of me like the tough girl I definitely wasn't feeling. "You done?" I cocked my head at him and hoped I sounded more confident than I felt.

He smiled, and the fluttering intensified, sending tendrils of heat to my skin. "Not nearly. You?"

I arched an eyebrow at him. It was a move I'd perfected as part of my intimidation repertoire. My thirteen-year-old self had practiced in a mirror until disdain oozed from my eyes when the eyebrow went up. I wondered whether it was as effective without the disdain, since I couldn't seem to muster any for this man.

"Maybe." I had no idea what I was equivocating about, but he wasn't going to win this … whatever it was.

"With Quimby?"

I shuddered involuntarily. "Definitely."

His smile got bigger and held the glint of something … appreciative? "See you around, then." He turned and continued walking down the path, the wrecked bicycle on his shoulder as if it weighed nothing.

See me around? How? He didn't know my name, didn't know anything about me. Chicago was a big city. How in the hell did he think he was going to see me around?

I watched him for another ten steps, half-expecting him to turn back and speak to me again.

He didn't, and I was absurdly disappointed.

[4]
GABRIEL

"Speak up or risk becoming background noise." – Kendra Eze

I woke up feeling like I'd been beaten with a cricket bat.

Nothing was broken that I could tell, but one whole side of my body felt like a slab of meat to which someone had taken a tenderizing mallet, and the bruises would be a sight in a couple of days.

The alarm went off on my mobile phone – currently set to the *Hamilton* soundtrack, which amused my twin, Kendra, to no end. She laughed at my show tunes, but I just shrugged and turned them up louder.

An image of the beautiful brunette with the bloody dangerous dog suddenly filled my head, and I had the thought that I wouldn't mind if she knew I sang to *Hamilton* in the shower. Which led to thoughts of her in a shower, which led to thoughts … and a long time spent in the shower having those thoughts.

The hot shower did make me feel better about the bruises, at least until I walked into the kitchen table and had to swear a streak so blue my mum would have reached for a flip-flop if I'd been in her flat. It was either that or cry, and I didn't cry.

After a painkillers-and-coffee breakfast and quick heart emoji proof-of-life texts to Kendra and Mum, I made my way downtown to the main office of Cipher Security Systems. Stan raised his coffee cup to me as I passed his desk in the lobby. All agents put time in at the front desk, and my three days there the week prior had been a much-appreciated chance to catch up on the latest *Rivers of London* mystery.

"O'Malley wants to see you," Stan said gruffly. He had the face and physique of a prize-fighter, but I suspected a jelly-filled center under the hard exterior.

"Right," I said. I squared my shoulders and decidedly *did not* limp to the elevator.

Dan O'Malley and Quinn Sullivan were equal partners in Cipher Security, though they oversaw different elements of the business. Sullivan was the corporate face who regularly took meetings in Washington, New York, and London with CEOs, heads of banks, and high-powered government officials. O'Malley was the head of operations, and he preferred to be the man on the street. Given the direction Sullivan had been taking the company, there was far less street and far more boardroom to cover, but O'Malley had an instinct for dirty dealing, white or blue collar, that put the finest police forces to shame.

Sullivan was in O'Malley's office when I knocked on the door, and they both looked up from the files they held. O'Malley said to Sullivan, by way of explanation, "Gabriel came up with the girlfriend-stole-for-the-wife theory on the missing money, and I feel like it's the right call."

"I assume Quimby called in local law enforcement?"

O'Malley shook his head. "Shit-heel says he wants us to handle it. Says he has an insurance clause with us that makes it as much our problem as his."

Sullivan looked pained. "He's not wrong. ADDATA was one of our first contracts, from the days when we were hungry for corporate business. Unless we can prove criminality on Quimby's part, we insured any assets we agreed to protect."

O'Malley looked pointedly at me to weigh in, so I did. "Honestly, it would be difficult for him to bring the police in as his mobile appears to have been the access point. Not that it would have been particularly difficult otherwise as he has no password security and easy entry to banking applications. If the transfer had been made via hack we could have stopped it. As it was, we were aware of it the moment the money was moved and we contacted him immediately. Apparently we missed the girlfriend by only a few minutes, though I believe I may have seen her outside the restaurant when we arrived."

O'Malley looked up from the file he was holding. "What'd she look like?"

"Caucasian female, about six feet tall, long brunette hair, perhaps late-twenties, wearing denim jeans, boots, and a gray sweater."

O'Malley snorted. "No way a piss-ant like Quimby'd date a tall chick. He's maybe five-eight and doesn't have the fucking balls."

"Unless he met her online and last night was their first face-to-face encounter," I said quietly.

Sullivan addressed me. "Find out what you can about the girlfriend."

O'Malley added, "Use Alex for the internet shit if you need to. He digs kicking over digital rocks to expose all the fucking creepers to the light."

Sullivan held out his hand to shake mine. "You were military police before joining the Peacekeepers, right?"

"Royal Military Police for three years, UN Peacekeeper in Ethiopia and Cambodia for two."

O'Malley looked at me oddly. "You spent time in Nigeria though."

"With forces from that country. Not on an official mission." Sullivan no doubt saw my hand tighten on the back of the chair, but he said nothing.

O'Malley merely nodded. "Nigeria is where you met Fiona Archer?" he asked, citing the name of a former CIA agent I knew was a personal friend of theirs.

"That's correct."

Sullivan clapped me on the shoulder. "Good. I'm glad she

connected you with us, and I appreciate you taking the lead on this. I want to drop Quimby from our client roster, but he can't have any possible claim against us when I do."

"Yes, sir," I said automatically.

Sullivan's mouth twitched in what I thought might be a partial smile. "I'm not sir to you, Gabriel."

"Habits die hard … Quinn," I said as I nodded to them both and left the office.

I preferred to work in one of the three large conference rooms on the third floor of the Cipher building. They were well-stocked with coffee, and I could generally spread out with my laptop and notes at one end of the massive table.

It was a challenge not to sing along with the *Hamilton* soundtrack playing in my headphones as I worked. The music brought the founding fathers of the U.S. to life in a way that made me almost imagine they *had* been black.

I flexed my fingers over my keyboard with something suspiciously like relish as I pictured the mystery woman as she had looked the previous night in running tights and a black hooded sweatshirt, her prosthetic leg glinting like something slightly dangerous, and her eyes flashing at me as though deciding whether to run or fight.

It was the flashing eyes that got me. She hadn't been afraid, she'd been fierce. Fierce women fascinated me. This fierce woman dared me to discover who she was.

I began with prosthetists in the Chicago area. There weren't many, so finding a patient of theirs might not be such a needle in a haystack. I logged the information and then did a search for Dane Quimby on every online dating site I could find. He had accounts on several, but cross-referencing location, age, and interests didn't bring up any women who looked like the lovely one I'd encountered on the bike path.

"Gabriel? Dan said you might be working in here." Alex Greene, the information systems expert of Cipher Security entered the boardroom and gestured to a chair at the table where I was working. "Mind if I join you?"

"I'd be glad if you would. I'm capable of a fair amount of internet work, but I've heard you see the world in code."

He scoffed. "If only the world was that easy to navigate."

I believed he truly meant it. "I have a woman to track down. She was at the Northside Cafe around seven forty-five last night, slender brunette, about six feet tall, late twenties, wearing custom riding boots and fitted jeans."

Alex quirked an eyebrow up. "Are you always so observant?"

"Saved my life more than once in Africa."

"Right. Fiona said you were a Peacekeeper." He opened his laptop and typed while he spoke. "Why Chicago?"

"My sister is in law school at the University of Chicago, and my mother moved here to take care of my nephew." I shrugged. "The job was offered, so I took it."

"This your woman?" Alex turned his laptop to face me. It was security camera footage from a pawnshop on the corner captured right after she left me standing in front of the restaurant.

"That's her."

I scanned every inch of the image, absorbing all visible details. No purse, no jacket, nothing in her front pockets, no rings of any kind, small hoop earrings – the kind that don't get accidentally pulled out in a fight.

"Is there another image?" I asked him.

Alex took the computer back and scrolled through the footage. "Just the rear view."

There was no "just" about her rear view. He turned the computer back to me, and I could see the outline of things in her back pockets. A phone in her right pocket, and possibly its battery in the left? Could that be? If she carried money or keys, they weren't visible in the security camera image.

"She's paranoid," Alex said.

"The battery removed from her phone?"

He nodded and zoomed in, but the details were lost to pixilation.

"She left on foot? Let's see where the nearest public transportation is." He entered information into the search bar, pulled up two more

29

screens, then scrolled through more camera footage from the closest bus stop. "There," he pointed. "She got on the 74 bus toward ..." He zoomed in on the front of the bus. "Halstead."

"Can you follow it?" I asked. Alex glanced sideways at me, but scrolled through the camera footage at high speed.

After a few minutes of mouse clicks and otherwise silent searching, Alex spoke again. "She got off at Fullerton and Sheffield."

"She's headed for the L," I said as I studied her confident stride captured on what looked like a storefront security camera.

"Fullerton station. Red, brown, or purple line?" Alex asked as he switched cameras and we scanned the footage.

"There." I pointed to the woman on the screen. "Red line to Howard."

Alex's fingers flew over his keyboard as he changed cameras again. "Okay, now we go station by station."

I was the one who spotted her a few minutes later. "Got her. Bryn Mawr station." I knew her walk now, and I hadn't imagined the slight hitch in her step. "She turned left out of the west exit. I don't know the area."

Alex was back on the keyboard, presumably cross-referencing security cameras with an area map. "It's residential and starting to gentrify. Not high-end enough to have cameras at the doors, not criminal enough to have them on the streets."

He closed the lid on his laptop and stood to go. "I'll run the tapes at the Bryn Mawr station to see if your woman has a schedule. Maybe we'll get an image that can be run through facial recognition."

It wasn't lost on me that Alex was calling her my woman. It also wasn't lost on me that I hadn't corrected him, or mentioned her prosthetic leg as an identifying feature.

I shook his hand. "Thanks for the time you're putting into finding her."

Alex shrugged. "Beats internet chess against Google."

"Against ... Google? The search engine?"

"Search engine is just the term people use to make artificial intelligence sound like it works for us."

"Google is AI?"

"Biggest there is," he said as he headed out.

"That is a remarkably disturbing thought."

"Isn't it?" There was a smile in Alex's voice, and I wondered at the sanguinity of a man who played chess with the world's biggest inorganic brain.

I pulled up a map of the neighborhoods around the Bryn Mawr L and studied the satellite imagery of the area to get a feel for who lived there. Large turn-of-the-century residential hotels seemed to anchor Bryn Mawr Avenue, and the commercial areas around the Historic District were shifting away from 1950s coffee shops to boutiques and cafes.

I decided I'd done enough satellite recon and certainly wouldn't be finding my mystery woman from a conference table in a posh downtown high-rise. I packed up my computer and went in search of O'Malley. I finally found him getting ready to head out.

"Good, you're here," he said to me. "Quimby's losing his shit, and we may need to go after the wife."

"What has changed since this morning?"

O'Malley tossed me the keys to his favorite SUV and said grimly, "She's missing."

[5]
SHANE

"Never let them see you sweat. Because if they see it, they're close enough to smell it, and that's just gross." – Shane, P.I.

H e was in there somewhere.

I stood in the downtown plaza outside Cipher's building and looked up at the windows that reflected the puffy white clouds of a beautiful spring day. I told myself I'd gone to the business district to do a property records search for a client, but standing outside the imposing offices of one of the top private security firms in the country, I knew I was there hoping for a glimpse of *him*. I just wanted to make sure he hadn't been badly injured the night before. I even convinced myself that I could walk in and charm his name out of the front desk personnel, and then I'd send flowers or something.

I scoffed at myself. *Or something.*

I didn't feel guilty about taking Dane Quimby's money. He had cheated on his wife, and he'd hidden money from her – money she was entitled to according to the law. A lot of money, granted, but that was the wife's problem now. I hadn't spent a lot of time talking to Denise

Quimby when she hired me, but I knew the number it did on a person's self-esteem to be cheated on.

I also hadn't *technically* broken the law – at least not in any way that was traceable back to me. The money transfer had been done from Dane's device to Dane's wife. Those two salient facts meant the difference between something mischievous and something criminal, and no matter how annoying mischief might be, it wasn't enough to trouble my conscience.

I did, however, feel guilty about causing a very sexy Cipher agent to fly ass-over-teakettle off his racing bike. I was sipping coffee from a to-go cup, wincing because I'd let it go cold while I stood outside the office building trying to decide exactly how chicken I actually was, when the man himself walked out of the building.

My breath caught, and I once again had the insane instinct to wave at him. Fortunately, years of acquired habit kicked in, and I froze in place and studied him. He was in a well-cut, dark gray suit, and he wore a heavy, waxed canvas bag or maybe photographer's case, with the strap slung diagonally across his chest. Nothing about the bag fit the fine material of the suit, but it fit *him* somehow, as though he'd always carried a bag like that.

He walked with another man – the one with the neck tattoos I'd caught a glimpse of outside the Northside Cafe – to a big SUV parked at the curb. My guy unslung his bag, tossed it in back, and then got into the driver's seat. A moment later they'd pulled away into traffic.

I watched the SUV until it was out of sight, trying not to obsess about the fact that I'd mentally called the man *my guy*, then dumped my cold coffee into a nearby bin, took a breath, and entered the Cipher Security building.

The lobby had the warm tones of modern money and good taste, and it smelled like wood polish and leather furniture. I was still running through all possible scenarios for information extraction as I approached the desk, and it wasn't until the man behind it spoke that I finally settled on my strategy.

He was all business, with no trace of flirtation or friendliness in sight. "Yes?" he said. He didn't ask, despite the implied question mark of his tone – it wasn't "tell me how I can help you," but rather "what do I need to do to see you on your way." He had just taken the lid off a Dark Matter Coffee cup, and judging by the opened sugar packs, had just dumped four sugars into the black coffee and was stirring it carefully.

This man was leaner than my agent, and darker-skinned, and his accent was pure Chicago. His badge said Van Hayden, and he looked vaguely annoyed in a way I recognized as defensive. Attempting to flirt or charm him would probably backfire spectacularly.

I took a deep breath and exhaled shakily as I braced my hands on the desk. "The two guys who just left – the Brit and the one with the neck tattoos – they said I should see you for their contact info. My purse was just stolen by a guy on a bike, and they took off after him in their SUV."

The guy studied me, looking for telltale flickers of lies, I supposed. "Are you hurt?" he finally asked.

I shook my head. "I had the bag off my shoulder to get my sunglasses, so it was easy to grab from my hands. I tried to run after the guy, but the Brit said they were on it and I should come and see you."

He pulled out a slip of paper and a pencil, and I held my breath. Then he slid them across the desk to me, and my heart sank. "Write down your name and contact info. I'll have them call you when they get back."

Damn! This one would have none of my damsel in distress nonsense. I sighed and wrote the name *Sophie* on the paper. It was the name I'd used in my online dating profile, and hopefully the only one he had for me.

I tried one last tactic. "What's with the bag the British guy carries? It looks like something from a surplus store."

The guy behind the desk snorted with something that sounded suspiciously like derision. "Probably military. Looks like shit with the suit, but he doesn't care."

"What is it, a briefcase? Photographer's bag?" I asked, trying to sound casual as I debated what number to write down. My friend the

35

bankruptcy specialist? A proctologist's office I saved for persistent drunks? The combo to my high school locker?

"Eze doesn't keep an office, so he carries all his crap with him in that bag everywhere he goes. He's a walking target for a messenger jack, just like what happened to you."

Ayzay? Was it a nickname? Last name? I wished I could see it spelled. Impulsively, probably stupidly, I wrote down my own cell phone number on the paper and slid it back across the desk. I instantly wanted to snatch it back and throw it away, but somehow I didn't think Van Hayden was the type to let suspicious behavior go unnoticed, and I definitely didn't need that kind of interest from another Cipher employee.

Just then, two men exited the elevator and strode toward the front door. They were both ridiculously handsome, but where one was tall, dark-haired and lean, the other was pure power, and I fought the instinct to duck away from his gaze. He wasn't looking at me though.

"Hey Van. Did Gabriel and Dan just leave?

"Just missed them." Van said.

"Get them on the phone, would you?" The powerful one said. "They're after Quimby's missing wife, but Alex needs to get whatever they know to look for her online."

Van nodded and picked up the phone. I was torn between wanting to watch his fingers dial and needing to get away before someone actually noticed me.

"Dan, Quinn and Alex are standing in front of me. Alex needs info from you to work on finding Quimby's wife." He paused while the person on the phone spoke, and I took that as my cue to leave. I backed out of direct view of the two men standing at the counter, then turned and started toward the door. Van must have seen me leave, because I could just hear his next question into the phone. "Hey, by the way, did you guys catch the thief?"

I pretended I'd heard nothing and left the building without a backward glance, although I didn't really do too much breathing until I was outside and around the corner. The smart move would have been to leave the area altogether, though part of me wanted the handsome Brit to come screeching around the corner looking for me.

Did I really want that?

Was I actually insane, or did the camera just put ten pounds of crazy on? And by camera, I meant the memory of the way the man had studied me. People didn't usually see me. They saw my face and my height if my prosthetic was out of sight, or they saw the fake leg and only the fake leg if it wasn't. I hadn't really felt seen as a whole person in a very long time, and this guy had taken his time perusing me from head to toe and back up again.

The novelty of it was a little bit thrilling.

It was also incredibly disconcerting.

I had a couple of names to check out now. My guy was either Gabriel or Dan "Ayzay," though the last name could probably be spelled any number of ways. He was British and had spent some time in the military, and I had a vivid physical description to match against photos.

I stopped and sighed. I also apparently had a missing client whose cheating husband had just been relieved of half his disposable cash. I needed to get to a secure computer to determine if a: Denise had contacted me, and b: if the money from Dane's secret stash was still in her new account.

To top it all off, my walking leg was starting to hurt, and it made my limp more pronounced, which in turn made me more noticeable to strangers and people who might be looking for me. I changed direction and headed west toward the warehouse district. I could use Sparky's computer while he worked on my leg, and maybe if I was busy trying to find Denise Quimby, I wouldn't be waiting for my phone to ring.

[6]
SHANE

"You wouldn't trust an engineer to cut off a real leg. Why the hell would you trust a doctor to fix a fake one?" – Bill "Sparky" Spracher, prosthetics inventor and engineer

---

"So, this is more of a pull-up condom instead of the roll-on kind." Sparky demonstrated on his own fist with a completely inappropriate thrusting gesture. This, of course, caused me to spit-take the milk I'd just gulped, which led to the inevitably giggled comments about the wisdom of swallowing. Despite his physical age, which was twenty-five, and his engineering genius, which was off the charts, Sparky had the sense of humor and sensibilities of a Comic-Con-aspiring, fourteen-year-old Marvel superhero fanboy.

He was also my best friend, prosthetist, and all-around MacGyverist.

"Quit putting your sweaty fist inside my new leg liner," I snorted as he continued to point out the benefits of the new silicone.

"Seriously though, this stuff doesn't tear. Some little company in Santa Barbara has figured out how to add nylon to the silicone. I want their recipe."

"I like their logo," I said, checking out the package the new liner, socket, and sleeve had arrived in. "AMP'D Gear. One of the owners is an amputee stuntman, and his partner designs all his movie legs," I read.

"Kind of like us," Sparky grinned. "Except you're Nebula, only not as mean, and I'm like Rocket, but less hairy, if Rocket looked like Star-Lord."

"Because you look like Star-Lord," I deadpanned.

"Well, yeah." Sparky wasn't kidding, and I was going to lose the battle to keep a straight face.

"I need your computer." I changed the subject so I didn't laugh out loud, though to be fair, Sparky did look a tiny bit like the *Parks and Rec* version of Chris Pratt, or like the teddy bear version of Star-Lord.

He absently waved me toward his gaming laptop which was, I knew, possibly even more secure than my own. Gamers are pretty life-and-death about their security. They have to be, in a world where swatters – people who make 911 calls about fake crimes to bring police down on innocent people – have the technology and social engineering skills to find the addresses of their virtual enemies.

"Can you put me on your VPN?" I asked him.

He scoffed, not looking up from the silicone into which he was attempting to poke holes. "It's always on. I have it routed through double encryption unless I'm gaming and I need the speed, so if you're streaming, I'll take it off."

VPN servers mask a computer's IP address so activity can't be traced, and I knew the server that Sparky used was in Panama and didn't log its users' activity.

I checked my e-mail and found nothing from Denise Quimby – no message, no payment for services, nothing. I sent her an e-mail, then checked her social media accounts for any recent activity. Nothing had been posted for more than a week, and unless I paid for a credit card search, hacked my way into her bank, or went out and canvassed her neighborhood, my search for her was limited by her own willingness to communicate.

So instead I began looking for Gabriel or Dan Ayzay.

"How would you spell a last name that sounds like 'ayzay'?"

He shrugged. "If it's African, it's the Igbo word for king, spelled E Z E."

I stared at him in stunned silence long enough that he looked up from the socket in his hands. "What?" he asked defensively.

"It isn't enough to carry around an entire Wiki file on every Marvel character ever invented, you have to know the origin of obscure foreign words too?"

He ignored my sarcasm. "Not Marvel. I got that from Comic Republic. Either way, you spell it E Z E."

"Thank you," I said as I typed "Gabriel Eze" into Google. I scrolled through the pages that came up. "What's Igbo?"

"An ethnic group and language in Nigeria."

"Oh, thanks."

I tried Google Images first, but they quickly devolved into photos of famous men named Gabriel. Finally, way down on the bottom of the fifth page, I found a photo of some men wearing light blue helmets. One of those men was in profile, and he looked like my Brit, but younger. The man was Lieutenant Eze according to the article attached to it, and he was a Peacekeeper in a mostly Nigerian squad.

Fascinating.

"Blue helmets," I said, turning the computer so that Sparky could see the photo. "Those are UN Peacekeepers, right?"

He shrugged. "Marvel made a deal in 2008 to make educational comics with Spiderman and UN Peacekeepers, but they never followed through, so my blue hat knowledge is pretty limited."

I scoffed. "So if it doesn't exist in the world of comics, you don't know it?"

Sparky picked up a socket wrench and adjusted something on the fin of a diving leg he was working on. "Sounds about right."

"So why do you know so much about prosthetic legs?"

He stared at me with a *you can't be serious* look. "Cyborg, Bucky Barnes, Atom Eve, Flash Thompson, Forge, Nebula, Misty Knight ..." He was counting down on his fingers, and I held up my hands in surrender.

"Okay, okay, got it. I'm just your willing guinea pig, is that it?" I said, laughing.

Sparky's expression turned serious. "You're my muse."

He held my gaze for a long moment. "Oh," I said, inadequately.

He raised an eyebrow as a mischievous grin broke across his face. "You're also either brave or dumb enough to be my crash test dummy."

I snickered. "Right, there's that."

The next page in my Gabriel Eze search revealed a five-year-old article from a London newspaper about an investigation the Royal Military Police had conducted into the death of a soldier on the base. Lieutenant Gabriel Eze was mentioned as a witness. I couldn't find anything else about that case or any other mentions of MP Eze, but it felt like it fit.

If my guy had joined the British army right out of high school, he could have reached the rank of Lieutenant by twenty or twenty-one. He could have done some time with the UN Peacekeepers, maybe fit in a couple of years of university in no particular order, and then joined the private sector as a security agent.

No searches of his name in conjunction with Chicago resulted in any hits, but there was a Kendra Eze at University of Chicago. I had no way of knowing if she was connected to Gabriel at all. For all I knew, Eze could be the equivalent of Smith. I sensed that I'd gone as far as I could with the information I had.

I closed the lid of the laptop and spent the next hour trying various leg components Sparky had been playing with, and he surprised me with a liner, socket, and sleeve from the Santa Barbara company that he'd already fitted to my titanium walking leg. It made the limp almost imperceptible and was way more comfortable than even my cheetah leg socket.

I gave him an impulsive hug and then poked him in the ribs when he sniffed my hair and said I smelled like the vanilla air freshener realtors use when they want to sell a house.

Dork.

[7]

SHANE

"Why did you wait two days to call her? She gave you her number, right? Call her as you're walking away and tell her how nice it was to meet her." – Overheard on the basketball court

---

I was startled to realize it had gotten dark while I'd been working in the warehouse, and a pang of guilt hit me. Oscar would be hungry, so I texted my neighbor's son. Jorge was a senior in high school and always took my dog out for a walk when he got home from school. He could also be counted on to feed him if I was late.

You got it, was the reply.

Thanks. How did the comp-sci test go? I texted back.

He responded with an eye-roll emoji that he'd programmed to actually roll its eyes. I wanted it, but he was holding out to use it as currency someday.

Jorge was taking computer science from a high school STEM teacher who had stopped advancing his own education around the time the internet was invented, which meant Jorge had been teaching himself using YouTube videos and reading programmer message boards. He was the one who had set me up with my own VPN service, and he could generally be counted on to fill the gaps in my programming education. He was also one of the few people who was possibly more paranoid than me. Oscar and I were both going to miss him when he went away to MIT.

I took the L back to Bryn Mawr station and made it home about twenty minutes later. Jorge was still in my apartment wrestling on the floor with my giant, hairy dog.

"Hey," he said, looking up from under piles of fur. Oscar gave his face a tongue-swipe and then leapt up to greet me.

I grinned as Jorge picked dog hair out of his mouth. He was a stringy cross-country runner, and one of the few people I knew who could keep up with me and the cheetah leg.

"I got a new socket. Want to go for a run later?"

"I gotta work tonight, so I'll be up at five tomorrow to run. Want to go then?" Jorge stood up in that graceful way only teenagers and yoga instructors can manage and attempted to brush off the dog coat he'd cleaned off my floor.

I made a noise somewhere between a scoff and a snort. "Pre-crack is not something I experience on purpose. I need to wake up slowly, with copious amounts of coffee, preferably administered intravenously."

Jorge laughed and scratched Oscar's ears on his way to the door. "Have a good night."

"Thanks for taking care of my dog," I called to him.

"He's my dog. He just lives with you," he called back as the door shut behind him.

I heated up some leftover rice and Moroccan chicken and scrolled through Twitter for a few minutes while I ate. I used social media mostly as a way to see what people were talking about, since I didn't have water cooler conversations in my line of work. The political news depressed me, the random bits of activism gave me hope, and I scrolled past way too many fake news claims and comment trolls for comfort. It was getting harder and harder to find the kind of conversations people actually used to have at the water cooler. Even TV shows were binge-watched, so there weren't collective Friday morning "can you believe what Ross and Rachel did?" moments anymore. The last time I remember people actively suppressing spoilers was when the Bruce Willis movie *The Sixth Sense* came out and nobody gave the secret away.

Also, every social media account I had was under a different name, because my paranoia was that big. I never clicked on anything as I scrolled, no matter how tempting the quiz to reveal my Hogwarts House was (I was pretty sure I was a Ravenclaw, but I had hopes for a little Gryffindor too), and I refused every overture of Facebook friendship I received. Social media was a tool for my work, just like property searches and the County Recorder's Office, which meant the less I exposed of myself, the more anonymous I could remain.

I ran my fingers through Oscar's fur with one hand as I scrolled through Facebook on my phone with the other. My hand would likely be gray with dog dust, but he was in that blissed out space hounds get where tongues loll and eyes glaze in ecstasy, and consequently he shot me a glaring stink-eye when I stopped ruffling his fur.

I'd just scrolled past a quiz that promised to reveal your personality type. Even more striking to my eyes than the click-bait photo of the woman yelling, was the fact that it was powered by ADDATA, which was Dane Quimby's company. From my research I knew they scraped data from social media to predict market reception for ad sales, but this was something completely different.

I debated for a long moment – to click or not to click. On the one hand, I had every reason in the world not to break my cardinal rule about anonymity and invisibility, but on the other hand, I had the curiosity of a cat with all the survival instincts that went along with it. I could always delete that account, create a new e-mail address, and start over.

Curiosity won. I clicked the app and then actually read the terms and agreements. Everything was pretty standard except for the tiny little clause that gave ADDATA the right to use my data and that of my friends, in the event I had any, for their research.

That was interesting. As far as I knew, Facebook hadn't allowed friends' data to be accessed by third-party applications since 2014, which was approximately the year I removed my actual name from most online public records.

It was much more difficult to click the "agree" button, but I consoled myself with the thought that I'd be deleting this account tomorrow – and the fact that I had no friends.

It was a clever quiz, and if the first question was any indication of the rest of them, I knew they'd be able to guess my age and gender and then have a fair degree of information to guess education, interests, and leisure-time activities.

I was trying to decide between the truth and complete fiction when my cell phone rang. I answered on speakerphone without thinking. "Hello?"

There was a pause. I looked at the number and realized I didn't know it. My hand was just reaching for the disconnect button when a deep British voice said, "Sophie?"

And I promptly dropped the phone.

"Shit!" I mumbled under my breath as I grabbed for it, then, "Sorry."

Oscar gave me a side-eye look before hmphing himself back to sleep, and I heard a low chuckle as I put the phone to my ear. "Tell Oscar he'll be getting the bill for my bike."

"How do you know his name?" I asked without thinking. I was actually doing a lot of not-thinking – far more than I was comfortable with.

"It's what you called him. I briefly considered searching the veterinarians in the city for patients named Oscar to find you, so I appreciated the note."

"I didn't actually mean to give you my real number."

"Well, I assume Sophie's not your real name, and the number's unlisted, so perhaps we're even?" His voice was very smooth and deep, and I pressed the phone to my ear to get closer to it, which hurt.

"Hold on, let me get headphones," I said as I grabbed a pair of earbuds from the coffee table. When I could see my phone screen again, I took a screenshot of the phone number as backup. "Give me the address of your bike shop, and I'll go in and pay the bill," I said.

"Don't worry about it. I'll just straighten the rim and it'll be fine."

"I'm really sorry about what happened. Are you okay?" I played with the cord of the headphones and tried to picture him as he answered.

"I'm pretty sure they're going to have to amputate," he said significantly.

"Smart ass," I said. "You're walking just fine."

"Really? And how might you know that?" Gabriel Eze sounded relaxed and amused, and I settled back into the couch and absently ran my fingers through Oscar's fur.

"I spied on you at work. I thought about sending you flowers, but I couldn't very well address them to the hot guy my dog smashed into."

His low chuckle rumbled through me as I winced at my un-filtered mouth.

"Why did you call?" I finally asked.

"You gave me your number." There was a note of laughter in his tone, and I pictured him lounging back on a sofa. "We didn't catch your thief, by the way."

"Oh, well, thanks for trying." I played idly with my phone, and the Facebook quiz screen sprang back to life.

"I'm not done. The thief's still out there, and I'm still searching for her," he said quietly. My hand stilled, and I might have held my breath a little. "She seems to have found an account worth a million that didn't belong to her – an account under our protection."

"A million dollars? That's a lot. You sure that much went missing?" I tried to keep my tone airy and unconcerned.

"The account holder implied so," he said carefully.

"Hmm. You've got your work cut out for you. I'd better let you get to it, then."

This time, Gabriel was the one to change the subject. "What were you doing when I called? You sounded distracted."

I smiled. "I was about to take a personality quiz on Facebook. It's on an app run by ADDATA. You may have heard of them?"

I could hear his sharp intake of breath. "I may have. Why might ADDATA be running a personality quiz? Don't they sell digital ad space?"

"It's something I've been asking myself too. Why don't you take the quiz with me and maybe we can figure it out?"

There was silence on the other end of the phone, and then another low chuckle. His laughter did very strange but not unpleasant things to my insides. "Okay," he finally said. "You read the questions, and we'll answer them out loud."

I exhaled sharply. "I was just trying to decide whether to answer them honestly or make something up when you called."

"Oh, honesty is always the best policy," he said.

"I will if you will." I closed my eyes and thought I heard a smile in his tone.

"Deal."

Of course either of us could lie at any point and the other person wouldn't know, but I thought it might actually be fun to tell the whole truth and nothing but the truth for once.

"Okay, question one. You're stranded on a desert island. Which would you rather have with you – your favorite book, your favorite music album, your favorite video game, or your favorite movie?"

"We're assuming the requisite electronics accompany said choice?" he asked.

"We are assuming so, yes." I smiled.

"You first."

"Book," I said quickly.

"Why?" he asked.

"Because when I've read it through so many times that I've memorized it, I can use the pages for toilet paper or to light signal fires."

Gabriel burst out laughing, and there went my insides again. "What about you?" I grinned. His laughter was infectious.

He thought for a moment, then answered, "Music album."

"Okay, why?"

"Because music is my escape, and no matter where I am or what I'm doing, I can be transported someplace else."

Oh.

"There's a second part to the question. Which album would you choose?"

"Really? That's rather detailed for a personality quiz. It provides quite a lot of information, don't you think?"

"I do think. It's also not as easy to collate fill-in-the-blank as multiple choice questions, which means they're matching specific information with specific people – people they can track and potentially target."

"That's interesting, and not a little bit frightening."

"My thoughts exactly," I said as I considered the scope of the implications.

"So, which book would you bring?" The smile was back in his voice.

"An anthology. Something big, with all the stories. Maybe Jack London or Arthur Conan Doyle."

"Somehow I think *Call of the Wild* might be a bit more useful than *Sherlock Holmes* on a deserted island."

"Maybe. But survival requires cleverness too, not just resources."

"I'd say survival is ninety percent cleverness and ten percent resources," he said with a degree of seriousness in his tone that suggested personal experience.

"Which album would you bring?"

"The soundtrack to *Hamilton*," Gabriel said, without hesitation. I was so startled I laughed. "You think that's funny?"

"I think that's excellent. Why *Hamilton*?"

I could hear the smile again. "There's music, there's singing, there's implied dancing, and perhaps more importantly, it's a display of the promise of what's possible. Also, I'd be lying if I didn't say the emphasis on immigrants getting the job done appeals to me."

There was a notification ding on his phone. "Hang on a second," he said. I heard him type something, and then he was back. "Sorry about that."

"It's okay. You have to go?"

"No, it was just my sister letting me know she survived another day."

"That sounds ominous. Was her survival uncertain?" I was joking, but then I realized it might not be a joke for him at all. I had no idea what her life looked like, or where she lived, or what her circumstances were, and I held my breath, waiting to hear if I'd offended him.

"Survival is usually guaranteed in my family. We're rather hard to kill. Sanity, however, remains a daily question."

"Should I be worried?" I exhaled quietly, hoping my relief wasn't audible.

I could hear the long, slow smile in his voice again, and imagining it on his face made my heart pound. "I don't know. Should you?"

I practically leapt off the couch, and Oscar grumbled at me for the disturbance. "So, I have some work to do. I don't suppose I'll see you out on the Lakefront Trail anytime soon, right?"

I wasn't sure why I'd just gotten so panicky, but I suddenly felt the need to end this call. I paced my small living room and felt Oscar's eyes track my progress as I circled the coffee table.

Gabriel's voice got sharper, and his British accent was more clipped and formal. "I won't be cycling for a few days, if that's what you're asking."

"Good. I mean, I'm sorry, not good, I just …" I didn't know what I just. I just …

"What just happened?" he asked carefully.

I exhaled sharply. "I don't know. I have to go though, okay?"

"Okay." He didn't sound sure, he sounded … disappointed?

"Goodnight, Gabriel," I whispered.

There was a long pause on the other end of the phone. "Goodnight."

[8]

GABRIEL

"A word only has the power you give it. Truth is just five letters unless the promise of it is honored, and trust – those five letters are meaningless without a whole lifetime of evidence to back it up." – Gabriel Eze

---

She knew my name. Hearing it in her slight whiskey voice did something ... odd to me.

Van Hayden may have told her my name, but for some reason I wanted to believe she'd ferreted it out for herself.

I didn't like how quickly things had become strange between us. I didn't like not being able to see her face when she withdrew, to know what had affected her. Was it jokes about madness? About Kendra?

I busied myself with the damaged wheel from my bicycle. Truing a bent rim without a stand is a bit of a trick, but a Jamaican-Nigerian boy from Peckham had no choice but to learn it if he wanted to work in any South London neighborhood other than his own. I turned on the *Hamilton* soundtrack, got myself a Red Stripe beer, dug up a spoke key, and got to work.

The woman was a mystery – the good kind of mystery, with intrigue and hidden bits to tease and tempt a man into uncovering her secrets. And no doubt the secrets ran deep. Every search I'd run on her identity had failed, and failure was not something I was particularly familiar with. So, after working on my bike for a bit, I decided to make a nighttime visit to the neighborhood near Bryn Mawr station, in the event she planned another midnight run. I didn't generally choose after-dark visits to unfamiliar neighborhoods, but something in me rebelled against the idea that this woman could remain anonymous.

I slipped on a dark warmup jacket, but left the hood down. My body still ached from deep bruises that would likely go dark brown in a day or two, but I was fit enough to pose as a runner if I needed the cover. I had no intention of actually running up to the north side neighborhood, but I would use the disguise if someone questioned my presence there.

The L train was still running, but the station at Bryn Mawr was nearly deserted. I followed the direction out of the station that she'd taken and found myself walking down a main street that felt like a hybrid between centuries. Storefronts from the 1950s were interspersed with a growing hipster influence of boutiques and cafes of the variety that posted signs about mobile phone use and refused to have internet on the principle that it discouraged conversation, all the while disdaining customers for their lack of cool.

I took note of several cameras above storefronts in the event that I needed more of Greene's eyes on the street to discover which way she walked. There was an Armenian market on one corner with a particularly fine display of fresh produce in front and what looked like a hot food counter inside. I stood across the street from it, studying the side streets and their various styles of housing. Most were converted hotels from the 1940s and 1950s, with blocky, post-war construction that promised utilitarian rooms with requisite windows and little else to recommend them.

I continued down the street toward an older apartment building constructed sometime near the beginning of the twentieth century. A center courtyard gave it a peaceful air, and its mere four stories made it feel positively quaint in this city of sky-rises. It's where I would choose to live if I were in this neighborhood.

I pulled up the address on my mobile and saw that it had been converted to condominiums in the last decade. One was currently for sale, and I made an impulsive decision to send a query to the listing agent about it. If I'd been certain this was where she lived, it might have been dodgy for me to look at a flat here. But having stumbled upon the building in the course of an investigation made it fair game. I could assuage my conscience with the fact that I was still new to Chicago, and my family's plans meant I'd be settled here for at least the next three years.

It was late, and my bruises ached. I'd discovered a few cameras to check, and I'd taken the measure of an interesting neighborhood where a man could walk alone at night for a time without difficulty, and where a woman with a large dog felt safe enough to go for midnight runs. It wasn't an admission of defeat to go home without finding her, but I was still left with the unsettled feeling that had come over me ever since I'd hung up the phone.

Sullivan and O'Malley found me in a conference room the next day. I'd sent a list of business names to Greene to see if he could access their camera footage and hopefully find a good quality image of my woman's face for identification purposes, and I was currently searching all the businesses within a two-mile radius of the Bryn Mawr station to check on veterinarians, emergency animal hospitals, and prosthetists.

"We found a bank account at the same branch as Quimby's," O'Malley said brusquely as he and Quinn walked into the room. "It was opened by Denise Quimby last week and funded to the tune of five hundred k two nights ago by direct transfer from Quimby's account. Yesterday, it was emptied."

I studied the two men in front of me – so different from each other in appearance, but so alike in posture and attitude. "Was that before or after the last time Quimby says he saw his wife?"

"After," grumbled Sullivan. "He says she was gone when he got home after meeting our mystery woman, but he only realized it when she didn't come home for dinner the next night."

"Do we think Quimby had anything to do with the wife's disappearance?"

"Nah, he doesn't have it in him," O'Malley said as he spun a conference table chair around and straddled it with the ease of an athlete. "Most likely she took the money and ran."

Sullivan studied me for a moment. "You're still looking for the girlfriend?"

I nodded. "I am, though I have the sense that she's less a girlfriend, and more ... opportunistic."

"You think she targeted him specifically for this job?" Sullivan asked.

"I do. And the fact that I haven't discovered her identity yet makes me think she's somewhat professional at it."

"A P.I. maybe, or someone in one of the government services?" O'Malley was thoughtful, but Sullivan shook his head.

"Not federal. This is too small and stinks of payback. We know Quimby cheats on his wife; it wouldn't take much for the wife to hire someone to find the money," he said.

"Finding the money is one thing – not easy, but doable. Having balls big and hairy enough to take it is something else," O'Malley said with something like admiration.

I pictured the beautiful woman with the enormous dog, sprinting on a cheetah leg at midnight, and I thought one could make a case for some variation of that, minus the dangling bits.

Sullivan stood decisively. "Frankly, I don't particularly care about the money. Cheat on your wife, you deserve to lose half of everything. He's lucky she didn't go for half his company while she was at it. My problem is that he's being a pain in my ass now. I've got our lawyers working on it, but at this point, I'm looking for any way to shake him loose without having to pay him off. Whether it's getting the money back or finding enough dirt on him to shut him up, I'm open to anything."

I looked up at him and took a breath. "I'm working on another angle, in addition to finding the woman."

"Yeah? What do you have?" O'Malley leaned forward, and I included him in my gaze.

"Quimby's company, ADDATA. There's something going on that doesn't fit. I'd like to use Greene's particular skills to follow a lead on this as well, if I may?"

"Alex is in D.C. on something for me. You can have him when he gets back, and I can probably find a couple other agents with decent computer skills if that'll help," said Sullivan. "Also, he accessed the wife's e-mail account and said to give you this." He tossed a thumb drive in my direction, and I snatched it from the air.

"Thanks. I can make do with my resources until he returns," I said, thinking of a whiskey voice and her personality quiz.

"Whatever you need, man. Let's just make this go away," said O'Malley as he rose from the table. The two men left the conference room together, and my thoughts returned to the woman who left the north side restaurant two nights ago. She carried herself with the confidence of the athlete she obviously was, despite the loss of a leg, which perhaps meant she'd lost the leg after she'd grown into her athleticism. She was clearly educated and had a detailed understanding of the ramifications of something as specialized as data scraping and social engineering.

My mobile phone rang, and I checked the screen. The name "Sophie" winked at me as though daring me to answer, and I smiled.

"What a lovely coincidence," I said into the phone when the call connected.

[9]

SHANE

"Sometimes it's better to ask forgiveness rather than permission." – Shane, P.I.

"I'm curious what name came up on your screen," I said, unable to keep from smiling at the sound of his deep, cultured voice.

"Sadly, not the one that belongs to your number."

"So I remain a mystery? Oh good. No one likes to be a foregone conclusion."

"And yet, I need to call you something. Sophie is the name by which Quimby knows you, therefore it doesn't fit who you are."

"What are you going to call me then?"

"Some random term of endearment will have to do until I learn otherwise." I could hear the smile in his voice, as though he dared me to contradict him. Honestly, a part of me wanted to hang up. No one used endearments with me, and it confronted everything I'd been trying to escape when I ran away to Chicago.

I took a deep breath instead. "Are you at Cipher?"

"I am." The brief moment of playfulness was gone from his voice.

"Do you have access to Quimby's accounts?"

"I do." His voice had a note of sternness.

"What about the wife's account. Can you access hers?" I kept my tone as even as possible to cover up the shakiness I felt.

"What are you asking?"

I was standing outside the Quimbys' house in the leafy suburb of River Forest. There were two cars in the driveway, and as I watched the house from behind a nearby hedge, Dane Quimby exited the front door, got into a new red Tesla Model S, and drove away. The other car, a new Lexus SUV, remained in the driveway alone.

"Did Denise Quimby ever return home?" I asked quietly.

"What do you know about her disappearance?" His voice was gentle, even if his question was accusatory.

"Nothing, but it doesn't surprise me. Her car's still in the driveway though, and she's the type of person who would leave it in the airport lot and make him pay the ticket. If she left him, which I suspect she did, someone came and picked her up."

"Five hundred thousand dollars was withdrawn from her account yesterday."

"Is his account still funded?" I asked.

"We put a block on it so money can't be moved in or out."

I scoffed. "I'm sure he loved that. I assume you guys are looking for Denise?" I studied the neighborhood around the Quimbys' house. It was the time of day when all the CEOs had gone to their companies and all their wives had gone to the country clubs. I slipped around the back of the house and scanned for cameras. There were none in sight, and no signs of a dog, so I only had to worry about a motion-detection alarm.

"We are." Gabriel's tone was careful, and I thought there was a lot he wasn't saying.

"Good. Me too." I spotted a downstairs window that had been left partially open. I pulled my knife out of its sheath on my leg and slid it between the screen and the window casement.

"Where are you, Darling?" He sounded different. Concerned, maybe.

"You shouldn't call me that," I said, as the catch lifted and the screen came loose.

"Until I know your true name, it's who you are to me."

I didn't stop to examine that statement, it was too fraught with … stuff. I slipped the window screen from its frame and set it carefully against the house, then slid the window further open, half-expecting an alarm to blare. The only sound was Gabriel in my ear.

"Darling?"

I didn't say anything as I hoisted myself up on the window ledge, poked my head into what appeared to be a laundry room bigger than the kitchen in my condo, and climbed inside.

"I have to go," I whispered before I ended the connection and pulled the earbuds out of my ears. The phone in my pocket buzzed again immediately, but I ignored it and slid the window closed behind me.

I crept down the hall, automatically turned off the coffee pot that had been left on, and then stayed away from the windows in the front of the house as I explored the ground floor. The square footage was astounding, especially for just two people. Entire suites of rooms looked untouched by human habitation.

I wondered if Cipher had done any poking around into Dane's personal finances recently and thought I might plant that bug in Gabriel's ear the next time we talked. I could do it myself, but the searches would cost me, and it didn't look like I was going to get paid for the work I'd already done.

The next time we talked. It was an odd thought. It almost felt normal to imagine phone conversations with Gabriel Eze. I shoved that thought firmly down around my ankles as I slipped into the front hall-way, took note of the inactive alarm system, and climbed the stairs. I wondered at the man who installed an alarm he didn't use, and decided that Dane Quimby, with his dishonorable discharge from the military, might be the kind of guy who kept a gun. It was a disquieting thought for a home invader to carry on tiptoe with her through the man's house.

The upstairs was carpeted in plush, white wool, and I wrinkled my nose in disgust. I hated wall-to-wall carpet. No matter how luxurious it might feel under bare feet, it always stank of fire retardants and chemical cleaners. This was fairly new and still hadn't fully off-gassed its original chemical smell, but it did make my passage utterly silent.

The first two rooms were guest rooms, but one was actually empty, as though the designer hadn't even bothered to pretend it was an office. In the back of the house there were two master suites – his and hers bedrooms as though this were the nineteenth century and the lord and lady of the manor didn't actually know each other well enough to share a bed.

Dane's room was obvious from the mess. Two different jacket/trouser combinations lay crumpled on his bed. I'd never actually known a guy who couldn't decide what to wear, and it made me chuckle to imagine him holding the fabric up to his face in the mirror. His walk-in closet was the size of my living room, and at least three days' worth of clothes had been flung over the armchair haphazardly. I recognized the jacket he'd worn on our "date," and wondered what day the housekeeper came. I didn't think the Quimbys had much to do with the toilet-cleaning aspects of home ownership.

The other bedroom was decorated simply in pale, anemic colors. There were several old lace pillows on the bed that looked scratchy and uncomfortable, and everything matched at least one other design element perfectly. The room looked like it had been decorated by someone with a need for perfect symmetry. It was the kind of space that would make me nuts to sleep in.

The closet was like one of those perfectly organized rooms where everything was arranged by color palate. Denise Quimby had left more clothes behind than I had in my whole wardrobe, but I got the sense from the space that it was by no means all she owned. I studied the photos of Denise and Dane that were artfully placed in beautiful frames, and noted that she always wore pale colors, while he wore vibrant jewel tones like the peacock he was. I found myself wondering why she'd stayed as long as she had.

Up high in the closet was a shelf that housed an incomplete, matched set of Louis Vuitton luggage. I found no sign of a jewelry box, and the velvet-lined drawer hidden in the bottom trim of the ornate dresser was empty except for a single pearl earring way at the back. A casual observer might have thought Dane's wife had taken nothing with her and conclude that she'd been forced or otherwise coerced into leaving, but I saw things differently.

It was time to go. I'd already pushed my luck by entering the house, and every passing minute made discovery more likely. Fortunately, the carpet upstairs hadn't been vacuumed so recently that my footprints would stand out, but I was nonetheless careful to wipe down anything I'd touched with the edge of my t-shirt.

A few minutes later I'd slipped back out of the laundry room window and replaced the screen. I didn't bother to re-latch it, but I did take a moment to close the window itself all the way. I doubted Dane spent much time in the laundry room, but I thought the open window might invite investigation.

Ten minutes later I was another anonymous passenger on the train, making mental lists of the assets in the Quimbys' house and wondering where Dane had found a million dollars.

[10]
GABRIEL

"A house is a place. A home is a haven." – Miri Eze

"Hello, Darling," I said, only half-surprised to see her turn the corner.

She literally stopped in her tracks, and I fancied I heard the screech in the sound effects track of her day. "What are you doing here?" She stared at me, but she didn't seem afraid, which pleased me.

"Waiting for you, of course." I was actually waiting for the realtor with whom I'd made an appointment to show me the condo for sale, but I was early, and I'd been enjoying the sun for a moment. If my eyes had remained closed a second longer she'd have seen me before I saw her, and she might have bolted.

I studied her as she approached. To be fair, I felt studied as well. She had on a black linen t-shirt and black jeans and wore her hair in a single braid over one shoulder. Low, flat boots completed the ensemble, and her prosthetic was invisible even to one who looked for signs of it.

"And now that I'm here, what are we going to do?" she said. She was playing her cards close to the chest, giving me nothing useful. She was very good at whatever it was she did.

"There's a condo for sale in this building." I indicated the building in front of us. "I'd like your help deciding whether to buy it."

"In *this* building?" It might have been my imagination, but I thought she squeaked, and I studied her even more closely. Damn, this woman was fascinating, and I still didn't even know her name.

A slight flush rose on her cheeks, and an idea began to rise in my brain. "What can you tell me about the building?"

Her mouth opened, but no sound came out. Sadly, my question was answered by a woman I presumed was the realtor.

"It was built in 1908 by Pridewater in the Tudor style. There are some who believe it was once the British embassy. You must be Mr. Eze." The woman wore a yellow suit that clashed with her sallow skin, but apart from the unfortunate color choice, everything about her was pulled together to "professional attire" perfection. She had already assessed the cut and quality of my suit and was turning her attention to my companion. The realtor held out her hand to shake Darling's, and I struggled to keep my expression blank.

"I'm Trisha Blake," she said brusquely.

"Good to meet you, Trisha. What can you tell Gabriel about the neighborhood?" Darling said with a pleasant smile. Damn. Still no name.

Trisha proceeded to describe the historical preservation of Edgewater and the gentrification of the area in general as she led us inside the courtyard and into the red brick building. I indicated that Darling should go ahead of me, and I found my hand naturally going to the small of her back as I held open the door.

I could feel the heat from her skin through the thin linen of her t-shirt, and I let my hand linger beyond what was polite or appropriate. She looked into my eyes and said thank you, and a queer, giddy sensation washed over me.

Trisha nattered on about architectural features, but my focus had somehow narrowed to the woman at my side. She was nearly my height, with eyes that changed color according to the light. At the moment they were green, and I very nearly tripped up the stairs as I studied them.

She wore some indescribable fragrance – some combination of vanilla and amber that might have been soap, or skin crème, or essential oil. I caught rare hints of it when she turned, or when I was close enough to catch the color of her eyes, and I found myself leaning close, even when she was in front of me, just to inhale.

We'd stopped outside a door, and I snapped back to myself in time to remember why I'd asked Trisha to come. "This," she said with a dramatic flourish, "is the apartment."

She opened the door and stepped inside, presumably to turn on lights and make the place look welcoming. I'm sure it did, though I couldn't say for sure. My focus was on the other woman with me. She'd lost the nervousness she'd worn when I first encountered her outside the building, and her expression had opened into something like peace, and maybe wonder.

"Do you like it?" I murmured to her as she stopped to admire what was admittedly an intriguing view from the big windows in the tower room.

"The light is beautiful," she breathed, as she took in the view.

The glow of sunlight on her skin showed the remnants of a tan, and tiny freckles dotted her nose and cheeks as her eyes, again green, took in the scene.

"Beautiful," I agreed, and she looked at me. I was too close, I knew, but I couldn't make myself step back. She didn't blink or look away, and I was drawn to her as though she was a magnet and I was iron.

"There are two bedrooms through here if you'd like to take a look," Trisha buzzed, somewhere near my ear like a fly. I blinked and realized that the realtor was on the other side of the room waiting for us to join her for the rest of the tour.

I smiled slowly and answered Trisha, but spoke to the woman next to me. "Right. The bedrooms."

Darling flushed, and I wanted to touch her face, to feel the heat of her cheeks. Then her eyebrow quirked up and a gleam of mischievousness lit her eyes.

"Wouldn't want to miss ... the bedrooms," she said, dropping her voice dramatically.

She spun to follow Trisha through the apartment, and I watched her walk away with extreme appreciation for the excellent view. Then she tossed a look over her shoulder that made me swallow tightly.

The larger of the two bedrooms had a fireplace that may have been original to the building, and a big window that overlooked the peaceful courtyard. Despite my preoccupation with my lovely companion, I actually took a moment to notice the details of the apartment. 1908 was young by London standards, but the building had been renovated in the last ten years, and the attention to period details was done with a light but sure touch. The spaces had great natural light, the rooms were large enough for a person of my height to feel comfortable, and it was elegant and clean without fussiness.

Darling was standing at the bedroom window pointedly avoiding my gaze, so I finally directed my attention to Trisha. "What can you tell me about the other tenants in the building?" I asked.

Darling's shoulders tensed so slightly I would have missed it if I hadn't been looking for it.

"Lots of young professional couples, a few with children, mostly owners. Some of the owners have leased their apartments, but those tend to be the smaller ones."

"Are dogs allowed in the building?" I asked.

I definitely wasn't imagining the catch in Darling's breath.

"Yes, but to my knowledge, there are only one or two. They're well-behaved, and the owners are quite conscientious about making sure they're quiet."

"Any big dogs?" I asked.

"I believe so. A Bernese mountain dog. I've seen him in the courtyard with his owner ..." Trisha trailed off and turned her attention to Darling. "Of course, you're a tenant in the building. I'm so sorry, I thought you looked familiar, but I couldn't place you."

Darling's voice was tight, but she smiled convincingly. "It's no problem. I didn't expect you'd know me."

"Oh, but no one could forget your beautiful dog. Oscar, isn't it? I'm friends with Jorge's mother, and she said he just dotes on that dog."

Who the hell was Jorge, and why did he dote on Darling's dog?

"Well, speaking of my dog, I need to take him for a walk. It was nice to see you again, Trisha," Darling said to the realtor with a brightness that sounded brittle to my ears. She turned to me, her smile tight in a way that made her eyes go stormy. "Gabriel, thank you for letting me see the apartment with you. I'd always wondered what these big places looked like."

She left the room before I could answer, and I trailed her to the door. "Let me walk you home."

She turned to face me. "No."

"It'll take five minutes to find out which apartment you're in," I said inanely, as if that could make a difference.

She reached out and I flinched, thinking I'd be slapped. Instead, she touched my cheek with a wry shake of her head. "Have a good day, Gabriel."

I exhaled in defeat. "You never said if I should take the apartment."

She looked surprised at that. "You're actually considering it?"

"It's why I'm here." She could believe me or not, but it was true.

Darling crossed her arms in front of her and looked past me into the grand living space with its big windows and lovely light. She seemed to choose honesty rather than convenience. "If you can afford it, you won't find anything nicer for the price." She turned to head down the stairs. "I've heard the neighbors are pretty rough, though," she said, without looking back.

[11]
SHANE

"Fear and excitement produce the exact same physiological response. It's what you do with all that adrenaline that makes things interesting." – Shane, P.I.

I took Oscar out for a run immediately. I didn't want to take the chance that Gabriel would ask for my apartment number or wait for me outside the building, so my hound and I did ten easy miles along Lakefront Trail. About mile five I stopped being annoyed, and by mile eight I was smiling through the pain.

I was smitten. More than smitten, actually. Probably something closer to besotted, with a side of lustful thoughts for added intrigue.

Oh my.

There was something about the way Gabriel looked at me, like I didn't quite fit his world view, or maybe as though I were a fascinating new species of bird – something about the way his eyes found mine and held me … not captive, but safe.

I didn't know what to do with the thought that someone else could keep me safe. No one had done that in a long time, and honestly, the job hadn't really been open for applicants.

"Hey!" Some guy yelled at me from the street. I was almost to the intersection of Bryn Mawr and Sheridan, my muscles ached, my lungs hurt, and I wanted to go home and soak in a bath. I ignored the guy, turned left, and tightened Oscar's lead to adjust for traffic. I heard a horn honk behind me, and the squeal of tires, and the same guy called out, "Hey, Sophie!"

Uh oh.

I side-eyed a look at the car edging up next to me. It was a new, red Tesla Model S, and the passenger window rolled down so the driver could see me.

Abruptly I turned right and sprinted down an alley across from the old Edgewater Beach Apartments. Dane Quimby swore and slammed on his brakes. Someone was going to hit him if he drove like a moron, but that would keep him busy enough for me to disappear. I turned onto a side street and pulled Oscar even closer. He sensed my urgency and picked up his pace, though we were both near the end of our reserves.

The Tesla turned the corner, and I ducked down a different alley, changing directions so abruptly that I had to yank Oscar with me.

"Sorry, baby. I'll make it up to you," I gasped to him as we darted back toward Edgewater.

I could hear tires squealing on the next block, but it was a one-way street, and I thought we could make it to our building before he could turn another corner to spot us. It was a huge risk, because I *really* didn't want Quimby to know where I lived. It was bad enough he knew where I ran and what my dog looked like. Somehow, having Gabriel discover those same things hadn't felt nearly as dangerous to my well-being, though my freedom was potentially at stake with either man.

I didn't wait for the light, and I silently prayed to the traffic gods to keep my dog safe as we bolted across the avenue and into the service alley behind my building. I heard squealing tires from the street. I pressed myself into the service entry, punched the code, and pulled Oscar inside the vestibule just as the car nose slid past the alley entrance. My heart was pounding from much more than the ten miles we'd just run, but I didn't wait for the elevator. Oscar and I raced up the stairs to the second floor, and we were both breathing hard when I finally unlocked my apartment door.

I shot the deadbolt home behind me, unclipped Oscar's leash and got him a giant bowl of fresh water. Finally, I collapsed on the couch in a sweaty, panting mess of shaking muscles.

I held up my right leg and studied the cheetah leg/tights combo I wore. Dane hadn't known I was an amputee, and I wondered if he did now. The tights were black, the leg was black. There was no shoe on the end, which might have caught his attention, but he'd been driving on my left side, and that was the side I kept Oscar on so I didn't accidentally kick him with a leg I couldn't feel.

I decided that Dane had been studying my face to make sure I was actually the woman he knew as Sophie. And studying my face meant he hadn't noticed my leg.

I pulled up the bottom of the tights and peeled off the sleeve, socket, and liner. I was using the new ones Sparky had gotten from AMP'D Gear, and I'd just done ten miles without a hot spot on my stump. The politically correct term was residual limb, but that was too many syllables for the seven inches of lower leg that remained attached to my knee. I flexed the knee and was happy to feel nothing beyond the ache of hard use. There'd been so much pain the first year that I still anticipated agony every time I tried a new prosthetic.

I wanted to call Gabriel. I wanted to feel safe. But that was just crazy – Gabriel Eze had as much reason to find me as Dane did – Dane's company was Cipher's client, and Dane's bank account had been lightened on their watch. Gabriel knew I was responsible for that, but he had no legal proof, and I wasn't about to hand him any.

I peeled my tights the rest of the way off, then hopped down the hall to the bathroom. The tub was an old-fashioned clawfoot which the owner had re-enameled, and it was the best thing about the apartment – long and wide enough to lie down in, and with one leg folded in half, I could be fully covered in water.

I pulled up the audio version of the newest *Iron Druid* book, turned my phone on speaker, and when the tub was full, I sank into the hot water with a sigh. Luke Daniels could read a shampoo bottle and I'd listen, but my mind kept drifting off of Atticus' and Oberon's adventures, and was instead hopping from rock to rock in the garden of ADDATA, the Quimbys, and Gabriel. I wasn't even annoyed when the phone rang and interrupted the story, because I knew I'd have to go back to the beginning of the chapter anyway.

It was on its fourth ring when I finally dried off my hand and reached to answer it, so I hit the speaker button just as I looked at the screen.

Gabriel's name startled me so much I didn't say anything – I just sat up in the tub and stared at the phone.

"Please say you're not in the bath." Gabriel's voice was quiet, deep, and had a note of pleading in it.

"What do you want, Gabriel?" I moved again, and the water sloshed around me. I knew he could hear it because he groaned softly.

"Where to begin." It was almost a whisper, and the words sent a shiver through me. He cleared his throat and continued in his normal, beautiful voice. "We had a call from Quimby. He said he'd found you and wondered what we were going to do about it." I didn't say anything, and the silence lasted two long heartbeats. "Are you okay?" he finally asked, quietly.

"He saw me turn from Bryn Mawr onto Sheridan. I lost him in the alleys."

Gabriel exhaled. "Good."

"Aren't you supposed to be finding his money? Or his wife? Or something else he misplaced?"

"Do you have his money or his wife?" he asked.

"No."

"Okay."

"Okay? What exactly do you want from me, Gabriel?" I sat forward and the water sloshed again. I traced the ripples with my fingers as I heard his sigh.

"I don't know. I just know that every time you move, I hear the water in your bath, and I imagine ..." He exhaled sharply. "Be careful, darling. I don't trust Quimby not to try to hurt you if he can. Don't let him catch you."

"You haven't caught me yet, and you're far more resourceful than that little man."

He chuckled softly. "*Yet.*" He hung up the phone without saying goodbye, and Luke Daniels' voice returned, continuing the story as I sank down in the water and let its heat lap over the chills on my skin.

[12]
GABRIEL

"Don't shit on a plate and tell me it's fudge." – Dan O'Malley

---

I put my phone down and sat back from the conference table. What *did* I want from her, this woman who had captured my imagination such that even the sound of her bathwater made my heart pound uncomfortably. Or perhaps *especially* the sound of her in the bath. That would be simpler, of course. Pure lust would be much simpler to take in hand …

I winced at the bad pun and then chuckled at myself. *Wanker*.

A heart emoji dinged on the screen of my phone. My sister, Kendra, checking in.

How goes the American justice system? I typed.

My con law prof is an originalist who ignores the social context of the framers, she wrote.

Second Amendment?

Indeed. I could practically hear the disgust behind the word.

Can't win that one in this country, I wrote.

The kids might, she rejoined.

I sent her a heart in return and signed off. My sister had found her passion in U.S. Constitutional law, which was the source for no end of jokes from her British friends. But I believed that at heart she was merely a humanist in the classic sense of the word, with an abiding belief in the responsibility and right of all people to lead meaningful, ethical lives capable of adding to the greater good of humanity. The original framers of the U.S. Constitution had been rare visionaries for their time who had managed to turn their ideas into ideals by which a nation formed. I think that appealed to her sense that anything was possible to one willing to put mind, body, and soul into it.

It also made me wonder about some logistics as they concerned one Dane Quimby. I got up and went in search of O'Malley.

I found him in the kitchen making himself a cup of tea. He looked up when I came in, and my eyebrows rose in surprise. "Tea? You strike me as a coffee man through and through."

He snorted. "I take my coffee black, and I wanted something sweet. The options were tea and hot chocolate, and the fake marshmallows in the packaged shit taste like freeze-dried ass pellets, so tea it is."

I bit back the bark of laughter at his tirade and managed to keep a straight face. "Now that you mention it, the powdered chocolate *is* a rather distressing shade of brown."

O'Malley smirked and added four lumps of brown sugar to his tea. I refrained from comment. "Do we have access to information on weapons license holders for the State of Illinois?"

"To carry a gun here you gotta have a FOID card – a Firearm Owner's Identification – issued by the Illinois State Police. Yeah, we can run searches on those, but the state doesn't require individual weapons registration, so even if someone has a FOID card or a concealed carry permit, there's no proof they have a gun."

"Right. Do we know if Quimby has a FOID card?" I poured myself a cup of black coffee as O'Malley dumped his tea bag in the bin and took a sip.

"Huh. Interesting." I assumed he was talking about the question of Quimby having a weapons permit, not the tea-flavored simple syrup he'd concocted. "I guess we might have run a search on the partners when we first took on ADDATA's account, but that was a couple years ago."

"Quimby has a partner?" I hadn't actually done the research into Quimby's company, just the man himself. That was an oversight I would correct as soon as I got back to my computer.

"On paper anyway. Guy's a researcher at U of C. Teaches psychometry or some-fucking-thing like that." He had his phone out and was doing a search.

"Who partnered whom?" I asked, taking a sip of the foul brew that masqueraded as coffee after four hours in the pot.

O'Malley smirked. "Listen to you – 'whom.' The 'who' in this case was the fucking researcher guy, Karpov."

"Russian?"

He shrugged. "I guess. Name like that, someone on the family fucking tree was. My guess is Quimby was the hype man Karpov needed to turn his data science into cash money. Look 'em up – there's a file."

He gulped his tea, then navigated to a screen on his phone and passed it to me. "There – Quimby's got a FOID card. Picked it up three months ago."

I examined the date on the listing next to Dane Quimby's name, and it seemed familiar. I pulled out my own phone to check the case file. "That's the same week the secret account was opened."

"No shit?" O'Malley asked.

"No shit."

"Sounds like something spooked old Quimby, huh?"

"It does indeed."

[13]
SHANE

"I cook with wine. Sometimes I even add it to the food." –
Shane, P.I.

The adrenaline spike Quimby inspired had made me hungry, but none of the food in my kitchen appealed to me for dinner. I was not generally a picky eater, in fact I was the opposite of picky when it came to food. Food was good. Fried food was better. Food with bacon or butter (or both) was best. But general dissatisfaction had a way of making what should have been a simple decision (yes, corn chips and tuna sounded like a great combination, thank you very much) turn into a case of standing in front of the open refrigerator waiting for something to reach out and embrace me.

I was getting cold and annoyed, and I finally closed the fridge in disgust. A very small voice in the back of my head told me not to leave the apartment in case Dane Quimby was driving around my neighborhood waiting to spot me. Which was exactly why I wasn't going to take the easy way out and order a delivery. Fear pissed me off in principle, and I refused to allow it any control over my actions.

I pulled my hair up in a ponytail and debated my leg choices. No cheetah – I planned to wear shoes – but maybe I'd try one of the new superhero legs Sparky had designed for me. I had three of them: two had normal feet with titanium pole legs equipped with various MacGyver-inspired attachments, and one had a foot designed for a high-heeled shoe with a natural-looking leg that could be worn with a skirt. I'd never tested that leg, but tonight wasn't the night for a skirt or heels.

I picked a leg with a couple of screwdrivers, a sheath for my knife, and a kinetic energy-powered flashlight. Imagining the scenario in which I might need to use all those tools made me smile as I pulled on sweats and trainers over the prosthetic.

Oscar grumbled as he got to his feet, which was dog for "I haven't napped nearly long enough after our run, but you're going out aren't you, so I'm coming too." I leashed him for his last walk of the evening, and pocketed phone, keys, and cash. I figured I'd find inspiration for my dinner from whatever smelled good at the Armenian market on the corner.

I loved my neighborhood at night. There was a comedy theater a half a block away, and I loved catching the audience coming out of a show. People were always smiling and laughing as they recounted their favorite bits, and things occasionally got a little hot when the comedians were political. The cafe and bar near the theater stayed open late, and sidewalk conversations there were some of my favorites to eavesdrop on as Oscar and I walked toward the park.

Despite the darkness, it was still early and the theater crowd hadn't emerged yet. Oscar took me to all his favorite trees, and I let my brain wander around the problem of Dane Quimby.

"I thought to myself, if I owned a dog as big as that one, where would I go for his walks?"

I jumped at the deep voice that came at me from a bench about ten feet away, and if I hadn't immediately recognized it, my fight or flight instinct would have kicked in hard. As it was, my hand had tightened on Oscar's leash, and my brain had already plotted my escape route.

I reached down, pulled up the leg of my sweats, and unclipped the flashlight. It took effort to get my beating heart under control and I covered for it by flicking the flashlight on and shining it at the bench where Gabriel sat in the near pitch black night. He blinked but didn't wince away, and I gave him points for self-control By the time I'd sat down next to him, I'd managed to make my voice sound normal and calm. "I guess I should give you props for not actively stalking me, but after this afternoon's cat and mouse game with Quimby, I'll admit to being a little jumpy."

I was watching Oscar sniff around the bench before he casually nosed Gabriel's hand and accepted ear scratches as his due. I flicked the flashlight off and stowed it back on the leg. Gabriel noticed the motion with what looked like interest, but he didn't comment on my built-in tool kit.

"Sorry about that," he said. "I figured I'd be less likely to have the police called on me if I waited here rather than outside our building." His voice was like a caress on my slightly frazzled nerves.

"*Our* building?" I asked, incredulous.

"I couldn't pass up that apartment, could I? Despite the slightly dodgy neighbor with the enormous, bicycle-crushing hound, it suits me quite well."

I opened my mouth to say something that I'm sure would have been clever and scathing if I'd actually been able to think, but my mind had gone completely blank. So I closed my mouth, and turned on the bench to look at Gabriel.

In the dark, his eyes shone pale and serious. I'd expected him to laugh at me, but there was nothing mocking in his gaze.

"What are you doing?" I whispered.

"I don't know," he murmured back.

Oscar barked, and I jumped back. Apparently I'd been leaning forward, almost as if I'd wanted to kiss the man who kept finding me. Gabriel had gone still at the bark, and he searched the darkness for signs of whatever had startled my dog. Nothing else moved around us, and after a moment of alertness, Oscar went back to nosing the ground for signs of squirrels.

Gabriel stood and held his hand out to me. "I haven't eaten yet. Are you hungry?"

I hesitated, then took his hand, and he helped me to my feet. His skin was warm and callused, and that seemed to fit better with the jeans and cashmere sweater he was wearing now than it did with the suit I'd seen him in earlier.

"I was going to pick something up from the Armenian market on the corner," I said. I let him keep my hand about five seconds longer than I ever let anyone touch me, but instinct kicked in and I pulled it back. He let go, but he walked close enough to me that our hands continued to bump into each other.

"Mind if I join you?" he asked.

I shrugged and then remembered it was too dark to see. "When do you get the keys to your new place?" I asked instead of answering.

"I'm going to rent it for the month it's in escrow, so I'll move some things in this weekend."

I stopped before we got back to the street, and I stared at Gabriel. "That's really fast." My tone came out somewhere between panicked and angry, and he must have sensed it because he took his own volume down to something quiet and calming.

"I don't know why I keep calling, or why I want to run into you, or even why I'm waiting for you to tell me your name," he said. "I do know that even though you've managed the job just fine all these years without me, somehow I feel responsible for your safety where Dane Quimby is concerned."

"So, it's a job?" I asked, and then immediately wished I'd kept my mouth shut, because I didn't really want to hear the answer.

"No. It's personal."

I turned to keep walking, and Gabriel kept pace beside me. After half a block, I spoke.

"Dane Quimby thinks I have his money," I said.

"As long as his wife is missing, you're his only link to it," Gabriel agreed.

"I refuse to be afraid." I might have snarled a little. I hated feeling even a tiny bit of fear, and I generally went out of my way to avoid it whenever possible. "I guess I need to find Denise Quimby," I mumbled.

"Do you know where she is?" he asked quietly.

"No. Nor do I really want to throw her to the wolf that is her husband, but I don't need him breathing down my neck in her absence. I have work to do, especially since she stiffed me on my bill before she left town."

"Ah, I had wondered," he said.

"What did you wonder?"

"Whether you'd been hired by the wife, or whether you worked for a government agency of some variety."

"Why would a government agency be interested in Dane Quimby?"

He was silent for a few steps. "You may have noticed there's something a little … off."

"You mean besides the fact that he's an indiscriminate wharf rat with a Napoleon complex and a bad dye job."

Gabriel laughed, and I got a warm and fuzzy feeling, like I'd just done something wonderful.

We stopped at the light, and I nodded. "He is a little … desperate," I said.

"I was tasked with finding you," he said. I tensed and he saw it, but he continued speaking as though everything was just fine. "My bosses want to fire Quimby and ADDATA from their client roster, but since the money went missing on our watch, they can't cut him loose yet."

"Until the money's found, or until you can dig up something bigger on him to make him go away?"

"Just so." We crossed the street and continued on to the Armenian market. Gabriel held the door open for me, then grabbed a shopping basket as though we did this every Thursday night. I handed Oscar's leash to Mr. Basmian behind the counter and told my dog to lie down. He did so immediately, and Mr. Basmian slipped him a piece of jerky, as he did every time I brought Oscar into the market.

Gabriel smiled at Mr. Basmian and followed me down the produce aisle. We were next to the apples when I finally turned to face him. "This is weird," I said.

He stood at eye level with me, and the distance between us was no more than a few inches. He studied my eyes for a moment, and then he smiled. "I propose," he paused, and my eyes widened. He smiled and continued, "that we get enough food for a picnic, and then find someplace quiet to discuss just how weird this is."

I studied his face for another moment and then answered with my own smile. "We're going to need wine."

"Without a doubt," he said.

I turned and picked up a honey crisp apple, then placed it in the basket and continued down the aisle. He added a salami and sharp cheese, and I contributed rosemary crackers, fig jam, and a mild brie. He grabbed a package of chopped salad vegetables, and I added cucumbers, feta, and garbanzo beans. The roasted chicken was by mutual choice, and we both reached for the same bar of hazelnut chocolate. He stood back and let me choose the wine – a full-bodied red blend – but he blocked me out at the register when it was time to pay. I didn't argue; I just poked him in the ribs and whispered, "Next time."

He shrugged, took the bags, and said, "Sure," but I saw the smile, and Mr. Basmian winked at me when he handed over Oscar's leash. I took the lead and walked us to the door of my ... our building. I said nothing as I let him in and directed him toward the stairs and up one flight.

He was silent when we stopped outside my apartment and I unlocked the front door. It was nothing he couldn't have found out from the realtor, but it was still significant that Gabriel Eze now knew where I lived. He seemed to realize it too and was properly respectful of the fact that I'd let him in on another piece of information about me.

I refilled Oscar's water dish while Gabriel plated the salami, cheese, and crackers. We made the salad together, exchanging just enough words to find knives, the can opener, and ingredients for dressing. He carved up the roasted chicken and plated that too, while I tossed the salad and opened the wine.

"Can you pair your phone with the speaker and put on music?" I asked. It was presumptuous of me, but I hadn't shaken the feeling that the whole night straddled the line between work and something way too strange to contemplate. I didn't want to choose the music – I didn't want to inadvertently pick something romantic, or angsty, or just wrong – because I honestly didn't know what could be right. Country music was out, because everyone was either cheating or getting left, rap music was definitely out because I really only liked Eminem, and I shuddered to think what that said about me, and I definitely wasn't putting on one of my mixes, because there were at least two bagpipes tunes, an Indigo Girls song, and an angry female rocker in every one of them. I could probably get away with classic rock, but by this point, the overthinking was working its way into my confidence and taking big, toothy mouthfuls of its fleshy bits.

The fact that I was wildly attracted to this very random Englishman I knew almost nothing about was the most disconcerting thing of all.

I carried dishes to the table while he fussed with the music. He had the speaker paired just as I added napkins and silverware to the place settings. I collected handmade pottery and stoneware from art fairs and second-hand stores, so nothing matched, but I liked the way the table looked – sort of rustic with a mid-century modern vibe.

I looked up at him in surprise when the first notes of the music played. "*Hamilton*?" I grinned.

He answered with a smile of his own. "It was either that or *Jesus Christ Superstar. Book of Mormon* would have been too much, and *Greatest Showman* is better for cleaning dishes than for dinner."

I laughed in delight, and just like that, all my overthinking disappeared.

[14]
GABRIEL

"Live a life that lets you sleep at night, but if you dream, make sure you can live with yourself in the morning too." – Miri Eze

---

Her eyes laughed even when her expression gave nothing else away. She'd moved two electric pillar candles into the middle of the table, and they gave her skin the glow of summers spent outdoors. I served her some chicken and a large portion of the salad.

"Dane Quimby has a partner in ADDATA," I told her as I served myself. "A post-doctoral student from University of Chicago named Karpov."

She grabbed her phone from the table and typed in a search. My sister always did the same – instantly accessed information – and it impressed me every time. The years I'd spent with the Peacekeepers, where internet was often a luxury, hadn't trained me to expect to have information at my fingertips at all times.

I watched her face as she scanned the screen intently. "Alex Karpov did his doctoral thesis on psychometric applications of beliefs and thought processes on consumer behavior. He developed a person-

89

ality quiz that provided his research team information on individual demographics, income, and interests which could predict trends among specific data sets. Then he applied for and received permission from various social media platforms to collect the data from among their users for research purposes." She looked up from the phone to meet my eyes. "It's a whole different deal to use that data for commerce though. If Karpov is partnered with Quimby in ADDATA, which sells ad space, is he using his research access to predict buying trends for the clients of their company?"

"It would explain the ADDATA questionnaire on Facebook," I said.

"It would also be super unethical."

"And possibly illegal." I considered the implications, both to Cipher's relationship with ADDATA and to her involvement in moving Quimby's money for his wife. "Would you consider working with me on that angle?"

She took a sip of wine and contemplated me over the rim of her glass. "We haven't addressed the elephant in the room," she said finally.

"Which one?" I asked. "The really big one about the fact that you appear to have taken something that doesn't belong to you, and my job is to find you and get it back? Or the obvious one that is the fairly significant attraction between us, despite the fact that we know almost nothing about each other?"

I could see her smile behind the rim of her glass. "Part of me is hoping I don't actually have to tell you my name – that you'll figure it out for yourself."

"I know the name you go by ... *Shane,*" I said significantly, "but it's not your name."

Her eyes widened and she tilted her head. "Hmm. Interesting. My mail, my neighbor, or something else?"

"We have a rather extraordinary computer genius in the office—"

"And by computer genius you mean hacker?" she said with an arched eyebrow.

"That is information I can neither confirm nor deny," I said with an answering smile. "I can, however, suggest that your client's e-mails were accessed in order to determine whether there was foul play involved in her disappearance. Your final bill for service was among her unopened messages."

She scoffed. "Apparently the wife's security is as stellar as Quimby's."

"Remarkable, isn't it? Almost makes one wish for the days of clandestine meetings and telephone conversations instead of the 'anonymous' internet of today."

"Why do you assume I go by Shane?" she asked.

I studied her for a moment, and her eyes held mine. "It's effectively gender-neutral and therefore relatively anonymous. According to your invoice, you accept checks under the name S. Hane, which must be some form of your legal name, though I find no record of it in Illinois combined with a date of birth or address that could possibly be yours, and finally, Mr. Basmian at the Armenian market, heard your neighbor, a young Hispanic man, greet you by the name Shane when he returned Oscar to you one evening last month."

"Mr. Basmian told you that?"

"No, his daughter did. Her father had been very excited to finally learn the name of the mysterious, beautiful woman he'd seen nearly every day for a year, but who had never actually introduced herself." I helped myself to a piece of chicken and took a bite with extra skin, which was crispy and excellent.

She poured more wine into our glasses, then finally met my eyes again. "I don't have many friends, Gabriel, and the few I have know me as Shane."

"Is it a name you'd allow me to call you, or do I need to keep digging?"

"It's the name I chose for myself, so if you think we can be friends, you can use it." Her tone was careful, and I thought that she was protecting herself. I wanted to ask who had hurt her, but I wasn't even sure what I'd do with the information if she gave it to me. Not that she would – she looked ready to ask me to leave, and again I wondered what had caused such mistrust that even the possibility of friendship was so tentatively offered.

"I would like to be your friend," I said solemnly. I held my hand out to her across the table. "I'm Gabriel Eze. It's nice to finally meet you."

She hesitated for the space of one breath, then shook my hand. "I'm Shane."

Her hand was cold, and I wanted to keep it in mine to warm her skin, but she let go, so I reluctantly released her.

"I guess we should start with ADDATA's finances," she said as she made herself a bite of cheese and salami.

I hid the smile provoked by the "we" in her statement with a sip of wine, and managed a serious tone. "I can get our man at Cipher on it tomorrow."

She picked up her phone and navigated through a few screens. "Or … I can get us in."

She handed the phone to me, open to Dane Quimby's ADDATA bank account page. I stared at her. "You didn't hack this, because my own phone would be buzzing off the hook if you had."

"No, the bank believes it's Dane accessing his own account. And I assume that as long as there aren't any big withdrawals, you guys won't be alerted."

I finally allowed myself the grin that had been threatening since she agreed that we'd work together. "Greene, in our office, has set up an alarm system on every client account we monitor."

"Probably somewhere around ten grand right? That's the federal reporting threshold, so most people don't move more than that in any one transaction." She'd taken her phone back and scrolled through the account activity.

"Do you find it strange that a guy who drives a brand new, hundred-thousand-dollar car, whose wife left her brand new Lexus SUV sitting in the driveway, and whose home is worth more than two million dollars, is sweating the fact that his wife left with half-a-million dollars, despite walking away from the car and the house? It's almost as if they both know nothing but the cash is worth anything."

I'd been staring at her lips as she spoke, and I suddenly realized she was expecting an intelligent response. "Quimby took out a FOID card the same week he opened the secret account," I said.

She looked up from the phone in surprise. "A gun license? That's terrifying."

"That he can carry a gun? Yes, I agree."

"You ever notice that it's the people who are most afraid who are also the most dangerous with weapons?"

I scoffed. "I went from a country with incredibly strict gun laws into the UN Peacekeepers, which arms anyone who wants to don the helmet, and everyone who doesn't. I felt like one of the few people who wasn't in it for the firepower."

She put down her phone and regarded me. "Why the Peacekeepers? That's how I found your name, by the way – from a captioned photo taken in Africa."

I felt the familiar prickly sweat that had plagued my dreams whenever they took me back to my time in the country of my father's heritage, and I unconsciously sat back.

Shane stiffened and spoke quickly. "You don't have to tell me." I could practically see the protective shell she was wrapping herself up in.

"No, it's okay," I exhaled. "I just don't generally talk about it."

She bit her lip and then pushed back from the table and grabbed the dishes. "Will you pour us more wine while I put away the food?"

This woman had spikes on her armor, and I could almost picture them flaring out like the spines on a porcupine when she felt threatened or insecure. I did as she asked and then carried dishes into the kitchen while she wrapped up the food. "Dear Theodosia" was playing on the speaker, and I sang along with Leslie Odom, Jr. as he crooned to his baby daughter, promising to make the world safe and sound for her.

And then my voice broke, and Shane spun to look at me.

I closed my eyes for a moment to get my breathing under control. When I opened them again I saw Shane's gaze locked on mine. She hadn't moved, and I leaned back against the counter.

"My heritage is Nigerian and Jamaican. The Jamaican is on my mother's side. My grandmother was born in Jamaica, and she came to

London when she was a child, right after the war. She and my mother raised us on stories of her childhood, so the Jamaican side of me I know quite well."

Shane retrieved our wine glasses from the table and handed me mine. She remained silent, waiting for me to continue. "There have been Nigerian Peacekeepers for more than fifty years, and at first, joining them was a way to connect with my father's heritage. There aren't any official peacekeeping missions in Nigeria, but some of the men in our unit were personally affected by Boko Haram operating out of the north. When Boko Haram kidnapped the schoolgirls a few years ago, my Nigerian mates decided to do something."

Her eyes searched mine as she waited for me to continue. I took another sip of wine to try to swallow the remembered horror.

"We were a small unit, officially unsanctioned, but they weren't expecting us, so we were effective. We removed twenty girls from the Boko Haram compound." My voice broke again, and Shane closed her eyes against my words. "Some were as young as eight or nine. One of them was the little sister of a Peacekeeper in my unit."

"Oh, Gabriel." She reached out to hold my hand, and my heart pounded in gratitude at her touch.

"I left the Peacekeepers after that. It was just too ... hard." I rubbed the back of my neck and turned back to the table to clear more dishes. "I guess that's more why not the Peacekeepers than why."

"I suppose a better question would be why Chicago?" she said, accepting my subject change without digging into the things I hadn't said.

I shrugged. "That's easy. My twin sister, Kendra, got into law school at University of Chicago, and my mum moved with her to take care of my nephew. I was just back from Africa and couldn't imagine being anywhere they weren't, so I made a call to someone I'd met when I was a Peacekeeper, introductions were made to Cipher, and I got here a month ago."

Her expression softened, and it made her look young. She didn't appear to be much younger than I, but then I'd always held that one's experiences are often much more aging than one's years. I generally felt decades older than my actual age.

"How old is your nephew?" she asked.

"Mika's four. His dad, Jackson, and I were in the Royal MPs together."

That simple statement was like taking a dagger in hand and slitting my chest open from sternum to navel, and I felt as though I'd peeled back the skin to expose far more of myself than anyone should ever have to see. I carefully set the wine glass down on the counter, then took Shane's hand and lifted it to my lips. Her eyes didn't leave mine.

"Thank you for dinner," I said quietly.

She started to speak, but her voice broke so she cleared her throat to try again. "I'll work on Quimby's finances."

I nodded, relieved that I could tuck my discomfort back out of sight. "And I'll see what we have on ADDATA."

I finally let go of her hand, bent to give Oscar a belly rub on my way past the sofa, and turned to meet her eyes just before I left the apartment.

"Good night, darling," I said quietly, meaning the endearment not the nickname.

She gave me a wry smile and closed the door behind me.

[15]

SHANE

"I don't want to sound like a badass, but I eject my USB without removing it safely." – Shane, P.I.

I t was almost noon when I finally closed my laptop and left my apartment, which was an excellent time to lurk outside the ADDATA office building. In my experience as a spy for marital fidelity, the lowest-paid staff of any company were typically the least loyal to the executives in charge of it. They were also the most likely to race out of the building at noon to get the tables at the good eateries.

I'd once had a client who lived near the ADDATA offices, and we used to meet at a taqueria that made perfect street tacos – the little kind with meat sliced off the stacked roasting spit. That taqueria was directly opposite the office building, and I was willing to bet there was a line out the door every day at 12:05.

I turned the corner just as a group of twenty-something guys exited the ADDATA building and strode toward tacos. One doesn't amble toward tacos of such quality, and my own long legs carried me with velocity into the line just behind them.

They appeared to be programmers, as evidenced by the t-shirt on one that proclaimed, "There is no cloud, it's just someone else's computer." Also, they appeared to be speaking recognizably English words, but not in any order that made sense to the casual, or even astute listener. It wasn't until Cloud T-shirt Guy began discussing the demographics of the red state data sets that I tuned in.

"They've got me coding micro data sets by location and specialized interest. I'm pretty sure they're looking for gun-owning rednecks."

"Dude, you can't say redneck," the shorter one in front of him whispered.

"Sorry. I meant white guys from the rural South with interests in hunting, big trucks, gun shows, and the NRA," the guy in the cloud t-shirt said, with a shake of his head.

"I've got a really broad group to scrape. They want pretty much anyone in California or New York with a college degree isolated into a subset," said the third guy.

"So ... the opposite of my set," said Cloud T-shirt Guy.

"Hey, did you hear about Mickey Collins?" the short guy asked. "Steve said he dumped his girlfriend and went to California with the boss's wife."

"Shut up!" said the third guy.

"Dude, his girlfriend is hot," said the short one. "And now she's available."

"I heard the reason Mickey left Tomi is because she's seeing some married guy, so when the boss's rich wife hit on him, it was karma." The third guy shrugged.

"No, it was stupid," said Cloud T-shirt Guy. "If the wife was going to leave Quimby anyway, she should've waited until Karpov's politico deal goes through. She would have left with a helluva lot more."

It was their turn to order, so the conversation shifted to food, and then to weekend plans, but I made a note of Cloud T-shirt Guy's name – Nathan – when he gave his order. I ordered my own *tacos al pastor*, then drifted near a table where a couple of young women sat oblivious to the stolen glances they got from the programmers. They were discussing books, and I almost jumped in a couple of times on the relative worth of the blockbuster vs. the indie, but I managed to restrain myself. With effort.

When the guys got up and dumped their trash, I moved fast to get to the door in front of them. I looked back as the guys approached. "You're Nathan, right?" I said to Cloud T-shirt Guy.

He smiled without a trace of wariness. Oh, to be a young, white guy with no natural predators. "Yeah."

I held out my hand to shake his and tossed my head in the direction of the girls' table. "Kylie said I should talk to you." I pulled the girl's name out of thin air, hoping Nathan didn't actually know any of the girls he'd been leering at.

He held the door for me, and I walked with the guys as they headed toward the office building. "Oh yeah, what about?"

"That political deal Karpov brought in? How can I get on that team?"

Nathan scoffed. "Talk to Quimby. No one ever sees Karpov anymore, and Quimby's got us running around like chickens trying to please him. You'd never know they were partners the way Quimby drives us on data sets and target pops."

"Target pops?" I asked, as though that was the only confusing thing he'd said.

"Target populations." He looked at me oddly. "You're not a programmer though, are you?"

"I'm looking for ways to monetize each client relationship to its maximum potential," I said brightly, hoping to dazzle them with the pure bullshit of that statement.

"Well, good luck monetizing the politicos. I'm not sure where the money's actually coming from, but if we don't see some more soon, Quimby's going to lose a lot of really good people."

We got to the front door of ADDATA, and Nathan held it open for me. "You coming in?"

I checked my watch. "Crap! I have to run. Here," I said, thrusting my cell phone at him. "Give me your number and I'll come find you later, okay?"

Nathan looked bemused as he typed in his cell phone number. He was a computer nerd, so he wouldn't be nearly as easy to hack as Quimby had been, but I'd take whatever access I could get. When he handed my phone back, I waved with another bright smile, and then hurried around the building without a backward glance.

As I walked, I sifted through the bits of disjointed information I'd gotten from the young programmers. I memorized the names for my notes, saw with satisfaction that Nathan Yorn had added his last name to his phone contact, and resolved to dig a little deeper on Quimby's partner's political dealings.

[16]
SHANE

"There are actually seven food groups if you count coffee, chocolate, and wine." – Shane, P.I.

I stopped at Dark Matter Coffee for a to-go cup, black with four sugars. It was a gamble, and not one I was sure would pan out well for me, but I understood enough about people to have worked up some apology hacks.

Van Hayden was behind the front desk of Cipher Security Systems, and he watched me enter the building through narrowed eyes.

"Another bike messenger steal your bag?" he said in a voice devoid of humor.

I held up my bag and kept my expression neutral. "Not today." Then I put the coffee and sugars on the desk in front of him. "Brought you something to apologize for lying to you before."

That got his attention in a fairly big way, and I could see him chewing over which question to ask first as he studied me in silence. "You want to talk to Eze," he finally said in that not-a-question way he used so effectively.

"If he's available, that would be great," I answered quickly to cover my surprise at the restraint Van was showing.

He picked up the phone on the desk and punched in a number. "She's here." He scowled as he said it, then hung up. He met my eyes and nodded to the elevator. "Third floor."

The surprises just kept coming, and I struggled to keep my face from giving anything away. I must have failed though, because Van's scowl became the ghost of a smirk. "His neck's out pretty far on you."

"Is it just me you dislike, or people in general?" I retorted, and the smirk disappeared.

He let his expressionless stare be his answer. "Thank you for the coffee," he said in a tone that was drier than the Sahara Desert. I turned to walk to the elevator, and his gaze itched between my shoulder blades. I had a feeling he was mentally mapping all my kill zones as I waited for the elevator. I was avoiding his eyes so studiously that I missed the entrance of the woman who called to Van in a voice that sounded like a combination of lace and fine suit wool. "Hello, handsome."

Shockingly, there was a chuckle in Van's voice as he answered. "Alex is working in the vault today, Sandra."

I turned just as a stunning redhead blew Van a kiss. "He's lucky he saw me first, or you'd be in trouble," she said as she strolled past the desk toward me.

The fact that it was the elevator she strolled toward, and not actually me didn't seem to matter. She was like a curvy magnetic neutron star, with the strength of a hundred billion Teslas. She smiled at me, probably because I was staring and it was either smile or flee, and the room lit up a thousand candle watts brighter.

I finally found my words when the elevator opened and we stepped inside. I stared straight ahead so I didn't get burned by her sunlight. "You must be one of the two people in the world Van likes."

She laughed, and silk joined the lace in her voice. "Being scary is a sport to him."

"Well, he has Olympic-level skills," I said.

"Abusive fathers tend to bring that out in men who fear losing control," Sandra said, and then she gasped and turned toward me. "I'm sorry, that was TMI on an epic scale, and pure speculation on my part."

Somehow, her mea culpa diminished her candle wattage by just enough that I could properly look at her without fear of getting fried by pure luminescence. "I do it all the time," I said, the same chagrin in my own voice. "I make up stories in my head about who someone is based on what they look like, what they're wearing, how they walk. It's a terrible habit, made even worse because I'm usually right."

Sandra exhaled with a quiet chuckle and held her closed fist up for a fist bump. "Sisterhood," she said, when I bumped knuckles with her.

The elevator dinged at the third floor and the doors opened, and Gabriel stood there waiting for me. "Hey," he said in low tones that made my toes curl up in my boot.

I gave Sandra a quick smile as I stepped out of the elevator, and she winked back at me before the doors closed.

Gabriel was wearing another gorgeous suit – light gray with a lavender shirt and a purple-and-silver tie – and I suddenly felt under-dressed, even in my favorite long coral cardigan with a Chinese silk scarf that made my eyes go really green.

"I'm glad you're here," he said, as he gestured for me to precede him, and then guided me with a hand at my low back. I could feel the heat of his hand through the thin knit of my sweater, and he smelled faintly of something spicy. I tried to pay attention to the room we walked through – I really did – but two of my senses were busy trying to pretend they weren't captivated by him, and the other three were wishing they could be wrapped up in essence of Gabriel too.

I was in serious trouble.

Gabriel directed me toward a conference room with a long table and a big window that looked out onto open space. His waxed canvas bag was on the table next to a laptop and a stack of files, and he pulled out the chair for me at the end of the table, next to his seat. Then he moved his laptop out of the way and studied me with searching eyes.

"You came," he said, almost as if he couldn't believe it.

"You expected me," I answered, a little defensively.

"I hoped."

103

Oh.

All those stern lectures to myself about how this wasn't a thing and thinking otherwise was just setting myself up for disappointment flew out of my brain and landed, flopping like a fish, on the table between us. I had to look away from his gaze so I didn't accidentally lean over the flopping fish of managed expectations and kiss him.

Because I really, really wanted to kiss Gabriel Eze.

And to make sure I didn't do something stupid and impetuous, like actually kiss him, I did something even dumber.

"Do you want to run with me tonight?" I asked, before I had the sense to bite my tongue. And then I winced and screwed my eyes shut. "No, never mind. It's a bad idea—"

"Yes," he said quickly, cutting me off.

I opened my eyes and peered at him warily. "Why?"

I clearly had no business opening my mouth around him, because only the most inane things managed to find their way out. I shook my head at my own idiocy. "No, don't say anything else. I'll just answer with something ridiculous and embarrassing, and I won't be able to look you in the eye." I was already having trouble seeing past the haze of mortification that blurred my vision and knocked whatever discretion I might have had right off my tongue.

Gabriel laughed, and the sound was velvety and smooth.

"I like watching you run. You're fast, probably faster than me, and that intrigues me," he said, his gaze never leaving mine. "*You* intrigue me."

My heart was beating too fast. I blew out a breath and looked away. "Okay," I whispered, not really sure why I said it.

A knock sounded on the glass, and I was grateful for the interruption. I looked up to see the tattoo-necked guy standing in the open doorway.

Gabriel didn't shift away from me, though I had the sense we were sitting much too close for casual conversation, but his expression held no guilt when he looked up at the guy.

"Come in."

The guy, whose name I assumed was Dan based on my former

deductions, flicked a look at me. What was probably meant as a casual glance turned into laser focus when Dan realized who I was. "You're Quimby's date," he said in a distinctively Bostonian growl.

"What do you need, O'Malley?" Gabriel said. There was an edge to his voice that hadn't been there before, and it got Dan's attention.

"I need you to tell me what the fuck's going on," he responded, minus the growl. Then, improbably, Dan held a hand out to me. "Dan O'Malley, Cipher Security."

I took his hand and shook it, surprisingly not intimidated by him despite the gruff street manner – or maybe because of it. "Shane. P.I."

He smirked. "Shane P.I.? That a name, or a string of single-syllables to confuse perps into forgetting they didn't get a straight answer?"

My scoff had a smile attached. "Both. You can call me Shane, and I'm a licensed private investigator."

Dan's eyes flicked to Gabriel's, and I followed his gaze. Gabriel was stone-faced.

"So, Shane of the no-last-name, what brings you to Cipher?" Dan said, ignoring Gabriel. He spun a chair around backward and dropped onto it.

The tension seeping off Gabriel raised the temperature in the room, and I knew Dan wasn't oblivious to it. The neck tattoos stood in stark contrast to his crisp white dress shirt, and I thought that contrast was exactly who Dan was – a ruffian in a nice suit, and the kind of guy who deliberately pushed buttons just to see what a person was made of.

I leaned forward, and I heard Gabriel inhale softly. "I'm here to see Gabriel." I held Dan's gaze deliberately, with an appearance of ease I didn't actually feel, and the moment stretched far beyond the realm of a comfortable pause in conversation. I sensed that Gabriel's gaze was locked on Dan, but I didn't dare break my eye contact in this dominance game. I wondered where Gabriel stood in this particular pack, considering that his hands twitched like he wanted to clench his fists.

"Enough, O'Malley," Gabriel growled, and Dan suddenly broke into a beatific smile. I could see hints of the scruffy little boy he'd been who used smiles like that to get out of punishments he'd undeniably earned.

Dan pushed back from the table and stood in a fluid motion, breaking eye contact, the dominance game done. "Nice to meet you, Shane P.I."

"Really?" I asked. I watched myself inserting my own foot into my mouth, and yet seemed powerless to stop my own snark. "Was it really nice to meet me? Because I felt like you just sniffed my ass and raised your hackles to see if I'd submit."

I had clearly been reading too many dog training manuals and needed to rethink my whole going-out-in-public strategy. Both men stared at me for the one second it took me to flush in mortification from head to toe, and I stood up quickly. "Sorry, I'm going to go now."

"No, I'm sorry," Dan said, taking a step backward. "You're right. It's a fucking bad habit, and my wife keeps calling me out on it. I apologize, Shane P.I. Hackles and ass-sniffing I'm good at, polite conversations, not so much."

He shot Gabriel a contrite look over my shoulder, then gave me a quick nod and left the room. Gabriel had gotten to his feet when I did, and he touched my hand. "Don't go."

I turned to face him. His expression was stony and grim, and the part of me that hated confrontation was yelling "run away!" in my brain. I inhaled and forced my legs to lock so I didn't head straight for the door.

"How long did you say you've worked here?" I asked.

"A month." His voice grated, and he was still trying not to clench his hands.

"You're pissed that you let him do that." It wasn't a question.

"Yes," he said.

I really looked at him – not just the tension in his face and body. His bronze skin stretched tightly over sharp cheekbones and a strong jaw that clenched with tension. His black hair was cropped short and looked like a leftover military habit, and his broad shoulders filled out his well-cut suit as powerfully as they would have filled fatigues. This was a strong man who had taken orders he didn't like from men he maybe didn't respect, and some part of him was still locked in that pattern.

I sat down with a sigh. "The rules are different for both of us, and I can't pretend to know what your rules are, just as mine must be baffling to you. I assume you've never been a woman—" he smiled at that, which let some of the tension seep out of his features "—and you appear to be in possession of all of your limbs, while I have no idea what it's like to be black in America, nor how an English Jamaican Nigerian man navigates a landscape full of assumptions that have nothing to do with who he actually is."

Gabriel finally sat down next to me again and allowed his hands to rest on the table without involuntarily clenching into fists. His expression had relaxed into attentiveness and interest rather than the fight-or-flight look he'd been sporting a moment before.

I kept my tone conversational. "What Dan did was just a version of the basic assessments humans do to other humans to categorize them into friend or foe, safe or dangerous, tribe or stranger. As a white man in America, he's at the top of the food chain, so his check was for dominance. Mine as a woman is usually for threat level, and I can only guess at yours."

He was silent for a long moment – long enough that all my noisy self-doubt conversations started talking at once, mostly about how I had no business discussing race because I couldn't understand what his experience had been.

"I look for their fear," he said quietly.

A whole chasm of unspoken words yawned between us, but he stepped around the edge without looking down.

"You found something about Quimby's finances?" His change of subject was smooth, and if he hadn't just been so tense, it would have seemed completely natural in the flow of conversation.

"I talked to some guys at ADDATA. They have the programmers scraping data into subsets with a political slant. One set sounded clearly conservative, and another was obviously liberal. The programmers I talked to said Karpov had brought political clients into ADDATA, but the money was getting scarce, and they were likely to start losing people."

About halfway through my recitation, Gabriel began taking notes, and when I was done, he stared at the pages he'd written for a long moment before finally meeting my eyes. "This is good work."

"Thank you."

Gabriel stood and held his hand out to me. I took it, and then felt absurdly like a princess rising from her throne, if the princess was standing on a stick and the throne was hard plastic. "I think it's time I introduce Alex Greene to you."

I raised an eyebrow and balked as Gabriel indicated I should precede him from the room. He smirked. "He's suspicious of everyone, says almost nothing about himself, has superpowers at which no one can even guess, and he's a genius. Also, he's a criminal, so you have that in common too."

I narrowed my eyes at him. "He's your hacker, isn't he?"

Gabriel just smiled cheerfully and closed the door behind us.

[17]

GABRIEL

"Yesterday I changed my wifi password to hackifyoucan. When I checked it today, it was challengeaccepted." – Sandra Greene's T-shirt

---

It was a tactical decision to direct Shane to the elevators and then walk behind her – not only was the view one to be appreciated, it was an excellent vantage point from which to watch others' reactions to her. And make no mistake, people reacted to her. It was rare to see a woman of her height, much less one with so much natural grace. Something was different about her walk as well – the limp that had been slight before was nearly indiscernible now.

Alone in the elevator together, we both stood in the middle, closer than strangers would, but not as close as I wanted to. She smelled good, like vanilla and something tropical, and I imagined her with sun-warmed skin, the gold in her hair glinting on the beach.

"Have you ever been to California?" I said impulsively. The easy silence between us disappeared, and the question hung in the air like a bad smell.

She took a quick breath, as though steeling herself, then turned to look at me. "I don't tell people my stories. They're done, and I've moved on."

Her voice was too quiet, and I thought it had cost her something to even say the words. I stepped back from her to give her the space she seemed to require, and her shoulders tensed. The elevator doors opened on the fourth floor. "This is us," I said. She suddenly seemed fragile in a way I didn't understand, and I stopped her before she could step out.

"Wait," I touched her arm, and she finally met my eyes. "Whatever it was that just happened, I'm sorry. I didn't mean to pry."

She exhaled sharply. "I don't know why I'm here. Whatever this job is, it's not mine – I'm not getting paid for it, and I haven't even been paid for the initial work I did. This isn't personal, Gabriel, it's a job, and I don't work for free."

I studied her for a long moment, and though she met my eyes, she wouldn't hold my gaze. The elevator doors began to close, so I thrust out an arm to hold them open.

"Okay," I said quietly. She did meet my eyes then, and she looked equal parts fierce and vulnerable. I wanted to gather her into my arms and protect her from whatever haunted her, even as I knew she'd never allow it. I reached in front of her and pressed the button for the lobby.

"Thank you for all your help. The information you gave me today was excellent, and I'll pass it along to Greene and O'Malley myself."

She nodded and then pressed the button to close the doors as I stepped back out of the way.

"Hold that elevator, please!" A woman's voice called from the hallway. My arm automatically shot into the closing doors, halting their path again as I turned to see Greene escorting a beautiful redhead to the elevator. She smiled at me with the kind of gaze that made a man feel seen, then slid into the elevator next to Shane.

The redhead grinned at Shane and said, "We meet again," as I let the doors close. I turned to see Greene's eyes lingering where the redhead and Shane had just been.

"Was that your wife?" I asked.

He nodded, and I thought I caught the hint of a smile on his preternaturally stoic face.

"That your woman?" he asked me. I knew he referred to the woman he had tracked for me on security cameras throughout Chicago.

I shrugged with no trace of a smile, because honestly, I didn't know.

[18]

SHANE

Everyone: *"Are you a natural redhead?"*
Me: *"No, I soak my hair every night in the blood of my enemies."*
– Sandra Greene's tote bag

The stunning woman next to me stuck out her hand. "I'm Sandra, and I think we're meant to be friends, don't you?"

I had just badly overreacted to Gabriel's question, and I desperately needed to get out of my head. Sandra had just provided me with a welcome distraction, and I shook her hand. "I'm Shane. It's nice to meet you."

Sandra scoffed dramatically and grinned. "You say that now. Get a lemon drop or two into you, and I'll make you cry."

I laughed, and the tightness that had been squeezing my chest eased. "Is that your superpower?"

"One of them. What's yours?" Sandra's magnetic appeal was on full strength again, but actually talking to her instead of gawking at her made it feel slightly less irresistible.

"Intimidation," I said, not feeling the slightest bit intimidating, despite the five or six inches I had on her in height.

She looked me up and down critically. "I can see that. You'd intimidate the hell out of competitive women and short men. Fortunately for us, given the number of lemon drops we're going to be consuming, I'm neither." Then she pulled out her phone and handed it to me. "Your number, please."

I tried not to laugh and/or stare at her while I typed in my name and actual phone number. I handed the phone back to her and she looked at it.

"No last name? Whoever you're hiding from won't be joining us for lemon drops, just so you know."

I definitely did stare at her then and almost let the elevator doors close on me when she disembarked in the lobby. Sandra was already walking toward the front doors when I finally made my legs move again.

She blew Van a kiss. "See you soon, handsome."

"Not soon enough, Mrs. Greene," Van said with a grin that lit up his eyes, and maybe a tiny corner of his mouth.

Mrs. Greene? As in Alex Greene's wife? Huh. I stored that information away in the mental file I kept on everyone I'd ever met, not sure what I would do with it given the unlikelihood that I would ever run into the magnetic Sandra Greene again. I was just passing Van's desk when Sandra called back over her shoulder to me.

"Expect my call tomorrow, Shane."

I halted in mid-stride for a second, mentally adjusting to the idea that perhaps I would see Sandra Greene again. Van Hayden sucked his teeth and smirked at the shocked expression that must have been on my face.

"She makes men cry," he said.

I leaned down to adjust the cuff on my pants. There was a smirk in my voice as I answered without meeting his eyes. "So do I."

Sparky was in when I let myself into his warehouse. The soundtrack to *Guardians of the Galaxy* was playing on the speaker, and he was belting along as out of tune as it was possible for a human to sing. There's something about singing off-key at the top of one's lungs that simultaneously inspires laughter and cringing pain in one's audience, but it was the perfectly executed spinning-in-place dance move that finally tipped the scales in favor of laughter.

He grinned at me like a pre-teen boy caught dancing in a mirror. "'Sup, Shane?"

"'Sup? Is that a greeting or a command to eat?" I dropped my bag on the desk where his computer sat. "Can I …?" I indicated the laptop, and he waved me to it.

"Help yourself. There's leftover Chinese in the fridge if the command to eat is more interesting than my feeble attempt at youthful vernacular."

I laughed at the pompous tone he adopted to go along with the fifty-cent words, and booted up his computer.

"Whatcha looking for?" he asked as he worked on something that looked vaguely bionic.

What was I looking for? I'd gone to Sparky's to use his secure system out of habit, but was I actually going to do more poking around ADDATA? I'd surprised myself with the level of my annoyance at the fact that I was essentially working for Cipher without a paycheck, even though I was self-aware enough to get that it was the comment about California that set me off. Did Gabriel actually know my history? I'd been doing a great job of existing in the moment since I'd moved to Chicago, and it pissed me off that one question sent me spiraling back into all the feelings that made me leave California.

I typed in a name before I was even aware my fingers were on the keyboard. *Marquette Hane.* The list that populated Google was the same it had always been over the years: the Yellow Pages, LinkedIn, and old articles from the *Sacramento Bee* about both accidents. My mom hadn't made the news since I left, and she didn't seem to be on social media at all. Like mother like daughter, at least in that respect.

When I reached the bottom of page three, I quickly slid the cursor back up to the top and typed in another name. *Sandra Greene.* The page loaded slowly and I almost navigated away, but then a business website came up and my eye was caught by a title. Doctor of Psychiatry.

Of course she was. I clicked on the website, and a photo of the stunning redhead filled the upper left corner of the screen. Sandra Greene was a psychiatrist, which explained why she made people cry. She uncovered their deepest, darkest secrets, just like I did. The difference was that people handed her the keys to the vaults where they stored their skeletons, while I had to dig up the skeletons myself – by hand – with a dull spoon.

I navigated to the contact page on her website, but it was the fill-in-the-blank kind that kept her phone and e-mail private. Smart – especially since her picture was on the website – but not useful for my purposes. I doubted I'd get anywhere with a search on Alex Greene, if he was, in fact, her husband, so I went back to the initial Google results and tried two Yellow Pages searches looking for Sandra's contact info. Finally, I clicked on her LinkedIn page. The site didn't even have a chance to load when a red warning flashed on the screen.

"Uh, Sparky? You may want to take a look …"

I backed away from the computer as he rushed over. "What did you click on?" he said, frantically navigating away and shutting down screens.

"Nothing. I was doing a Google search on someone and I hit their LinkedIn page." I didn't like how panicked he suddenly was.

"I haven't heard of any LinkedIn Trojan horses, so it must be something else. Where were you right before that?"

"On the business page of a psychiatrist," I answered.

Sparky looked sideways at me even as his fingers roved the keyboard faster than I'd ever seen anyone type.

I snarled at his side-eye. "Not for me, you dork, for work." Well, not for that either, but definitely not for me.

He shrugged. "I wasn't judging. Or, rather, I was judging, but it was good. You should see a therapist. Everyone should at least once in their lives, just to know what it feels like to talk to someone who's really listening."

"I listen to you," I said, way more defensively than the statement warranted.

"Really? Who is my favorite superhero, then?" he asked, finally clearing the screen before he shut the lid on his laptop.

"Star-Lord," I shot back.

"Wrong. And by the way, you're banned from the laptop. You can bring your own, but you can't network with mine."

"Why not?"

"Because you just unleashed a worm that I need to go in and neutralize sometime when you're not sitting here."

"What does me sitting here have to do with a worm?"

"I can't curse you with full invectives if you're looking at me."

"But you can and presumably do when I'm not here?"

Sparky sighed and looked pained. "Something like that."

I rolled my eyes and threw up my hands in disgust. "Ugh. I'm sorry my simple Google search seems to have generated a worm, although how, I have no idea, unless all your digital protection is just for show." I grabbed my bag off the table then turned to him, suddenly contrite. "I really am sorry. I wasn't careless, I promise."

He scrubbed his hands through his hair, which had the effect of turning perfectly nice boy hair into porcupine meets light socket locks. "I know you didn't do it on purpose."

I caught sight of the bionic ... thing Sparky had been working on when I came in. "Making a Terminator?"

He shrugged. "I have nightmares about Skynet."

I stared at him. "You do?"

He looked up sharply. "You don't?"

I was not going to debate the relative safety of artificial intelligence with a man who had nightmares about a fictional corporation from a film released in 1984. I looked around the workshop at the various leg and arm parts in different stages of assembly. "I don't suppose you've done any new running legs, have you?"

"I'm working on a formula for carbon fiber that will make cheetah blades extra bouncy," he said without looking up.

I grinned on my way to the door. "You'll call it the Tigger leg, and you'll make millions."

He snorted and re-opened his laptop. I headed for the door to leave just as he called out. "You."

"What?" I couldn't tell if it was a command or a declaration.

Sparky finally looked up from his computer screen, looking adorably tousled, like the man-sized version of a scruffy teen. "You're my favorite superhero. Now get out so I can curse you properly."

[19]
SHANE

"There is a unique brand of awkward that lives in mortification central and can usually be found on the Why? aisle right next to the pictures of me." – Shane, P.I.

A t 7 p.m. I got a text from Gabriel. *Run at 11?* I ignored it.

At 8 p.m., as I was eating leftover chicken, another text. *Meet you at the park or outside our building?* I snorted at that. *Our* building indeed. I ignored that text too.

At 9 p.m., as I wrote up the day's work at ADDATA in the Quimby file, a third text. *If I have to come to your door, I'm bringing balloons.* I smirked at that one. Yeah, right. Where was he going to get balloons at eleven o'clock at night? *The Party Store is open until midnight,* he texted a moment later.

At 10 p.m. I closed the lid of my laptop just as my phone chimed. *Never mind, I'm coming up now. I have paperwork for your services as an independent contractor.*

Bullshit, I thought. Oscar snarfled in his sleep as I got up and pulled on running tights over my bare legs. I couldn't help it – prosthetic and pants always came off the minute I got home. I had the habits of a two-year-old who strips to underwear and actually prefers nothing at all. I hopped to the kitchen, and Oscar cracked an eyelid in acknowledgement that movement was happening. He groaned as he got to his feet and padded behind me in hopes that manna from the kitchen gods would fall in his path. I opened bubbly water and drank directly from the bottle.

There was a knock on the door, and Oscar's head came up in anticipation of Jorge, who often dropped by for some dog love on his way home from the library. I called out, "Come in," as I put the lid on the bubbly water and stashed it back in the fridge.

"Do you always leave your door unlocked?" asked a voice that sent a shiver across my skin.

I straightened and turned to see Gabriel, wearing running shorts and a University of Chicago sweatshirt, entering my apartment with an envelope in one hand and a water bottle in the other.

My shock must have been obvious. "You're not Jorge," I said, inanely, given that he clearly was not my young neighbor.

"No, I'm not. Is it odd that I now have an intense desire to know this Jorge and his intentions toward you?" he asked as he closed the door behind him.

I stifled the smile that his words provoked so he didn't get the idea that I kind of liked caveman proclamations made in such cultured tones.

I also stifled the playful comeback his comment deserved. I didn't want to play with Gabriel. Or maybe I wanted it too much. "Why are you here?" I asked. I realized I was still leaning against the kitchen counter, and I didn't want him to come in there to speak to me. It was too small, and I could be cornered too easily.

I felt Gabriel's eyes on me the whole way as I hopped into the living room and to the sofa where my cheetah leg had been left the night before. The attention made me bristle because I assumed it was focused on the ungraceful way I moved.

He took the seat across from me and put the envelope on the coffee

120

table. "Cipher Security is offering you a consulting fee to work with us on this ADDATA case." His voice was easy, but his gaze was locked on my hands as they worked automatically to attach the cheetah leg to the sleeve on the end of my residual limb. I was far more self-conscious than was comfortable.

"You know, there's a whole subset of sexual deviants called stump-humpers," I said casually to cover my awkwardness. I flexed my knee to check the fit of the leg, then pulled the end of my modified running tights down over the socket, annoyed with myself at how relieved I was to cover up.

His eyes met mine again. "I didn't know that. I confess I am completely fascinated by the mechanics of your legs. Obviously this one's designed for running, but it wouldn't fit into the boots you wore the other day. Do you have different foot attachments, or are the legs entirely unique according to your needs?"

I scowled. I'd tried to shock him, and all he wanted to discuss was the mechanics of my prosthetics. To cover my discomfiture, I grabbed the envelope from the table and opened it. *Dear Ms. P.I.*, it began, and I smirked. "O'Malley wrote this?" I asked.

"He's a partner in the company," Gabriel confirmed with a nod.

The typewritten note was brief and to the point. *Cipher Security is offering you three thousand dollars per week for your services as a consulting investigator. Eze showed us his notes on your work to date and pointed out that you deserve compensation, so you can thank or blame him as you see fit. To cover my own ass, this engagement can be terminated by either party with no notice and for no specific reason, but I hate firing people, so don't do something stupid.* I looked up from the paper and scoffed. "Doesn't mince words, does he?"

"Not usually." Gabriel nodded toward the envelope. "There's a check in there for your first week's compensation if you accept the job."

I removed the check, written out to S.HANE Information Services in the amount of three grand, and a wave of relief hit me, quickly followed by a confusing mix of anger and something warm and fuzzy.

"I don't want to owe you," I said grumpily.

121

"You don't," Gabriel shrugged.

I looked at him a long moment, then finally sighed. "I'm being a moody bitch, and that pisses me off too."

"Then get your shoe on, grab the beast, and let's go run it off."

"You're awfully presumptuous, aren't you?" Some of the tightness in my chest let go, and I decided I was tired of fighting. I grabbed my shoe from where I'd kicked it off next to my leg, and laced it up.

Gabriel had Oscar sit, then clipped on his leash and scratched his ears. I was impressed. Most non dog-owners wouldn't know to make dogs work for their leash so it's a privilege instead of something to pull against.

I grabbed my running key and pulled it on over my head, then took Oscar's leash from him. Gabriel hadn't moved from his place just inside the door, and his eyes were on me as I stopped in front of him.

"Thank you for getting them to hire me," I said quietly.

He shrugged. "You're doing the work. I just reminded them to pay the right person for it."

The flecks of gold in his eyes fascinated me a little too much. The fact that I could see them meant I was standing much too close, and the slow smile he gave me meant he knew it too. I stepped back, right into the coat rack, and when I jumped forward to keep from knocking it over, I impacted with his chest while an umbrella hooked onto my socket, pulled out of the rack, and clattered to the floor.

My entryway had just become mortification central, and my face flamed horrendously. So I did the only thing one can do when one makes a complete ass of oneself. I kissed him.

[20]

GABRIEL

"Obviously, The Princess Bride has a movie quote for every occasion, but you might be surprised to know that Bull Durham comes in a close second." – Shane, P.I.

She kissed me.

And for one stunned moment, I kissed her back.

It was only one moment because the next moment she broke the kiss and nearly collided with the coat rack again in her haste to back away.

"Don't—" I said quickly.

"I'm sorry, that was totally inappropriate," she stammered.

"—stop," I finished.

That arrested her apology mid-word, and she stared at me with an open mouth.

"Or if you must, then I need to run, otherwise I may not leave." I wasn't sure what possessed me to be quite so honest, but her kiss had rattled me. It had been unexpected, but it lit a fire that made my hands burn to touch her.

She exhaled and dipped her gaze down to her dog. "Come on, Oscar, let's run."

I opened the door to her flat, and she stepped past me into the hall. After I pulled the door shut behind me, she locked the deadbolt using the key around her neck. I was pleased to see it would have been reasonably difficult for someone to break in.

I was a master at mental avoidance.

She saw me study the lock. "Lock picks won't work on it. I've tried," she said, a note of something less than confidence in her voice, as though she, too, were unsettled. I didn't like that she could ever be less than fully confident.

"You have lock picks?" The thought was possibly even more arousing than the collision of our mouths had been. Actually not, but it was close.

She pulled her confidence back on and scoffed. "You don't?"

"I never needed them. I've always been more of the kick-in-the-door type."

She preceded me down the hall, but not before I caught the smirk on her face. "So door-kicking is a Peacekeeper thing?"

The table tennis nature of our conversation was an excellent distraction from the persistent erection battle I was losing.

"It's actually more of a suicidal sister thing," I said, which well and truly derailed my arousal, as I knew it would. Then I sighed, because I also knew I'd have to explain. "Kendra had fairly severe post-partum depression. Then when Mika was three months old, her husband died, which sent her over the edge. She got help, and she's doing great now, but it was a rough couple of months in an already difficult year."

She turned to face me on the landing of the stairs, and her hand flinched, like she held back from touching me. I wished she had given in to the impulse. "We are full of landmines, you and me. I keep stepping on yours, and mine seem to have hair triggers that explode when I least expect them to. So I'm going to try to stop apologizing for putting my foot in it, and hopefully we can get through a run without the pavement blowing up around us?"

She looked so earnest and beautiful, and I just barely managed not to kiss her again.

Shane's eyes flicked to my mouth before she turned and sprinted down the stairs. Her beast was happy to lead the way and didn't stop pulling until we got outside.

The night had just enough chill to keep us cool as we ran, and the lake breeze washed away some of the stench of city traffic. We didn't speak again until we got to the Lakefront Trail and had settled into a comfortable pace.

"I feel like I need to explain my reaction earlier, when you asked about California," she said as we turned to run south. I put her on the lake side of me – an old habit of situating myself between potential danger and the person I was with.

I didn't confirm or deny, and she continued. "I grew up there, and left under less than ideal circumstances." She inhaled, hesitated, and then spoke her words in a rush, as though ripping off a bandage. "I was cheated on pretty badly by someone I thought was special, and when I ran away from California, I was running away from him and every one of the ugly memories associated with that break-up." She sighed and then shook her head. "Essentially, I broke up with my state, not just my boyfriend, and I guess there are still a couple things I'm incomplete with about that."

The slap of our feet on the pavement blended musically with the softer tread of Oscar's paws and Shane's cheetah leg. I let her words echo in my head with the cadence, and she didn't fill the silence.

"I've never been to California, but I guessed you were from some-place where the sun always shines and where much more of life is lived outdoors than in."

"My life was," she said, and I hoped it was a smile I heard in her voice. I didn't look over at her, not wanting to break the fragile thread of honest conversation between us. "I grew up in the mountains, where I spent every weekend backpacking with my dad before ..." She trailed off. I said nothing, and finally, after a bit, she picked up the thread in a stronger tone. "But in high school, the minute sixth period was done, I was at my car and gone to the lake every sunny day. It was the days of coconut oil tans instead of sunscreen, and I still think of lake parties when I smell the stuff."

"When I smell coconut, I'm transported to my mother's galley kitchen in South London. She made coconut cake for every one of Nana the Great's birthdays, even long after she died," I said.

"Nana the Great?"

"My great-grandmother," I said. "She came from Jamaica on the *Windrush* right after the war, and then married an Englishman and settled in Southwark. She came to live with us after her husband died, and she taught Mum all the island recipes she learned as a little girl. You've never known a tougher or more loving household than one run by Jamaican women," I sucked on my teeth at the memory of the trouble I could get into for putting even one ounce of sass in my voice with my mother. "When Mum would yell, Nana would pat her knee for me to sit on, put a fritter on my plate, and then have another go at me for causing trouble."

Shane laughed softly, and the sound soothed the deep ache of missing my Nana, her wide lap, and her island cooking. "They were the best of friends, and my mum mourns Nana the Great to this day. We all do."

We ran in silence for a few hundred feet before Shane spoke again. "I love the easy way you talk about your family."

The fact that it was remarkable to her in any way made me sad for her. It also made me curious as hell, but I knew better than to open that conversational minefield. If she wanted to tell me, she'd have to do the talking. I shut my mouth against the questions that burned my tongue, and instead, I kept my comment general. "I have an easy relationship with them most of the time. Doesn't mean they don't drive me crazy on occasion, but my mum and Kendra are the only ones left who knew me before I got so respectable."

"Oh, is that what you are?" She laughed and gave me an exaggerated once-over look. I really liked this woman's laugh, and I wanted to make it happen often.

"You should see me in a suit—" I began, but she cut me off.

"I *have* seen you in a suit, but respectable isn't the word I would choose for how you look in it." There was a playful smirk growing in her voice, and it sounded good on her. "Especially when you wear that canvas bag slung over your shoulder."

"What's wrong with my satchel? I love that satchel. I traded my last night's stay in a hotel room in Benin to a Croatian photojournalist for it," I protested.

Her eyebrows rose. "A Croatian— in *Benin*? Where did *you* stay?"

"I slept at the train station," I said.

"You traded a hotel room for a train station bench and a canvas bag?" I couldn't quite tell if it was actual outrage in her voice.

"Have you ever really looked at a photojournalist's satchel? It's like the roll-top desk of satchels. It has a sleeve, a pouch, or a pocket for everything you can imagine, as well as things you never thought you'd need. Truly, it's a marvel of design and engineering in waxed canvas and leather."

She laughed again, and I didn't even mind that she was laughing at me. "You sound like you're in love."

"More like a deep, abiding appreciation with perhaps a little passion thrown in."

"Passion ... for a bag." She played up the skepticism, and her expression was adorable.

I sighed dramatically. "Lacking the luggage lust gene – you have no idea what you're missing."

She snorted a laugh, and I think I fell a little bit in love with her for that utterly ridiculous sound. "Luggage lust? That's a thing?"

We passed one of the art installations along the trail, and the breeze had stilled in the park. "It is but one form of the more prevalent leather lust, a close cousin to shoe and boot lust, and distantly related to old-fashioned shaving brush lust. Of course it can't hold a candle to wristwatch lust, or even fine linen lust, but it certainly has its devotees."

She was laughing in earnest now, and my lust-filled heart thumped hard. It wasn't the only thing hard, which, as any man knows, is indescribably uncomfortable while running.

There was a water fountain nearby, and I slowed. "I'm just going to get some water. Should we turn around, or are you determined to make me pay for the excess male pride that won't let me quit until you do?"

She matched my pace, and we veered toward the water. She filled the water bowl below the fountain for Oscar before drinking herself. The brief pause gave me much needed adjustment and lust-suppression time, but it also allowed for face-to-face contact, which threatened to undermine all of my newly restored self-control. Shane was a truly beautiful woman who was all the more intriguing – if somewhat infuriating – for her very private nature. The women of my family all believed that secrets were just lies waiting to happen, and problems were to be aired out like musty rooms with the dust covers ripped off for everyone to see the state of your furniture.

She smiled at me, an echo of her earlier laughter. "I might have a little boot lust."

I chuckled. "You might? I've seen your boots – a different pair every day I've known you. My favorites are the custom riding boots you wore the night we first saw each other."

She arched an eyebrow. "You noticed my boots?"

"I notice everything about you."

I made the mistake of looking at her lips then. We were both still breathing hard from the run, and I automatically moved closer to see better in the darkness. Her eyes were on mine, and I felt rather than saw her gaze as she licked the sweat from her mouth.

Exactly one second before mine crashed into hers.

[21]

SHANE

"Long, slow, wet kisses that last three days. See? I told you Bull Durham could be relevant." – Shane, P.I.

Liquid heat. That's all I was – the sum total of my being. I was on fire and melting from the inside out. Gabriel's hands burned my face where he held me, his lips singed and his tongue teased mine.

My heart slammed in my chest, and I gasped as I tore myself back from him. "I …" I faltered, because I didn't know what came next.

"Shane …" Gabriel groaned, in his deep voice with the accent that made the breath catch. He pressed the heel of one hand against his forehead, and then after too many heartbeats pounded my ribs, he met my eyes.

"I'll see you home," he said.

Did that mean he would come in? Take off his shoes? Maybe the rest of his clothes? Oscar would eat his underwear for sure, he'd be weirded out by the stump of my leg, and then, if he actually spent the night – and that was a big if – he'd remember how different our lives are, how screwed up I am, and he'd duck out while I was in the

129

shower. Then Van wouldn't let me go up, the check from Cipher Systems would have a stop payment put on it, and someone would accidentally leak my address to Quimby, who would wait for me outside my building with his gun.

"Don't," he said, slashing through my thoughts like a knife through a shower curtain. I looked at him like a deer in headlights.

"Don't go wherever you're going right now," he said. His voice had gentled, and I felt like a skittish horse being coaxed into a stall where the door would clang shut behind me.

"I'm not—"

"You are. Whatever you just made up about that …" He inhaled sharply, and his voice dropped even lower. "About kissing me," his voice had reached caressing tones, and I shivered with want, or possibly fear. "Just don't."

He met my eyes directly, and his hands went to my upper arms. "I want you far too much to stand out here on the Lakefront Trail and kiss you like that. I need some time to think about what the hell I'm doing, and I suspect you do too. I do *not*—" he emphasized the word so I couldn't mistake his meaning, "regret one moment of kissing you, nor do I wish myself anyplace other than right here next to you where I can see and hear and occasionally touch you as I attempt to make some sort of sense in my own brain."

I leaned down to scratch Oscar's ears. He had sprawled, panting, on the grass at my feet, and it gave me a moment to school my expression. I spoke to Oscar. "Let's go."

He lumbered to his feet with a grunt, and I carefully avoided Gabriel's gaze as I turned back toward the trail.

Gabriel stopped me with one hand on my arm, which he slowly moved up to my cheek. I couldn't avoid his eyes when he touched me like that, and the intensity of his look made me want to run? Throw myself at him? Hide?

And then he smiled. It was a tentative thing, almost as though he could wipe it off at the slightest hint it was unwelcome, but it did fluttery things to my insides. "Race you back," he said, and just like that, the smile turned into a diabolical smirk, and I could see twelve-year-old Gabriel daring me to run.

So I did.

I didn't bother with the mental gymnastics I knew were inevitable and would quite likely wake me up at 3 a.m. I just put feet to pavement and ran. Oscar was at a full sprint next to me, his tongue lolling happily as he flew down the trail. I pushed myself to the limit of my speed, and when I hit the wall of pain, I broke through it and kept going. I ran like I was falling – a controlled, forward free-fall, and by the last mile, I had left gravity behind and was in a state of euphoric weightlessness that I've only ever experienced at the end of long distance races.

Gabriel stayed by my side and seemed to be as silent, determined, and focused on the run as I was. We didn't stop until we reached the front door of our building, and once inside, we both bent over double to catch our breath.

"That ... was ... insane," he gasped.

I grinned at him. "Yep."

He laughed. "You have amazing endurance."

I pushed sweaty hair off my face and unclipped Oscar's leash. "Except in the mornings – I'm terrible at them, so I'll be into the office by ten, if that's okay?"

Gabriel held my gaze a long moment as he seemed to realize we'd be parting ways in the lobby, and then he finally nodded. "Your badge will be at the front desk. I typically work in the third-floor conference room where the Nespresso machine is, so I'll see you whenever you get in."

I smiled at the man with proper caffeination priorities. "Thank you, Gabriel." Then I looked down at my hound and said, "Come." It was all he needed to hear. He bounded up the staircase, and I smiled one last time at Gabriel before I followed my dog home.

[22]
SHANE

"When you wear black clothes and someone asks whose funeral it is, look around the room and tell them you haven't decided yet." – Shane, P.I.

As I suspected, I spent the hour between 3 and 4 a.m. awake and mentally spinning on the electric attraction between Gabriel and myself, which had an unfortunate alternating current effect – positive vs. negative –that made restful sleep impossible.

So, rather than exhaust myself failing to sleep, I sat up, turned on the light, and pulled my computer onto my lap. By 8 a.m. I had a fairly comprehensive file on Alex Karpov and a more in-depth financial one on Quimby. I also had a fairly decent idea that the political group using ADDATA's tech was a front for Karpov's own radically conservative leanings.

I was feeling pretty black-ops when I got dressed, so I chose black skinny jeans, a black t-shirt with a fairly subtle *Star Wars* Rebel Alliance symbol on the front in gunmetal gray, and black pointy-toed boots. As a nod to the fact that I was going to an office, I wore a long, lightweight jacket that hit me about mid-thigh and looked a little like a Victorian man's frock coat. It was not a particularly feminine outfit, but it suited my need for personal control and had an effect similar to armor in making me feel invulnerable.

I gave Oscar a quick walk to the park, texted Jorge that my hound would welcome his company today should he choose to bestow it, then shoved my laptop and the hard drive with all the Quimby files into my briefcase and locked the door behind me.

I stopped at the Armenian market for an almond börek to go, teased Mr. Basmian about the state of his fruit display, then made the 9:17 train to downtown.

It was a minute before ten when I walked into the Cipher Security building, and I was almost disappointed that Van wasn't at the front desk to snarl at me. A friendly guy named Stan handed me a badge that he said would work on the door locks.

"Dan O'Malley said to find him if you need an office, otherwise you're free to work in any open space in the building."

My disbelief must have shown on my face, because Stan continued. "Don't worry. He can find you if he needs to." He leaned in like he was imparting something top secret. "O'Malley's a little scary that way."

"Good to know," I said, in what I hoped was a neutral tone.

I might have accidentally taken a half-step back in the direction of the front doors when Van Hayden walked in. "Hey Stan, don't believe anything she says unless it comes with coffee," he said as he headed for the elevator.

Stan turned laughing eyes to me, and I couldn't help the smile that accompanied my dramatic sigh. "Pull one over on him *one* time," I said, indicating Van, "and the only way back through the door comes with four sugars."

Stan grinned and leaned forward with another secret whisper. "You're going to fit right in here."

Van held the elevator for me and pushed the third-floor button when I stepped in. "Good morning, Van."

He grumbled at me, but there was a hint of a smile under the gruffness. "Made anyone cry yet today, Shane?"

"Not yet, but it's still early."

When the elevator stopped at the third floor, I turned as I got off just in time to see Van throw me a half-smile salute. It did more to quell the nerves than even Stan's teasing had.

Gabriel didn't meet me at the elevator, which either meant he hadn't been warned about my arrival, or he was letting me walk in like I already belonged. I got a couple of curious glances from people as I made my way to the conference room, but no one stopped me ... or called security, so I had that going for me.

Gabriel sat alone at the long conference table, a computer and a cup of coffee in front of him, and a steaming coffee at the place where I'd been seated the day before. So he had been warned, but chose not to make a thing of my arrival.

"Good morning," I said as I set my bag on a chair and pulled out my computer. I was going for a purely professional tone and kept my eyes focused on what I was doing until I sat down.

Then I made the mistake of looking into his eyes, and I couldn't look away.

Gabriel held my gaze with an expression that felt warm and inviting. He seemed to notice everything about me in one sweeping look, and he seemed to like what he saw.

"Nice t-shirt," he said with a smile, his eyes never leaving mine. "Rebelling already?"

My own smile was an involuntary response to his. "I didn't figure you for a *Star Wars* nerd."

"Original three only. I actually still have a VHS copy that proves Han shot first," he said proudly.

I gaped. "No you don't!"

"A 1982 rental video from my cousin's shop."

"Have you digitized it?" I knew how rare the original videotape release of *Star Wars* was because Sparky had been on the hunt for one with matching serial numbers since I'd known him.

Gabriel shook his head, clearly amused that I understood the significance. "It's PAL, and I only have access to NTSC machines here."

"Will you let me borrow it? I have a friend with all the electronic toys who can probably do it."

His eyes were laughing, even as his mouth only smirked. "Why would you go to the trouble of helping me digitize a VHS tape that's older than you and has probably degraded to the point of unwatchability?"

I smiled and shook my head. "You know the answer just as well as I do. Han shot first. That's a crucial fact that no amount of CGI can change. He starts out as the profiteer without a conscience who preemptively shoots Greedo, and then turns into a guy willing to sacrifice himself for people he loves. He's the one character who really, fundamentally changes. That's why Han is the romantic lead of the movie."

I couldn't tell if I'd shocked, horrified, or amused Gabriel, so I busied myself with my computer rather than look at him.

"I have questions," he finally said. I looked up to see a smirk punctuated by laughing eyes.

I arched an eyebrow in response.

"*Star Wars* isn't a romance. How is Han the romantic lead?"

I rolled my eyes. "Everything's a romance. Every good story worth telling has a romantic element – it's what makes us want to watch them, want to *be* them. You can't possibly tell me you had little boy aspirations of growing up to be Luke? Everyone wanted to be Han. *I* wanted to be Han, although Leia was pretty badass despite the breakfast bun hair."

Gabriel watched me with something more than amusement, and it disconcerted me, especially after what had happened the night before.

"So, I think I probably figured out which political group Karpov is connected to," I said, in the non-sequitur of the century.

Gabriel stood suddenly, as though he had just remembered an appointment. "Come. I promised Greene I'd introduce you when you got in." He held his hand out for me to take in a gesture I'd always associated with Victorian gentlemen. I was perfectly capable of standing up from my seat without help, but I wanted to touch him again, for no other reason than that I would be touching *him*.

So I took a sip of the coffee he'd made me, then took his hand and stood. His gaze held mine for a long moment before he let go of my hand and indicated that I should precede him through the door.

"What can you tell me about your hacker before I meet him?" I asked as we stepped into the elevator. He waited until the doors closed before he answered.

"There's a rumor that he invented bitcoin."

I snorted my derision, but Gabriel's expression didn't change.

"You're serious?" I asked.

He shrugged. "For a guy who plays chess against Google, I'd say it's not outside the realm of possibility."

"Why does he want to meet me?" I asked, suddenly nervous.

Gabriel turned a serious gaze to me. "It was a condition of your hiring."

The elevator doors opened on the fourth floor, and he directed me to an office at the back. I thought I'd managed to keep a serene expression on my face, but inside I was reeling. A condition of my hiring? I wasn't a hacker, but I'd been reasonably good at erasing my own trail. Either Alex Greene had figured out my story or he hadn't, and no amount of nerves would change whatever came next.

Dan O'Malley pulled the door open just as Gabriel knocked on it. His gaze flicked from Gabriel to me, lingered on my face for exactly one second, then back to Gabriel. "Quinn wants to see us in his office," he said.

"I'll just see Shane back down to the conference room after she meets with—"

"Now," O'Malley said in a tone that confirmed the command. "She's a big girl, and Greene's only a little scary. She can handle him."

Ha! That's what he thought. But I put on my best unconcerned expression and nodded at Gabriel. "I'll meet you downstairs."

He hesitated too long, and I could see O'Malley tense, so I slipped past them both into the office and shut the door behind me.

The first thing that struck me about Alex Greene's office was how spare it was. The only décor in it seemed to be the furniture that likely came with the office. The walls were empty of art, or anything at all –

not even the sticky notes I half-expected from the mad hacking genius who played chess with Google. I wasn't even sure why I expected hand-written sticky notes. Maybe because unlike digital ones, paper notes could actually be destroyed.

The man who sat behind the utilitarian desk in the otherwise empty room seemed to simultaneously take up all the space and none at all, and I didn't have time to examine that thought before he looked up from the computer at which he'd been working.

"Hello, Samantha."

[23]
SHANE

"Names are like superhero suits – they have to fit right to have power, and sometimes they just don't work off the rack." – Shane, P.I.

Samantha.

The name sucked all the oxygen from the air and replaced it with a black hole where my lungs had been.

It also had the effect of triggering my fight or flight mode. I must have twitched, because Alex stood suddenly, as though to block my exit. My heart pounded, and my situational awareness suddenly kicked in hard as I tried to calm my pulse.

I saw the fancy green lunch-sized Thermos that had a fork attached to it with a thick, yellow rubber band – the kind of rubber band that held bunches of broccoli together at the supermarket. It sat on a yellow cloth napkin with a three-letter monogram, *A G S*, in green embroidery thread. It looked hand-stitched, as did the cable-knit turtleneck sweater Alex wore.

Assessing my surroundings allowed me to take a breath, and I made my voice deliberately casual. "It's very cute that your wife makes you a hot lunch, *and* finds time to knit you sweaters. You must not be quite the bastard you seem to be."

I thought he would blow up at me – yell or throw me out of his office – anything but what he actually did, which was cock his head to one side and study me.

"Sandra wants to drink lemon drops with you," he finally said, as though he couldn't imagine why his wife would do such a thing. Then he nodded once and indicated I should sit in the only other chair in the office. I perched on the edge of it, poised to flee at a moment's notice if the conversation warranted it.

Alex studied his fingernails for long enough that I began to relax infinitesimally, which was a mistake, of course, as his next words illustrated when he finally looked up.

"Samantha Hane. S. Hane. Licensed as a private investigator in California three years ago, worked for The Agency in Los Angeles. Born and raised in Auburn, California. Father, deceased—"

I held a hand up to stop him. "Your point?"

"I don't like mysteries, Miss Hane. I particularly don't like lies."

"I've never lied to you," I said. I was defensive as hell, but I kept my tone even.

He considered me with an intensity that would have been swoony on any other man. On Alex Greene it bordered on psychopathic. "I tend to see things in zeroes and ones, Miss Hane. There are no degrees of truth. There is truth, and everything not true. When there are blanks, I fill them in. Mostly, I fill them in with the truth, but sometimes, when there isn't enough truth, I get bored and creative, and that's usually when people end up going to jail."

My stomach lurched uncomfortably, and I felt cornered. "Why threaten me? Why even hire me?" I asked. "If you can hack someone so thoroughly, why don't you just plant something on Quimby and take him down?" My voice was rising, and I struggled to get it back under control.

Alex quirked an eyebrow as though the question surprised him. "I don't want to take Quimby down."

"Why not? He's definitely guilty of fraud, probably theft, certainly adultery, and God knows what else he's into."

Just then the door opened, and the very tall man I'd seen with Alex the day I accidentally left my real phone number for Gabriel entered the room. He filled it with his shoulders first and then with an aura that fairly screamed power, and I recognized him from my research about the company. He had also clearly been listening to our conversation somehow, because he didn't miss a beat.

"It's the 'what else' that is concerning," Quinn Sullivan said quietly. "Alex can follow the cyber trails, but you seem to have the people skills to deal with the unpredictable human element, as you've already proven by the very efficient way you separated Quimby from his money."

I stood as gracefully as I could manage to given the adrenaline that pumped through my body. I did it so I could look him in the eyes, but also so I didn't feel like a little kid about to get punished. I inclined my head and reached out my hand to shake. "Quinn Sullivan," I stated directly.

"Samantha Hane," he answered as he shook my hand, our identities firmly established. The man was distractingly handsome, but all I could think about was how fragile my hand felt in his. I wasn't fond of feeling fragile.

"Shane is fine."

"Thank you for working with us, Shane. I've seen what you can do, and it's impressive," Quinn said solemnly.

"Really? Is that why the hacker here decided to investigate me?" I tossed my head aggressively in Alex's direction. I was taking my digital life into my hands, but I was still rattled by the use of my real name – a name I'd taken pains to bury along with the memories of the girl who'd been born to it.

"Our contractors are subject to the same rigorous background checks as our employees. There were gaps in yours. Alex merely filled them," Quinn explained with what might have been patience, in a voice threaded with steel. I realized I'd lose if I held on to my indignation, so I let it go.

"I've buried that information for a reason. I'd appreciate if it remains confidential," I said in a tone that was as business-neutral as I could manage. My acquiescence seemed to surprise Quinn. I doubted Alex even noticed my tone shift. His attention had returned to his computer screen, and Quinn and I had become background noise.

"As are all employment files at Cipher," Quinn said evenly.

I nodded. "Well then, since you obviously have a super-hacker on the case already, what do you need from me?"

There might have been the hint of a smile at the corner of Alex's mouth, but it was gone before I could confirm its existence.

Quinn answered as he turned toward the door to leave. "From what you've gathered already, it appears that we need to focus your efforts on the bigger picture of ADDATA's recent activity as it relates to Quimby's finances. You appear to work well with Gabriel Eze – please continue to do so. I think you'll find that you have compatible survival skills and complementary tactical ones."

He nodded at me in farewell as he closed the door behind himself. Alex's desk phone rang, and I turned to acknowledge the end of the meeting. He seemed focused on his computer screen and didn't pick up. On the third ring I finally said something.

"Are you going to get that, or should I?" I couldn't successfully hide the snark in my voice, but Alex seemed unaffected by it.

"It's for you," he said.

Staring at him in shock for two more rings didn't result in the call being answered, so I finally picked up the receiver.

"This is Shane," I said, trying to sound like I meant it.

"Shane! This is Sandra. Can you come tonight for cocktails? Kat has a new recipe for lemon drops that uses thyme-infused vodka, and I promised we'd make them, but only if we have an impartial taster, and since you're fabulous and I want to know you better, I want it to be you. Say yes?"

I tried not to stare at the phone. All those words sounded like they'd been spoken in one breath.

"Shane? Are you there?" Sandra asked.

"Sorry, I think I was waiting to see if you were done. That was …

impressive." This time I wasn't mistaken about the smile lifting the corner of Alex's mouth.

I half expected her to huff and hang up, but she didn't even pause before she laughed. "You're going to fit right in. Get the address from Alex and come at seven, okay?"

"Okay?" I couldn't help the question on the end of the confirmation, because honestly, I had no idea what I'd just agreed to, and she hung up before I could ask.

I replaced the phone in its cradle. "Apparently I'm having drinks with your wife and someone named Kat tonight."

Alex didn't even meet my eyes as he placed a sticky note with an address on the edge of the desk for me. The half-smile was still there though, and on the face of this emotionless man, it was practically a declaration of love for the outrageous and seemingly remarkable woman that was his wife.

"Good luck," he said quietly.

I left the office thinking that the hacker might not actually be the dangerous one in the Greene family.

[24]
SHANE

"Girls night? Dude, it's an actual thing. When guys aren't around, they all strip down to bras and panties and have tickle fights." – Overheard at a muffler shop

---

The rest of my day at Cipher Security was spent searching for any digital trace of Denise Quimby and gathering all the information we could find about ADDATA. Gabriel was called into a meeting with Quinn and Dan, and I left the office before he returned so I'd have time to shower and change before meeting Sandra and Kat.

Jorge was happy to study at my house after he took Oscar for a run, and his willingness to keep my hound company for the evening was the deciding factor that led to my presence outside the luxury condo building with security features that rivaled most foreign embassies.

I was expected, however, and the guard had even been given my description – or, considering the hacker and his skills, probably a photo from a security camera somewhere.

"Go right up, Miss Hane." The guard smiled disarmingly as he swiped his card key on the lock and pressed number four. "Enjoy the lemon drops."

His friendliness startled me into returning the smile. "Thanks."

He gave me a small salute as the doors closed, and when they opened again on the fourth floor, Sandra was just walking down the hallway to meet me.

"Shane! I'm so glad you came!" She leaned in for an air kiss and then surprised me with a second one on the other side like Europeans do.

"I have to admit, there was an element of fear as I made my decision," I smiled to lighten the statement, but it was utterly true.

Sandra laughed as she steered me toward a door with no number on it. "Alex is a teddy bear when you get to know him."

"Oh, I wasn't talking about the hacker," I said, which made Sandra burst into a fresh peal of laughter as she led me inside their apartment.

The door was reinforced with something heavy, and the latch caught with a solid click. The room opened up into a long living room, with big, loungy sofas and low slipper chairs in neutral grays. The apartment had likely been designed by the same person who did the Cipher building lobby – warm wood tones and clean lines like a yacht from the 1930s – with bright accents that looked like light shining through stained glass around the room. Colorful art and pillows made of gorgeous woven fabric made the space feel like someone interesting lived there, and a remarkable Stormtrooper Sugar Skull print hanging behind the long sofa sealed the deal.

A lovely, lithe brunette sat on the sofa. She was younger than me, with doe eyes and stylishly messy hair that probably looked the same on the beach as it did in the boardroom. Her style was curiously buttoned up, despite having a face and figure that begged for bohemian bangles and flowing dresses.

Sandra introduced us as though we should already be friends. "Kat, this is the woman who is working with Gabriel and Dan on something for Quinn. Shane, this is Dan's wife, Kat."

That surprised me. This pearls-and-silk waif woman was married to the tattooed bruiser from South Boston? Fascinating. I crossed the room to shake her hand, and Kat looked up at me from the sofa with a careful expression and a genuine smile. "Dan said you were smart and fierce. He forgot to mention lovely."

I scoffed in surprise. "I'll take smart and fierce. Coming from him those are huge compliments."

Sandra was pouring a drink from a pitcher on the sideboard. "Alex said Gabriel's in trouble. I'm inclined to agree," she said with a grin as she handed the cocktail to me and raised her own glass. "Welcome to Cipher, Shane."

I raised my own glass and thanked them. The thyme-infused lemon drop was fantastic, and I knew it would be dangerous to do more than sip. I sat on one of the slipper chairs across from Sandra and Kat and had the fleeting instinct to bolt from the room. Why was I in a fabulous apartment with the fabulous wife of a hacker and her fabulous friend who just happened to be the boss's wife?

Apparently my face must have given away my momentary panic because Kat's voice held the soothing tones of someone speaking to a cornered wild animal. "We're actually not terrifying, I promise."

I shook my head with a chuckle, then took a deep breath. "I'm going to have to respectfully disagree about that. You have no idea the willpower it's taking to sit here and calmly sip this amazing cocktail."

Sandra laughed. "Which part takes the willpower, sipping, or sitting?"

"Both?" I grinned back with surprising sincerity.

"Alex told me he pissed you off today." Sandra sat criss-cross-applesauce on the sofa, and the position made her seem slightly more human.

"He's … very good at his job," I said carefully.

"Apparently, so are you. He actually had to do more than three searches to find you." Sandra raised her glass to me again before taking a sip. "It's an impressive feat for someone so clearly visible—" she waved her hand up and down in my direction, "to hide as well as you do."

I winced, and Kat smiled at me. Her tone held sympathy. "Everything about this conversation is hard for you."

I took a fortifying sip of my lemon drop. Layers of lemon, thyme, and vodka danced on my tongue as I dug for the courage I generally saved for things like breaking and entering, or blind dates with cheaters. I hadn't been friends with women in so long that I felt out of my league, and that propelled me forward just on principle. "In my experience, women don't generally like me. I'm too tall, or seem too confident, or I'm friends with their boyfriend. Whatever the reason, I've learned to avoid women before they turn on me, so I haven't really developed good girlfriend skills. I had that going for me even before your husband hired me," I looked at Kat, then turned to Sandra, "and your husband hacked me. So yeah, every molecule in my body is screaming at me to run before things get ugly."

Those weren't just flippant words. I'd chosen to isolate myself when I'd moved to Chicago, and eventually alone became a habit instead of a choice. I didn't want that for myself, but I was the only one who could change it.

Sandra studied me over the rim of her glass. "So, you know I'm a therapist, right?"

I huffed a laugh and wondered if telepathy was one of her super-powers. "Van mentioned that you make men cry."

Kat smirked at that, and Sandra smiled. "A useful skill, at times. What I don't do is analyze my friends."

"Why not?" I said, genuinely curious. "I mean, I assume you know them well enough to see all the cracks."

She smiled. "Someone very dear to me once pointed out that supporting someone and fixing them are two different things. Loving and accepting all the broken pieces is the very definition of friendship."

"That's a good one," I said. "The advice I got was 'always know where your exits are'."

Kat burst out laughing, and I was surprised at how honest the sound was. What had seemed improbable about her marriage to Dan suddenly made sense in a way that defied explanation. I'd had a similar discon-nect with the idea of spectacular Sandra with scary hacker Alex, but watching him talk to her on the phone had helped clear up that one too.

Kat leaned forward. "You really are a private investigator?"

I nodded as I sipped the cocktail. "I needed a job when I got out of college, and my cousin a couple of times removed had a P.I. agency. He hired me for minimum wage and trained me to investigate personal injury claims. I worked under his license for three years until I had the hours to take the California license test." I took a breath and found my courage. "Insurance fraud cases sucked though, so after my ex cheated on me, it was a pretty easy leap into tracking jerks like him."

Sandra waved her hand at me and swallowed the sip she'd just taken. "Don't even think you're going to drop that bomb and walk away whistling. Spill."

I'd underestimated my ability to remain carefully detached with these women. The honesty in Kat's eyes was utterly disarming, and Sandra was so magnetic it was like my cast-iron secrets wanted to fly across the room to her. It was somehow easier to just surrender the truth rather than try to hide it behind rules of socially acceptable sharing. "He and I had been together since my senior year of high school. I tried to break up before I went to college, but he convinced me we should stay together, and later, when he proposed, I said yes. One night while I was still away at college, I decided to go home and surprise him. I drove all night to get there. I thought that somehow maybe he'd been expecting me, because I found his front door unlocked. Except it wasn't me he'd been expecting."

Kat's expression battled between sympathy and anger. Sympathy won. "Oh no," she said sadly.

I scoffed a little at my own overshare, but also at how much the memory still ached. "You know that feeling you get on a twisty road when you've been reading, the first time you look up and realize you're about to puke? It was like that when I walked into his bedroom and saw some short-haired blond chick on my side of his bed. I must have gasped or something, because they both woke right up."

I could still picture the expression on Mitch's face when he saw me standing in the open door to his bedroom. He had looked sick, and he might have even said my name, but the only thing I truly remembered was feeling like I was going to throw up.

"I turned and left, and then I sat in my car until my hands stopped shaking enough to drive. And while I sat there, I mentally played back every phone call, every date, every interaction we ever had, trying to find the clues that he was cheating on me."

"Did you find them?" Sandra asked, as though it was inevitable that I would.

I gave a mirthless laugh. "Once I started looking, that was all I could see. In fact, the next two guys I dated after Mitch had no chance. Every time they were late from work, every cagey answer, every unanswered phone call was them cheating on me. It was pretty awful – *I* was pretty awful. It wasn't until I started catching other people's cheating spouses that I could finally distinguish normal human failings from infidelity."

"No wonder you look for the exits," said Sandra. "The rhetorical question I'm not asking is if just knowing the exit exists is enough, or do you have to go rattle the handle and try the door to make sure you can get out."

I raised my glass to Sandra and took another sip, feeling a bit of confidence settle under me. "Good thing you're not asking, because I've exceeded my quota of self-revelation for about the next decade, and I'm fresh out of navel-gazing."

"How gross are fuzzy navels?" Kat asked in a voice that instantly revealed how very tiny she was in relation to the strength of the alcohol in her glass.

"Grosser than gross," announced Sandra.

"What's grosser than that?" I chimed in. Adolescent jokes were an excellent way to deflect from probing questions, and I sensed that these women would let me.

"What?" Sandra asked, looking gleefully like she expected something highly inappropriate to come out of my mouth.

"When you open your oven door and your rump roast farts." The fifth-grade humor was followed by too much laughter and a round of frog-in-a-blender jokes followed by the completely random assortment of topics that make the best conversations memorable. I was finishing my second lemon drop when I realized I genuinely liked these women.

That revelation was immediately followed by the sound of the front door opening and Sandra's voice calling out.

"Don't come in, we're having a panty dance party."

Sandra and Kat dissolved into giggles, and I melted backward into my chair as though I could possibly become invisible.

"As Shane is still here, I find that amusing, but unlikely," Alex's voice rumbled from the hallway.

I was instantly, unaccountably offended. "Why wouldn't I be wearing panties?" And then I clapped my hand to my mouth and stared at Sandra with horrified eyes. "Oh crap," I whispered, which set off a whole new wave of giggles from the other two women.

I got to my feet in what I hoped was a dignified manner, considering that my real foot had gone to sleep, and I couldn't feel the other one anyway.

Alex appeared, wearing a half smirk. "Hello, Shane."

I smiled at Sandra and Kat, who were still giggling helplessly. "Thank you so much for tonight. You have a gorgeous home, you make a fantastic drink, and you even manage to make oversharing feel slightly less painful than a poke with a sharp stick."

"You're coming back," said Sandra with the kind of confidence a person could be envious of.

I grinned. "Probably. I get the feeling you don't hear 'no' very well." I looked at Alex as I passed him in the doorway. "You have excellent timing. We had moved off the dirty jokes and were headed down the path toward truth or dare."

"Never play truth or dare with my wife," rumbled Alex with a smirk. "She doesn't pull punches."

"Somehow, that doesn't surprise me." I gave Alex a brief smile, then slipped past him down the hall and out of the apartment. It was bad enough to discover I actually liked Sandra and Kat, but to find the hacker tolerable too? That was going too far.

[25]
SHANE

"It's the differences between men and women that keep things interesting. " – Gabriel Eze

---

I had an appointment to meet a client at ten the next morning, and even though her apartment was only two L stops from mine, I was very nearly late. First, my alarm bitch-slapped me awake, which, with a lemon drop hangover and a side of overshare, was just rude. Then Oscar had spent twenty minutes on our walk in the park daring a squirrel to come down and face him like the rodent it was. When I finally wrestled him back home, my hound promptly curled up on the sofa and was already asleep as I raced out of my building.

Rose Hawkins surprised me. She was in her forties, super fit, and seemed confident in the way of a star athlete. She'd gotten my number from a friend whose sister-in-law left her husband because I'd taken photos of him kissing his secretary. I remembered the case, even though a husband kissing his secretary was like generic brand toilet paper – common, cheap, surprisingly uncomfortable, and likely to result in skidmarks.

Rose put a cup of black coffee in front of me and sat across from me at her kitchen table. "I want you to warn Barry's girlfriend about his blood pressure," she said without preamble.

I was blowing on my coffee to cool it down and nearly spluttered it onto the table.

"You want me to *warn* her?" I asked.

She sipped her own coffee with an air of casualness that made her words seem entirely reasonable. "He hasn't been taking his blood pressure meds, and it's too high without them. On one hand, regular sex is probably a good thing, but she's in her twenties, and I'm concerned he's putting on a good show for the hot, young girlfriend that he just can't sustain."

I cocked my head to one side as I looked at her. "You do know that I'm the kind of P.I. who catches the cheaters at the cheating, right?"

She shrugged. "It's not cheating if he has my permission."

"If you don't mind me asking, if it's an open relationship, why do you need my help?"

"We both know that there are people in this world who are excited by forbidden things. Barry is one of those people, and the young woman he's currently dating – her name is Tomi – she seems to be interested in him primarily because he 'belongs' to someone else. I love my husband, and I want him to be happy. I'm afraid if I tell Tomi about his blood pressure, she'll dump him because it's not exciting enough to be with a guy who has permission."

"Or she'll dump him because he's a bad risk," I said wryly.

She winced. "I guess there's that."

I spent the rest of the meeting trying to convince Rose not to hire me, but she insisted I take a check as a retainer. She hugged me when I left, and I thought about how strange my life had become. I thought I could actually be friends with Rose, and just last night I'd had drinks with women I genuinely liked. When I left California, I left all my high school and college friendships behind. Sparky had become a friend of sorts, and Jorge too, but women were harder for me. Because of the work I'd spent the last few years doing, the only women I'd met were either suspicious or vindictive, and those weren't healthy friends to cultivate.

I wondered where Gabriel fit into this puzzle that had become my life. We ran together, we had significant conversations about *Star Wars* and *Hamilton* and hacking into people's finances, and the attraction between us felt like a downed electrical wire, all sparky and dangerous to get close to. I worked with the man, and I needed the money from this job too much to risk it over a guy. But probably more importantly, Gabriel was nice and normal, with normal family relationships and a normal background that didn't include hauling a hundred pounds of emotional baggage wherever he went. The minute he figured out what was hiding in my closets, he'd be out the door so fast I'd barely even feel the breeze.

I said all that out loud to myself even as I practically ran to catch the L downtown in my hurry to get to Cipher and see Gabriel.

"I think I have a way to track down Quimby's wife," I announced when I sat down at the boardroom table. A coffee waited for me, and I plunked a bag of fresh croissants between us. Gabriel opened the bag with the relish of a hungry kid. It was at such odds with his handsome dignity that I had to take a sip of coffee to keep from smiling at him.

"Everything Greene found is up on the board," he said, nodding toward our corkboard pinned with note cards. "Denise Quimby hasn't used her credit cards, and there've been no hits on her name since she left."

"I might know who she went with," I said as I pulled my laptop out of its sleeve and booted it up.

A raised eyebrow was all the answer I got because he had a mouth full of croissant.

I pulled up the notes from my impromptu visit to ADDATA and the various snippets of conversation I'd overheard. "You remember the ADDATA programmers I ran into?"

"At the taqueria," he confirmed.

"Right. One of the people they gossiped about was a guy named Mickey Collins who'd run away with the boss's wife."

Gabriel nodded. "Yeah, we ran the name down, but there were too many to get a definite hit, so Greene shelved it until we have more to go on."

"I might have a lead on Mickey's ex-girlfriend," I said, glancing across my coffee at him as I sipped it. I liked watching his face change with his thoughts. I was able to read each one as it crossed his mind, and I wondered if he was just that expressive, or if I had a superpower where Gabriel Eze's face was concerned. At the moment, his face registered surprise and admiration.

"Tell me," he said as he wiped his hands on a napkin and got up to refill my coffee cup without asking, a very attractive trait in a man.

I accepted the full cup with thanks and held it with both hands while I blew across the top. "I have a new client whose husband's young girlfriend is named Tomi," I said. Gabriel's eyebrow arched at that. "The programmers mentioned that this guy, Mickey, had just broken up with his girlfriend, Tomi, because she had gotten together with a married guy. I realize it's the equivalent of a circus contortionist's maneuver, but I have some girlfriend-tracking to do."

Gabriel didn't hesitate. "Do you want company?" he asked.

I shook my head. "This is the boring part of my job, all computer searches and legwork. What are you going to do while I'm tracking down the alley cat?"

"You're fairly judgmental about infidelity, aren't you," he said.

"You would be too if you got to witness as much home-wreckage as I do."

He studied me. "Why do it then?"

"It pays the bills," I said.

"So does dog walking, and substitute teaching, and exotic dancing, and washing cars."

I narrowed my eyes. "Are those suggestions for alternate employment?"

"Why? Do you fancy dog walking as a career?"

"Actually, I was thinking a car wash staffed with exotic dancers would probably make millions, but stripper poles get slippery when they're wet, so maybe not." I appeared to give it serious thought and enjoyed the sharpening of his gaze on me.

"And now I have that image with which to torture myself. Thank you so much."

"You're welcome." I smiled innocently and stood up to leave.

"Where are you going?" he asked quickly.

"To catch Denise Quimby."

"I'll walk you downstairs," he said as he stood and pulled the strap of his canvas bag over his head and across one shoulder.

I studied the bag, and then I sighed. It was going to pain me to give him this point. "All right, you win. Show me the inside of your magic bag before we go." Ever since he'd waxed poetic about the glories of the photojournalist bag he'd taken in exchange for a fancy hotel room, I'd been dying to see inside it.

He grinned and pulled the bag off over his head and unbuckled the leather straps. Then he hesitated and said seriously, "I'm not sure you're ready for this. To be honest, it's a bit like showing you the inside of my drawers."

I arched an eyebrow and buried my smirk beneath a solemn expression. "You wear drawers? I figured you more as the commando type."

He looked confused for one moment, and then laughed. "Do Americans even say drawers anymore? In England, a person's underthings are called pants, which, I must say, causes no small amount of merriment when shopping for trousers in this country."

"You're ridiculous," I said, peering into the bag as he flipped back the canvas flap. He made a show of covering the opening.

"Huh uh. No peeking. I'm giving the tour."

I scowled at him and waved my hand. "Get to it then, before I lose interest."

He then proceeded to extol the virtues of the waxed canvas and leather bag like it was an Italian sports car. The Velcro camera compartment separators to hold lenses and filters – repurposed for computer, water bottle, wallet, and keys – were actually pretty cool, but my favorite elements were the hidden pockets on either end of the bag. Gabriel looked confused, so I explained.

"Hidden pockets are to women what little red dresses cut down to Argentina and slit up to Canada are to straight men. They are the fiction of fashion, the unicorn of usefulness, and almost impossible to spot in the wild."

"I wore a kilt once with hidden pockets," he said.

"You ... a kilt." I struggled for words while my brain processed the image of Gabriel in a kilt. "Most women's skirts won't hide a panty line, but a man's skirt gets hidden pockets?"

"It's only called a skirt if you wear something under it," he said with a sly grin.

Gah! His smile was playful, but his laser-sharp gaze didn't let me look away, and I felt a betraying flush creep across my cheeks.

"Okay, I'm leaving now," I said, finally tearing my eyes away and shouldering my briefcase.

As we left the conference room, Gabriel asked, "Are you coming back today, or shall we plan to debrief tonight?"

My gaze narrowed. "I'll text you when I'm home."

The elevator opened when I hit the button, and he stepped inside with me and pressed *L*. When the doors closed, Gabriel spoke. "Come up to my place if you'd like. We can work there."

I turned to face him with wide eyes. "You've moved in?"

A smile crept onto his face as he shrugged. "My partner lives in the building. It's convenient."

I was still staring at him when the elevator doors opened, which is why I saw his expression harden to granite. He grabbed my hand and pulled me forcefully out of the elevator and around the far side, out of sight of the lobby desk.

"Wha—" I began, but he made a silencing gesture and instinct took over. I hugged the wall to my back and caught Gabriel's eye as I heard the sound of men's voices. He mouthed the word "Quimby" and then motioned for me to move past him so I could hear what was being said. I nodded my assent, and somewhere past my pounding heart, near the back of my brain, I had the thought that *this* was Gabriel in full commando mode.

"I need to talk to O'Malley," Quimby snarled. He must have been standing at the desk with his back to the elevators, otherwise he would have seen us when the doors opened.

The sound of a receiver being replaced in its cradle was followed by Van's emotionless tone. "He's not picking up, Mr. Quimby."

Quimby gave a giant sigh. "Then get me that other one."

"Which other one, sir?"

"The black one," he said impatiently.

An edge laced Van's voice. "*Which* black one. There are several of us."

"God! The one with the accent!" Quimby was losing control of whatever small hold he had on his temper, and I might have smiled in anticipation of Van's wrath if my stomach hadn't been tied up in so many knots.

It sounded like Van spoke through a clenched jaw. "Would that be a Southern accent, a New York accent, one from the Bahamas, from Chicago, or from the UK?" he asked. "Because we have a whole lot of accents here." Now Van was messing with him.

"I don't know accents, I just know he has one. And a weird name … Easy, or something like that." I looked over at Gabriel. He seemed watchful and alert, but not overly concerned about Quimby's interest in him.

Van picked up the phone again and dialed a number. "I'll just see if he's in."

Quimby didn't bother to ask for Gabriel's name, and I moved closer to the corner where I could see the edge of his shoulder. He was tapping his fingers on the counter in a way that seemed impatient and anxious.

The phone was replaced in the cradle again. "I'm sorry, he's not answering his phone." I noticed that Van hadn't revealed Gabriel's name to Quimby.

"Well, tell them I need answers. How hard can it possibly be to find the bitch who stole my money?" Quimby hurled.

Gabriel tensed next to me, and I put my hand on his arm. I didn't bother examining the instinct too closely because it calmed my own anger to touch him.

"I'll give them the message, Mr. Quimby," Van said, his voice tightening to a degree that a person with the smallest bit of sense would have known meant it was time to back out of there. Quimby did not have that sense.

"On second thought, get me Sullivan. He'll sort this out if I have sue him to do it."

That did it. I slipped my phone from my pocket and pulled up Quimby's number, dialed the code to mask my caller ID, and texted him the message, *I hear your wife's missing. Meet me at the Market Grill, north side in twenty minutes.*

I hit *send* and a moment later heard Quimby's text alert. He cut off his own tirade to read the text, and Gabriel reached over and tilted my hand to see what I'd written on my phone. His expression was grim when he let go of my hand.

"You people are useless. Make sure O'Malley gets that message, right?" Quimby said as he moved toward the doors.

"He'll get the message," Van said in a tone that told me what kind of earful O'Malley would be getting about asshole clients.

The door opened to the sounds of traffic and then closed behind Quimby, shutting the room into peaceful silence once more. I let my hand fall from Gabriel's arm with a sigh.

"You can come out now. He's gone," Van called from the reception desk.

We emerged from the elevator alcove. My eyes immediately went to the glass doors, and I exhaled quietly when I confirmed that Quimby wasn't in sight.

Van studied me. "Know anything about the 'bitch' he was talking about?"

Gabriel tensed, but I straightened my shoulders automatically. "You're looking at her."

His gaze narrowed, and he nodded. "Right." He looked at Gabriel, then back to me. "That little shit know you work here?"

I shook my head. "We need a tracker on his car," he said to Gabriel. His eyes were locked on Van's. "Apparently we do."

"I'll tell Sullivan about the threats. He'll authorize it," Van said, as if that ended the conversation. He made a note on the pad in front of him and then picked up the phone.

Gabriel steered me outside with his hand at my low back, and I was absurdly comforted by his touch. Neither of us spoke until we'd turned the corner down a side street.

"Quimby's a little nuts," I said, the understatement of the year.

"I don't want you to go back to ADDATA," Gabriel said grimly.

"I don't want global warming or stump-ache, but we don't always get what we want, do we?"

"Stump-ache is a thing?" he asked.

I rolled my eyes. "It's a daily thing, like tired feet and itchy eyes. You get used to it."

"Do you have a cream or something that helps?"

I shot him a pointed look. "Why are we talking about my leg?"

"To distract you from my autocratic tendencies," he said.

"Hmm, you noticed it, so I'll let it pass – this time." I held up a finger before he could interrupt. "But here's the thing. You suit-types hired me to talk to people. I can't do that from glass towers."

"Quimby is afraid of you—" he began.

"And I'll be honest, it makes me nervous that a guy with a Napoleon complex and a firearms permit is afraid. I also don't like that he knows the neighborhood where I walk my dog, but I'm not going to let him make me afraid too."

"Can I make a request?" Gabriel asked. His seriousness startled me.

"Sure."

"When you and Oscar go out for walks or runs, will you text me when you go, and when you come back? I realize it's very mother-hen of me to ask, but I find ridiculous amounts of comfort in proof-of-life emojis."

I laughed, and was surprised at how not-annoyed I was by the request. "Fine. But no hearts. I'll figure out something better."

[26]

GABRIEL

"The most valuable treasures are the ones you didn't know you were seeking." – Miri Eze

---

I'd been home for an hour when she texted me a prosthetic leg and a Bernese mountain dog emoji at 7:30 p.m. I was almost out my door when I realized what I was doing. If I met her in the lobby, she would feel as though I was stalking her. It was bad enough I had asked her to text me her plans, but using the knowledge to spend time with her wasn't appropriate, or perhaps even welcome.

I looked around the apartment for something with which to occupy my brain or hands so I didn't get twitchy and follow her to the park. Sullivan had indeed approved the tracker for Quimby's car, so I'd spent the afternoon learning how to use it. I was debating between a night-time plant at Quimby's house, thereby risking a nosy neighbor's call to the police, or a daytime public garage plant at ADDATA. I decided the odds against an arrest were likely better during the day, particularly if I wore a suit.

I had *Hamilton* in my earbuds as I dismantled and reassembled the tracking device for the fifth time, which meant I almost didn't hear the knock on my door as the last pieces were going back into place.

I checked my phone, surprised to see that an hour had passed since Shane's text. I disliked the worry that wound its way past my reason, and got up to answer the door with the dread of someone for whom nighttime knocks on the door had been the portend of bad news.

Shane stood there, holding Oscar's leash. "I half expected you to follow me out," she said.

"I almost did," I admitted.

She took a breath, hesitated, then said, "I set up a meeting with the ex-girlfriend at ten tomorrow."

"That was fast. Would you like company?"

"Actually, yeah, come with me." She looked uncertain.

I stepped back. "Do you and the beast want to come in?"

"Do you mind? I can keep him on leash if you don't want him to give himself the tour."

"Let him off. He can check the place for brownies and house elves." I gave Oscar's ears a scratch as he strolled in like he owned the place.

Shane was dressed all in black, and I remembered the handy flashlight attachment she had on her prosthetic. I struggled to contain my dislike at the idea of her alone in the dark at the park, and I gave Oscar an extra rub for protecting his mistress.

"Brownies and house elves? Those sound like distinctly British problems. I don't think this building is old enough for an infestation of magical creatures." She looked around at the few furnishings I'd moved into the flat. "If you have them though, they came from that cabinet."

She stood in front of the antique secretary I'd inherited from my nana – the one piece of furniture that her father had brought with the family from Jamaica, and which had moved with us from flat to flat. I'd had it shipped from London when Mum followed Kendra to Chicago, and it finally rested in a flat that felt worthy of its age and dignity.

"I think I understand your fascination with your photographer's bag," she said as she ran her fingers lightly across the wood. "This probably has about ten secret compartments."

"It has six, actually," I said. Her expression was like a curious child, and I smiled. "See if you can find them."

"Really?" It was a rhetorical question, because she was already searching the cubbies and drawers. Oscar emerged from the hall and came over to sniff the secretary to determine the source of his mistress's interest. Apparently finding nothing to intrigue him, he came to me for the attention she wasn't giving him.

Shane quickly found the two most obvious compartments – behind decorative panels in the cabinetry. She searched carefully and methodically, and her searching fingers mesmerized me with their thoroughness. I shook myself out of the fantasy of being caressed by those fingers, and sat back to enjoy each of her triumphs as she found three more compartments.

The last one eluded her, as I knew it would. Nonetheless, I was impressed with her persistence. She had been over every square inch of the secretary, and even measured the depth of it against her arm before feeling around in the back of every drawer. The various views of her, from bent over the top of the desk to crawling beneath were sending my imagination into overdrive, and I finally spoke up, just to save myself from the embarrassment of the near-constant erection I was having in her presence.

"Shall I show you?"

She blew a piece of hair out of her eyes and regarded me mischievously. "I'm not giving up."

I raised an eyebrow and sat back. "Fine. I'll just sit here and enjoy the view."

She looked down at herself and scoffed. "Of me on my knees?"

"You said it, not me."

She laughed playfully. "You didn't have to." Then she sat back and regarded the secretary. "What do you know about the history of this?"

"I know it came from Jamaica on the *Windrush* with my nana's family, and Kendra and I used to hide messages for each other in it when we were small, but beyond that, I don't know its story."

"Hmm. Then I'm going to make up that it was built for a ship, because it looks the right size for a captain's cabin." She began to push on the decorative woodwork scrolls that did look rather like waves. "And if it had belonged to a ship's captain, he would have required a locked drawer." She found the loose bit of trim, and with a little jiggling, was able to slide it to the side to reveal a hidden keyhole.

Shane looked up at me with an expression of delight that punched me right in the solar plexus. I grinned back at her and indicated a leather box on the desk.

"The key's in there."

She found the small iron key and fitted it into the tiny lock, which turned with only a little difficulty. The slim drawer that was hidden behind the decorative scrollwork slid open, and she gasped with pleasure. "See? Just right for maps or letters."

"I found it when I was about twelve, but it was empty." I said, enjoying the way Shane stroked the velvet tray of the shallow drawer. Her eyebrow raised, and she did a more thorough search of the edge of the velvet with her fingertips.

"There's something here though – a tiny catch," she said. "Can you feel it?"

She drew my hand to the drawer and ran my finger tip along the edge of the trim. Her hand guiding mine was the most erotic thing I'd ever felt, and through the haze of desire, I did, indeed feel a small depression in the wood.

She pulled up the right leg of her trousers, and I was almost surprised to see the prosthetic leg underneath. I'd been so intent on the soft shape of her curves and the touch of her hand that I'd forgotten about the hard metal bits she wore.

She extracted a sliver of metal from somewhere inside the prosthetic and carefully slipped it into the catch. She twisted gently, and the velvet drawer liner released.

"You're quite handy with that, aren't you?" I said, impressed.

"You have no idea," she said, concentrating on the careful extraction of a bit of paper from under the old velvet. When enough had been revealed, she reached for her prosthetic and pulled out a long pair of tweezers and used them to inch the paper out.

"I don't know what impresses me more – the sheer quantity of hardware you carry around with you in the most remarkable places," she looked up at me with a smile that nearly made me lose track of my voice, "or the care with which you are handling both the desk and that paper."

"I used to dream of being an underwater archaeologist," she said, concentrating on pulling the last of the paper free from beneath the velvet.

That fascinated me. "Why didn't you?"

"I can't clear my ears underwater. It's hard to explore deep wrecks when you can't dive, you know? And despite the thrill of the hunt and the satisfaction of solving the puzzle, just finding the wrecks wasn't going to be enough." Shane carefully laid an envelope, yellow with age, on the top of the desk with her tweezers. She studied it thoughtfully while I studied her.

"Probably reveals a lot more about myself than I want it to," she said finally, meeting my eyes.

"It explains your profession perhaps," I allowed, "but I'd like to think our childhood dreams of romantic or heroic futures can be allowed to fade quietly into the background of who we become."

She looked sharply at me. "Have you allowed your childhood dream to fade then?"

I thought about the South London streets where I'd spent my childhood, and the Nigerian man who fathered me and Kendra but stuck around only long enough to get his citizenship. "When my dad still lived with us, I dreamed of being a firefighter like he was. He'd come home from work with stories of saving lives, saving buildings, saving cats from tall trees …"

She smiled at the stereotype, and Oscar moved over to lay his head on her lap as she sat cross-legged on the floor. I leaned forward in my chair and rested my forearms on my knees. "But then he went back to Nigeria, and I spent the next six years angry at everyone and everything. The British military managed to kick that out of me with impressive haste, and then I put myself through university to make up for the angry years of dismal scholarship. Whatever childhood dreams I might have resurrected at uni were effectively diminished to just one during my Peacekeeper years – stay alive to care for my family."

I glanced at Shane, suddenly self-conscious about how much of myself I'd revealed – things I wasn't proud of – and then looked away so I didn't have to see what she thought of it all.

"I think we should go plant that tracking device on Quimby's car tonight," she announced. My eyes snapped back to hers.

"Tonight?" I asked, dumbly. "I'd been thinking tomorrow at his office garage."

She checked her watch. "It's eleven on a weeknight. Still a plausible time to be getting home from work, but late enough that the casual looky-loos will be asleep."

She stood up and brushed off her trousers. "Aren't you going to open that?" I asked, indicating the letter she'd left on the desk.

"I'd love to, but it's yours, and it should be done with gloves on to try to preserve the paper. It looks pretty old; oils from our skin would potentially damage it." She looked longingly at the letter, but then snapped her fingers for Oscar, and he lumbered to his feet.

"I can't believe you can just walk away. I would think the archaeologist-dreamer in you would be swooning at the romance of it."

She smirked. "I'm not really the swoony type. Probably not too romantic either, if I'm honest."

I stepped closer – likely too close, but she didn't back away. "And how do you feel about adrenaline? Risk? Danger?" I couldn't help looking at her lips, nor at the pulse I saw beating in her neck.

"There *was* that whole underwater component to my dream of being an archaeologist," she said in a volume that was only a little more than a whisper.

"Where it's dark…" I said, my eyes catching hers in a gaze that didn't let go. "And deep…." I said, even more quietly.

Then a smile played on her lips as she said, "And wet."

And I was done. Well and truly gone.

I swallowed hard, and Shane's smile grew bigger as she watched me stumble for the next words. She didn't let me say them though, because she whispered, inches away from my mouth. "Let's go bug a car."

[27]
SHANE

"You can teach a cat to do anything ... that it wants to do." –
Shane, P.I.

Quimby's house was dark when we pulled up to it in Gabriel's hybrid car. It was a new enough car not to raise eyebrows in the neighborhood, which was why we decided to take it.

We parked in front of a house under construction three doors away from Quimby's, and we sat in the dark for a few minutes listening to the silence. Quimby's red Tesla was parked in his driveway, but Denise's Lexus was gone.

"I need to check Quimby's garage for the Lexus," I whispered to Gabriel.

"Why?" He had the remarkable ability to speak in such a low tone that it sounded like a whisper but felt like the brush of his skin on mine.

"To see if it's still here. He wouldn't get rid of his wife's car if he was hoping she'd be back."

Gabriel studied the attached garage. "Is there another door besides the roll-up one?"

"There's got to be one inside the house."

"No," he said.

I bristled but kept the bristle to myself, storing it away for use in the wall I'd eventually build to brick off the part of me that was attracted to him.

Then he sighed and said, "Sorry. How can I help is what I mean to ask."

Just like that, the bristly brick was discarded. "There's a window to the laundry room in the back. It was unlocked when I was here a couple of days ago, and there's no alarm. If you'll set the tracker on his car and then keep watch, I'll get in, check the garage, and get out. We can be gone in ten minutes."

His mouth was tense, but he nodded. "Take your phone."

"I'd better set it to silent mode then, or the sexy sigh I use as your ringtone will get us caught."

He looked sharply at me, and I grinned to show him I was messing with him to break the tension. A tiny smirk hit one corner of his mouth. "As it would," he said, but then he turned serious. His hand reached for me, as though of its own volition, and then settled lightly on my arm. Even through the long-sleeved fabric of my black t-shirt, his touch burned. "Be careful," he said.

I swallowed against the urge to kiss him, and nodded. "You too."

The dome light remained dark as we opened the car doors, got out, and then pushed them closed behind us with a soft click.

A car turned onto the street and Gabriel quickly put his arm around me and pulled me to his side so we could walk as though we were a couple coming home from an evening out. As the car drove past us, I leaned my head onto his shoulder and inhaled the warm scent of his skin as I felt his lips in my hair.

"You ready?" he asked in the barely-there voice that sent a shiver across my skin.

"Yeah," I whispered back.

He kissed my head. "Go," he said, and I moved quickly, before I could think about how much I missed the heat of his body next to mine.

Gabriel slid around the Tesla and crouched down low while I ran to the back of the house. The only sound I could hear were crickets in the yard and the whooshing sound of blood in my ears. I slipped along the wall, dipping below a window I remembered was a bathroom until I reached the laundry room window I'd gone through before. I hoped it was still unlocked as I'd left it. I removed the screen quickly and found the crack under the window with my knife, wedging it up until I could work my fingers in. Then I raised the glass by inches, moving as swiftly and silently as I could, until there was enough room for my body to slither in.

Inside the laundry room I stood motionless for the length of time it took my eyes to adjust to the dark. I knew I could use my phone for light if I needed to, but that light would be even more suspicious-looking from the street than an overhead light would be. When the silence remained absolute, I stepped out into the hall and turned right, past the powder room, to the door that had to lead to the garage.

A creak upstairs stopped me in my tracks, and I froze to listen, frantically trying to remember the floor plan. One of the master bathrooms was overhead, and my heart slammed in my throat as I waited for more footsteps. I reached for the deadbolt on the garage door, and it turned with a quiet click.

A toilet flushed, and I quickly opened the door, hoping the sound upstairs would mask the noise I made. It was pitch black inside the garage, and the scent of motor oil, cement, and something that smelled suspiciously like feces assaulted me. I pulled out my phone and hit the button to illuminate the screen just as a text came through from Gabriel. *Light on upstairs*, it read. I shone the light into the garage, which was empty of anything but a pair of eyes that glowed yellow in the dark. I barely stifled my scream as a creature yowled and flew past me into the hallway.

"Cat?" a male voice called from upstairs.

"Shit," I breathed as I got the hell out of the garage, shut the door behind me, and flung the deadbolt closed.

I darted back into the laundry room as footsteps stumbled down the stairs, and Quimby's voice murmured, "Damn cat."

I slid out the window, and a hard body wrapped around me from behind.

I took a breath to scream, and the arm around me tightened. "Shhh, there's a neighbor out front," Gabriel whispered into my ear. He must have sensed my panic, because he spun me to face him and then pulled me down to sink below the edge of the window as the light went on in the hallway.

Gabriel held my face in his hands and locked his eyes onto mine. My panicked breath and racing heart began to calm as if by the force of his will, and I gradually realized his fingers stroked my hair as he whispered hushing sounds.

I nodded to let him know I could be trusted not to scream. The sound of Quimby's voice carried through the still-open laundry room window. "Where the hell have you been, dumb ass? You haven't touched your food in days."

I swallowed a gasp. Had the cat actually been locked in the garage for days? Hopefully Quimby had mice. Lots of them.

When the hall light went out and the sounds of Quimby's mumbled conversation ceased, Gabriel reached up and inched the window closed. I studied his face, still so close to mine, and his gaze left the window's progress and returned to me. One of his hands still cupped my cheek, and I became aware that he'd pulled me across him, as though to shield me with his body.

I touched his face, felt the planes of high cheekbones and a strong jaw under skin rough with the day's stubble. His gaze dropped to my lips, and a flush of heat spread through me.

My mouth opened, to say … something, I didn't know what. But then his thumb slid to my bottom lip, as though he couldn't help touching it. He stroked it softly, gently, and I watched him study the contour of my lips until wanting him was unbearable. I closed my eyes and savored his touch. I felt adored, and protected, and desired.

He groaned and pulled me to him. His lips met mine, and then he kissed me as though starved for the taste of me. My hand wrapped around his neck and slid down his back, drawing me closer to him.

He groaned again, deep in his throat, and I pressed myself into him. His heartbeat became mine, my breath became his, until our lips, our tongues were the source of *us*. I felt so light, like the only thing tethering me to the ground were his arms around me. Nothing existed outside of us, nothing mattered, nothing counted except the feeling of our mouths tasting, exploring, demanding each other.

When our lips finally parted, I rested my forehead against his and just inhaled him – eyes closed, fingers clutching his shirt, pulse pounding. I gradually opened my eyes to find him watching me. His gaze felt like a caress, and I wanted to wrap myself in it.

So of course I did the logical thing and pulled away.

"We need to go," I whispered as I peeled myself off his lap. My muscles resisted – my skin didn't want to let go of the contact – but my brain stubbornly refused to give into the impulse to seek more of his touch. Timing ... location ... everything but the company was a bad idea.

Gabriel exhaled, then nodded and held a hand out to me. I was confused for the barest second, because he was still on the ground and I was rising to my feet, but then I took his hand and pulled him up with me.

He grinned at me. "That's a first," he whispered.

"Being helped up by a woman?" I was irrationally disappointed.

He gave me a strange look. "No, Kendra and I help each other up all the time."

Oh. Right.

He put his finger to his lips, and we peeked around the side of the house. The road was deserted, so Gabriel took my hand then pulled me in close to him for the walk back to the car. Looking like lovers seemed like the best way to cover our presence on the street at that hour. Feeling like lovers seemed not safe at all.

"What's a first?" I asked when we were in the car.

Gabriel gave me a quick look, then looked away and seemed captivated by the top of the steering wheel. He finally spoke, playing absently with the leather bracelet around his wrist, still not meeting my eyes.

"When my mum gave Kendra and me the talk about sex, she sat us down together and made us each listen to both sides – male and female," he began.

Whatever I'd been expecting, it certainly hadn't been this conversation, and I was pretty sure my mouth fell open as I stared at him.

He looked sideways at me, caught my expression, and gave a self-deprecating scoff. "Yeah, that's exactly what we looked like while Mum talked. I suppose she thought we could ask each other questions about girlfriends or boyfriends later, which was, of course, the last thing either of us wanted to discuss with our sibling."

"I can imagine." I actually couldn't imagine, and even trying to was like standing at the edge of a chasm looking down into the nothingness.

"Do you have a brother?" Gabriel asked with sudden interest.

"Oh no you don't. No deflecting," I said, totally deflecting. "You were saying something about a first?"

He sighed and smiled. "One of the things Mum told us was that there are different kinds of kisses. There are the cheek kisses for greeting friends, goodnight kisses for family, goodbye kisses for loved ones, foreplay kisses and sex kisses—"

Gabriel was back to watching his own hands, as if the conversation was making him shy. *That* almost made me laugh out loud. The idea that this imposing, confident, magnetic man could ever be shy was almost too cute for words, and I felt an ache of tenderness in my chest.

He took a breath, as if steeling himself for saying something out loud. "And she talked about flying kisses and falling kisses."

I raised an eyebrow, and he stole another sideways glance at me. "Flying kisses are ones that make your insides feel like you're accelerating to reach altitude, and the moment you begin to soar, your chest can fill with air again, and your body floats free. I never had a flying kiss and always thought Mum was talking romantic nonsense." He took a deep breath, looked back at his hands, and smiled. "Apparently, it wasn't nonsense."

He started the car and pulled away from the curb before I could formulate the words to respond to that breathtaking statement.

I watched him drive for a long time, and then when he looked over, presumably to gauge my reaction, I looked away. We rode in silence, and the longer we said nothing, the bigger the silence grew, until it was an entity in itself, filling the spaces around us and swallowing all the possible words.

When Gabriel parked his car in the lot reserved for our building, he turned to me and faced me full-on for the first time since we'd kissed. "I'd like to know you, Shane. Will you allow me to try?"

"What's a falling kiss?" I blurted, maybe so I didn't have to answer the questions he'd been asking all night.

He held my gaze for a long moment, then finally looked away. "I don't know. I've never had one."

[28]

SHANE

"Today my brain asked, 'ne yapiyorsun?' – what are you doing? *in Turkish – and I couldn't answer it."* – Shane, P.I.

I was freaking out, and it pissed me off.

I spent most of the night watching my favorite Turkish TV show just to avoid the inevitable toilet spiral that my thoughts had become. It didn't help, because the main romance of the show kept getting cock-blocked by everything the two leads *didn't* say to each other. Not to mention all the kisses they *almost* had. And of course, there was a whole soaring albatross element to the Turkish story that was definitely *not* helping me block thoughts of flying kisses from my head.

GAH!

The worst thing was that I knew I was doing a number on myself – no one was sitting me down to tell me "don't get involved, it's not going to work, he's just going to leave anyway." That was all me and my twisty brain.

It was going to be a bad day if Turkish TV couldn't override twisty-brain.

I finally gave up trying to sleep and dragged myself out for an early morning run with Oscar in a fairly futile attempt to clear the noise from my brain. Jorge was doing pull-ups from a conveniently-positioned bar in the courtyard when we got back, and Oscar danced in excitement to see his friend.

"You went for a run?" he asked, after giving Oscar the greeting he demanded. "I mean, aren't you afraid you'll incinerate in daylight or something?"

"You're just lucky I'm too tired to bite," I grumbled.

"How's the new gig?"

Since Jorge was probably smarter than me and Gabriel combined, I tossed him a question while I stretched. "Know anything about a guy name Alex Karpov or heard of a company called ADDATA?"

He shook his head as he wrestled with my dog. "No. Should I?"

I gave Jorge the bare bones outline of the connections we'd drawn between the data-scraping they were doing with online personality tests and the data sets the programmers were setting up for the political think tank.

"Politics, huh?" Jorge asked, and I nodded. "So it's probably safe to assume that the data they're harvesting is going into whatever propaganda machine they're running," he continued.

"Theoretically, yeah. Although I took one of ADDATA's personality quizzes. There are places to write in a unique answer, and they can't possibly collate that kind of data into something useful."

"Sure they can," Jorge said. "Data scraping like that just requires Crystal Report or SAS and a sequel back-end."

"In English, please." I finished the last of the water in my bottle while he dusted the dog hair off his hands.

"It's just about how the information gets processed and turned into something useful. The problem with a personality quiz is that only a really small cross-section of the population will even see the link, much less click on it. Unless, of course, there's a social media algorithm deliberately putting it in people's feeds."

"I read the terms of service for the quiz," I said.

Jorge scoffed. "I thought I was the only dork who did things like that."

"No, there are two of us. But get this, the terms of service was from 2013, and it gave the developers access to the user's friends list and all *their* information."

"Shane," Jorge said quietly. He held himself very still, and I almost looked behind me.

"What? What's wrong?"

"That kind of data access is ... dangerous."

"But the friends aren't the ones answering the personality quiz questions," I argued.

"It doesn't matter," he said, shaking his head. "I just took a US Government and Politics in the Information Age class, and we had a whole section on how the media impacts voter perceptions. To change politics, you have to change culture, and what are the units of culture? People are." He paused to let that sink in, then continued. "When you have that kind of access to the things people like and share, and to the comments they make, you can micro-target your message. If they create the right content, it's like whispering into the ear of each and every voter, and they'll never know it's happening."

I stared at him. "You're scary."

He smirked. "They see a skinny brown boy and they have no clue who's coming for them."

"And by 'them' you mean ..."

He shrugged and grinned. "I haven't decided yet."

I narrowed my eyes at my friend. "What can we do about it?"

Jorge shrugged. "Dude, I'm eighteen. I might think I know everything, and I might even convince you that I do, but I leave the heavy lifting to the adults."

I scoffed. "You say adults like there's one around here."

Jorge laughed. "You thought I meant you? You maybe need to rethink that," he said, ducking away from me as he led the way into the lobby.

Gabriel stood by his open mailbox and looked startled to see me.

"Hey," I said to him as Oscar bounded over. I looked at Jorge and said, "It's okay. Oscar knows him."

My dog swirled around Gabriel for a rubbed-ear greeting as I made introductions. "This is Jorge," I said to Gabriel, and then I turned to my young friend. "Jorge, this is Gabriel."

"The cop in 3C," said Jorge.

A half-smile lifted Gabriel's lips. "Former British Army. But I've been accused of standing like I've a stick up my arse, so I suppose old habits die hard," he said, his clipped English accent making the crude statement sound almost elegant.

Jorge bit back a grin and he held out his hand. "Oscar likes you," he said. "It's high praise."

"I imagine it is," Gabriel said, shaking his hand with a smile.

Gabriel's gaze flicked to Oscar and then moved across my face like a caress. I could feel my skin warming in response, and the glint in his eye told me he saw it.

"Jorge has some interesting ideas about the political influence ADDATA could have with the information they're gathering," I said, to redirect my thoughts from things like caresses and warm skin.

"Oh?" Gabriel's gaze sharpened.

"If you have time, why don't you two talk at my place while I shower, and then you and I can go meet the ex-girlfriend together," I said to Gabriel, before turning to Jorge. "Is that cool?"

He shrugged. "I can spare fifteen."

"Thanks." I nodded at both men then sprinted up the stairs ahead of them. I left my door unlocked and pulled my t-shirt off as I headed down the hall to the shower. Gabriel must have entered my apartment right on my heels because his voice sounded a little strangled as he called from the kitchen.

"Mind if we drink the last of your coffee?"

"Help yourself," I called from the bathroom as I stripped off the cheetah leg and tights and stepped into the scalding spray. I smiled at the thought that Gabriel was probably picturing me naked as he heard the shower running.

I have excellent balance on one leg, and I've become a very efficient shower-taker. My shower is tiny, so I can brace myself on a tiled wall for all things except hair-washing, which takes two hands to be effective. I have to extend my elbows like wings when I shampoo my hair, just to stay upright long enough to rinse, so I've gotten fast. I was out, dry, and dressed in my uniform of jeans and boots in under ten minutes. I wound my hair into a French twist, which meant it would dry curly, and chose a linen t-shirt the color of red wine. I figured I'd been wearing so much black recently that I was in danger of becoming predictable. I grabbed a tapestry coat with autumn shades of wine, rust, and green from the closet before heading out to the living room.

Gabriel and Jorge sat at the dining table, empty coffee cups in front of them, talking about cyber security and encryption algorithms. Gabriel's gaze lingered on me as I entered the room.

"That was fast," he said.

I shrugged. "I'm fairly low maintenance. Did you guys figure out how to take down the world's financial systems yet?"

"Is that what we were doing?" Gabriel smiled.

"Nah, that's small time. Anonymous is the one to hack. They're way more dark web than even the NSA," Jorge said as he rose to his feet.

I studied my friend whom I'd first met just over two years ago, before he'd gotten stringy height, whipcord muscles, and whiskers on his chin. He was not quite as quick to smile as he'd been as a fifteen-year-old boy, nor quite as easy in his skin, but most notably, some-where along the way he'd gotten just a little dangerous.

"Remind me to stay on your good side, Gonzales," I said as I walked him to the door.

Jorge's toss of the head toward Gabriel was friendly, and he gave Oscar a final scratch behind his ears. "You assume I have one." He smirked. "That's your first mistake."

He threw a final wave at us and closed the door softly behind him.

"I think Greene needs to meet that kid," said Gabriel, with some-thing like admiration in his tone.

"Right? Between the two of them, they'd get in and change the nuclear codes just for fun."

Gabriel stood and cleared both coffee mugs from the table. He rinsed them in the kitchen sink and then turned off the coffee pot, dumped the dregs, and rinsed that too.

"You've been domesticated," I said drily.

"You try being feral in a home full of women." He dried his hands and then met my eyes. "Jorge's theories are sound. I think you and I should sit down with Sullivan and O'Malley, and maybe Greene, to discuss our options."

I leaned against the doorway. "I got weird last night, and I'm sorry."

He seemed to freeze in place for the space of a breath, and then he smiled. "You *are* weird, and I'm not sorry."

I stared at him open-mouthed as a huff of surprised laughter escaped. "I'm not quite sure what to do with that."

He shrugged, and somehow it was the very best thing he could have done, because I could feel myself relax under the warmth of his smile. "I'm sure you'll figure out some way to twist it up in your head. I have the feeling you do that a lot."

I could easily have taken offense at his easy words, but precisely because they were so easy, I didn't. "Yeah, my head's a pretty uncomfortable place to be a lot of the time."

He stepped out of the kitchen and picked up his bag to sling over his chest. His voice was warm and comforting. "Well, if you decide not to invent things I didn't mean, here's the straight truth. I like you. I think about you a lot," he sighed, almost as if it frustrated him, "and last night's kiss was probably the best of my life. I'm not really doing a lot of thinking beyond that for reasons I haven't fully considered, but I know I'd like to kiss you again."

At least my mouth had closed, even though my eyes were trapped in his gaze and my muscles had locked into place. I finally swallowed and managed a nod. "Okay."

Only then could I see that the easy confidence he'd been wearing when he'd spoken had masked something a little fragile, because he exhaled softly. "Okay," he said, as he ruffled the fur behind Oscar's ears and held my front door open for me. "My mum invited you to dinner tonight. Can you come?"

I let my amusement at the way my inner fourteen-year-old twisted his words twinkle in my eyes. "Yes," I grinned.

His eyebrow raised in an "I see what you just did there" expression. "Good. I'll pick up the wine."

I gave my dog a two-handed ear scratch, kissed him on the head, grabbed my bag, and then Gabriel and I left for work, together.

[29]
SHANE

"Payback and Karma are the bitchy little sisters of Revenge, and I promise you, it's not a family you want to mess with." – Shane, P.I.

G abriel drove to the outer edge of one of the neighborhoods around the University of Chicago. It was full of overpriced apartments in converted hotels that should probably have been condemned but were still getting top dollar because of their proximity to one of the finest institutions of higher learning in the country.

It had taken three internet searches and one in-person visit to a former workplace to get contact information for Tomi – current paramour of Rose Hawkins' husband, and Mickey Collins' ex-girlfriend. I would only be charging Rose half my normal rate since I was doing double duty on this case.

Tomi met us in the courtyard of an Italian coffeehouse that served almond cappuccinos in pint glasses, with enough sugar and caffeine to give a person the jitters after just one. She was a pretty, petite blonde who looked a little like Nicky Hilton, and she caught my eye and gave me a tentative wave when we walked in.

Gabriel asked Tomi what he could get her. She asked for an almond cappuccino, then turned to me with a raised eyebrow when he left to order our drinks.

"I guess you're the one who found out about me and Barry?"

I smiled. This girl was pretty bold, and considering she was probably only twenty-two or three, she would be formidable when she grew into it. "Actually, his wife already knew about you. She wanted me to tell you about her husband's blood pressure so you'd be careful."

Tomi scoffed just as Gabriel sat her coffee drink in front of her and handed me an Americano like he had. "That's pretty messed up. It's not 'don't screw my husband,' it's 'don't screw him so hard he dies.'" Tomi's voice held a note of respect though, and I suppressed a smile at the expression on Gabriel's face.

"Yeah, definitely not my typical client. But that's not the only reason I asked to meet you," I said.

She seemed to consider us both for a long moment, then said, "You want to know about Mickey."

That surprised me. "Yes. How did you know?"

"Because Mickey owes people money and you're a P.I., so someone probably hired you to find him." She took a gulp of her sweet coffee drink and swiveled her eyes to Gabriel. "You a P.I. too?" she asked him.

"Her partner," he said simply, and I was not prepared to like the sound of that as much as I did.

"Who do you work for?" she asked, returning her attention to me.

"A private security firm. We're actually trying to find the woman Mickey ran off with."

Tomi scowled. "Quimby's wife. Serves him right she left, even if it was Mickey she took with her."

"Did you ever work for Quimby?" Gabriel asked her.

She shook her head. "No, but he hit on me every time Mickey took me to a company thing. The guy's gross."

I huffed a laugh in solidarity. "So gross."

She looked a little surprised at my ready agreement, and I could see a slightly reassessing focus as she studied me for a minute. Then she leaned in and dropped her voice. "Quimby's in trouble. Money trouble, and maybe something else. Mickey put himself in hock to get the wife out of there."

Mickey was an idiot then, because Mrs. Quimby had five hundred grand in her pocket, courtesy of me. Gabriel's mouth twitched, and I knew he was thinking the same thing.

"Who is Mickey in hock to?" I asked.

She shrugged. "Who knows? I got tired of the robo-calls, so I moved."

"You moved to escape the telephone?" Gabriel asked in astonishment.

I shot him a look laden with *duh*. "Sometimes it's easier."

Tomi sipped her drink, oblivious to Gabriel's bafflement, and I turned my attention back to her. "I'm guessing Mickey got rid of his cell?"

She shrugged. "Probably. I did. Collections is a bitch, you know?"

"I assume you have a burner phone?" I asked.

"Have to. Can't get work if you don't have a number."

"If you had to get in touch with him, what would you do?"

"Talk to his Aunt Shelley. She lives up in Northport, Michigan, and every time things get tough, Mickey runs to her," she said. Her tone was remarkably free from judgment.

"You've met Aunt Shelley, I take it?" I asked.

Tomi nodded. "Once. She's a photographer, and Mickey wanted her to take our engagement photos."

"You were engaged?" I think my mouth might have even fallen open at that.

Tomi nodded again with a shrug. "Like I said, Mickey runs to his dad's sister every time things get weird. Getting engaged to me was definitely on his scale of weird, and Aunt Shelley had a pretty cool way of making me see why it was a bad idea for us to get married." Tomi finished her coffee drink in one last gulp, then stood up to go. "She wasn't wrong, was she?"

Gabriel was already on his feet, ready to block Tomi's exit at the slightest look from me. "Wait, Tomi, how can I find Aunt Shelley?"

She rolled her eyes. "I told you. Northport, Michigan. It's a small town. Just ask."

She deftly slipped around Gabriel and out of the cafe, and although my instinct was to go after her and wring her for every bit of information she had, I doubted it would do more than piss her off. So instead, I just sighed and took a sip of my coffee.

Gabriel dropped into the seat Tomi had just vacated. "What do you think?" he asked.

"I think it's pretty interesting that Mickey's ex-girlfriend knows Quimby's in trouble. And I think it's even more interesting that Denise Quimby left with half-a-million dollars, leaving behind a new luxury car, a matched set of Louis Vuitton luggage, and a wardrobe of expensive clothes."

"Then two days later, the car's gone." Gabriel's low voice sent a shiver across my skin. The good kind that came with heat, not chill.

"We should run a credit check on Quimby. It might have been repossessed," I said.

Gabriel had his phone out and was texting something. "Just sending the credit check request to Greene," he said.

I finished my coffee and stood to go. "Let's go talk to your bosses about Jorge's theory and see what kind of research we can do on Karpov and his organization."

My phone buzzed in my pocket, and I checked my messages. There was just one, from Sparky. *Whatever you did the other day locked me out of everything. Get over here!*

I spoke as I typed a response. "Do you mind if we make a quick stop on our way?"

"No problem. I'll just let O'Malley know we'll be in in about an hour."

As we made our way to Sparky's loft, we talked through the various bits of information we'd learned about Quimby, his wife, and his company. Talking to Gabriel was like taking notes on a case out loud, and I thought that report-writing, which was only slightly less painful than flea-combing my dog, would actually be kind of fun with him.

"Oh, I forgot to tell you. I gave the letter you found in my desk to a friend of Kendra's in the rare documents department at the university library. I'll let you know what she says," Gabriel said as I opened the door and we entered the cool, dark lobby of Sparky's loft. The freight elevator waited, and I pulled the gate down to go up five floors to his space.

"Who the hell did you search on my computer, Shane?" Sparky yelled when I opened the elevator doors directly into his space. He stalked across the loft to get right up in my face.

Gabriel instantly put himself between us as Sparky continued to snarl at me. "Whoever you unleashed on me has now managed to get my gas turned off and my bank account frozen. What. The. HELL!"

"Easy, friend." Gabriel's voice sounded soothing on the surface, but underneath I could hear the steel.

"Who the hell are you?!" Sparky said fiercely.

I stepped in front of Gabriel and turned to face him. "I've got this," I said firmly. His gaze was locked on Sparky, and it took a minute for him to meet my eyes. Finally he did, and then he nodded.

I exhaled, and then turned back to Sparky, who was practically vibrating with rage.

"I don't know what you're talking about, Spark. Walk me through what happened."

My friend seemed to realize he needed to calm down, because he backed up a step, then turned and leaned against a work table. He took a deep breath and spoke without looking up.

"You ran whatever search you ran the other day, and it set off some kind of alert," he said as Gabriel stepped to the side of the table, within Sparky's view but not in his space. It was a good move, designed to put him at ease while also making him aware that he couldn't freak out on me again.

"Yeah, I remember, and I told you I'm sorry," I said, not quite as generously as I should have. "I thought you have super-security so none of your game nerds can swat you."

"I'm not actually a big enough jerk to be at risk for swatting, believe it or not," he said acidly.

Gabriel watched us interact through narrowed eyes, and I wondered what he was thinking. I knew I was in a defensive snit because I'd screwed up and Sparky was mad at me, so I made myself take a deep breath and calm down.

"I'm sorry, Sparky. I know you're not a jerk. I'm just being prickly because something I did jacked up your computer."

His eyes widened, and I could see his temper flare. "You didn't just jack up my computer, Shane. You left a door wide open, and now someone's fucking with my life!"

Sparky's hands ran through his hair like he wanted to tear it out, and he stormed away across the loft. I could see Gabriel start for him as Sparky passed me, but I quelled him with a look. I sat very still on my stool, my back to the room, waiting for the crash.

Aaaanndd... CRASH! "Fuck!" There it was. The kicked chair and the jammed toe I was waiting for. Gabriel watched Sparky warily, but I turned on my stool and then got up to help Sparky hobble to a chair.

"Dude, I think I broke it," he gasped as he sat heavily and let me pick up his injured foot.

"Why do you wear Crocs around heavy machinery?" I asked, pulling the hot pink foam shoe from his foot.

"I wasn't working yet." He sucked in a breath as I probed his big toe.

"Wiggle it," I commanded. He did, wincing, but able to move all five toes.

"You need a pedicure," I said with a wrinkled nose as I eased the pink monstrosity back on his foot.

"You suck dog's balls," he mumbled.

I ignored the snicker from the peanut gallery.

"Now that you've gotten the destruction portion of the program out of the way, tell me what happened." I righted the chair he'd kicked and sat across from him, knee to knee. Sparky was gingerly testing his weight on his injured foot, and I caught Gabriel's gaze as he watched us from a spot behind Sparky where he wouldn't be noticed.

Sparky took a shaky breath. "I don't exactly know. I'm not a hacker like you."

"I'm not a hacker," I said automatically.

"You understand how it's done. I just know that I always turn off the VPN when I pay my bills because it's a pain in the ass to remember every single password and deal with the 'you're not in the country' b.s. at the bank and the gas company. The day you opened whatever back door you did, I spent hours scrubbing everything I could think of to scrub. I ran all the software, Nortoned the hell out of the thing, and finally, that night, it booted up just like normal. The next day I had money to move and a bill to pay, so I turned off the VPN, did my business, and then got to work. This morning, I get e-mail notices that my bank account is frozen by some government agency bullshit that sends me in a phone-recorded spiral, and my gas has been turned off because of six months of non-payment." He stared at me. "Six fucking months they say I haven't paid a bill, when I know for certain I paid a $45 bill the day before."

Sparky's expression was bleak as he got up and hobbled to a counter where his laptop sat open. He swiped the touchpad and the screen lit up. "And now this."

I moved closer to look at the background photo of the Avengers I knew was Sparky's boot-up screen. The whole thing had a filter over the top that looked vaguely like The Hulk's skin. "Is it usually so green?" I asked as I swiped the trackpad again to see if it would wake up further.

"It's green?" Gabriel asked, his deep voice suddenly at my left ear as he looked over my shoulder at the computer.

"Like I asked before, who the hell *are* you?" Sparky asked, startled out of his bleak apathy.

"Shane's partner." Gabriel didn't look at him – just studied the screen. He typed in a couple of commands I knew would reboot a frozen screen, but nothing changed.

"The green screen looks like a locked Photoshop layer," I said to Gabriel.

"I don't have Photoshop on that laptop," Sparky said. "I didn't

193

know you had a partner," he added quietly to me, and I could hear the accusation in his tone.

I opened my mouth to respond to Sparky, except it suddenly registered what had gotten Gabriel's attention. I took a step back from him because if I was right, I might have wanted to accidentally punch him. "Why is the screen green, Gabriel?"

He didn't say anything as he typed another ineffective command into the laptop, but neither did he meet my eyes.

"Gabriel?" I could feel the accusations blooming like toxic flowers in my lungs. "Does he leave a calling card when he hacks in? Something pretty, and poisonous, and deadly – like a *green* screen?"

He inhaled as if steeling himself, and then faced me. "It's possible," he said quietly.

"FUCKING HACKER!" I roared, utterly and completely furious.

Gabriel flinched, and Sparky stared at me as though Medusa snakes had just sprouted from my head. "You *know* this guy?" he squeaked.

"We may," Gabriel answered quietly.

[30]
GABRIEL

"Things that are equally inadvisable: sliding down a 50-foot razor blade and pissing off a hacker." – Billy "Sparky" Spracher

---

S hane was shaking with anger as she sat down in front of the laptop and opened an e-mail server.

"Wait, Shane, what are you doing?" The prosthetist, aptly called Sparky, seemed to come back to consciousness all at once. He reached for the keyboard of his laptop, but she batted his hand away as if it were a fly.

"Pissing off a hacker," she growled.

"Wait, wha... don't do that!" Sparky sounded frantic, and she batted his hand away again as he tried to reach for the laptop.

"Go sit down, Spark!" she snarled, typing furiously. She was likely playing with the digital equivalent of rocket fuel, but somehow, I didn't think Shane would back down from taking on Alex Greene.

She hit *send* and then pushed back from the computer. She was scowling. "Did you know?" she asked quietly. She didn't look at me, but I knew she was talking to me.

"I didn't." My voice held a quiet note of urgency. I needed her to believe me, but she was so angry. I straightened and held my hand out to Sparky.

"I'm Gabriel Eze," I said quietly. "I work with Shane in a private security firm, and with the man who may have been responsible for hacking your accounts."

"Billy Spracher," Sparky said automatically, shaking my hand. Shane snorted. "I build Shane's legs," he finished, lamely.

Shane scoffed. "You have a bio-mechanical engineering degree from University of Chicago and a graduate degree in bionics. You design prosthetic prototypes for some of the biggest manufacturers in the country, and I'm lucky to be your crash test dummy."

Sparky smirked faintly at her, and I sensed a long-standing relationship with layers that might have included friendship, humor, comradery, and possibly a little attraction, at least on his side. "You're a good dummy," he said.

She inhaled deeply. "I'm really sorry I brought the hacker down on you, Sparky. I'll make him put it all back to rights."

"Forgive me for asking what may be a foolish question," I interrupted, "but why would Greene interfere with Mr. Spracher's finances?"

"Because I used Mr. Spracher's computer to find out what I could about the hacker's wife," she said, disgust evident in her voice.

My eyebrows arched up in surprise. "Truly?"

"The guy's a psychopath," she said, swiping the trackpad to keep the computer from going to sleep.

"He would probably argue high-functioning sociopath with overactive protective instincts," I said evenly. I was familiar enough with my own protective instincts to diagnose the condition in others.

She looked up at Sparky. "I'll fix this," she promised him.

"I gotta admit," he said with a nervous laugh, "I was more pissed than scared until you mentioned mental disorders."

"High-functioning is definitely the key to him, Spark," she said. "The guy plays chess against Google."

"No kidding?" I could see the first vestiges of admiration in Sparky's expression, but his next question was mercifully interrupted by the chime of his e-mail.

Sparky reached for the keyboard, and Shane once more batted his hand away as she opened the message and read. *Dear Ms. Hane*, it began. I skimmed the message over her shoulder as she read out loud. "*I apologize for any inconvenience Mr. Spracher may have experienced, and am assured that the affected funds and accounts have been restored. I believe I have met your terms satisfactorily and look forward to no further mention of this incident. Best, Alex.*"

"That's the hacker?" Sparky spluttered. "He sounds like a suit."

"If by suit you mean the nerd-side-of-goth, that's him," she said with satisfaction as the green film that had covered Sparky's laptop screen blinked out of existence. The machine's fan spun up as if in a sigh of relief, and Shane stood to relinquish her chair.

"Check your accounts, but I'm pretty sure everything's back the way it was. Leave it running for another ten minutes so he can also close whatever backdoor I accidentally opened." She leaned over and kissed Sparky on the cheek, and I beat down an utterly irrational surge of jealousy.

"Sorry, bud. I'll bring my own laptop from now on," she said with a wince.

Sparky stared at the laptop as if he wasn't quite brave enough to touch it.

"It was nice to meet you," I said as I steered Shane toward the door with a light touch on her lower back.

"Hey Shane," Sparky called out as we reached the door. She turned back to see him still staring at the computer but finally sitting down to type.

"Yeah?"

"Come back next week. I'm working on a dive leg you can walk on."

She grinned, and I felt her whole body finally relax in relief. "Nice!"

We stepped into the freight elevator and closed the gate, and it wasn't until we were outside Sparky's building that I finally spoke again.

"How did you get Greene to back off?"

"I threatened to tell his wife."

She explained her logic as we made our way, via public transportation, to the luxuriously modern building in which we worked. Alex wasn't actively monitoring each individual search on his wife's name – he didn't have time for that – so he had alerts in place, a lot like Google alerts – with a specific attack sequence set to trigger after a certain number of searches from the same source. Shane didn't think Sandra would tolerate that kind of over-protectiveness from a mate, no matter how well-meaning he was, which made her threat effective.

"If you were a man, I'd say you have a set of very large balls," I said in awe.

She smirked. "Ovaries the size of cantaloupes, and I defy you to tell me how big balls are anything other than a complete liability. The bigger the balls, the larger the target for a well-aimed kick, and who wants that business dangling between their legs, getting in the way and slapping up against parts?"

And now I had the image of slapping parts to contend with in my already overactive imagination.

"I assume Mr. Spracher is the designer of all of your high-tech prosthetic limbs?" I said to distract myself with a subject change.

"He is now. My prosthetist in California suffered from a distinct lack of imagination. He was one of the 'if you mess with the leg you void the warranty' types. Sparky was trying to interest him in a rock climbing foot he'd designed, and when I came limping out of my appointment, Sparky whipped out a tool kit and made adjustments to my leg right there in the waiting room. My doc came out all blustery, and Sparky just told him to shut up and quit trying to make the woman fit the leg. Everything felt better the minute he adjusted my leg, and he's part of the reason I moved to Chicago."

We entered the Cipher building and greeted Stan at the front desk. "Quinn and Dan wanted to know when you got here. They'll meet you in your conference room as soon as they're free," Stan informed us as he picked up the phone, presumably to tell my bosses we'd arrived.

"Right, thanks," I said as I held the elevator door for Shane. She touched my hand as she entered, and I caught the scent of amber. Everything about this woman intrigued me, and I allowed myself a moment to enjoy the small contact.

The conference room we'd taken over with our colorful sticky notes was empty, and I made us each a coffee while Shane set up her laptop. We'd been using green sticky notes to represent the trail of money, and she wrote the information that Tomi gave us on green and added it to the line of stickies below Quimby's name. She studied the board for a minute while I studied her.

She stood tall and confident, with the easy grace of an athlete. I knew tall people who hunched, as though they'd spent a lifetime uncomfortable with the idea of being visible. For the most part, I tended to be unconscious of my size – my height and strength were just tools to keep me off the target list of the kinds of people who seek targets. But Shane wielded her size as though it were her right – as though she had chosen her height for its advantages and would be using each one as it pleased her to do. It was a degree of confidence that could look like arrogance on some, but on the woman in front of me, it fit her like a second skin.

She looked over her coffee mug at me. "I can feel you studying me," she said.

I shook myself out of my contemplation. "You hold yourself like an athlete, and I was wondering what sport you played in school."

"Basketball."

I smiled at the obviousness of it. "Were you good?"

"I was good because I worked at it. I didn't have the natural talent to play beyond high school, even if I'd been able to." She made a vague gesture toward her leg.

"How did you lose it?"

"Cliff jumping."

"Really? Where?" The image of long, coltish legs leaping from a cliff somewhere in the Mediterranean filled my brain.

"Cliffs of Insanity. Right after a sword fight with Inigo Montoya. He won, clearly." She was utterly straight-faced, and I suppressed the creeping disappointment that she still didn't trust me with her story.

"Right. How old were you when you leapt from said cliffs to escape the Dread Pirate Roberts, who was presumably right on your heels?" I was pleased to see the hint of an appreciative smile at the corners of her mouth.

"I was nineteen," she said after a pause, and I thought she might finally be telling the truth.

"My battles at nineteen were not of the sword-fighting variety, though I think I would have preferred swords," I said in a feeble attempt to distract her from the inevitable overshare shutdown.

"You must have been in basic training then?" she asked.

I shook my head. "I began basic training at age seventeen. By nineteen, I'd just left the Defense College of Policing and Guarding and was posted to an operational unit as a probationer with the C.S.I."

She looked impressed. "It sounds like you were quite the grown-up."

I scoffed. "I thought I was. In reality, I was a lost boy hiding behind a uniform and a purpose, terrified someone would call me out as a fraud."

"Does that feeling ever go away?" she asked with a wince.

I thought about that for a moment, and my silence seemed to embarrass Shane, because she looked away and busied herself writing notes.

"I don't feel like a fraud anymore," I said quietly. Shane met my eyes, and I continued. "I have survived enough now to feel entitled to call myself a man."

"Sometimes I still feel nineteen," she didn't meet my eyes, but she didn't stop there. "And my survival is relative."

A knock on the door interrupted whatever else she might have said, and I wanted to lock everyone out of the room so she'd finish her thought. Shane looked grateful for the reprieve though, and turned her attention to Sullivan and O'Malley as they entered the conference room.

"The tracker you set on Quimby's car is transmitting fine," O'Malley said. "He spent two hours at the gym while his car got new tires and a detail, then stopped by his tailor to pick up a couple suits and a half-dozen shirts that still had tags on them, flirted with the meter maid outside the tailor's to get out of a ticket, went for coffee, and just finally rolled into work."

"Do you have a tail on him?" Shane sounded startled. "How do you know about the tags and the flirting?"

"Alex occasionally hacks into surveillance cameras," I said.

She looked thoughtful but didn't comment.

"Did he do a financial check to see about the wife's car?" I asked O'Malley.

"Repo'd," answered Sullivan. I'd had a commanding officer in the Royal MPs with the same brusque manner, so I'd long since stopped taking his tone personally. Shane didn't have the same experience of our boss. I saw her flinch and then straighten her spine as if to defend against whatever came next.

"The bank took it two days ago," O'Malley added.

"Who'd he meet for coffee?" asked Shane. Sullivan arched an eyebrow in question and then picked up the conference room phone.

"Check the cameras in the cafe." He listened briefly, then hung up.

"Alex will be right down." Sullivan got up to make himself a coffee and then wandered over to the wall of sticky notes while it brewed.

"What are you thinking?" I murmured to Shane.

"I think they're coming for the house next," she whispered back. I liked the feeling of sharing secrets with her, and I loved seeing the glow of intrigue in her eyes. She knew something, and the confidence of it looked stunning on her.

"Talk to me about your system here," Sullivan said. Shane met my eyes, and I nodded to her. She moved next to him so she could point to the various color systems on our board.

"Orange is for anything directly associated with Quimby." She pointed to a line of sticky notes that ran down one side. "Blue is ADDATA, which is why the orange notes connect with a lot of it. And green—"

"Is the money," Sullivan said, nodding thoughtfully. He was impressed, and I was glad. The colored sticky notes had been all Shane, and the minute they were up I saw them for the genius they were. Things could be moved around or added to with each new bit of information. Facts could be as simple as a single word, and yet, when they went on the wall they represented part of a visual pattern. The amount of green on the wall had become quite striking, and Shane took a moment to write another green sticky and add it to the orange side. *Denise Quimby's car repossessed,* it said.

There was a perfunctory knock on the door as Greene walked into our conference room. He looked directly at Shane. "He met with his accountant."

She nodded. "Yeah. He's about to lose the house too."

"The guy just bought a bunch of new suits. That doesn't sound like someone afraid he's going to lose his house," said O'Malley.

Shane spoke clearly and with confidence. "When someone is going to declare bankruptcy, their attorney tells them to stop paying their credit card bills. That debt will always get wiped out anyway, and it's just throwing good money after bad, so he's running them up to their limits while he still can. He has too much equity in his house for the bankruptcy trustees to let him keep it, so it's either short sale or foreclosure. The market has dipped, so foreclosure is most likely, which is probably why Quimby moved the million dollars into the hidden account, and why he's ready to hunt me down to get it back. Denise must have known this was coming, or she'd have taken her car. She walked away with half his escape-hatch money and her personal jewelry, and if I were her, I'd change my name and start over."

O'Malley raised an eyebrow. "That's a fuckin' impressive bit of bankruptcy law."

Shane met Greene's eyes as she answered O'Malley. "My mother is a bankruptcy law specialist."

Greene didn't blink, but his carefully schooled expression said "I know" just the same. She shot me a quick glance too, and I realized the information about her mother must be another way to trace her true name. As much as I wanted to know her story, I refused to dig for it myself. If she wanted me to know, she'd tell me.

"I'm guessing a douchebag poser like Quimby's not gonna want his financials splashed all over the business news. This info is probably enough to get him to back the fuck off so we can close the account and be done with his bullshit." O'Malley's colorful lexicon rivaled the toughest London dockworker for expressiveness.

"I want to take down ADDATA," Shane said quietly.

The room stilled, and I realized Shane was looking not at the men who paid her consulting fee, but at me, her partner.

"Why?" asked Sullivan. I didn't hear irony or challenge in his tone, just a genuine question.

"Because they're cheating," she said.

Sullivan sat at the table across from her and leaned forward. "Why does this offend you?"

Shane took a sip of her coffee as she gathered her thoughts. O'Malley sat down near her, and Greene leaned back against the wall, waiting to hear the rest. She looked up and met the eyes of four men without flinching.

"I've spied on a lot of people. I've followed them, made notes about their habits, investigated who they talked to, where they went, who they called. I can tell you three are married," she looked at Sullivan, Greene, and O'Malley, "and the smallest things tell me your wives love you. You're a new dad," she said to Sullivan, "and you're thinking about it," her eyes flicked to Alex, "and it freaks you out that I can tell things like that just from looking at you." O'Malley opened his mouth to speak but closed it again as Shane resumed.

"ADDATA is doing exactly what I do. But it's cheating on the rules it tacitly agreed to with the person who casually scrolls through social media. The implied rules say 'use my platform and I will sell things to you.' But they're doing more than that. They're finding out what music you like, whether you vote, what you're afraid of, and who your friends are. And they're looking at your friends and finding those things out about them too. But the biggest cheat of all is that they're not just selling products, they're selling ideas. They're selling things to embrace, and things to fear. They might even be selling lies and hate, and they're hiding behind this idea that it's fair because *you knew* they were going to sell you something."

She looked directly at me then. "I became a P.I. because I got hurt by a cheater. This cheater might have the power to hurt all of us. I can't stand by and let that happen."

I wanted to kiss her so badly I ached with it. But more than that, I wanted to hold her in my arms and protect her from the hurts of her past. My hand twitched toward her before I could still it, and my wish was approximately as useful as wishing to change history, so instead, I poured all that feeling into one very small smile.

"We're not generally in the social justice business here at Cipher Security," said Sullivan, rising to his feet once more.

Greene stepped forward off the wall. "I'll help," he said quickly. Shane stared at him as she stood, and O'Malley and I were up a moment later.

Sullivan shot Greene an unreadable look, then returned his attention to Shane. "You make a compelling argument, however, and admittedly, you could very well continue the investigation without Cipher's sponsorship." He looked at me, then at Greene. "You also appear to have a team, with or without my support."

Shane took a deep breath and stood straight as Sullivan drilled her with his eyes. "You remain, however, a target of a man this company should have cut loose years ago. I dislike retaining him as a client for even one more day, but I do believe that whatever remains of his self-control will snap when we drop him. Please finish this quickly and in a manner that removes the risk to yourself."

Shane nodded. "Thank you," she said quietly. Sullivan raised one eyebrow in response, then checked his watch and left the conference room.

O'Malley considered Shane, myself, and Greene for a long moment before he directed his comments to Shane. "For what it's worth, I say go after the wife."

"She's probably up in Northport, Michigan. Or at least someone there knows where she is," I said.

Shane nodded once. "I can leave today."

O'Malley scowled. "Eze's got weapons training, so take him with you." She looked about to protest, but O'Malley quelled it with his parting shot. "It wasn't a suggestion," he said as he left the room.

For once, I was grateful to O'Malley for being a bossy prick.

Greene pushed himself off the wall he'd been holding up. "It's time for me to get inside ADDATA."

Shane looked ready to protest that too, but then seemed to realize her mistake. "You don't mean you're going to physically walk inside the building, do you?"

His expression was incredulous. "Why would I do that?"

Shane smiled at Greene, which was possibly the first smile I'd ever seen her wear in his presence. She pulled out her cell phone and wrote down a name and phone number, which she handed to Greene. "Here's the cell phone number for Nathan Yorn, one of the ADDATA programmers working on the data sets. I don't have access to CCSS7, but I assume you've already got something set up on Quimby's phone, so you might as well monitor their programming department too."

"What's CCSS7?" I asked.

Greene seemed startled to be handed something physical, and he answered the question with a distracted air. "Common Channel Signaling System 7 in the U.S., or just SS7 in the U.K."

"You say that as though I should know what it means."

Shane answered with a smile that went straight to my groin. "It's a network interchange program that acts as a broker between mobile phone networks. There are rumors that the NSA uses it to hack and snoop on targets." Smart was unbelievably sexy on her, and it took me a moment to actually focus on what her words meant.

Hacking a cell phone number? I shuddered to think of the possibilities.

Meanwhile, Greene chuckled in the sort of tone generally reserved for evil masterminds as he pocketed the number. "My wife wants you to meet her friends," he said to Shane.

It was her turn to look startled. "I already met Kat. She has more?"

The expression Greene wore was as baffled as Shane's. "She can't seem to help herself," he said just before he left the room.

[31]

SHANE

"Things are different in the north, where body heat is a precious commodity and spring break-up is an annual thing." – Aunt Shelley

---

I couldn't shake the feeling of unreality that had been creeping up on me since the conversation in the boardroom had begun. I was so glad Gabriel had been there next to me, and that was freaking me out too.

I'd become far too attached to the comfort of knowing Gabriel was there, and I watched him as I contemplated the likelihood that this thing between us would go the way of my past relationship.

Gabriel dialed his cell phone and smiled quickly at me as he waited for someone to answer.

"Hi, Mum. How's Mika?" he said, then smiled at her answer. "Can you put him on please?" A pause, and then, "Small Man, it's Big Man." His tone was serious. "I have news. My partner and I have to go out of town to investigate a law-breaker, so we won't make it to dinner at Gran's tonight." He took a breath, clearly hating to disappoint his nephew. "Can you make sure we get invited to dinner the next time Gran makes suya? She's going to grumble about me under her breath after I break the news to her, so I wanted you to hear it first."

I loved how serious this whole conversation was, and Gabriel met my eyes as he smiled at something his nephew said. "Yeah, your mum will let us come back over. She wants me to bring Shane to meet you. She knows you make me look good."

His nephew said something, and Gabriel smiled again. "Yeah, I like her." I had to look away from his face then because I was in danger of going gooey. He wrapped up his conversation with Mika, and I busied myself with packing up my laptop as Gabriel finished his brief conversation with his mother. When he hung up, he shook his head.

"I'm going to get dish duty for the next five family dinners for that one. She spent all morning making sticky toffee pudding and insists that we come to dinner tomorrow night while it's still good to eat."

"We should be back from Northpoint tonight, right?" I asked.

"It's almost a six-hour drive. If Jorge can cover Oscar tonight, it's probably safer if we come back tomorrow," he said.

The idea that I might be staying overnight with Gabriel Eze struck me right in the solar plexus, and my shock must have shown on my face because he took a step backward. "Or we can drive back tonight if you'd prefer."

I felt betrayed by my physical reactions, and I controlled my expression with effort. "We'll play it by ear. At this rate we should get there by dinner, so hopefully the gallery will still be open and we won't have to track down Aunt Shelley at her home."

Gabriel studied me as he packed up his bag. I watched his hands rather than having to look in his eyes, but I could feel them on me nonetheless. "I will admit to a growing fascination with your bag," I said, to distract myself.

"It would suit you," he said. "I'd give it to you, but I'm not sure you have anything with which to negotiate."

That statement startled me right out of my weird mood. I couldn't ignore that kind of challenge. "Oh really? There's nothing I have that could entice you?" I added enough edge to my voice that it didn't seem quite as flirty as it sounded, and Gabriel pretended to consider.

"Let's see … hmm, no, nothing comes to mind." He grinned as he slung the bag over his chest. "Shall we head back to our building? Ten dollars says I can be packed and ready to go before you are."

I smirked. "You're on." He had no idea who he was dealing with. I was the queen of low-maintenance travel. For one night I could tuck a pair of underwear and a credit card in my pockets and be ready to go.

I blew a kiss to Stan on our way out of Cipher, and called Jorge about Oscar on our way home. He welcomed the chance to stay at my place with my dog, because I had faster internet than he did, and I was still in the free premium channels part of my satellite subscription.

When we got to our building, I stood in the lobby and smiled at Gabriel. "Okay, I'm ready to go." I held out my hand. "Ten bucks, please."

He stared at me. "We're probably going to be spending the night. You're not ready for that."

I shrugged. "Sure I am."

"Prove it," he said, which didn't actually annoy me at all. I liked being able to surprise him.

I opened my leather messenger bag. "Computer, wallet, battery charger for my phone, contact lens solution and case, glasses, tooth-brush, hair band, and deodorant. I'll wash my underwear in the hotel sink, and I'll sleep naked. I could get by on just a credit card, but I usually carry the basics so I don't have to use it on stupid stuff."

He stared at me, and finally shook himself. "Sorry, I got hung up on the sleep naked part."

"I get the sense you'd be fairly easy to distract," I said with a grin. "Mental images of nudity to you are kind of like shouting 'squirrel' to a hunting dog."

"Not nudity in the abstract, I'll have you know," he started for the stairs. "Come on, you win – spectacularly, I might add. But you should spend the time cuddling the beast while I get some things together."

I followed him up. "So, naked people in general don't do it for you?"

He scoffed. "There is nothing fascinating about the male body. It is, as they say, a meat wagon to carry around a consciousness."

I shuddered at the mental image. "I might have to agree to disagree about that, but how is a female body not just a meat wagon too?"

"I refuse to reveal the baseness of my thoughts and say out loud something utterly offensive about wagons for meat."

I groaned at that, just as it deserved. "You do that well – say you're not going to say a thing as you say it anyway."

"I'm British," he shrugged. "It comes with the accent. I'll be down in a few minutes. Pack your running gear so we can go for a night run up there." He left me outside my apartment and took the staircase up to his at a sprint.

Oscar thumped his tail from the couch, where he'd snuggled in for his day nap. He got up and stretched slowly, half-on and half-off the couch, until I dropped next to him and gave his belly the appropriate level of attention. I told him Jorge would be taking him on a run later, and he could probably sleep with him on the couch if he didn't take up the whole thing. I was fairly certain all the important words, like "run" and "Jorge" and "couch" got through.

I got up to grab a sling bag from the hall closet, tossed my cheetah leg and running shoe into it, and then despite my earlier bravado. I broke down and packed a change of underwear and another t-shirt in addition to running tights. I kept the tapestry coat on because it was warm and stylish enough to work for most scenarios, but I added a cashmere scarf to my bag in case I needed to dress it up even more.

Gabriel was scratching Oscar's ears when I came out of the bedroom, and he nodded at the sling bag. "You broke down and packed something to sleep in?"

"Nope. You said pack running shoes. In here is one shoe and one leg. Not nearly as sexy as you were hoping for."

"Aaaand… squirrel!" he said with a sigh. "No pajamas equals naked in bed. It's about as sexy as packing can get."

And since there was nothing I could say to refute that, I kissed my dog on the head, grabbed two water bottles from the fridge, and then locked my apartment door behind us.

There was a bunch of construction on the I-90 East out of Chicago, but once we hit the I-94, things picked up. Gabriel let me drive the first part, since I offered, and I was happy to hand over the wheel when we stopped for gas in Grand Rapids. He was a good road trip companion, just as easy to talk to as to be silent with. We spent most of the trip either listening to history podcasts or discussing them, and things got particularly lively after a podcast about the technological inventions that caused historical swerves. I pointed out that the producers hadn't done a particularly good job of seeking female representation among their innovators, and he challenged me to name three black ones. We both agreed that it would be far more interesting if more of history was written by someone other than the victorious white guys.

I slept for a little while on the way to Traverse City, and Gabriel listened to the soundtrack of *Moana*, which was oddly soothing. I woke up to a very different landscape as we traveled along the west arm of the Grand Traverse Bay. It was breathtaking, and I must have made a sound, because Gabriel turned off the music.

"It's different than I expected up here," he said.

I nodded as I took in the view. "I grew up in the Sierra Mountains, which are full of tall, old-growth trees. This landscape is so flat and almost barren, even though we're surrounded by water. It's beautiful and desolate at the same time." I felt a kinship with it that surprised me.

"I was a city kid, through and through. The first time I saw mountains was on maneuvers in Scotland. I tried to run up to the top of one, and nearly killed myself in weather that changed on a dime. When I'd recovered, I made it my mission to learn to climb them properly, and then spent every weekend as high as I could climb." He smiled at the memory, and I was struck by how relaxed it made him look, as though even the memory of being outside in nature calmed him.

"I spent almost every weekend backpacking when I was a kid. We'd get home from school on Friday, Dad would tell us to pack extra socks, a toothbrush, and a down coat with our sleeping bag and pad, and by dark on Friday night we'd be setting up camp somewhere."

211

"So that's where you got your superior packing skills?" he asked with a grin.

I shrugged. "That happens when you're expected to carry your own pack from the age of six. You also learn what's necessary when you decide a sleeping pad is too heavy and you don't want to bring it. It only takes one night of hard, cold ground to understand what is and isn't worth the effort."

"I've had a lot of nights on cold, hard ground. When you're tired enough, you sleep, and if you don't, those are the nights you should be awake anyway."

"From your time in the military?" I asked.

He shook his head. "Believe it or not, the British military is actually fairly considerate of its soldiers. The Peacekeepers are less so. Or perhaps the pretense of British civility has no place in the war zones of the rest of the world." His words faded to silence, and he seemed lost in thought for several minutes.

"How long has it been since you've been backpacking?" he asked me, probably just to change the channel on his own thoughts, since he couldn't know how fraught that question was for me.

"Since I was sixteen. I bought myself a new pack for my twenty-third birthday, but it's still in my closet with the tags on." I felt oddly guilty whenever I thought of my unused backpack, like I was letting my dad down.

"Apparently, there are some great backpacking trails in the Huron-Manistee National Forests, which we went through about an hour ago. We should go sometime." Gabriel's tone was perfectly casual, and somehow I managed to twist the words around in my head.

Why did I always have to make things complicated? I had never gone backpacking without my dad, and I didn't even know how my leg would react to a thirty pound pack on my back. I should have been jumping at the chance to do something I used to love, instead of yelling at myself to get over it already.

"…Or not," he finally said.

I realized my arguments had all been internal, and he hadn't had the benefit of my brain on loudspeaker to know that I'd even heard him. "Sorry. Yeah, that would be nice."

"Really? Because on the scale of one to enthusiastic, that answer rated deep in the negative numbers. It's fine if you're not interested. I've just always preferred actual conversation with another human in the woods rather than talking to myself to keep the bears away."

"I've never backpacked alone," I admitted.

"I don't recommend it except as an antidote to family reunions. The silence can make your thoughts alarmingly loud."

I smiled wanly. "I don't have family reunions either."

He glanced at me quickly, then returned his focus to the road, but not before I caught his look of surprise. After a moment he said, "Dinner with my family is never just a spectator sport, nor is it for the fainthearted."

He'd hesitated just long enough that I knew it wasn't what he'd originally wanted to say.

"I look forward to dinner with your family," I said, with an intentionally bright smile.

Gabriel sighed and rubbed the back of his neck with one hand. "I've become gun-shy about asking anything personal of you. I've come to expect silence and withdrawal. I have to tell you, it feels awful to run every question through a 'will this piss her off?' filter."

I stared at the road ahead of us, and the silence stretched between us as I probed his words like a tongue does a cavity. The self-indulgence of it made me want to scream, and I finally had to speak or be consumed by the silence.

"When I ran away from California, I left everyone behind – friends, co-workers, family, the cheating ex – everyone. Other people knew Mitch was cheating on me, and when I finally figured it out, I realized the look I'd been seeing in their eyes was pity. And then, because I stayed with him after discovering him in bed with the other woman, I became someone even *I* didn't like or respect very much. When I finally did leave, the only way I could find my confidence again was to shut the door on all of it – on every person who said nothing, on everyone who had seen me strip myself of my dignity and turn into that naked, mewling baby Voldemort thing from the last Harry Potter movie."

Gabriel barked a startled laugh, and it made me feel good that I could lift a little significance out of the gut-spill.

"It took about six months for me to hold my head above water, and another six before I felt like I could swim back to shore. I guess part of me is afraid that if I connect with any part of that past, the memories of who I let myself turn into will suck me back into the deep end. Unfortunately, it's made me pretty rigid about even sticking my toes in."

The view of the lake outside had clearly affected my metaphoric speech center, but it was a pretty appropriate description of what it had felt like to lose myself. It was not a place to which I would ever willingly return, and I thought Gabriel's own statement about being gun-shy fit me far too well.

"Does your family know you're alive?" he asked after several minutes of silence.

"I send my mom a Christmas card every year." I didn't mention that the first year I drove across state lines to mail it so the postmark wouldn't give me away. I didn't actually hate my mother; I just felt betrayed by her.

"I won't pretend to understand your relationship with your family – I suppose that requires details you're not willing to share. I do understand a bit of your reaction to the place, and the person you let yourself become while you were there. I suppose I've done something similar about my time in Nigeria."

He let the words fade into silence, and another mile passed before I finally pulled up my big girl panties to speak. "So, here's the thing. My normal M.O. is to let something like what you just said slide, even though I'm totally intrigued and want to ask all the questions. Because I know that if I start digging, then you get to ask questions in return, and before you know it, we're having an actual conversation with sharing and stuff."

I deliberately allowed my speech to reflect the teenaged girl I felt like – nervous, twisty, and far too self-conscious for comfort. But nothing in this moment was comfortable, so I soldiered on, silently blessing Gabriel for keeping his expression impassive.

"But you just called me out on something I deserved, and I have to tell you, it doesn't feel good to know I've gotten so touchy and stand-offish that you feel like you have to run things through a filter before you say them to me." I inhaled as though I could draw courage from the air. "So, I'm just going to plow ahead and ask. You don't have to answer, obviously, but if you do, and it turns into an actual dialogue, I promise to do my best not to shut it down if it gets too personal."

His eyes stayed on the road, and the headlights from oncoming traffic sent spotlights across them that made them sparkle.

"What happened in Nigeria?"

[32]
GABRIEL

"The most painful beatings are the self-inflicted ones." –
Miri Eze

Her question felt like opening the locked door to the room that stood between us, only to find the room haunted by screaming demons, and I forced my grip on the steering wheel to loosen. I had to do the same with my clenched teeth. I wanted her to ask for all the reasons about which she'd spoken, but answering meant stepping into the room with the demons and looking them in the eye.

I exhaled slowly to buy time to find the words. "I told you that a group of us went on an unsanctioned mission to rescue the sister of one of my Peacekeeper mates. She had been kidnapped by Boko Haram with other girls from an NGO-sponsored school in their village," I began tentatively.

"Boko Haram are … terrorists?" Her voice was soft and coaxing, and gave me a chance to answer with confidence.

"Technically they are a jihadist militant group based in northern Nigeria whose name literally declares that Western education is forbidden." Memories threatened like dark clouds overhead, and I felt as though I were facing a hurricane with nothing more in my arsenal than an umbrella. "And yes, one of their aims is to terrorize families into keeping their children away from Western schools."

I took a fortifying breath and then continued. "There was a Boko Haram compound hidden deep in the woods, about eight miles off the main road. Five of us walked in one night with plans to find the sister and nineteen other girls – four for each of us – to give us the best chance to get them, and ourselves, out alive. My mate found his sister in the first hut – each hut held fifteen or twenty girls – and the rest of us had to pick which girls we would take out with us." My voice broke on the last word as I remembered the pleading faces of children looking at us with desperation. "We had agreed to leave behind any girl with a baby at her breast—" I swallowed painfully "—there were dogs – German shepherds. We didn't think we could keep the babies quiet as we ran, and we were so outnumbered by boys and men with AK-47s in the camp that stealth was our only chance."

Shane's hand touched the back of my neck, and I was grateful for the warmth of it. I took another breath and willed my voice to work. "One little girl, maybe ten or eleven years old, followed me and the four bigger girls I'd chosen out of a hut. I decided to take her too, even though four was supposed to be the limit. She had a bundle strapped to her back that I thought was clothes, but when I touched her back to help her through the fence, the bundle moved."

I wanted to close my eyes against the memory, but driving forced me to keep them open and focused. "I made her stay inside the compound while the bigger girls slipped out to join the ones already waiting in the forest." My voice broke, and I cleared my throat. "She didn't say a word, but her eyes told me that she would die if she stayed. I almost pulled her through the fence with me, but then a dog started barking somewhere in the camp, and I pushed her back toward the hut and walked away. It was the hardest thing I've ever had to do."

"Christ," she whispered, and then was silent for a long time.

It was several miles before I found my voice again. "We got all twenty girls to safety, carrying two at a time while two walked in listless silence until we'd gone eight miles back to where we'd hidden our vehicles. They were so weak and malnourished they weighed almost nothing ..." My voice trailed off as I thought about how different my solid little nephew felt when I gave him piggy back rides. At four years old he probably weighed more than the little girl with her own baby bundled to her back would have.

"You got your friend's sister out." Shane's voice was soothing, like the touch of her hand against the back of my neck.

"Kesandu. Yeah, she was twelve," I answered. "She was tough and strong. She'd been given a gun for raids on villages."

"Oh no," Shane whispered.

"Yeah. The girl with the baby – she was one of the girls they chose for *camp* life." I could still hear the echo of Kesandu's fear and revulsion in my memory. "I promised myself then that even if it meant my own life was in danger, I could never again choose not to help someone who needed it."

We passed a sign welcoming us to Northport. "We're here," I said as I slowed the car to look for a commercial district, very happy for the change in subject. Shane looked as though there was more to say, but I'd used up all the words I had about my time in Nigeria. Looking that particular monster in the eye had taken more courage than I had reserves for, so I firmly shut the door on the memory of the dark eyes that haunted my dreams, and turned, instead, to the bright green ones next to me.

Before we'd left Chicago, Shane had looked up *Shelley Photographer Northport* and got a hit on a gallery show at the Willowbrook Mill. "Turn right up ahead, and then left, and it should be on the left side," she said. Her voice was still quiet and her tone subdued. I didn't want to think about her opinion of my character now that she knew what I'd done.

We pulled into the parking lot of an elegantly rustic building surrounded by trees. A bridge crossed a chasm where presumably a stream had once powered the namesake mill, and strings of lights directed us to the front door. The lot was nearly full of cars, and music could be heard from inside the building.

I ignored the hollow feeling in my gut as I got out of the car, but oddly, breathing was somehow easier, and my partner was just the distraction I needed from tedious introspection.

I tried not to be too obvious in my appreciation for the way Shane stretched the stiffness from her long body, but bending to touch her toes required a proper look, and it was a view which inspired my already creative imagination. She swung her long coat on with a flourish that added to the superhero illusion she seemed to carry with her, and then she looked over at me with a smile.

"So, do we have a story, or do we tell the truth?"

I didn't realize how much I'd needed that smile until I felt my jaw unclench and my own smile answer. "You're the expert at people. Why don't you read the room and then decide?" She gave me a speculative look that I thought might have been appreciative, and I gestured for her to precede me across the bridge.

The interior of the Willowbrook Mill was lit with chandeliers suspended from the ceiling of the main room. It was full of people in clothing that varied from jeans to cocktail attire, holding glasses of red and white wine, and taking polite little appetizers from wandering servers with silver trays. The walls were hung with black and white photographs, and about half of the guests were actually looking at them.

"Wow," Shane said quietly to me. Her eyes were on the photos, and I gave them a closer look. The subjects were men or women in varying states of undress – some were blatantly sexual, but most appeared to be people captured in their daily lives.

"It's like the *Women Before 10 a.m.* series, but at night," Shane said in surprise.

I had no idea what she was talking about, but she'd already crossed the room to study a photograph before I could ask. A voice at my shoulder kept me from following her.

"She's not wrong, but I would not have expected someone her age to get the connection." I turned to see a woman in her sixties with black and silver hair, horn-rimmed glasses, and a dramatic turquoise necklace smiling at me. She held out her hand. "I'm Shelley Thorpe," she said as I shook her hand.

"Gabriel Eze," I answered.

"You're not from Northport, Gabriel, or I'd have photographed you already." Shelley Thorpe had a direct gaze, a strong grip, and a voice that sounded as though she were close to laughter. I liked her immediately.

"This is your show," I looked around the room, wishing Shane were still next to me. Shelley noticed.

"That one's not from here either," she said appreciatively, following my gaze to Shane.

"We came up from Chicago."

Shelley studied my partner. "Did you?" She turned her gaze to me. "Will you introduce me to your friend, Gabriel? I think I need to meet her."

I didn't think many people said no to Shelley Thorpe. Something about her reminded me of my nana, which told me I wouldn't get very far with a "no" even if I was foolish enough to attempt one.

Shane was studying a striking photo of a young man lacing up his running shoes. He wore shorts, shoes, and nothing else, and he had the lean lankiness of a distance runner.

She turned to greet me as I approached, and her eyes widened at the sight of Shelley with me. "Your work is spectacular," she said simply.

I was surprised that she knew who Shelley was until I realized she held a program in her hand that was emblazoned with Shelley's photograph.

"Thank you. I'm Shelley."

Shane shook Shelley's hand and introduced herself. Shelley smiled at her. "I heard you mention Veronique's work. How do you know it?"

"I inherited my dad's photo books. *Women Before 10 a.m.* is one of my favorites."

"I thought her work with models and celebrities was inspired, but I wondered if the stories of people who aren't famous would have the same impact on the viewer. So rather than go to an actress's home to surprise her as she got ready for her day, I decided to photograph ordinary people later, when the day has decided the mood."

Shane turned back to the photo of the young man. "I see myself in him. The set of his shoulders and grim determination tells me he's going to run off the frustration and let go of the anger. It's a moving photograph."

Shelley studied Shane as she admired the photo. "Do you run, Shane?"

"I do. Usually at night, probably for the same reasons as he does."

Shelley tilted her head as she regarded her. "May I photograph you running sometime? I feel as though I'd like to capture you in motion."

Shane made a self-deprecating sound. "We're only up here for the night, but thank you, I'm flattered."

"Then let me photograph you tonight," Shelley said.

I could see the mental debate Shane engaged in. Shelley Thorpe was very likely the Aunt Shelley who might know where Mickey Collins and Denise Quimby could be found. If she said no to a photograph, it would be pretty awkward to then ask where Shelley's nephew was, but if she said yes, she could perhaps use the time as an excuse to get the information without alerting Mickey.

"We don't have a hotel room yet, so I'm not sure when we're going out to run—" Shane began.

"Then stay here," Shelley interrupted. "There are rental cottages next door, and I know the owner."

Shane gave me a look that said *help me*, and I gave her one back that said *your call*. Then she sighed and turned back to Shelley. "We'd be very happy to talk to your friend about one of the rental cottages, thank you."

I tried not to notice the jump in my pulse at the fact that Shane had just said "one" of the rentals, but I failed miserably.

"So, you'll do it? You'll let me photograph you tonight?" Shelley asked with what seemed like undue excitement given the nature of the request.

Shane smiled graciously. "Yeah. If you can point us in the direction of food and a place to sleep, we're going to run anyway, so ..." She shrugged. "It would be kind of cool to have such an amazing artist shoot a photo of me."

Shelley clapped her hands in excitement and rushed away to arrange a cottage for us. I stepped closer to Shane and murmured, "Are you sure you're okay with this?" I didn't just mean the photo, and she knew it.

"I'm a grown-up. I can deal," she said.

We wandered around the room looking at Shelley's photographs. They were startlingly good, and I considered buying one for my new flat, though Shane and I had different opinions about which one I should get. She thought I needed the boxer, sitting alone in his room after a fight. I argued for the woman strapping a high-heeled shoe onto her foot. Her face was out of focus, but her leg was shapely and strong.

Shelley returned with the key to a cottage and directions to a seafood restaurant in town. Our meal was good, but somewhat quiet and tense, as though the unspoken things were louder than the small talk we used to fill the silence.

The parking lot at the Willowbrook Mill was nearly empty when we got back, though it was barely past nine o'clock. "I'll go find Shelley and tell her to meet us at the cottage," Shane said just before she disappeared into the mill. I retrieved our bags from the trunk and took them to the cottage Shelley had pointed out when she'd given us the key.

It was rustic and charming and fit the décor of the Willowbrook Mill. A four-poster queen-sized bed dominated the room, and the doors of one of the built-in closets had been removed to make room for a bookshelf and a twin bed with big pillows against the wall. The effect was of a reading nook or space for a child to sleep, or, in this case, space for a man unsure of his footing around a woman to whom he was wildly attracted.

The reading nook and the bathroom were the only semi-private spaces in the otherwise large, wide-open room, and I tossed my bag and myself down on the twin bed to await Shane's arrival. Dinner had been awkward enough that I was debating the wisdom of staying in Northport after Shane's photo session with Shelley. I couldn't help feeling that my revelations in the car had put her off. It didn't surprise me. I didn't much care for that part of myself either, but I'd hoped she would understand a little, and perhaps be able to forgive ... enough.

I heard the door, and I sat up and rubbed the back of my neck self-consciously. Shane was staring around the room in surprise.

"It's bigger than I thought it would be. And nice," she said.

"Did you find Shelley?" I swung my legs off the twin bed. She caught my gaze but looked away before I could sense what she was thinking.

"She'll meet me here in fifteen."

"Just you?" I stared at her, but she wouldn't meet my eyes.

"I didn't want to assume ..." She faltered as she pulled her cheetah leg, single shoe, and tights out of her bag.

I didn't even know what to say. She sat on the queen-sized bed and bent down to unzip her boot, and I was reminded of the photograph of the woman buckling her high heel. That boot came off, but she didn't bother unzipping the other one. Instead, she pulled the leg up on her jeans and unhooked the socket from her leg so the whole thing detached.

Shane didn't look at me as she stood on one leg and unzipped her jeans. I was mesmerized as she slid the tight jeans off her hips and down past the stump of her leg. Once that was free, she sat back down and stripped off the other leg.

Her underwear were black boy shorts and hot as hell. I was staring and I knew it, but she was determined to avoid acknowledging it, or me, as she folded her jeans and reached for her running tights.

"You are so fucking sexy," I breathed, only half-aware that I'd spoken out loud.

Shane's head came up sharply, and she looked surprised. She flexed her right knee – the one with the sleeve on the stump – and it seemed like an unconscious gesture in response to my eyes on her. I wanted to peel the tight neoprene sleeve away from her skin, to soothe the lines that indented the flesh just above it. My hands itched to run down the length of her legs, hips to thighs to foot, and I clenched the bed cover in my fists to keep from reaching for her. Just so I didn't make a fool of myself, I grabbed my own bag to get my shorts and shoes. Shane remained frozen, her eyes still wide, until I stood and turned my back to her. I stepped out of my trousers quickly so she wouldn't see the evidence of my attraction to her. Thankfully, she moved again, presumably to finish dressing, while I pulled on my shorts and willed my erection to subside.

When my shoes were on and I could stand without tenting my shorts, I turned my attention back to Shane. She wore her black running tights and a black sport bra, and she stood by the door, watching me warily.

I couldn't take my eyes off her, the way the Lycra fit her curves and skimmed her long legs. My gaze devoured her, and I felt my own skin heat in response to the blush that crept up her neck.

I swallowed hard and opened my mouth to say ... something, but all the words got muddled in my head, and the only thought that rang clearly through them was, *I want you.*

[33]

SHANE

"House cats are the most ruthless predators in the animal kingdom." – Gabriel Eze

---

Gabriel's gaze hunted me. His eyes slid down my body with a slow deliberateness that felt sensual and predatory, as though I was being stalked by something feline and shockingly dangerous.

I'd lost my breath when I'd turned to see him staring, and I felt utterly trapped in his attention. When I found it again, it came fast and shallow, and my heart thudded in response to the intensity of his look as he studied me.

He'd seen me in running clothes before, and he'd even seen me once without my leg, but it had been a calculated risk to change in front of him – a risk that was heightened because he'd been so taken with the image of the woman's leg in the gallery photograph – a leg I clearly didn't have.

My disappointment had been acute, and I knew he'd noticed my silence at dinner. Maybe the revelation he'd trusted me with on our drive was a signal that we were friends and nothing more, and certainly the fact that he'd found the leg photograph so appealing had pricked at the insecurity I carried shackled to me like handcuffs – that I wasn't ... *enough* for him to appreciate in the same way.

So why did he look at me with the kind of hunger I expected from a panther lurking in a tree as it studies the gazelle on the ground below?

Heat raced across my skin, and I had the sense that he could smell it on the air, as though fear and confusion and desire combined to make me smell like prey. I thought I could see the pulse in his neck, and then he swallowed, hard.

A knock on the door made me jump, and a flash of something primal crossed Gabriel's face before something else that looked like relief settled in.

I turned to answer it, glad for a reason to tear my eyes away from his gaze. I could still feel his eyes on me, and I pushed down the desire for something *more* that threatened the boundaries of my comfort zone.

Shelley stood at the door with a camera slung around her neck. "You ready?" she asked with a glance down at my running gear. Her gaze faltered, arrested on my cheetah leg, and then slammed back up to my face. "You're an amputee?" Her voice held surprise and wonder, and possibly delight.

"I actually have two legs. One just likes to dress up as a steampunk Goth." I honestly couldn't help the snark, and I heard a snicker behind me. Gabriel drew Shelley's attention too, and the appreciation in her look was almost annoying.

"You're coming too, I hope?"

Gabriel flicked a glance at me. "Am I?"

I almost snarled at him, still affected by the earlier heat between us, but turned my attention back to Shelley. "Where's a good place for us to run?"

"If you go down to the marina, I can set up by the pier and catch you under the lights," she said, her eyes lingering on my cheetah leg. "Oh, and Gabriel?"

He looked up from his water bottle in response.

"Lose the shirt, please?"

Definitely annoying, but Shelley smiled charmingly, then gave us quick directions and took off in her car to meet us down there.

Gabriel stripped off his t-shirt and tossed it on the twin bed. My mouth went dry at the sight of hard muscle that looked like it had been carved from a slab of mahogany. I grabbed his water bottle because it was handy, and because I wouldn't be able to speak without help.

He let me exit the cottage first and then locked it behind us. I started to run slowly in the direction Shelley had indicated, and Gabriel kept an easy pace next to me. We didn't speak until we could see the marina in front of us.

"I'm sorry I was a jerk earlier, at dinner," I finally said.

"You weren't a jerk." He sounded wary, and then exhaled. "I know you're probably disgusted with the choices I made in Africa, but I'd like to think you'd give me a chance to prove I'm different now."

I stared at him, openmouthed. "Disgusted? My God, Gabriel! I'm horrified at what you had to do to get those girls to safety, and I'm so, so sorry for the choices you had to make. But I think you're a hero, and I'm kind of wondering why you're even here with me right now."

"What are you talking about? Where else would I be?" His voice had gone deep and growly and was threaded with some emotion I couldn't read.

I shook my head and turned to run again. "Nothing. It's nothing."

He kept pace with me, and I could feel his gaze burning my face. "*Something* happened. Something made you pull away from me. What was it, Shane?"

"It's stupid," I murmured. It wasn't stupid, but I didn't want to say it out loud, because then it would be.

"Tell me." His voice had an edge of command, and I bristled. "Please." I could feel his eyes searching my face.

I finally exhaled in frustration. "The photograph. Of the woman's leg."

"What about it?" He sounded confused, and I hated him in that moment for making me explain.

"You like it."

"Yeah, so? I like the boxer too."

229

"I don't wear heels," I said quietly.

"You'd be six-four if you did. Not that I'd mind. I'm a particular fan of tall women."

I stopped again, hands on my hips, and glared at him. "I'll never be like the woman in that photo. I'll never wear sexy high heels and short skirts, and all the things that make someone normal." I was angry, but only because he made me spell out my self-consciousness. I started running toward the marina again, but Gabriel reached out and grabbed me before I could pass him.

His mouth crashed into mine, and I fell against his bare chest. He held my upper arms, and after one shocked moment, my hands snaked around his waist as he kissed me. His heart beat a tattoo against mine, and the bare skin of our stomachs felt as though it had fused together.

"I taste you in my dreams," he murmured against my mouth. "I think about kissing you ten, fifty, a hundred times a day."

My breath caught in my throat as his mouth slid from mine to the space just below my earlobe, where he whispered, "When I saw you tonight, without your jeans, without the leg, I wanted to kiss every inch of your skin. Every..." he kissed the hollow beneath my ear, "damn..." he gently bit my earlobe, "inch."

It was a good thing he held my arms, because I could feel my knees buckle as I melted into his skin. I took a ragged breath, and Gabriel pulled back enough to look into my eyes. "You could never be normal. Extraordinary is not normal. Stunning is not normal. Brilliant is. Not. Normal."

His hands went to my face and cupped my cheeks. "I want to make love to you, Shane. But more than that, I want to talk, and run, and laugh, and wake up with you."

He kissed me again, hard, and then let go of my face, inhaled sharply, and looked away toward the marina. "We have a job to do, so I can wait." He captured my gaze again. "But not for long. And not patiently."

We resumed our run to the marina without another word, and my own brain, usually full of denial, insecurity, and excuses, had gone utterly silent. The only thing left was electricity that zinged through me on an alternating current. Even the space between us had its own atmosphere – the kind of meteoric storm that shorted out radios and fried computers.

I could see Shelley halfway down the pier, just under the yellow haze of a streetlight. I debated calling Gabriel out on a race in an attempt to snap the tension between us, but then realized I didn't want to. I liked the tension, and I used it to pick up speed as we ran across the parking lot to the pier. Gabriel matched me stride for stride. By the time we blew past the spot where Shelley crouched with her camera on a tripod, the shutter firing on automatic, we were at a full sprint, and I was laughing.

We crossed the invisible line at the end of the pier within half a step of each other and crashed into the railing with gasping laughter, hearts pounding, sweat slicking our skin. Shelley arrived a minute later running with her tripod.

"That was amazing! I could shoot you both all night!"

I caught Gabriel's eye and guessed he was thinking the same thing I was, which was *I really wish we could go back to the room right this minute, but we have work to do.*

I stood up and met Shelley's admiring gaze. "Shelley, you're an amazing artist, and we're really honored to be your subjects. But the main reason we drove up here was to find your nephew, Mickey."

Shelley's eyebrows raised, and she took a small step backward as her smile faded.

I held up my hands in supplication. "Denise is a client of mine, and I need to warn her about her husband. We're not here to cause trouble for them, but Denise has information that we think can help us and also keep her safe from Quimby. We need to talk to her."

"Do you have a card or something?" Shelley asked suspiciously.

I nodded. "Back at the cottage. I'm a P.I., and I just did some work for Denise to prove her husband was cheating on her. She knows me."

Shelley considered us for a long, silent moment. I stretched so I didn't stiffen up while she made her decision, and maybe it helped convince her that I was just a regular person. "Give me your cell phone number," she finally said to me. "If Denise wants to talk to you, she'll call."

It wasn't a great option – Denise already had my cell number and hadn't bothered calling. Nor had she bothered to pay my bill, so I wasn't holding my breath.

"Ask Denise why her husband got a FOID card three months ago," I said.

That got her attention. "Her husband carries a gun?"

I nodded. "I don't trust him, and I'm trying to keep us all safe."

Gabriel knelt down to re-tie his shoe, and I knew it was an excuse to look up to Shelley so she wouldn't be threatened by his size when he spoke. "We work for a security company in Chicago tasked with neutralizing threats, and we believe Quimby is a threat."

Shelley exhaled. "And if you could find them here, so could he." She nodded thoughtfully. "Meet us at the mill in twenty minutes." Her tone was resigned, and she left the pier without a backward glance.

When Shelley was out of earshot, Gabriel murmured to me, "I'm impressed."

I looked him straight in the eyes and dared him boldly. "First one back gets the big bed." And then I sprinted past him and up the hill.

[34]
GABRIEL

"What would you ask for if you knew the answer was yes?" –
Shane, P.I.

S he probably would have won anyway, because she'd surprised me
with the taunt that we wouldn't be sharing the bed, but I let her
win by enough that the shower was running when I entered the cottage.

I'd just kicked off my shoes when I heard a thud coming from the
bathroom.

"Ow!" Shane's curse was muffled by the running water.

"Shane?" I called. She didn't answer.

Another thud. I was on my feet and at the bathroom door before I
was even aware I'd moved.

And another thud. Had she fallen? I opened the door without
thinking and nearly tripped over the cheetah leg on the floor. My gaze
was caught on the sight of Shane behind the glass door of the very
large shower, standing on one foot with her eyes closed under the

233

spray, holding the tiled wall with one hand, and trying to wash her hair with the other.

"Shit," she muttered under her breath, unaware that I was there.

I'd dislocated a shoulder once and had to wash one-handed for three weeks. It was hard to get short hair clean with one hand – long hair like Shane's must have been impossible. I didn't stop to consider what she would think before I opened the glass door and, still in my shorts, stepped into the shower with her. Shane's eyes snapped open, and she stared at me as I put both hands on her waist to support her.

"Wash your hair," I said quietly.

Her eyes were wide and never left mine as I held her in place so she could use both hands to scrub the shampoo through her long hair. Even when she closed them to rinse, I didn't allow my gaze to drop below her face. Her small breasts teased my peripheral vision, and the rest of her taunted my imagination, but I did not look down. When her hair was free of soap and slicked off her face as though she were a mermaid risen from the sea, she opened her eyes and met my gaze.

"Thank you," she said softly.

I reached past her to turn off the water, and she held onto a wall as I handed her a towel. I tried to summon the fortitude to stay and dry her off, but my self-control was hanging on by a thread, so instead, I grabbed another towel for myself and left the room.

She met me outside the mill five minutes later, her wet hair twisted into a low knot, her face bare of make-up. My jeans felt tight; I was still half hard with the memory of water coursing down her naked skin, over curves and ridges that I wanted to trace with fingers, lips, and tongue.

She took a deep breath, and I felt the sear of it in my own lungs. "Shall we?" she said.

I indicated she should precede me across the bridge and into the main gallery room of the mill. Shelley emerged from a door at the far end of the room. Her expression was solemn, though she strode toward us without hesitation.

"Mickey and Denise will talk to you," she said in a stern voice, "but I want your word that they'll have no trouble from you or your firm."

"The firm has no quarrel with either of them," I said quietly.

"Nor do we," Shane added.

Shelley nodded and directed us to follow her.

The room at the far end of the main gallery was carpeted and softly lit by wall sconces on dimmers. A man and a woman, both in their early thirties, sat together on an elegant settee. They held hands, and I thought it said more about their nerves than their affection for each other.

"Hello, Denise," Shane said formally. Her tone wasn't cold, but it definitely wasn't warm and friendly either, and I remembered that Denise Quimby had skipped town without paying Shane's bill.

"Who is he?" Denise asked, indicating me.

Shane's tone cooled. "Gabriel is my partner," she answered.

"I didn't hire him. I don't want to talk to him." Denise wore surly anger as comfortably as the purple cashmere sweater she had on.

Shane's tone was innocuously pleasant, and she even managed a smile. "Considering that you haven't paid me for my services, you're not in a position to dictate terms, *Mrs. Quimby*." The emphasis on her name made Denise blanche, and I was impressed at the bloodless equivalent of a smack-down that Shane had just dealt her.

I nodded to Denise's boyfriend, whose nervousness had just increased exponentially at the traded barbs. "Mickey, I'm Gabriel." I stuck out my hand, and Mickey stood to take it. "Why don't we go for a walk and leave them to it for a bit."

He shot a quick look at the scowl on Denise's face. "Sounds good." He grabbed his leather jacket and then leaned in to kiss Shelley on the cheek.

"Back in a bit, Aunt Shelley."

"Oh no, I'm coming with you. You're not leaving me with the hissing cats," she said as she followed us from the room.

As we walked away, I heard Shane ask Denise about the money and what she knew. Their voices dropped to a murmur when we reached the large gallery room, so rather than go back out into the cold night air, I wandered past Shelley's photographs for the excuse to speak with Mickey. Any man who has ever had an honest conversation with another man knows they don't generally happen face-to-face unless dominance is at play. The best ones are in the car, or on a trail, or shoulder-to-shoulder at a football match. Voices are hard enough to navigate, but pain or confusion in another man's eyes make us too vulnerable to our own.

"Did she tell you about the money?" I asked him. We stood before a black and white photograph of a father bending over to kiss a sleeping child who reminded me forcibly of my nephew. Love flared hard and fast in my chest, and I shoved away thoughts of Mika's father who would never know his son.

"She told me he lost it all," Mickey said. He was a good-looking guy, almost my height, but lean and stringy, with dark hair worn too long in the way of musicians and artists. I could see how someone like cashmere Denise could find his slightly dangerous look appealing after the carefully cultivated gym rat appearance of Quimby.

"How?" I'd left my question deliberately ambiguous, just to see where Mickey's mind naturally went. I couldn't tell if he knew about the half million with which his girlfriend had absconded.

"Invested in a big infrastructure gamble at ADDATA for a client, then the client didn't pay as promised. I could see the writing on the wall when paychecks started bouncing and half the researchers got laid off."

"Why not go after the client in court?" I asked as we stopped at a photo of a shirtless guitar player on stage at a small club. The guy looked remarkably like Mickey, who suddenly seemed anxious to move on to the next image. Shelley trailed behind us, not speaking, but not obviously eavesdropping either.

Mickey shrugged as we stopped in front of a nude woman sitting at a dressing table putting on make-up. She had a beautifully proportioned shoulder-to-hips ratio that made her back look rather like a cello.

"Denise thinks the client is just a front for Karpov and that he has something on Quimby. She thinks Karpov keeps files on everyone, which is how he gets away with so much."

I knew Shane would be extracting this information from Denise first hand, so I didn't bother pursuing it with Mickey.

"Did you ever meet Karpov when you worked at ADDATA?"

Mickey sneered. "The guy's a real cheese-bucket poser. Always wore deck shoes and tucked-in collared shirts like he just stepped off a sailboat or something. He's ... oily; that's the only way to describe him. Makes Quimby look like a nice guy, if you know what I mean."

Mickey looked like he was itching for a cigarette. His fingers rubbed against each other as if he was holding one, and his eyes started getting twitchy. I figured I probably only had his attention for another few minutes.

"So, who's the bad guy in all this?"

"Karpov is for sure. And Quimby, for getting into bed with him. Not that I'm surprised. The guy gets into bed with anything with a pulse. Denise realized it was all going away when the repo notices started coming in. That's why she left."

I glanced at him from the corner of my eye so he didn't catch the pity in my look. Denise left because the money was gone. But then why run away with Mickey, who had creditors calling so often he got rid of his cell phone?

"So, what are your plans?" I asked him as we arrived in front of the photograph of the woman buckling her shoe. I now understood Shane's reaction, and the appeal of the photograph had diminished for me. We moved on to the boxer.

"Denise wants to go to Canada, and I have citizenship through my mom, so maybe we'll head up to Montreal. I heard the music scene is good up there."

Ah, now I understood what attracted Denise to the bad-boy musician – his passport. I pulled out a business card. "Let me know where you land. If there's anything left of Quimby's money when the dust clears, I'll see to it Denise knows where to look for it."

He pocketed the card. "Thanks, man. I appreciate it."

Mickey dropped his voice, as though his aunt wouldn't hear him.

"Hey, is she really your partner?" he asked, with a nod toward the room where Shane still sat with Denise.

"She is," I said simply.

"I'd be tapping that if I were you," he smirked.

I didn't punch him, because as misguided as he was, I knew that Mickey thought he was complimenting Shane, and perhaps me, with his comment. I caught a glimpse of the set of Shelley's mouth and knew she had overheard him.

Shelley reminded me of my own mother, with some of my sister and grandmother thrown in. Women who had taught me to value women. The time I'd spent with the Peacekeepers had shredded my faith in men, and I realized that was what I'd been rebuilding in myself since I returned from Africa.

I gave the boxer a last, lingering look. He held his head in his hands and was so tired I could almost feel it in my bones. But he wasn't beaten, and the proud strength of his shoulders spoke of resilience and determination. He'd fight again, just as soon as he decided he was ready. It was a powerful image of a powerful man, undaunted by momentary weakness.

I directed my comment to Shelley. "If it's for sale, I'd like to give the boxer a home."

[35]
SHANE

"Instinct is the equivalent of a Morse code message from our ancestors about how to survive." – Kendra Eze

---

When I got back to the cottage after the long interview with Denise, Gabriel was already asleep on the twin bed with a quilt pulled carelessly over him as he lay on his stomach, one arm hanging off the side. He was too big for a twin, and the view of his shoulders was far too distracting for the work I still had to do. I briefly considered waking him up to move him to the bigger bed, but that would have opened the door to the conversation we weren't having about the trajectory of our relationship.

And I was nothing if not an avoider of such conversations.

I considered this as I changed into a big, soft t-shirt and wrapped a throw from the chair around my shoulders. I believed people should trust their feelings, and I told that to my clients all the time. "If you believe he's cheating, he probably is" was my simple statement that almost always turned out to be true. But by definition, the inverse must be true too – if you believe you can trust him, you can. That simple statement was going to require some deeper probing than I had the inclination for though, so I let Gabriel continue to sleep in the tiny bed, and I sat in the bigger bed making notes on my computer and deliberately avoiding the view of the sleeping man.

I finally closed the lid of my laptop an hour later. Gabriel had turned over and tugged the quilt up to cover his shoulders, but that left his feet bare. The cottage had gotten colder, and even under the big duvet, the only warm spot was exactly where my legs were. No matter how twisty my brain was about Gabriel, he was also my friend. My conscience was not going to rest while my friend slept on a too-small bed under a too-small quilt in a too-cold room.

So I got up. If I whispered his name and he didn't wake up, I would cover his feet and go back to bed. If he did, well …

"Gabriel." My voice was barely audible to my own ears, but I stood close enough to him that I could see the pulse beat in his throat. His eyes snapped open so fast that I jumped back.

"Oh!" I gasped. "You scared me." I took a step back and retreated even as I spoke. "If you're cold, you can sleep in the big bed under the duvet with me."

I didn't wait to see what effect my invitation had, or even if he was awake enough to register my words. In my own ears, my heartbeat sounded like a basketball being dribbled down the court in an empty gym, and I was humiliatingly certain he could hear the echo. I got back into the queen-sized bed and almost knocked over the bedside lamp in my hurry to turn it off.

The room was dark, and I dove down under the covers, deliberately closing my eyes like a kid playing *if I can't see him, he can't see me* hide-and-seek. Gradually, my heartbeat slowed to something less turbulent, and I was able to convince myself he hadn't really been awake enough to hear my invitation and therefore it would be cruel to try to wake him up properly.

And then I heard him move, maybe sit up, maybe stand. Then the definite sound of bare feet on cold floorboards was followed by an unmistakable dip in the mattress next to me.

I was curled up on my side facing the nightstand with my back to the side of the bed that was about to be filled by a very large, shirtless and sockless and who knew what else-less man. Cold air followed him under the covers, and I shivered without thinking that it would give away the fact that I was only pretending to be asleep.

Either he didn't notice, which I thought was unlikely, or he was going to let me keep pretending, because he didn't speak and didn't try to get my attention. He just curled his body up against my back and legs, wrapped his arm around my waist, and exhaled quietly into my hair. I didn't move, he didn't move; my heart was back to slamming, and so was his.

I didn't hold my breath, because that would have been too obvious, and gradually I became aware of more than just … him. He was shirtless, which I already knew, but he wore some kind of soft flannel pajama pants, so between my t-shirt and his PJs, there was fabric covering every inch of where our bodies touched. I was aware of how warm he was, like he was fueled by a radioactive core, and the clothes we slept in were all that stood between me and a third-degree burn. Okay, not really, but that's what I was distracting my brain with so I didn't feel the hard length of him pressed against my backside. It was unmistakable evidence of his attraction to me – as if the flying kisses, and the lingering looks, and the hand at my back, and holding me steady in the shower so I could wash my hair weren't evidence enough.

The shower. Without a doubt the most intimate experience I'd had in years.

I hadn't even looked down to realize he was still dressed. My eyes had been locked to his until I closed them to wash my hair, and then all I could feel were his hands at my waist, keeping me upright.

I felt small in those hands – delicate, but not fragile. He supported me on my foot as though I weighed nothing and wasn't nearly as tall as he was. Delicate was not a word or a feeling I'd ever associated with myself, and it made me feel more feminine than I'd felt since I'd grown taller than the tallest boy in my third grade class.

I didn't think about what he saw at the bottom of my leg, or what he thought about my wide swimmer's shoulders, or my wide woman's hips, or my barely palm-sized breasts. I concentrated on the width of his hands spanning my ribs and the gentle strength in them as they held me.

Because if I had let myself think, I would have wondered why he didn't kiss me. Why his mouth hadn't trailed down my skin like the water running off my nipples and down between my legs. I would have thought he couldn't possibly be attracted to me if he had me naked in the shower and did *nothing*, because it was so easy to believe there was something wrong with me. It was so simple to look at the stump of my leg and believe the disgust on someone's face when he tells you you're crazy to think anyone would ever want to fuck you with *that* visible – when he says it's not cheating if he actually wants to be with her and only stayed with you out of pity.

I screwed my eyes shut and swallowed a sob against the memories of my ex-fiancé, Mitch. But then Gabriel's arm tightened around my waist, and I let myself relax into his hold until the pain of my thoughts receded.

His breath deepened and slowed, and when I finally fell asleep, it was long after the ache had dimmed and the cold had been banished by the heat of him around me like an electric blanket.

[36]

SHANE

"Sometimes the loudest things in the room are the words we don't say." – Gabriel Eze

---

Because I was a giant chicken, I ninja'd out of the room and went for coffee before Gabriel woke up. He was already dressed when I got back, and he sighed when I handed him his cup.

"A woman who understands," he said with a smile as he took a sip.

"You keep me so well-supplied with good coffee at the office, it would be hard not to," I said, trying not to notice how well he fit the dark gray denim shirt he wore, and quelling the irrational disappointment that he wore anything at all.

"Do you mind if we get on the road?" I asked. "I can run down everything Denise told me while we drive. The internet here isn't strong enough for me to do the searches I need to do."

If he was disappointed I didn't want to stay longer, he didn't show it, just like I didn't let him see that I was sorry he was dressed. "Sure.

I'll drive and you can talk." He grabbed both our bags and slung them over one shoulder to load into the car. We left the cottage key under the mat as we'd been instructed to and were soon back on the highway headed south, talking about safe work topics as our coffees cooled.

Denise had told me that Quimby's big client had hired ADDATA for contracts worth tens of millions of dollars. The client had only put down ten percent though, which wasn't enough to build up the ADDATA infrastructure to handle the workload. Quimby had put up their own personal assets and mortgaged them to the hilt in order to float the bills until the client paid.

All of that we knew, or had guessed. The part that Mickey had hinted at to Gabriel, and that Denise had confirmed outright, was that in order to grant ADDATA the contract, the political action firm had required background security checks on Quimby.

I'd been a P.I. far too long to ever trust someone else with the kind of information a person needs to pass a security check. I didn't even like answering census questions because it was just too much informa-tion to put out in the universe.

"So Karpov had enough information to get dirt on Quimby," Gabriel said, with a snort of something that sounded like disgust.

"And when Quimby made noise about getting paid for the work they'd already done, Karpov threatened to reveal whatever he had. According to Denise, Karpov has something big on her husband, but she doesn't know what."

Gabriel exhaled. "We could use that to get him to back off of you. Whatever Karpov has on Quimby was enough to inspire him to get a gun license." He let that delightful thought hang in the air for a long minute, then shot me a quick glance. "By the way, did you sort out your fee with Denise?"

"Yeah. She gave me cash."

His eyebrows rose. "She gave you cash?"

I smirked at him. "She said she doesn't trust banks."

"So where should we go?" he asked. "New York? San Francisco? Mexico? How do we spend your newfound wealth?" He had an infectious grin, and I let myself wish, for just a moment, that it could ever be that easy.

"Well, *this* part of *we* is going to pay my prosthetist for some of the legs he's designed for me on credit."

That statement sparked a whole conversation about the various MacGyver legs Sparky had successfully created, and some of his more spectacular failures, with me as his crash test dummy. Gabriel asked very technical questions about leg construction, from the first leg I ever wore, to the innovations Sparky brought to the devices.

"One of the guys in my unit in Ethiopia had his leg shattered in a fall, but he caught dengue fever while he was in the hospital, and it was three months before he could even sit up after the leg was amputated. By the time he was well enough to walk and try a prosthetic, his muscles had atrophied too much. He was never able to walk properly. Last I heard, he'd given up completely," Gabriel said. "Can something be designed to help him walk now?"

"Anything is possible, but it's so much harder the longer you wait. I'm sorry for your friend." I sat in silence for a long moment gathering my thoughts, or maybe my courage. It had been so long since I'd had a conversation like this – not even Sparky knew more than the basics. Gabriel left me to my silence, which is probably why I took a deep breath and broke it.

"There was a doctor doing a special series on amputations at the UC Davis Medical School who happened to be working with a group of students the night they brought me into the ER. He had just come back from Cambodia where he'd worked with landmine victims. He took one look at my leg and said 'cut it off.' He told me later that he probably could have saved the leg and the other ER doc had argued for keeping it. But, he said, it would never have been strong or pain-free, and would probably have needed five or six surgeries to repair to the point of usefulness. Better to get me up doing PT as soon as possible so I could use existing muscle tone to relearn how to walk with a prosthetic."

The words were so simple, and yet they weighed a thousand pounds, and I felt myself on the verge of gasping with the effort of them. But then Gabriel spoke, and the constriction in my chest loosened at the sound of his voice, as if the strings on a too-tight corset had just been cut.

"I was a fit, twenty-six-year-old RMP when I was shot," he said, and I whipped my head around to stare at him as he continued. "The bullet went in under my arm and punctured a lung. It was a fairly simple surgery, they said – out with the bullet, in with the chest tube – but it was two months before I was up and moving around again properly, and I've never felt so weak as I did then."

"Who shot you?" I asked before I could censor myself.

Gabriel hesitated only a fraction of a second, and to my ears it was as though he cracked open his chest and showed me his heart. "My best friend, Jackson. He shot me, right before he killed himself."

[37]

GABRIEL

"Feeling empty just means you're ready for filling." – Miri Eze

---

My chest hurt with phantom pain, but the memory of the physical wound from that day was the merest twinge in comparison to the empty hole Jackson's death had left in my life – in all our lives. It was an emptiness I'd run from as soon as I was strong enough, but nothing had ever filled it – not work with the Peacekeepers, not the Nigerian girls I'd been able to save, not even Mika, the little boy Jackson had left behind who filled my heart with such joy.

And yet this woman who sat beside me, who had so many twists and turns and hidden places of her own, somehow she'd crawled inside me and taken up residence in a corner of the cavern Jackson had left behind.

I could feel her eyes on my face, and although she didn't touch me, her warmth reached across the space between us. It took more effort than it should have to inhale the breath with which to speak, but I forced myself to say the words.

"I know he didn't mean to shoot me, and I'm not sure he really meant to shoot himself, but the gun was in his hand while he thought about it, and I made the mistake of trying to wrestle it from him." I took another ragged breath and shaped the memory into words. "If I had just talked to him instead, he might have put the gun down. But when I rushed him, he reacted in self-defense, and I got a bullet for my trouble."

I wiped my eye with the heel of my hand. "I'm fairly sure he thought he killed me, and it was too much responsibility to add to whatever it was that put the gun in his hand in the first place." Something like laughter that sounded more like a sob tore from my chest. "He preferred to die rather than tell my sister he'd killed her twin. So instead, he left the job to me."

I focused on the sound of the road beneath the tires, the drone of the engine, and the noise the trucks made as we passed them – anything to erase the crack of the gunshots in my memory.

"Oh God, Gabriel. He was Kendra's Jackson? Mika's dad?" Shane's gasp was the air my own lungs needed, and I finally inhaled deeply, drawing strength from her presence.

"He'd loved her since we were kids, but she never gave him the time of day until Jackson and I came home on leave. They got married when she discovered she was pregnant, but I think he was terrified of the responsibilities of being a husband and father. I don't actually know all the reasons Jackson had for putting a gun to his temple that night …" I left the sentence unfinished, and Shane allowed the words to fade away.

The miles passed in silence, and the turbulence in me began to calm. Jackson had been my best friend, no matter how much I'd hated him afterwards.

"I'm not sure when I finally let go of the anger," I said, as though Shane had been privy to the conversation in my head. "After Nigeria, I suspect, when I'd thoroughly beaten myself up over my prodigious failures as a savior."

"I'm still angry," she said quietly.

I glanced at her quickly, but her eyes were trained out the window, staring at nothing in particular, possibly not even seeing the view in front of her. I'd learned not to prompt Shane. She would speak if she wanted to. But with those three words, the door closed on my own pain, and somewhere inside the cavern Jackson's death had left behind, Shane took up a little more space.

She inhaled deeply and let the words escape one by one. "My dad and my little brother were killed by a drunk driver when I was sixteen. They were heading up to the mountains to go backpacking. I didn't go with them because I had a date with Mitch." The hitch in her breath sounded like swallowed tears, but I didn't turn to see. I would feel her eyes on me if she needed me to look at her.

Another mile passed in silence. "I stayed out after my curfew that night because my dad was the enforcer and my mom always went to sleep early, so I was still up when the police came to the door."

I reached for her hand and held it gently. She let me keep it for a time while she spoke. "The minute they left for the mountains, I felt guilty. I should have gone with them instead of going on a stupid date. And then when I found out they were dead, I got so mad. How dare they leave me with guilt as the last thing I remember feeling about them?"

The landscape was becoming more urban, and the navigation on my phone suddenly chimed in with my next move.

Shane gave a shaky laugh and pulled her hand from mine to wipe her eyes. "Guilt is my least favorite emotion," she said, finally meeting my eyes again.

I knew she had hit her revelations quota, and I matched her wry smile. "There's no problem so awful that you can't add some guilt to it and make it even worse."

Her laughter was genuine this time. "You're quoting Calvin and Hobbes to me?"

I grinned. "The fact that you could identify the quote speaks volumes about your excellent taste in comics."

We spent the rest of the drive talking about things that didn't hurt, and when we arrived at our building, we were laughing.

Shane's laugh was gorgeous – throaty and full of golden whiskey. I parked the car, then took her hand again and brought her knuckles to my lips. "You're a beautiful woman, Shane, but when you laugh, you're glorious."

She looked at me a long moment as the laughter slowly faded from the air but didn't leave her eyes. "Thank you," she said quietly, and I knew it wasn't for the compliment that she thanked me.

"Let's table all further discussions until after dinner tonight, shall we? I think that great beast of yours has missed you and could use a little time," I said.

"Sounds like an excellent plan," she said, and when we grabbed our bags and went inside, she let me keep hold of her hand.

[38]

SHANE

"Well, that escalated quickly." – Shane, P.I.

The condo Gabriel's sister shared with her mother and son was near the University of Chicago in graduate student housing. It was a two-bedroom place with a surprising amount of charm given its relatively anonymous architecture.

Spicy scents greeted us when Gabriel ushered me in. A beautiful boy I assumed was Mika jumped up from the blocks he'd been stacking on the living room floor and shouted, "Big Man!"

Gabriel dropped to his knees and threw his arms open. "Small Man!"

Mika barreled into his uncle's arms, and Gabriel held him so close I wondered at his ability to breathe. But then Mika looked up at me and shouted, "Mama, Big Man's friend came too!"

Gabriel's twin laughed as she came in from the kitchen wiping her hands on a dish towel. "You made it!" she said. She kissed her brother on the cheek and then turned to me with a smile. "And you're my brother's partner. It's nice to meet you, Shane." She was a couple of inches shorter than me and had the easy grace of a woman comfortable with herself. Her skin tone, like Gabriel's, was quite dark, and her long hair was streaked with copper highlights.

"Thank you so much for inviting me," I said, surprised by her automatic warmth.

Kendra waved dismissively. "The rule in this house is you're only a guest the first time, and you get invited back if you help yourself."

I grinned and held out the bottles of wine I'd brought, one red and one white. "I like that rule. Which one should I open?"

This time I got an eye-roll to go with the wave. "Both, obviously. Mika will show you to the kitchen while I grill my brother on why you cancelled dinner last night."

I chuckled at Gabriel's look of dismay, and the little boy grabbed my hand and pulled. "Come Gran's been waiting to meet you she says you must be special if Big Man brought you to dinner are you special?" The entire phrase was said in one long, adorable little British-accented phrase, without breath or pause to punctuate, and only because my arm was full of wine bottles did I not drop to the floor and gather the little man in for a hug.

The kitchen was the source of the good smells, and a striking woman standing at the stove was at the heart of it. She wore flowy, wide-legged pants with a pretty white linen tunic top. Her long braids were tied up in a high ponytail, and there was no hint, in either her hair or her skin, that she was old enough to be Gabriel's and Kendra's mother.

"Gran! She's here and Big Man is talking to Mum can I please have a taste?" Mika's enthusiasm was utterly infectious. Gabriel's mother winked at me quickly before she dipped a spoon into the pot on the stove and knelt down to hold it out for Mika.

"Slowly, my love. You blow just enough to cool the food, but not so much you cover Gran with it," she said, holding her other hand out under the spoon. Mika practically quivered with the effort it took to hold still and blow gently, and he gave the task a hundred percent concentration. "Okay, now see how it smells, and then test it with your tongue. Is it cool enough?"

He took a big sniff and then a quick, darting taste. "Yes, Gran."

The pride in her smile as the spoon disappeared into his mouth was a thing of loveliness. "Mmm," Mika said reverently, "that's the best bite I ever tasted."

She leaned in and sniffed his cheek, then kissed it. "And you're the best thing I ever tasted."

Mika flung his arms around his gran for a quick, exuberant hug, then ran out of the room. Gabriel's mother stood gracefully, dropped the spoon into the sink, and held both her hands out to me in greeting.

"Welcome, Shane. I'm Miriam, but please call me Miri or Mum as my children do." I put the wine down and took her hands, and she held them as she looked at me. "You are strong, and Gabriel says you're smart. That's good."

I didn't know what to say to that, so I blurted the first thing that came to mind. "I can see where your kids got their looks. You're beautiful." I promptly turned pink and winced. "Sorry."

"Don't be sorry, I'm not. That was the nicest thing anyone but Mika's said to me all day. I'll take it."

She let me have my hands back and then directed me to the wine opener. "I'll also take white wine please, but pour mine in something sturdy without a stem. My grandson likes to climb into laps when he's done eating, and I'm fairly certain his spirit animal is an octopus."

Miri continued speaking as I cut the foil from both bottles. "I think you like my son. Is that true?"

If I'd been drinking, I would have done a spit-take, but I managed to pull the cork on the first bottle without fumbling it. I looked up to find Gabriel's mum studying me. My instinct was to prevaricate, and with anyone else, I would have ducked the question or pretended it hadn't been asked. But I found myself responding to Miri's forthrightness.

I inhaled for courage and then met her gaze. "I do." My mouth opened again, because I had much more to say on the topic, but I closed it like a snapping turtle when I realized I had absolutely no idea where to begin, especially when most of the things that came to mind were not at all appropriate to say about a man to his mother.

So instead I said something much, much worse. "He makes me remember who I used to be."

Miri didn't flinch in surprise at my words, nor did she kick me out of her kitchen for being a psycho. She just let her gaze rest on me a long moment before she said quietly. "Who were you?"

I let the words go on a breath, almost as if they wore wings. "Strong. Fearless. Indomitable," and then, after a pause, "Trusting."

"Who are you now?" she asked softly, her eyes never leaving mine.

My heartbeat felt loud in my ears. "Afraid to trust."

Miri held a hand out to me, and again, running on pure instinct, I took it. She pulled me to her and held me tightly. I surrendered to this mother's hug in a way I hadn't since before my dad and brother had died – since I was sixteen years old. A sob choked my throat and tears gathered behind my eyes, but I held them back by matching my breaths to hers. She held me for a few more moments, then spoke into my hair just before she let me go. "You can be afraid and still strong, still fearless and indomitable. You can be afraid, *and* you can trust, and then when you're ready, you can let go of the fear. Fear muffles you. Let it go, and then you can live out loud again like you're meant to."

Her words slipped into the quiet spaces in my brain and found homes there. "Thank you," I whispered.

"You can thank me with wine, poppet." She gave me an extra squeeze and then stepped back to the stove. "Kendra will have white too," she said as she turned off the burner and removed the stew pot from the heat.

"And I will have red, if you're pouring," Gabriel said as he walked into the kitchen, swept the stew pot from his mother's hands, and kissed her affectionately.

I turned back to the wine so I could compose my expression as I processed Miri's words and reordered my heart to include them. I was glad to see my hands were steady as I pulled the second cork and bypassed the wine glasses to pull down five superhero juice glasses. Miri's gentle squeeze as she reached past me for a ladle grounded me, as did Gabriel's casual hand at my back as I poured red wine into a Batman glass for him. I took Spiderman for myself, then poured white wine into the Wonder Woman and Superman glasses for Miri and Kendra, and by the time I'd added lemonade to a Robin glass for Mika, I remembered that this was what family felt like.

Gabriel raised his glass to me, then raised an eyebrow at Kendra, who had just entered the kitchen. "DC comics, Sister?"

She shrugged. "They had Wonder Woman. And until Marvel comes out with the Black Panther set, she wins."

I raised my glass to her in a toast. "She always does."

We spent an entertaining few minutes on the topic of Wonder Woman versus any of the other DC or Marvel comic heroes, and I was very glad to have been properly educated by Sparky on their strengths and weaknesses.

Then Kendra and her brother launched into a discussion about the Black Panther comics, and Miri caught my eye. "They'll be at this for hours unless we change the subject," she said in a low tone.

"I kind of love it," I admitted with a grin.

She returned the smile and handed me a covered pot of rice. "Me too. Let's move them to the table, then, and continue it there."

Dinner was an easy affair, with reaches across the table, second helpings of the rice, stew, and roasted vegetables for everyone, and liberal splashes of laughter punctuating the non-stop conversation.

Mika made his way from lap to lap, sampling his uncle's stew, his mother's vegetables, and Miri's rice, before he climbed into my lap and wriggled into position. He finally found the right spot when I moved an arm to support him, and his head leaned back against me as he idly played with the leather wrap bracelet I wore on my wrist. The love in Miri's eyes as she watched her grandson fall asleep was breathtaking, and I wasn't even aware that I'd gone quiet until Gabriel looked over.

"Small Man's out cold," he whispered.

I nodded and realized I'd stopped talking when I felt him settle in, so that the rumble of my voice didn't wake him.

Gabriel started to get up to take him from me, but I shook my head. "Let him sleep." Mika twitched in a dream, and I was transported back to my own childhood. I was six when my brother Kieran was born, and ten when he was Mika's size. I remembered sitting around the firepit at my parents' parties when Kieran would find me on a lounge chair, curl up in my lap, and fall asleep to the sounds of our parents' voices.

I looked down at the top of Mika's curly head to hide the tears that filled my eyes, and a wave of hope for this little boy's life filled me. I wanted him to see his eleventh birthday, and then his twenty-first. I wanted him to have the chance to fall in love, and to hold his own child in his lap. After the night of the accident, I never let my mother see me cry for Kieran and my dad again, but every year on Kieran's birthday, I blew out a candle and sent a wish out to the universe for him.

I wiped the tears away and looked up to find that conversation around me had stopped. Kendra had a look of concern on her face, and Miri cleared her throat and stood to gather dishes. "Kendra, come help me clear the table."

She hesitated a moment, then filled her hands with plates to join her mother. Gabriel reached out to wipe an errant tear from my cheek.

"You okay?" he asked quietly.

I nodded. "Just remembering when my brother was this small."

"Do you want your own kids someday?" His voice seemed too blasé for the careful way he watched me, but I was tired of second-guessing everything I said around this man.

"Yeah, I do. I don't really have a plan for how or when, but I've always just kind of assumed it'll happen."

He exhaled so slightly I might have missed it if I hadn't seen his jaw unclench, and I wondered why that question had mattered to him so much.

Kendra came back into the room and over to where I sat. "Thank you for letting him sleep on you, Shane. I'll take him to bed now."

My lap felt cold and empty when she lifted her son off me, but I got to see his face before she carried him away, and the sight of long eyelashes against his skin reminded me forcibly of his uncle, who still watched me intently.

I turned to Gabriel. "You have a wonderful family."

His chair was next to mine, and he reached out for my hand, then brought it to his lips. "Thank you for being here with me. I feel like I got to show off all the special people in my life," he murmured against my knuckles as he held my gaze.

My heart lurched a little at the thought that I could be one of those special people, but I didn't have the courage to ask him. His lips glided over the backs of my fingers as he watched me, and my eyes flicked between his gaze, which burned my skin, and his mouth, that I suddenly needed very badly to kiss.

"I think," I said in a voice that surprised me with its huskiness, "that we should go."

The low tones of his murmur against my knuckles made my heart hammer. "It's time."

My breath left me in a whoosh. It was definitely time.

I hugged Miri and Kendra and vaguely remembered making promises to see them again soon. Gabriel kept my hand in his as we said goodbye, and I was so focused on the heat of his skin that I was barely aware of anything else around me.

He let go of my hand only to help me into the passenger seat of his car and then took it again as he drove. His eyes were locked on the road when he spoke. "You have fascinated me since I first laid eyes on you," he said quietly. "It's like I see you in infrared – your head and your heart burn bright white, and your whole heat signature draws me like a moth to a flame."

"Is that a good thing?" I whispered.

He smiled and pulled my palm up to his mouth to kiss it. "It's good, but it's not comfortable. I go to bed craving your heat, and I wake up wanting you next to me so badly my day feels empty until I see you again."

My skin felt flush, and the fire he described was real as it rushed through my body. We were stopped at the intersection just before our building, and my heart was already pounding in anticipation of what was about to happen between us.

I reached for the door and opened it. Gabriel looked over in surprise, and I met his gaze so he could see my words as well as hear them.

"Give me ten minutes before you come to my place." And then I bolted from his car and ran to the front door of our building. He didn't turn down the street toward the parking garage until I was safely inside the lobby, and I took the stairs two at a time up to my place.

Oscar greeted me in typical bouncy-ball fashion, but I didn't even give him a proper rub before I had his leash on him and was back out the door.

The titanium leg I'd worn to dinner was not so useful for running, but I was fast enough to get us to the park in record time. I wondered if I'd left clothes all over my bed in my what-to-wear-to-dinner wardrobe freak-out and whether I'd have time for a quick shower before Gabriel got there, when Oscar suddenly tensed and let out a low growl.

I spun around just as Dane Quimby stepped out of the trees. He held a gun in one hand, and its aim shifted between my dog and me.

Oscar must have sensed my fear, because at Quimby's next step, he started barking.

"Shut the dog up," Quimby snarled.

"Stop walking and he'll shut up," I said in a remarkably calm voice, considering the quaking of my guts.

He froze, but Oscar knew he was a threat and kept barking. "Where's my money?" Quimby sounded a little unhinged, and I wasn't quite sure how to play it – calm and "your wife has it," or nervous and "I don't know what you mean."

I studied his posture for clues to his mental balance. He was tense, and Oscar's barking was making it worse. The hand holding the gun could have been shaking, but he kept shifting his aim up and down, between my dog's head and my own, so I wasn't sure.

He was a small man who'd gambled big against someone much smarter than him, and he'd lost. His money was gone, his wife was gone, and his company would be gone soon too. Karpov had something on him, so the only revenge he could possibly get would be against me.

I realized I might not survive this night, and that thought made me mad.

"Shut that dog up!" Quimby yelled.

I jerked hard on Oscar's leash and made a *chhhtt* sound to quiet him. If Quimby shot my dog to stop the barking, the gunfire would draw immediate attention, but I didn't trust him to be sane enough to realize that at the moment.

"She doesn't have the money, Quimby, your wife does. Drop the gun."

[39]
GABRIEL

"As a black man, I hope one day I have as many rights as a gun." – Gabriel Eze

---

Quimby swung around, gun arm first, to find me in the dark. I was deep in the shadows, grateful I'd worn a black sweater to dinner, and terrified he'd turn back to Shane before she could run.

But she didn't run. She dropped Oscar's leash and launched herself forward – at the madman with the gun.

"Shane – no!" I yelled.

Quimby swung back around and fired wildly. I leapt forward to try to take him down before he could shoot again, but I'd hung too far back and I couldn't reach him in time.

Shane had dived out of the way of his first shot, but she got up and tried to tackle Quimby again. She missed, but Oscar didn't, and he took Quimby down. The handgun fired again, harmlessly, and by then I'd made it to them and punched Quimby in the jaw before kicking the gun out of his hand.

I dropped a knee on Quimby's chest and grappled with his flailing arms. Oscar was barking furiously as Quimby tried to buck me off of him. I was bigger and stronger, but he seemed to have the strength of a madman.

"Call the police!" I shouted at Shane, who I assumed was somewhere behind me still on the ground. But then she stepped past my shoulder and into my line of sight. She stood directly over Quimby's head and pointed his gun at his face.

"You were going to shoot my dog," she said in a voice so calm it sounded laced with ice.

"Where's my money, bitch!" Quimby spat at her, hatred shooting from his eyes like laser beams. I'd gotten one of his arms under control and was still wrestling with the other one.

Shane leaned down and pressed the barrel of the gun directly against Quimby's forehead. That got his attention, and he stilled.

"You cheated. You got caught. You forfeit half. That's the deal." Her voice was filled with loathing, and the look in his eyes was murderous.

Oscar stood over Quimby and snarled so menacingly I was worried he would attack.

"Give me the gun and get Oscar under control." I spoke quietly to Shane, and my voice seemed to cut through the haze of rage that shone in her eyes. She glanced at Oscar's rigid form, then handed me the gun so she could pick up his leash. She tugged him backward, but his growls were relentless. I stood up slowly, but my aim never wavered from Quimby's face.

And then we were surrounded.

"Police! Drop your weapon! NOW!"

It wasn't until we'd been put into individual interview rooms at the station that the adrenaline finally began to wear off. I sat alone at a table and wished Shane were next to me. I needed to see her, to know that she was alright. I took a deep breath and willed my hands to stop trembling.

The door opened and a uniformed officer entered the room. "Gabriel Eze," he said, pronouncing my name correctly. I nodded. "You may want to call a lawyer," he continued.

My eyebrows arched up. "Because Dane Quimby attempted to kill my partner?"

"Mr. Quimby says you and your girlfriend robbed him of five hundred grand."

I reached into the inside pocket of my coat and the officer's hand went to his gun. I looked coldly at him. "I was searched before I was left alone in this room, Officer." I pulled out my business card and slid it across the table to him.

"I am a security officer at Cipher Security. Please feel free to call Quinn Sullivan to confirm."

The police officer sighed and rubbed the back of his neck uncomfortably. "That's what your girlfriend said too."

"She's my partner. You should believe her." I used my poshest accent, and even I could admit it sounded intimidating.

"Quimby says you jumped him in the park and rolled him for more money than the five hundred k you already stole."

"*I* jumped Quimby with his own gun?"

"Officers on the scene said you were standing over him with the gun."

"I'd just disarmed him." It wasn't the first time I'd said those words and likely wouldn't be the last.

"He said he started carrying it after you stole his money."

"Where is Quimby now?" I asked calmly.

"Interview room, just like this one." The cop had remained standing, but when I leaned forward, he took a step back.

"Keep him away from Ms. Hane. He went to that park to kill her, as the two shots he fired at her can attest."

"Ballistics has the gun now," the officer grumbled.

"Call Mr. Sullivan, please." I struggled to maintain a polite tone.

He bent to retrieve the business card from the table and then backed toward the door. "Far as I can see, the only reason a little guy like that would go after a big guy like you is if you did something to deserve it."

I wanted to roar with frustration, but I kept my voice calm. "He didn't go after me. He went after Ms. Hane. I followed the sound of her barking dog and found him holding the gun on her." I was nearly quivering with tension at my need to see Shane and the effort it cost me to keep it invisible to Officer Just-doing-his-job.

"Yeah, well, it's his word against yours," the officer said smugly, "and I'm guessing he's got right on his side."

Right, or white? I didn't say it because I didn't have to. So instead, I did what I'd learned to do when fists and education and power didn't work – I smiled. I'd been told that my smile could be quite disconcerting. Apparently it was cold and flinty and fueled all manner of fears, and the officer was gone before the door had finished closing behind him.

Which meant I was out of my seat and across the room in time to catch it with my foot. I needed to find Shane. We'd gone to the station separately because an officer had stayed with her as she took Oscar back to her apartment, and the police had said they needed to interview me. I hadn't even thought to text O'Malley before they took my phone and put me in a room, and my only excuse for such thoughtlessness was pure adrenaline.

When Shane had rushed Quimby in the park, I'd gone right back to the moment I'd tried to take Jackson down instead of trying to talk him down. I'd been so certain Quimby's bullet had hit Shane like Jackson's shot hit me that I'd half-expected Quimby to turn the gun on himself next.

I opened the door to the interview room next to the one in which I'd been placed. It was empty, but I had the vague sense that I could smell the vanilla and amber scent Shane wore. Hopefully she was no longer being questioned.

I found Quimby sitting alone in the next room with a cup of coffee on the table in front of him. He stood up quickly when I opened the door, and we faced each other across the room. "Stay away from me," he said.

"Your wife has your money. Leave the P.I. out of it." I glared at him, and he took a step back.

"I heard you call her Shane, and I know where she walks her damn dog. How long do you think I'll actually be here, and how fast do you think she can run?"

I knew exactly how fast Shane could run, but she couldn't outrun a bullet, and I wasn't quite willing to trust Shane's life to the American legal system when any idiot could get a gun permit in this country, and the one in front of me already had one.

"What does Karpov have on you?" I asked him quietly.

Quimby blanched. "I don't know what you're talking about," he said sharply. But he wasn't nearly the actor he thought he was, and his fear stank of sweat and desperation.

"Go after Shane, and we go after Karpov," I said as I stepped out of the room and closed the door behind me with an audible snap.

Sullivan was just coming down the hall with the officer next to him. The cop's eyes went wide when he realized that I had just come from Quimby's room.

"Hello, Gabriel," Sullivan said darkly.

I nodded at him. "Thanks for coming."

"My wife sends her greetings," he said, with a glance at the wall clock. It was after three in the morning, and I suddenly remembered that the Sullivans had a young baby.

"Why are you out of your room?" the officer asked.

I ignored him. "Where's Shane?" I asked Sullivan.

"Van took her home. He'll stay outside until you get there, or I can leave him on until morning if you think you'll need it."

I didn't like anyone else but me protecting Shane, but I appreciated the security for her. "I'll take care of it," I said.

He turned and we headed down the hallway. "Get your phone and I'll see you outside," he said before he walked out of the station. He hadn't spared the officer another glance, and the guy scowled.

"You didn't say you worked for Quinn Fucking Sullivan," he said in disgust.

"You're right, I didn't use the expletive. And that's the only thing you've been right about so far tonight." I retrieved my phone from the duty cop and then turned to face the angry officer. I felt my composure finally slip. "I'm sure Mr. Sullivan mentioned his desire to see Dane Quimby arrested for attempted murder, but just in case he didn't, this is your gentle reminder to Do. Your. Fucking. Job." I punctuated my words with another smile, then pocketed my phone and left the station.

Sullivan waited for me in a black SUV, and I climbed into the passenger seat.

"Quimby is terrified, and it's not just the money. We need to find out what Karpov has on him," I said without preamble.

"Alex says whatever Karpov's got isn't online, which means there's a hard copy or a drive in a safe somewhere. He and Shane are working remotely tonight to find out everything they can about the man." Sullivan's cultured voice delivered information in a near-monotone. I found it almost soothing because it required no second-guessing.

"What happened to the tracker we planted on Quimby's car?" I asked.

"We don't know. Something in the Tesla's autopilot system may be interfering with the signal. Greene's working on that too."

A taxi drove past, and I watched the headlights paint shadows on the pavement. Sullivan broke the silence after a few blocks. "I understand you moved into the building where she lives."

"I did." I refused to get defensive.

"I'd like to set up a secure server in your place for remote work. I have it in my building of course, but as long as Quimby stays in custody, I don't feel Ms. Hane needs or would appreciate the security that comes with an apartment there. Obviously, keeping Quimby in custody is the priority." He drove in silence as I processed his words.

Give Shane a secure network from which to do her work, put it in my apartment, and guess where she spends her time?

"I'd appreciate it," I said sincerely.

"I'll send someone over tomorrow." Sullivan pulled up outside our building and turned to me. "Cipher takes care of its own, Gabriel. Ms. Hane is proving herself to be one of us – you don't need to do this alone."

I met his eyes with a nod and reached for the door handle. "Please apologize to Mrs. Sullivan for me."

Sullivan snorted in what I could only assume was his approximation of laughter. "She heard about the lemon drops night Sandra and Kat had with Shane. She told me to invite you both to dinner when you've decided you're willing to be seen together in public."

I stared at him. "I suddenly find myself terrified to meet your wife."

He glared at me. "You should be." Only the smallest hint of a smirk at the corner of his mouth softened the scowl in his words, and I thought Mrs. Sullivan must be a remarkable woman indeed.

Sullivan drove away as I entered the lobby of our building. Van Hayden stepped forward into the light from the shadows of the stairwell.

"Thank you. I'll take it from here." I knew my voice was frosty, but my ability to care had diminished with every hour I'd spent apart from Shane.

"Yeah? How'd he get the drop on her then?" Hayden crossed his arms and glared at me. He had about two inches and twenty pounds of muscle on me and was used to being the biggest man in the room, while I'd spent my life *not* fighting with men like him.

I took a step forward, deliberately within his reach. "I won't be questioned by you, nor will I accept your judgment. It seems I don't fit your idea of who I should be, but I find I don't particularly care." I took another step forward, now too close. "So thank you for being here when I couldn't, but I'm here now, and I've got this."

His eyes narrowed and his jaw clenched, and I was close enough for those signs of anger to matter, but I had my own frustrations to deal with, and I didn't give a rat's ass if he chose to swing. After a moment that stretched into two blinks, and then five, he finally took one step back. It was enough, and I went up the stairs without a backward glance.

[40]

SHANE

"What's the worst that can happen?" – Dan O'Malley

I'd called Jorge to stay with Oscar while I was at the police station, and he'd been curled up with the furry beast on my couch when I got back. I tried to make him go home, but he just went and got his laptop and joined me at the dining table.

I made Skype introductions between Jorge and the Hacker, and we both heard the keyboard clacking as soon as Alex had Jorge's full name. The kid impressed Alex by giving him a couple of dark web sites to search for Jorge's signature, just so he didn't waste time going down all the mole holes by which my friend traveled through the internet.

Of the three of us, I was the least adept at the dark web, but they both seemed to appreciate my instincts about both Quimby and Karpov.

From my internet research, I knew Karpov was in his thirties and tended to dress like a country club golfer in khakis, topsider shoes, and colorful name-brand shirts. His parents were Russian immigrants, he was an only child, and he'd gone to private school before ultimately graduating from Harvard. He'd served in the military and then used family money to partner in a video gaming company – strange career divergences in an otherwise unremarkably privileged upbringing. His most recent position was on the board of directors of a far right political "news" organization, which seemed to land him in the photo ops sections at swanky conservative fundraisers. From everything I could find about his current politics, Karpov stood firmly in the populist camp touting ideas of nationalism that were fueled by fear and distrust.

Video game development had seemed an odd choice for a nationalist, until I started poking around Reddit and 4Chan.

"Gross," I said as I stared at the four-year-old threads.

"What?" Jorge looked over at my screen. He made a face. "Careful, I've heard the viruses are catching down there."

"What did you find?" The Hacker's disembodied voice reminded me that I was sitting with some significant brain power, and testing my ideas out loud had merit.

There was a quiet tap on my door, and Gabriel opened it to step inside. I was unbelievably relieved to see him, as the unicorns and rainbows in my smile probably indicated, but I managed to keep talking like a rational person as I waved him in.

"You know that gaming company Karpov was a shareholder in a few years ago?" I said to the Hacker's image on my computer screen. I could see the big Stormtrooper Sugar Skull print in the shadows behind him.

"Yeah," he said without looking at me. "He sold his shares four years ago when he partnered with Quimby."

"The gaming company didn't make sense with the rest of the stuff we know about him," I said, including Gabriel in my gaze, "until you look at the message boards." Gabriel had gotten a bottle of sparkling water from the kitchen and refilled my glass before filling his own.

The clacking of keyboards told me the other two weren't just going to take my word for it, so I took a sip of my water and mouthed "thank you" to Gabriel while they caught up.

"Oh, right," said the Hacker.

Jorge's voice held just a touch of excitement. "He used the gaming company to reach all the white nationalist bottom-feeders in their basements. Damn! The guy's been playing a freaking long game."

"Stir up the basement-dwellers, then use the fear-mongers on the right to double down on the message through the news outlets, and suddenly Karpov's controlling a whole lot of information flow," I said in awed disgust.

"Well, this is interesting." The Hacker's voice had no inflection, but the pause in his typing was approximately as loud as a shout from the rooftops.

Gabriel moved into sight of my screen, and his motion must have caught the Hacker's eye because he glanced up. "Good, you're there."

Gabriel sat in the chair next to mine. "What did you find?" he asked.

"Karpov seems to have set up at least a dozen other 4Chan accounts under different names that he used to contribute to the conversations he, himself, stirred up. A couple of those troll accounts were eventually made moderators, so in effect, he was the controlling voice." The Hacker's attention had gone back to his computer screen, and I had the sense that video Skype was not his favorite. I left him on camera out of spite.

Then Jorge piped up from his seat on the couch. "Those moderator accounts were more than just information. Karpov was using them to direct black ops on major media outlets, Anonymous-style."

"What do you mean, Anonymous-style?" I asked.

"Anonymous is a decentralized international hacktivist group that's been operating since maybe about 2006?" He glanced up to my screen where the Hacker gave a curt nod. "Anyway, Anonymous puts out the call to run ops on international targets like ISIS in Operation Charlie Hebdo, or pedophile rings in Operation Deatheaters, and any hackers who want to participate can join in."

"It's far less organized than that, but much more insidious as there's no centralized head of operations," the Hacker added.

"Have you done ops for Anonymous?" I asked him.

He made eye contact with me through the camera on his

computer for exactly one second before he turned back to his computer screen. "I've found two ops – not associated with Anonymous – that Karpov seems to have directed – one against Al Jazeera, and one against AP."

"They also tried one against the DOJ, but they couldn't get in," Jorge added.

"What does any of this have to do with what Karpov might have on Quimby?" Gabriel growled.

"We've been all over Karpov's known storage sites, and have found nothing," Alex explained to Gabriel.

"So we go to his house and office and search there," Gabriel shrugged.

"Already did," Alex answered.

That surprised us both, so Alex continued. "While you were up north, we sent a team into ADDATA and Karpov's apartment. We found three safes and a safety deposit box, but the only thing of note was the amount of cash Karpov keeps on hand. No hard drives, thumb drives, physical servers, or paper files of any kind."

Something didn't sound right. "Karpov lives in an apartment?" I asked.

Alex grimaced. "Barely furnished even if it is prime real estate."

That didn't fit with the country club, photo op lifestyle he'd cultivated. "Have we done a property check on him in any other state?"

"Karpov's father was a Russian national," said Jorge as his fingers flew over the keyboard, "so … State Department?" I glanced at Alex, who had gone silent except for clacking keys. The State Department was a much bigger nut than I could ever hope to crack and therefore not my problem, so I turned to Gabriel and held out a hand. He took it in both of his big, calloused palms.

"Are you okay?" I murmured.

Something unreadable flitted across his face before he nodded at the computer screen where Alex's fingers on his keyboard had gone silent again. I returned my attention to my screen, and Gabriel kissed my knuckles and let go.

"Karpov owns a luxury yacht," Alex said quietly.

"What? Why?" I asked, before I could think about the inanity of the question.

"Registered in Canada without an easy trace to its real owner," Jorge finished. Alex nodded silent agreement.

Alex confirmed. "The money for it came through a shell company owned by Karpov's father."

A message from Alex pinged my inbox. I heard the same message hit Jorge's computer, and I opened it to find the registration details for the *Nachthexen*.

"He named his boat after the WWII Night Witches?" I asked, incredulous.

"The Russian women pilots who flew balsa wood airplanes to drop bombs on the Germans?" Gabriel made a face.

"Where is it?" I asked.

"On Lake Michigan," Alex said as another e-mail landed in our boxes with a satellite image of the Great Lakes attached. A red circle indicated a vessel just offshore about halfway up the coast on the Michigan side of the lake.

"The Great Lakes have some funky maritime laws," Jorge said, reading his screen. "They're considered the 'high seas,' and US and Canadian boats have the same uninhibited access to them."

"Which maybe explains the Canadian registration," I said, "but might put that boat in tricky legal water – excuse the pun – if there's any criminal activity aboard." Both Jorge and Gabriel winced at my word choice, but Gabriel gestured for me to finish my thought. "They could be under both state, provincial, and federal jurisdiction, which, depending on the crime, could be a giant pain in the propeller."

Jorge rolled his eyes at my cleverness, but Gabriel looked thoughtful.

Alex was still tapping away at his keyboard. "I'm into the *Nachthexen* satellite, so I've got navigation and ... communications."

"Can you get me in too? I'll help you look," Jorge said with that tiny edge of happiness he usually reserved for my dog.

While they geeked out on their hackery, I got up to put the electric kettle on for tea. Gabriel followed me into the kitchen.

"I feel like whatever they're hiding is on that boat," he said quietly.

"What happened at the police station?" I asked.

He shook his head dismissively. "It's fine. Sullivan threw his weight around and pissed off some cops."

I studied Gabriel by the dim under-cabinet lights. Long shadows rimmed his eyes, and he looked worn out. I touched his face, scruffy from two days-worth of beard growth. "You should sleep."

His eyes searched mine, and he turned his face to kiss my palm. "So should you."

"Not while there's a chance Quimby could get out," I said grimly. Quinn Sullivan had briefed me and Alex about the situation with Gabriel at the police station, and if Quimby somehow managed to get out of custody, it put Gabriel in line to go back in, according to the lies Quimby had fed them.

"Exactly," he said, his gaze locked on mine.

I inhaled deeply and closed my eyes. I was exhausted, and all I wanted to do was curl up in his arms and slip into a coma.

He pulled me in for a gentle kiss on the forehead then propelled me out of the kitchen. "Gentlemen?" Gabriel spoke to Alex on the screen of my computer, but included Jorge in his gaze. "We need to catch a couple hours of sleep. Do you mind if we grab it now while you're still here to wake us if things change?"

I almost pulled away from Gabriel's arm in protest at his assumption, but he wasn't wrong that we both needed sleep, and it would be better to do it now while the super-brains did their thing.

"Fine with me," Jorge said with a shrug. "I'll hang with the hound and take him out for a run when it gets light if you want."

I smiled at him in thanks, and he darted a quick glance at Gabriel as his lip quirked up in his version of a question mark.

Alex was still typing and didn't look up. "We'll wake you when we've found something useful."

Jorge had returned his focus to his computer screen, and Alex was clearly done communicating with words, so Gabriel stopped at the couch long enough to scratch my dog's ears before he gently pushed me out of the room.

I stumbled through tooth-brushing and contact lens removal and wondered if he would still be in my apartment when I emerged. He'd made a big assumption by forcing the issue of sleep, but it would be a massive one if he presumed we'd share a bed. I tried to examine the thought but couldn't hold it in my head long enough to decide how I felt about it.

Gabriel was still there when I was done in the bathroom, and he kissed me quickly on the lips as I passed him in the doorway. I liked that and decided to shut down all conversation in my brain that got in the way of keeping it simple.

He kissed me. I liked it. Simple.

I pulled off my clothes and leg, changed into a soft t-shirt and clean shorts, and then hopped over to open the heavy drapes. There were still two hours until dawn, and sunlight on my face would guarantee that I didn't oversleep.

I had just burrowed under the cold covers when Gabriel came out of the bathroom. I could hear the clank of his belt as he took off his jeans and listened for the rasp of his sweater as he pulled it over his head. A moment later he slid under the covers next to me.

"Roll over," he whispered into my hair.

In the interest of keeping it simple, I turned over so my back was to his front. He gathered me to him and fitted his body around mine, pulled me close at the waist, and curled his arm up against my chest.

He sighed deeply and whispered, "Good night." I felt my body settle into his like the pieces of a puzzle fitted together. I was asleep in the space between breaths.

[41]
SHANE

"Don't leave the dragon out of your calculations if you live near the treasure vault." – Jorge Gonzales

---

"Get up guys, He's out."

My eyelids snapped open at the sound of Jorge's slightly frantic whisper, and sunlight seared them temporarily blind.

I took stock in the moment it took me to regain my sight. I was in my room and had been dead asleep for … I squinted at the bright sunlight glaring into the room – maybe three hours? Gabriel's warm body was wrapped around me, and his heavy arm lay across my chest. His hand cupped one of my breasts, and I felt him harden against my back as he returned to consciousness. He didn't move his hand.

I didn't want him to.

I did, however, have to deal with the mortified eighteen-year-old in my bedroom.

"I'm awake," I croaked. "Say it again."

"It's Quimby – they let him go for lack of evidence. Some guy named Quinn just called Alex, and he told me to wake you up." Jorge was looking everywhere but at me, which meant his gaze kept getting snagged by things like my leg, my halfway open underwear drawer, and the bra I'd tossed onto the chair in the corner. I would have laughed if could have gotten past the clenching stomach his words had inspired.

"Shit," Gabriel murmured into my hair.

"Okay, out," I ordered Jorge. He scrambled out of the room so fast he practically lunged for the door. Gabriel rolled me over to face him, and my breath caught. The man was beautiful, even at close range after almost no sleep. It wasn't fair. He held my face in the hand that was still warm from my breast, and he looked at me as if he was devouring me with his eyes. I flushed with heat as his thumb traced my bottom lip, and I slid my hand up his side, amazed at how smooth his skin felt beneath my fingers. He made a sound deep in his throat and was about to kiss me when scrabbling claws on the wood floor made me clench my eyes shut in anticipation.

Whomp! Oscar landed on the bed like a furry bomb, and Gabriel grunted in surprise. "Get off, beast!" he said sharply, and Oscar froze for the span of one second before he swiped Gabriel in the face with his tongue and leapt off the bed.

"Ugh! I'm up." He sat up and wiped the slobber off his face with the back of his hand. I buried my face under the covers so he wouldn't see me laugh, but it was no good. My back shook with it, and he lifted the covers and got down under them with me.

It was pitch black under there, but I could feel his face about three inches from mine. I stifled my giggles, and he touched my face. "We need to get you out of the city," he said quietly.

"We need to get *you* out of the city," I said defiantly.

"I'm not the one the guy with the gun wants," he said with an edge of frustration that I ignored.

"No, you're the one the guy with the gun wants to frame. I'll go down there and give the cops Denise Quimby, and let them sort it all out."

I pulled the covers off our heads, which was a mistake because my eyes were immediately drawn to his very broad shoulders and very bare chest. God, he was beautiful. I sighed in appreciation, then dragged my eyes back up to his face to see a tiny, self-satisfied smirk.

I was still so tired that whatever filters I normally used had gone into hibernation. "It's very hard to concentrate with all your skin staring me in the face. You're going to have to cover up so I can argue with you properly."

Oscar stood at alert, and I realized the bedroom door was still open.

"Guys?" Jorge called down the hall. "There are people here. In suits." The way Jorge said "suits" was as though there were badges attached to them.

Oscar bolted out of the bedroom, and I was suddenly terrified that he'd bite someone and get taken from me. I threw off the covers and yelled for him as I struggled to my foot.

"Oscar! No!"

It would have taken too long to put my leg on, so I hopped to the bedroom door and called again. "Oscar!"

"He's fine, Shane," Jorge called from the living room, just as I got to the door frame.

I grabbed it and held myself upright, my breath coming hard from effort, and from a little panic at the thought that my dog could have gone after someone who could take him from me.

I rested my forehead against the wall to calm my pounding heart, then turned to find Gabriel right behind me. He held out my leg. "Here," he said quietly. "Use me for support if you need to."

I took the leg and hopped back to my bed where I sat on the edge and worked the sleeve onto the stump of my leg. "I thought he would bite someone," I said without looking at the man who'd stood in his underwear holding my leg out to me.

He hadn't jumped up and said, "I'll go get him." Instead, he'd brought me my leg and said with his actions, *I'll support you to go get him.*

I didn't know if it had been a conscious decision, or even if he was aware he'd done it, but I fought back tears and swallowed the frog that had crawled its way up from my chest to my throat and taken up residence there.

I felt Gabriel's eyes on me a long moment, and then he pulled on his jeans and sweater.

"There are clean socks in the top drawer," I said, finally looking up. "I can wash yours and get them back to you."

He opened his mouth to maybe protest, but then looked at the size of my foot, which was probably only a size smaller than his, and opened the drawer I had indicated. "Sorry, they're all singles, but they're mostly the same kind," I said.

"Do you want one?" he asked me.

"Yeah, thanks." I locked my normal walking leg into place and then got a clean pair of underwear out of my drawer. Gabriel noticed and turned to leave the room.

"I'll just ..." he said, indicating the bathroom down the hall. I nodded silently and he left, closing the door behind him.

I blew out a shaky breath. What was wrong with me? Why did I suddenly get so weepy and fragile?

I grabbed black jeans, a black t-shirt with *Fights Like a Girl* emblazoned on it, and combat boots. It was armor, and it worked. My spine straightened, my brain cleared, and my focus sharpened as I walked down the hall.

Gabriel was in the kitchen making coffee, and he caught my eye with a nod. Jorge stood by the dining table where he'd been presumably working. I saw that he'd showered and changed, which meant he must have taken Oscar for a run sometime while we slept.

There were three other men and two women in the room as well, and my small apartment was indeed full of suits. I scanned the room for familiar faces in the space it took me to inhale.

"Good morning, everyone," I said to the room at large, beginning with Dan O'Malley, whose smirk made me feel unaccountably feisty. "How can we help you?"

Van Hayden stood in a corner with his back to a wall, arms crossed in front of him. His eyebrow went up at the "we," and then he shot a glance at Gabriel as he came out of the kitchen with two cups of coffee. He handed me one and then sat on the couch next to Oscar with the other. "Coffee's ready if anyone wants some," he said to the room as he scratched Oscar's ears. My dog rolled over and presented his belly for a rub, which Gabriel provided.

I leaned against the arm of a chair and sipped my coffee.

A small, dark-haired woman a couple of years older than me stopped on her way to the kitchen. "I'm Fiona. Sorry about barging in, but Quinn thought it would be good for us to meet before tonight."

I shook her hand. *Tonight?* Her grip was shockingly strong, and I realized that despite her slight build, she was solid muscle. "Nice to meet you, Fiona. I'm Shane, and you already know Gabriel?" I said the last part hesitantly, but Fiona nodded with a smile.

"I met him in Nigeria a couple of years ago. It's my fault he got hooked up with this lot," she tossed her head at the rest of the suits in the room, and then looked down at my cup. "Mind if I go get some coffee? We have a new kitten, and my kids were up pre-crack to play with it."

"Please help yourself," I said as Dan emerged from the kitchen with a cup and sat down in the other chair, clearly intent on speaking to me.

"Quinn's talking to the chief of police about CPD's fuck up, so he couldn't be here. He wants you and Gabriel out of town, preferably within the hour if you can swing it. Alex and the wonder kid here," he indicated Jorge, who was blatantly eavesdropping, "have pinpointed the location of Karpov's yacht, which we're going to hit tonight once we determine how many bodies are on board to deal with."

Bodies? I must have looked shocked, because Fiona, who had returned with her own coffee, elbowed Dan in the ribs. "Ass. Don't make the woman think you're *actually* nuts."

"I'm a little bit nuts," Dan smirked, "because the thought of pitching bodies off that nutbag's boat gives me a thrill." He gave an exaggerated shiver, and Fiona caught my eye.

"We're not killing anyone," she said in a tone that I thought every mother should have in her arsenal.

"We're not? Well, damn!" Van said as he joined the conversation. "I was hoping that little shit Quimby would be there and I'd get some target practice in."

"You people are weird," Jorge said with a shake of his head.

Dan suddenly seemed to remember there was a youth in the room, and he straightened up. "So, Dallas and Darius, you guys are the only ones who don't know Shane, right?" He got the attention of the dark-haired, dark-eyed woman and the handsome, Disney prince talking to Gabriel. They looked over at me and nodded their greetings, and I tried not to notice how pretty Dallas was, or, for that matter, Darius either.

Dan continued talking to the room at large. "Shane and Gabriel are lead on this case. We brought you all in as support to finish this thing tonight, since the fucking CPD believed the squeaky little handjobber and let him go."

Fascinating. Dan O'Malley had established Gabriel and me at the head of a job for which we'd just been volun-told. So now, essentially, anything else he said would appear to be our idea that he was merely delivering to the troops. A startlingly effective tactic that I needed to learn.

Gabriel stepped into the fray and directed his words to the assembled group. "Could everyone run down your skill set and assets so the rest of the group knows who we're working with?"

Another solid tactic, and delivered in a quiet, confident voice that spoke of an easy relationship with command. It was ridiculously attractive.

Fiona looked around, then spoke. "Fiona Archer, electrical engineer by education, former CIA by training, now mom, wife, and occasional consultant for Cipher Security. I have black belts in Kendo and Brazilian Jiu-Jitsu, and in my previous life I was an Olympic gymnast."

Damn. I was impressed. Van went next. "Van Hayden, former criminal prosecutor, current Cipher Security agent. Firearms and explosives expert for SWAT training in Wisconsin and Minnesota. Basically, I blow shit up."

Gabriel glanced up sharply, and I was intrigued at the variety of credentials in the room.

The dark-eyed woman went next. She smirked at Van. "You blow shit up, I shoot it." She turned her attention to the rest of us. "Dallas

Profeit, hunter, survivalist, wilderness guide. My graduate degrees are in environmental science and botany, and I was recruited by the Canadian Olympic biathlon team before I came to the States to do close protection work for Cipher Security."

My mouth fell open, and I wasn't sure what surprised me more – that a wilderness guide would study engineering, or that the badass survivalist could stop her own heart to shoot a target 50 meters away.

Then the tall, dark, and handsome Disney prince spoke next. He had a very slight accent, and if money had a sound, it was Darius's voice. "Darius Masoud, architect and mechanical engineer. I design panic rooms and security systems for Cipher, though my primary qualification for this job is the 1954 Commander Express Cruiser on which I live."

Dan nodded and then looked directly at me. "Dan O'Malley. I used to be a street thug, now I'm a boardroom one. Skills include all the usual martial arts and self-defense training, plus a misguided youth in Boston and a bad fucking attitude."

Then Gabriel spoke, also directing his comments to me. "Gabriel Eze, former British Military Police, former UN Peacekeeper," he caught Fiona's eye with a small smile, "and a newly minted Cipher agent. Extensive hand-to-hand combat and weapons training, considerable investigative experience, and fair with computers. I'm excellent back-up in a fight, and I won't leave a partner behind." His gaze held mine for a long moment.

Jorge spoke before I could. "Jorge Gonzales, hacker, programmer, and reformed thief. If it's digital, I can find it."

There was laughter from the open laptop on the table, and Jorge turned it so the screen faced the room. Alex was there, still in his living room, still sitting under the Stormtrooper Sugar Skull print. "He's not wrong," he said with a nod to Dan. "The kid could be me in the field."

Dan growled at Jorge. "How old are you?"

"Eighteen."

"Shit."

I agreed with Dan, but Jorge was an adult, so I didn't get a say. And since apparently Alex wasn't introducing his skills, it was my turn now, and I refused to indulge in insecurity about my own relatively slim resume. "I'm Shane – licensed P.I. from California and a below-the-knee amputee. I've done two triathlons, climbed in the Himalayas, and I cycled across the U.S. just because they said I would never be able to walk without a limp. My superpowers are survival, the inability to hear the words 'no' and 'can't,' and a kick-ass prosthetist who builds me superhero legs. Also, I hate cheaters, so this is personal to me."

I tried to meet the eyes of everyone in the room, which was about as easy as tearing my fingernails out with pliers, but I somehow brazened my way through the eye-contact portion of the evening.

I saved Gabriel's eyes for last, and he held my gaze for an extra moment as he spoke to the assembled team. "I'm sure O'Malley has briefed everyone on what we've discovered so far. The fact that Dane Quimby has been released from police custody after holding a gun on Shane and myself is the reason for the urgency."

"We know his partner in ADDATA, Alexander Karpov, has potentially damning information about Quimby. It's enough to leash him, if not outright convict him of a crime." I added, "We believe Karpov may be holding that information and potentially much more in some form of hard copy on a yacht off the coast of Ludington State Park in Michigan."

Gabriel and I laid out the evidence we'd collected on ADDATA, Quimby, and the Karpov/right-wing political connection. Quimby's desperation, indicated by his attack on me, and Karpov's connections with angry nationalist groups were the biggest concerns because they spoke of unpredictability and the likelihood of firearms possession.

"Money troubles seem to be at the heart of Quimby's dive off the deep end," I said.

"Do we know where he got the million he stashed in the private account?" asked Fiona.

"It was a cash deposit. Essentially, the transfer of money from one account to another within the same bank." Alex's voice spoke through the speaker on Jorge's computer.

"Who owned the transferring account?" asked Darius.

"It was a business account owned by Galton Enterprises, and it was closed the same day," Alex said.

"What is Galton Enterprises?" Gabriel asked, but I already had my phone out and was searching.

"They do those genetic testing kits," I said, frowning. The name sounded disturbingly familiar.

"Genetic testing?" Gabriel growled, "By a company with the same name as the father of eugenics?"

"Sir Francis Galton." Darius's clipped tone was a sharp contrast to Gabriel's deep voice. "Victorian era statistician, psychologist, and psychometrician."

"Otherwise known as racist piece of shit," snorted Dan.

"Wait – psychometrician? As in the practice of psychometry?" Gabriel stared at Dan.

"Psychometry? Where the fuck did I hear that?" Dan retorted.

"It's what Karpov teaches at the University." Gabriel got up to pace. "We need corporate info on Galton."

"Already on it," Jorge said. "Galton Enterprises is registered in Connecticut and owned by Elena Karpova who is … a hundred and eight years old?"

"She would be, if she hadn't died fifteen years ago," Alex said.

"No death certificate," Jorge argued.

"He didn't file it with the County Recorder's office," Alex countered, "but there's an obituary."

"Who didn't file a death certificate?" I asked. Those two seemed unaware they had an audience.

"Elena's grandson and sole heir, Alex Karpov."

[42]
GABRIEL

"If it's ugly, make sure it's hot pink so everyone knows it's on purpose." – Billy "Sparky" Spracher.

Shane wanted to make a stop at her prosthetist's warehouse on our way out of the city. As I drove, she was quiet, but I recognized the signs of formulation rather than withdrawal, so I left her to it.

"Do you mind if I come up with you?" I asked, when I'd parked outside the building. She seemed surprised at the question.

"Of course not. I just need to borrow a leg."

I chuckled. "You just need to borrow a leg."

She smiled. "You know one of the things I really appreciate?"

"What's that?" We were in the freight elevator heading up to Sparky's flat.

"You don't make my missing leg significant."

"It's not. Your prosthetics, on the other hand, are brilliant, and the man who designed them is a god among engineers." We had emerged from the elevator, and I was grinning at Sparky as I said the words. I knew how important he was to Shane, and in the absence of her family, he and Jorge might be it.

He snorted. "A minor deity maybe. I'm more like Hephaestus with my robots, making precious jewels for a goddess. Oh look! Here she is."

Shane scoffed. "Goddess, my ass."

Sparky and I made an exaggerated point of looking at the part in question and silently agreeing. Shane laughed as she rolled her eyes at us.

I reached out to shake his hand. "It's good to see you again."

He took my grip. "Gabriel Eze, right? Was I right about your name being Igbo?"

I was surprised. "Yes. My father was Nigerian."

Sparky shot Shane a smug look. "See?"

"You are clearly the smartest pink-Croc-wearing man in the room, Spark," she said.

"I have to ask; why the pink shoes?" I looked down at the large, hot pink, injected-foam clog-type slippers he wore. If there were more horrible shoes in the world, I hadn't seen them.

"My niece picked them out for me so we could be twins," he said with a shrug. "And they're comfortable."

I gave him the raised eyebrows of respect, while Shane blinded him with her smile.

"I don't tell you often enough how cool you are."

"My coolness is so off the charts, you don't need to," he said with a grin. "Now, tell me what you need and get out, so I can be alone with my fantasies of goddesses who want me for more than my legs." He waggled his eyebrows at her suggestively, and she laughed.

"Can the diving leg you made be modified to fit me?"

"I made it *for* you. Here, try it," he said as he pulled a leg off a shelf. It was fitted with a swim fin that extended past a titanium peg that ended in a rubber stopper similar to the bit on the bottom of crutches.

Shane sat on a stool and pulled up the leg of her jeans to take off the walking leg she most often wore.

"The fin is on a hinge. Flip it up to walk on the peg," Sparky said as she attached the leg to the sleeve.

She did as he directed and stood easily on the peg. "I based it on the dimensions of the pirate peg leg you have."

"You have a pirate leg?" I said in awe.

Shane gave me a look that fairly scoffed *how can you even ask that*, and I smirked at her. "Fashion show."

"Not a chance," she said with a teasing smile.

"Dude, have her show you the Inspector Gadget leg." Sparky was adjusting a screw on the hinge as Shane tested her balance on the peg.

"The one with the torch and screwdrivers?" I asked.

"The flashlight is kinetically-powered, and it also has lock picks, tweezers, and a place to stash fishing line." The pride in Sparky's voice made Shane smile, and she met my eyes over his head.

"The leg is great, Spark. Can I borrow it for a couple of days?" She sat down to remove the dive leg and re-attach her walking one.

"Depends."

"On?"

He huffed a sigh. "I need you to model some legs for a promo video I want to do."

Shane looked warily at him. "I don't know—"

"I know you hate having your picture taken, but I made all my best legs for you, and you're the only person I know who can make them look like proper superhero limbs."

"Who will see the video?" she asked.

"Hopefully, everyone in the amputee community. C'mon, Shane, get over it already. You're an amputee, so what? I bet you haven't even worn the skirt leg I made you."

"You have a skirt leg?" I asked.

Sparky turned his plea to me. "I matched the calf size and skin color to her other leg exactly. It even has a flex foot that can fit into high heels."

I looked at the woman who was almost exactly my height, and the mental image of her in a short skirt and heels was the only excuse I had for saying the words out loud. "Definitely calls for a fashion show."

She scowled at me, then turned it back on Sparky. "I'll think about it."

He shrugged and suddenly looked bored. "I guess I'll think about letting you borrow the dive leg then."

"You're an ass."

"You're a chicken," he shot back.

"Child!" she spat.

"Bawk bawk!"

Shane glared ferociously, but Sparky just held her gaze with raised eyebrows. Finally, she sagged. "Fine."

He grinned brightly. "Good. Wear the leg in good health. I want to hear how it does in water."

"You haven't tested it yet?"

He scoffed. "No. That's your job."

I picked up the dive leg and steered Shane out of Sparky's warehouse before she could throw the punch that was building in her right arm.

"Good to see you again," I called to Sparky as we pulled the gate down on the freight elevator.

"Send photos," he called back.

I stifled a laugh as Shane growled something that sounded distinctly like a threat to remove body parts from the pink-Croc-wearing super-genius engineer.

[43]

SHANE

"The most powerful person in the world is the one standing on a street corner conducting traffic to move in the direction it's going." – Shane, P.I.

As we drove north, Gabriel and I sorted through all the pros and cons of the plan we'd designed with the rest of the group to find whatever Karpov had on Quimby. Our planning session that morning had been a true collaboration among remarkably creative people. Darius's 1954 wooden pleasure craft, affectionately known as the party boat, was retrieved from its mooring and stocked with a full bar. A surfboard was borrowed from Fiona's husband, wetsuits were rented, and Jorge turned my cell phone into some sort of super-spy device that only he knew how to properly utilize. The exchange of ideas flowed, and it was exhilarating to work with such fascinating people. I still had trouble believing I'd been invited into the room with them.

The goal of the mission was stealth, or, barring that, no witnesses. Since none of us were currently in the murder business – I assumed, and wasn't inclined to actually ask – leaving no witnesses was a bit more complicated than the piratical "throw them overboard!"

Step one involved Gabriel and me getting out of town. We had GPS coordinates for Karpov's yacht, which had been moored just offshore from Ludington State Park for the past week. Our immediate job was to get to the park and lay eyes on the yacht. Step two wouldn't happen until after dark, which allowed for contingencies as needed, and meant we would likely have a couple of hours to ourselves before Fiona arrived. We turned off the highway into what must have been the biggest wilderness area in all of Michigan. We saw no other vehicles at all as we wound our way through the forest on a single lane road. Finally, we'd gone as far as we could go on a paved road and parked the car in a deserted lot at the beach.

"Nothing's open here until May, so we should have the place to ourselves," Gabriel said as we stretched the long drive out of our legs.

"The GPS coordinates for the yacht are just north of here. Should we walk up there first and make sure we can find it before we haul everything in?"

"Sounds good to me." Gabriel took my hand in his as we stepped onto a wide, sandy trail. The gesture startled me after the hours of conversation about details, contingencies, and emergency plans, but I didn't pull away from him. His hand was warm and his grip was gentle, and walking beside him felt like the most natural thing in the world. Our shoulders bumped often enough that it wasn't accidental, and I was aware of every point of contact between our bodies.

We walked almost two miles along the deserted coastline on a path that skirted the edge of the woods. The tower of an old lighthouse came into view, and that became our destination. It sat on a rocky promontory at a spot that jutted into Lake Michigan, and there were no signs that anyone had been there in months.

We discovered the yacht moored about a half-mile off the coast when we walked around the lighthouse to the north side. Benches had been conveniently placed for guests to enjoy the view, and a fire escape ladder had been left fully extended against the wall. I grabbed a rung to support myself on one leg as I studied the outline of the fifty-foot pleasure craft. "The dimensions are right," I said to Gabriel, who had dropped his photojournalist's bag on the bench and was rummaging through it. I flexed my leg carefully – walking on sand was tiring with two legs, and brutal with just one. The new sleeve fit much better than the old ones ever had, but just like my dad always said about our feet when we backpacked as kids, I had to be ever vigilant for hot spots that could turn into blisters or open sores, because my ability to walk myself out of the wilderness could be the thing that would keep me alive.

Gabriel held up a pair of binoculars. "See if you can get an accurate ID while I take a look around and make sure the area is secure." Then he lingered, too close, and settled the binoculars around my neck. His eyes searched mine for a long moment before he smiled. "Wanting to kiss you is almost as much fun as actually doing it." Then he stepped back and was gone around the side of the building.

I trained the binoculars on the yacht and had to take a moment to calm my pounding heart before I found its name painted on the side in a vaguely Cyrillic font – *Nachthexen*. I couldn't see anyone moving around on deck, but the *Nachthexen* was a fifty-foot Prestige 500 with three staterooms, so there could be as many as five people on it, depending on their levels of coziness.

I heard Gabriel return but didn't remove the binoculars from my face. I told my brain I wasn't presenting myself as an open target for the arms that encircled my waist as he stepped up behind me, but I was a lying liar who lied, especially when I tried to pretend indifference.

I was powerless to stop myself from melting into his embrace, however, just as I was helpless against the shiver of desire that flamed my skin when he whispered in my ear, "All clear." I closed my eyes and leaned my head back on his shoulder while he held me.

"I woke up wanting you, and I haven't stopped," he said quietly.

My skin prickled with nerve endings everywhere his body touched mine. His desire rocked the control I'd been pretending to have since we'd left my bed, and I finally let myself feel *everything*. Strong arms encircled me, and breath warmed my neck. His heart beat against my shoulder blade, and his erection pressed against my backside.

I removed the binocular strap from around my neck and deliberately set it down on the bench that stood next to us. I ran down a mental list of supporting facts: the yacht was moored, we were out of casual sight, and it was still two hours until our plan kicked off. I was wildly attracted to Gabriel Eze, and I was so tired of dwelling on all the reasons it was a bad idea to be with him. That was enough to shut down the mental list-making at least, and I turned to face him and pressed my body against his.

"Me too," I breathed, as I touched his face.

He groaned and held me tightly to him as he kissed me. I savored his kiss, the sensation of his tongue, the taste of him, and the low hum in the back of his throat. I ran my hands down his shoulders and then slipped them around his back where I gripped his shirt to pull him closer.

It wasn't close enough. I slid my hands up under his shirt and over his smooth skin. I could feel goosebumps pebble on his back under my touch, and I smiled.

"My hands aren't that cold," I said against his mouth.

He growled and walked me back until I was up against the wall of the lighthouse – the ladder on one side of me, the bench on the other. He pushed his hips into mine, and the length of him pressed against the seam of my jeans. I wanted to feel *him* without clothes between us. I needed his skin directly against my own.

His hands lifted mine up to the ladder, and he wrapped my fingers around the rung above my head. His kisses were heady, and whatever focus I had left moved between his mouth on mine and his hands that trailed down my arms. He unbuttoned the black flannel shirt I'd worn over a black tank and then groaned deep in his throat when he realized I wore no bra underneath.

He tugged the fabric down and his mouth fastened on my nipple. I clutched the rung of the ladder above my head as he teased it with his teeth and tongue before taking it in his mouth and sucking hard. A bolt of pure desire flared between my legs, and I writhed against him with a soft moan. I dropped my hands to his back and clutched him to me. He kissed me again, deeply, and gently but firmly moved my grip back up to the rung above my head. My hands were free, but they felt fastened place as I clung to the ladder. He slid his mouth down again, and I squirmed under it as he exposed the other breast and gave it the same attention. I pressed myself against his hard length and moaned his name.

"Do you have a condom?" I whispered in a choked voice.

He kissed me then, deeply, and smiled against my lips. "I might."

My eyes flew open and I narrowed them at him. "Get it."

He unbuttoned my jeans and slipped a hand under my boy briefs, and I gasped as his finger slid inside me.

"I'm busy," he said against my mouth. I bit his lip, and he laughed.

The sensation of his hand and fingers against me – in me – made me bold. I wanted this man inside me. I'd imagined how he would feel and smell and taste since the first night we met. I let go of the rung and slid my hand down the rigid length of him over his jeans. He stopped laughing and ground the words out through clenched teeth. "Front pocket."

I lingered inside his pocket long enough to stroke him through the fabric, and he moaned and pushed another finger inside me. My breath caught as desire pulsed through me with each thrust of his fingers. When I had the foil packet in hand, I went to work on the button of his jeans, but I kept fumbling with the overwhelming sensation of *need*. He finally pulled my hands away, took the condom from me, and reattached my grip to the rung of the ladder.

"Hold on," he murmured against my mouth as he kissed me deeply.

I did as he said, and he tugged my jeans down. I couldn't kick off my boots, so I stepped on my jeans and pulled the legs inside out, trying unsuccessfully to get the pants off over the shoes. I reached for my feet to untangle them, frustrated at the delay, but Gabriel patiently moved my hand back up to the rung of the ladder.

"I've got this," he said, with a mischievous glint in his eyes. He unfastened his belt and jeans, rolled the condom onto himself, and then stepped over my inside-out jeans, which were still attached to my boots, and kicked them back so they circled behind him. He lifted my thighs and cupped my ass with one arm.

"Wrap your legs around me," he murmured as he kissed me.

No one had ever made me feel delicate enough to hold, but Gabriel was so strong he made it seem easy. I gripped his backside with my crossed legs as he guided himself halfway inside me. I didn't let go of the ladder, and he didn't let go of me. It was unbelievably sexy, and I squirmed on him, desperate to get closer.

He inhaled sharply and shuddered as he held me still. "God, Shane, you're killing me."

"I need more," I said with a gasp. The urge to grind against him made me tremble with need, and I closed my muscles around him to draw him in. He groaned raggedly and thrust into me.

He filled me completely, and the melding of our bodies became my sole focus. His hands gripped my bottom, pulling me closer. Pressure built, and heat suffused my skin. Each thrust ... every impact ... grinding... filling ...

Pleasure exploded through me with bright sparks of fire, and my orgasm left me gasping in surprise. I clutched the rung of the ladder over my head as he withdrew and thrust again, impossibly deeper, again and again. A second orgasm unfurled through me, and then he buried his groan against my neck as his own throbbed inside me.

He held onto me tightly, and when the shuddering in my body finally stopped, I let go of the ladder to wrap my arms around his shoulders. His strong arms held us both upright as our breathing slowed and our heartbeats returned to something that couldn't be seen on the surface of our skin. He kissed me again, hungrily, and I captured the taste of his lips to relive later. I memorized the scent of his skin, and the feeling of his body pressed against mine.

I finally broke the kiss to breathe. "Except for the fact that that may have just been the best sex of my life, ending up with my jeans around my ankles, trapping us both, is fucking undignified."

"What are the odds I can find a drugstore that's open up here?" he chuckled into my hair.

I pushed his shoulders back so I could look him in the eyes. "What? Why?" I demanded.

He leaned in and nibbled my earlobe as he whispered, "Because I only brought one condom, and I want to do that again."

The untangling of limbs and clothing was ridiculous and fun, and by the time we walked back to the car to retrieve the gear for our job, any possibility of afterglow awkwardness had disappeared. This time the shoulder bumps and accidental body contact felt like a promise rather than a wish, and I marveled at how easy it felt to be with him.

"For the record, if you ever decided to go back on the pill, I'm clean and healthy. I got checked when I left the UN."

"Duly noted," I said. "When was that?"

"Nine months ago," he said.

"You haven't had sex in nine months?" I scowled. "That doesn't seem possible."

"It's been more like two years, and why not? How long since you last had sex? Wait, no, I'm not sure I want to know the answer, because if he's in Chicago I might have to hunt him down and kill him."

"Are you reverting to your inner caveman again?" I teased, feeling absurdly pleased about his possessiveness, even if it was feigned.

"Reverting? No. It's always there. I'm just usually smarter about not letting it out to play."

"Well, if it makes a difference, it's been years," I said.

He utterly failed at hiding his smile. "The gentleman in me is immensely grateful to have been given the honor of your trust. The caveman just wants to puff up like a rooster and claim you as mine."

"Rooster is not the thing that comes to mind when I think of you. Now cock, on the other hand ..." I giggled and ducked away as he tickled me, and an unfamiliar warmth settled into my chest. I liked this man, and despite all the odds, he seemed to have a little bit of a thing for me too.

He reached for my hand and held it comfortably as we walked and talked about easy things. His favorite subject in school had been history, mine had been literature. He loved looking for mentions of black people in English history, I loved women authors who defied gender stereotypes. We were comparing our favorite books and had just switched to the fantasy genre when both our cell phones buzzed at once in our pockets. My phone had been quiet for hours, and the silence had allowed me to forget, just for a moment, why we were there. I was only sorry that the respite hadn't been real.

I looked at seven texts from Jorge and two from Fiona. "Crap," I said as I read them. "I didn't expect to hear from them yet, but they sent these over an hour ago."

Gabriel had his phone out and was reading the screen too. "Communication at the lighthouse must be non-existent. I didn't even notice." He looked up to meet my eyes. "I admit to being a little distracted."

"Just a little?" I grinned before my phone pinged again and another message loaded. "Fiona's already here, in the parking lot."

"Yeah," Gabriel said, in a voice that might have held a bit of disappointment. I appreciated it even as I had no idea what to do with the thought that he might prefer me over work.

We crested a dune and could see a dark green Subaru with a surfboard strapped to the roof parked next to Gabriel's car. I texted Jorge that we were back in range of communication just as Fiona exited the car.

"Communications are either shit, or you guys were frolicking naked in the waves without your phones," Fiona announced. "And because it's too freaking cold for naked wave-frolicking, I'm going to guess we've got shit comms."

I very carefully did not look in Gabriel's direction, and was proud of myself for not even twitching at Fiona's confident declaration as I pretended the activities of the last hour weren't flashing all over my face like a neon sign.

"We both got all your texts less than five minutes ago, so yeah, apparently the lighthouse where we'll station has shit comms."

"Well, that's not going to work at all," Fiona snarled. "I need to be able to coordinate between you and the other two while keeping an eye on the satellite so we're not completely blind."

"If you can talk to the party boat from here, I have a walkie set that could work between the lighthouse and this parking lot," Gabriel said as he went to his trunk and rummaged through it. He handed me a duffel bag and the case with Sparky's new dive leg, gave Fiona one walkie-talkie, and clipped the other to his belt.

"We won't know if this works until we can test it," Fiona argued as Gabriel went to work on the surfboard straps. I opened the rear door of the Subaru and pulled out a dive bag, which I added to my burden.

Gabriel shrugged. "Worst case scenario, you signal the party boat at —" he checked his watch, "7 p.m., and we'll meet them out there. We should be able to get a signal again through the yacht's satellite and we'll reconnect with you via our mobiles when we do. Does that work?"

Fiona glared at him, then included me in her focused gaze. I had the thought that she'd just fixed us with her "mom eyes," and they were pretty damn effective.

"I don't like it," she said. "You'll be without backup except when you're on the yacht. That's too much time on your own."

Gabriel could have been bad-tempered about her concern. I'd seen other men react that way when a woman called their decision into question, but, as I was coming to realize, Gabriel wasn't like other men. His voice dropped to the quiet one he chose when he wanted to make a point.

"We've got this, Fiona, and we're both very capable of taking care of ourselves. Thank you for having our backs, and I know how frustrating it is to be out of comms with one's team, but I promise, I'll keep us safe."

"We'll both keep us safe," I said quickly. Fiona's gaze went to me, and she finally nodded.

"Right, then. Keep talking as you head back to the lighthouse so we can determine the range of the walkies, and I'll wait here to run communications through the party boat. And Shane," she said pointedly to me, "sorry for getting bossy on this. It's a mom thing."

"Oddly, it doesn't suck to be mommed by you," I said with a smile. "I have the feeling you're pretty good at it."

Gabriel tucked the surfboard under his arm, and we left Fiona to her Thermos of coffee. The walkie-talkie at Gabriel's belt squawked as soon as we were out of sight. "Take care of my surfboard, Gabriel. My husband retains grand fantasies of the misspent youth he never had as a California surfer."

Gabriel pulled the walkie off his belt and spoke into it as we walked back to the lighthouse. "Trust is a two-way street, Fiona."

The sigh on the other end was audible. "I trust you."

He grinned. "The absence of an apology to me was noted, by the way."

Fiona must have heard the smirk in his voice, because she didn't take offence. "Good. Because you don't get one." The radio squawked unceremoniously.

"Might I inquire as to why that is?" He wore his Britishness as civility when he needed to.

Fiona laughed. "Don't think I'm susceptible to your proper English coldness, Eze – you forget, I married a Brit."

"Then perhaps you'll indulge me out of affection?"

She laughed again. "You don't bristle at being told what to do by women."

"And?"

"That means you've got bossy women in your life, and you're either immune or too smart to be threatened."

He burst out laughing. "My mum and sister would love you, Fiona," he said finally.

"I'm entirely loveable," she said with a smirk in her voice. "Just ask my—" And just like that, her voice cut out.

We stopped in our tracks not even halfway back to the lighthouse. "Fiona? Fiona?" Gabriel tried the walkie a couple of times, but there was nothing. I pulled my cell phone out of my back pocket and checked for bars.

"Phone's flatlined too," I said with a sigh.

"Does that bother you?" Gabriel's tone was curious rather than sharp.

"No," I said with a smile. "And if we hurry, we'll have time to get warm before we go in the water."

He grinned mischievously. "Cold?"

"I could be warmer," I said with eyebrows that added the word *naked* to the end of that sentence.

Gabriel feigned shock for exactly one second, right before he took off at a jog across the dunes.

[44]
SHANE

"Trust is more valuable than diamonds and as fragile as soap bubbles on a windy day." – Shane, P.I.

We got back to the lighthouse, and Gabriel started to get our water gear ready for use. I borrowed his binoculars and slipped around the north side of the building to check on the yacht. The evening light made everything blur into a non-descript gray on the water, but the yacht's running lights had already come on, which meant someone was definitely home. I just hoped it was a skeleton crew of only one or two people.

Our plan was designed to break as few laws as possible – an important distinction for Quinn and Dan, who didn't care to play as fast and loose with the rules as I usually did. If everything went perfectly tonight, we would be trespassing and committing petty theft, neither of which was likely to be reported given the nature of the materials we hoped to steal. Various ideas for how to deal with whatever crew was onboard had been discussed and rejected as either criminal, violent, or too risky. We'd finally settled on a plan that involved a manufactured breakdown on Darius' boat, an abundance of Dallas' flirtation skills, and a fair amount of alcoholic distraction.

I looked through the binoculars again and could just make out a crewman coiling lines while another one stowed bench cushions in the seat storage compartments.

"Gabriel!" I shout-whispered to him as I watched the two men work on the deck.

He came up behind me and wrapped his arms around my waist. I would have been startled if I hadn't felt the heat of him when he stepped close.

"Look," I handed the binoculars to him. "They're getting ready to leave."

He studied the scene for less than thirty seconds. "You're right." He handed the binoculars back to me. "Keep an eye on them. A yacht that size will take an hour to ready properly, so we need to move. I'll run back into walkie range and have Fiona alert the party boat."

"Right. I'll change," I said.

He gave me a quick kiss and then sprinted away. I took one last look through the binoculars, then left them on the bench and moved around to the back of the lighthouse to change into my wetsuit and dive leg.

I'd modified the wetsuit with a thick rubber band at the end of the leg opening to close the neoprene around the peg of Sparky's dive leg. Dry neoprene was warm enough, but a pain in the booty to pull on over goosebumps. The temperature had dropped as the sun went down, and I wasn't looking forward to my first few minutes in the water.

I flipped up the fin so I could stand on the peg leg, and I had the binoculars glued to my face again when Gabriel finally returned.

"What are they doing," he murmured in the low voice that warmed me to the core every time I heard it.

"Stowing gear."

I could hear him changing into his own wetsuit behind me, and it took every ounce of self-control I had not to watch. I resolved to contain my ogling to off-work hours, mostly because I doubted I'd ever get anything done otherwise.

"You ready?" he asked quietly.

The gray evening had dipped to dark, and the lake had gone quiet in the way water did after sunset. I whispered back, "Yeah."

He turned me toward him and took my face in his hands. "The Neanderthal in me has a request."

"The Neanderthal may make his request if he concludes it with a kiss." So much for my not-during-business-hours policy.

He searched my face in a way that made me wonder what he saw there. Nervousness? Fear? A zit growing on the side of my nose? I was on the verge of checking my teeth for spinach when he finally spoke. "I know how capable you are, and I know how prickly you can get when you think someone's about to tell you not to do something."

And just like that, my shoulders stiffened and I almost stepped back, but Gabriel didn't let go of my face. He smiled ruefully. "See? Even the suggestion of it puts your back up." He wasn't wrong, so I exhaled and forced my shoulders to relax. "All I'm asking," he continued, still looking into my eyes, "is that you trust the team to do its job. Every one of us is extremely capable – you don't have to carry us, and you don't have to do it all yourself. You can count on us to do our jobs just as we trust you to do yours. If something isn't safe or we need to make a different play, remember we're a team, and we'll make decisions on that basis."

I nodded automatically and met his eyes without blinking. He seemed to find what he needed in my gaze because he kissed me hard enough that my heart rate rose commensurately, and my hands reached out to steady myself on his waist.

"Let's do this," he growled into my lips. I smiled at the ferocity of his tone and turned toward the water. Gabriel picked up the surfboard and carried it under one arm as he walked beside me to the edge of the lake. It took more concentration to walk on sand with the peg leg, but it was surprisingly stable.

In the distance we could hear a boat engine, and a few minutes later when we were both wet and shivering – me in the water, Gabriel on the board – Darius's 1950s classic wooden party cruiser finally came into view.

"That's it," Gabriel said as I pushed off the ground and began to swim toward the *Nachthexen*. He lay on his stomach, paddling the board next to me.

I was a strong swimmer – I'd been a long-distance swimmer in high school and college. It was the one thing I could do to stay in shape during the long months of rehab after the leg came off. Sparky's fin prosthetic made me even faster, and within a few minutes I wasn't cold anymore.

As I swam, I occupied my brain with what we'd learned about Karpov. He was arrogant, enjoyed the finer things, and played a long game. In my head I pictured a sleekly modern yacht interior, with mirrored surfaces and blonde wood, or some combination of black, white, and chrome. He had invested in tech to exploit the masses, but he seemed to have gone old-school with storage of the potentially damning information he had on Quimby, so I thought Karpov would be the kind of guy who used a safe. Boats had lots of cleverly designed hiding spots, but a safe would have to be in a compartment in the center of the floor so the weight of it didn't throw the yacht's balance off kilter.

Gabriel reached through the water to tap me, and I looked up to see the party boat tied up alongside the *Nachthexen*. I could see Dallas standing on the wooden deck of Darius's boat chatting with two young white guys who were, presumably, the crew of Karpov's yacht. She laughed and played with her hair, and one of the guys leapt aboard the wooden boat. The other one said something and seemed to hesitate, but Dallas just smiled and beckoned to him before leading the way below decks. The first guy followed her like a baby duck. The second one looked around the yacht, then seemed to scan the lake for a few moments. Finally, he stepped aboard the party boat and dropped down out of sight.

Gabriel tapped my shoulder again, and we made directly for the stern of the yacht where a metal stepladder was affixed. Gabriel looped the collar of his board around one of the rails as I flipped up the fin on my swim leg and carefully pulled myself up the ladder. I moved slowly enough that I didn't rock it, just in case someone else was still on board, and then shifted to balance the boat as Gabriel pulled his heavier frame out of the water. He dropped a small wet bag on the deck between us.

I opened the wet bag and pulled out our cell phones and a small, super-absorbent camping towel which I used to sop up as much of the water running off my wetsuit as I could. Neither of us wanted a trail leading down into the yacht to show where we'd been. Gabriel dried off quickly, and less than a minute later, we stepped into the main deck of the luxurious yacht.

And luxurious it was. The image of sleek modernity I'd had in my mind disappeared in a puff of glitter. The interior of the yacht looked like something a Russian oligarch had done for his mistress's poodle. The sheer quantity of bling was nearly blinding.

"Good Lord," Gabriel said under his breath. The British understatement of it nearly made me giggle, and I moved past the gold-colored crushed-velvet settee with exaggerated care. A short staircase led down under the foredeck where the plans had shown two double staterooms. The third one, near the engine compartment, was a single, so I ignored it and led the way to the one which we assumed was the master. The door was locked, which didn't surprise me. I pulled a set of lock picks from the compartment Sparky had built into the peg of the dive leg, and Gabriel shone a light from his mini flashlight on the door handle. I felt him at my back as I worked, and it was comforting to know there was a set of eyes and ears behind me.

The lock was a fairly simple one meant to keep crewmen out of the master's chamber, and I had it open in less than a minute. Gabriel shone his flashlight around the room briefly to determine it was empty, and then we slipped inside and closed the door softly behind us. I turned the button on the handle to lock it, just for good measure.

If gilt-induced nausea was possible, I had it. The small room looked like Versailles and a jewelry box had a baby and dressed it up in purple velvet, and I had to put my hand on Gabriel's shoulder for a moment to keep the room from spinning.

"Check the floor for storage compartments. I bet there's a safe," I whispered to Gabriel. I pulled out my cell phone was pleased to see full bars when I texted Jorge. He was at my apartment with Oscar, monitoring the satellite for communications. *We're in the master bedroom.*

A moment later, Fiona texted. *Darius has one of the guys helping him with his "engine problem." Dallas is drinking with the other one. Only two on board.*

I exhaled. "There were only two of them, and they're still on the party boat," I murmured to Gabriel.

He had rolled up a thick Chinese silk rug and was tugging on a brass ring inset into the decking beneath it. The lid to the compartment pulled up, and inside was the door to a floor safe. I allowed myself a righteous smirk until I realized there was no combination wheel on the safe. It surprised me given Karpov's mistrust. Instead, the safe was locked with a digital combination.

"Shit." Gabriel exhaled sharply. "Harder to crack."

I texted Jorge. *Digital combo.*

He responded a second later. *Use the multi-meter probe I gave you, open the app, and go 1-9 on each key.*

Back in my apartment, as we'd gone through all the possible problems we might encounter, Jorge had given me a short cable that plugged into my super-spy phone. He downloaded a resistance-testing app and said he could turn my phone into a resistance multi-meter to open digital locks. I didn't really understand it at all, but Alex had been listening in over Skype, and it was clear he'd been impressed with Jorge's ingenuity. Apparently, the amount of current a lock battery drew varied according to whether the bits storing each number in the code were a 0 or a 1. By monitoring the multi-meter in my phone, Jorge could essentially spell out the correct key code until he got all six numbers, and all I had to do was hold the probe to the safe and punch numbers while I said them out loud. Gabriel opened a line to Jorge's phone and put it on speaker so I could whisper the numbers.

It took six minutes to get all six numbers of the combination. Fiona occasionally texted updates on the party boat happenings, and it seemed that both of the *Nachthexen's* crew members were quite happy to sample Darius's excellent whiskey and Dallas' considerable charm while one of them helped him fix the mechanical difficulty they'd manufactured.

The safe opened with a quiet snick, and Gabriel lifted the door carefully. Inside was a waterproof bag, which made sense for a boat, and inside that was a small case full of thumb drives and a packet of photographs. I opened the packet and was not startled to see images of Dane Quimby on a residential street wearing a black baseball cap and a dark jacket. The photos were obviously taken from a parked car by a camera able to shoot in low light. The pictures laid out a sequence of events – first, a full face shot of Quimby for identification, then his approach to a dark sedan. In the third photo, Quimby was pulling something out of his pocket, and in the fourth—"

"Shit!" I nearly dropped the photos when I realized what I was looking at. "Dane Quimby shot the driver of that car in the head."

I handed the prints to Gabriel and took a shaky breath. Whatever dirt I'd been expecting, that was not it. The Dane Quimby I'd investigated for cheating on his wife wasn't a killer, was he?

"When did he do it?" I asked, looking for a date on the photos. Nothing was burned into the print, and I couldn't tell the time of year from the image.

"There's a license plate visible on the car. We'll run the plate and find out who he shot."

"I can't believe I could have gotten a guy so wrong. He was a little desperate, and a jerk for sure, but I didn't have him pegged as a killer," I was whispering, but we were still on Gabriel's speaker phone.

"Give me the plate," said Jorge quietly.

Gabriel snapped a picture of the photograph and sent it to him. "Coming at you."

All right you two – party's winding down next door. Time to move. Fiona's text came through the phone in a clear command.

"Signing off," Gabriel answered quietly as I quickly packed my tools back into the dive leg. He tucked our phones and the photos into the dry bag, but I stopped him on the drives.

"Give me those. They're small enough to store in the leg."

He opened the little case they were stored in and dropped three drives into my hand. Then he closed the safe and rolled the rug back over it as I screwed the stopper back onto the shaft of my peg leg.

We made it back onto the deck of the yacht and had just eased ourselves into the water when the sounds of male voices came up from below decks on the party boat. Gabriel untied the surfboard using the side of the yacht to shield him from view and managed to push off toward the front just as the two crewmen emerged. I ducked under the water and swam back toward shore.

When I finally came up for air, I was fifty feet away from the yacht and, I hoped, invisible in the inky water. I could just make out the outline of Gabriel, still pretty close to the boat, as he paddled toward shore north of where we'd gone in. Good. He'd be less likely to be spotted bowside, and I appreciated that he didn't put himself at risk just to escort me back to the beach.

The party boat chugged away from the yacht, and I sent a silent salute to Dallas and Darius for their masterful distraction of the two crewmen. Whatever the conversation had been below decks, it did the trick and didn't seem to have raised any suspicions. I looked forward to the debrief back in Chicago, when Dane Quimby was safely in jail and the targets had been removed from Gabriel's and my backs.

I swam hard, and thoughts of warming up against the naked body of my handsome man kept my brain occupied the whole, shivery way back. I didn't even flinch at the possessive I'd added to "handsome man," though I shied away from anything that smacked of the word "future." I was getting the idea that I might have to rethink that someday.

I paused at the edge of the lake to flip the fin up on my peg leg and wring out my hair, and I caught the barest flicker of motion in the trees near the lighthouse. Could Gabriel have made it to the beach and walked back already, or was Fiona waiting for us to report in?

We'd left towels folded on the beach, and I dried my face and then flipped my hair over to squeeze out as much water as I could. I had the towel draped around my shoulders when I stood upright, and a feeling of disquiet hit me squarely between the shoulder blades. I turned to see what was behind me, but the beach was empty. I wrapped the towel tightly around my shoulders and started a fast walk back to the protection of the lighthouse where I wouldn't feel so much like prey in someone's gunsights.

I stepped up to the deck and had just started to unzip my wetsuit in anticipation of warm, dry clothes when an unpleasantly familiar voice stopped me in my tracks.

"Well, look at the trash that just washed up on my shore."

[45]
SHANE

"I'd like to think I will die a heroic death, but it's more likely I'll trip over my dog and choke on a spoonful of Nutella." – Shane, P.I.

Dane Quimby emerged from the shadow of the building. He held a type of handgun that I couldn't name because I'd never bothered to learn the differences between them. The business end was pointed at me though, and his finger was on the trigger in a tired echo of our last encounter. I might have sighed at the predictability of it if the circumstances hadn't been so dire.

The other piece of unassailable information to hit my brain was the expression of satisfaction on Quimby's face. He was going to kill me, and he looked forward to doing it. Unfortunately, the photos I'd seen confirmed he was capable of it.

"Oh, don't let me stop you from stripping off the wetsuit. You were off to such a promising start," he said with a leer.

I swiftly zipped the suit closed and glared at him. "Put the gun down, Dane."

Statements like "what the actual fuck do you think you're doing?" and "why are you here?" surged through my brain, but I didn't really want to know the answers to those questions, nor did I want to provoke him to come up with them, so I crossed my arms in front of my chest to keep from shivering and glared at him.

"Yeah, no, I'm not going to do that," he said, as though he'd given it thought.

I *really* didn't like Dane Quimby, but when he'd accosted us in the park and gotten us arrested along with him, he'd been more annoying than chilling. Now his voice, his sneer, and the leering look in his eyes made my skin crawl.

His gaze roved over my body in a way that made me feel like I'd just been slimed. "Take it off," he jerked his head at the wetsuit.

"Yeah, no, I'm not going to do that," I retorted, but in a way that made it clear I hadn't even considered the possibility.

His eyes narrowed, and the sneer was replaced by a scowl. He took a step forward as he raised the gun level with my head. "You'll do what I say."

"Or what? You'll kill me?" I scoffed, with a ridiculous amount of bravado given the circumstances.

"You have no idea what I'm capable of," he snarled, taking another step closer. I had a solid five inches on him in height, but his gym-buff body probably weighed at least twenty pounds more than mine did, which would count in a tackle.

"I thought I did," I said, edging around so my back was to the lighthouse. It wasn't the best defensive position in which to put myself, but it would force Dane to turn his back to the beach, and I sincerely hoped that Gabriel was on it somewhere heading this way.

He snorted. "You don't know me. You don't know anything about me."

"I know you're in trouble, and you're trying to find a way out. I can help you, Dane." I had no intention of helping the jerk out of his troubles, but I was stalling for time.

"You mean like you helped yourself to my money?" He took

another step closer. The gun was close now, too close to miss a shot, but too far to grab.

"I don't have your money. Your wife hired me to catch you cheating on her – that's my job. I'm a P.I. who catches cheaters. She's the one who has your money. She took it and ran to Canada."

I really wasn't throwing Denise under the bus, because Dane was going to jail. I just wanted to stay alive long enough to see it happen. I promised myself a panty dance party when it did.

"You catch guys by fucking them? Is that it? You trap them into sleeping with you, and then their wives take them for everything they've got?" He was snarling like a pissed-off wolverine, and I half expected rabid mouth-froth. "Well, I didn't get to sample the goods before I got screwed, so I'm going to say it again. Take off the fucking wetsuit before I cut it off."

"With what? Your sharp tongue? You're not going to rape me, Dane. You're not a rapist. You're an asshole, but all the women you sleep with seem to want to sleep with you, so that just makes you an inconceivably lucky asshole."

"Why are you up here? What were you doing in the lake?" he growled.

He wasn't arguing for rape, so I had that going for me. But where the hell was Gabriel, and how did Van Hayden manage to lose Quimby in Chicago?

"Diving shipwrecks. It's my hobby," I said evenly as I tried to surreptitiously scan the beach for any sort of movement that could indicate the presence of an ally.

"You were on Karpov's boat." He was back to snarling, and I didn't appreciate that the gun was still aimed directly at my right eye.

"Who's Karpov?"

He waved the gun at me in a gesture designed to make me wet my pants. It didn't work. My pants were already wet, and I was getting properly cold. "Did you go out there to meet him? No, he wouldn't care about you. He likes pretty blond men."

"You mean like you?" I asked sweetly. It was a mistake, and I knew it the minute the words left my mouth. Toxic masculinity went hand-in-hand with homophobia, and I'd just poked the wolverine with a long, sharp stick.

He shifted his aim two inches to the right and pulled the trigger, and I felt splinters of wood embed themselves in my cheek even as the boom of gunfire rang in my ears.

"Next time, I won't miss."

"I don't think you did this time," I said, as I pulled an inch-long bit of wood out of my skin. "Shit." It hurt, and I was pissed, because it was going to leave a mark. "What do you want, Dane?"

"I want to know why you're here?"

Finally, I saw something move in the darkness behind Dane. It was all I could do not to exhale in relief. The question was, would Gabriel risk a tackle from behind, which meant crossing a driftwood-littered bit of beach in the dark, or would he call out a distraction so I could disarm Dane myself?

"You're about to be two-for-two, Quimby. Drop the gun," Gabriel called out as he stepped forward from the line of trees. I tensed, ready to disarm.

But Dane didn't swivel around like I'd expected him to. He hunched his shoulders and narrowed his gaze at me as he yelled to Gabriel. "If you were armed, I'd be dead by now."

"Perhaps," Gabriel said, still moving at the same, seemingly unconcerned pace. His gaze was fixed on Dane's shoulders, and despite his casual air, I knew Gabriel was watching for the slightest twitch that would give away Dane's next move.

"Did you know Karpov had photos?" I asked, mostly to keep him distracted so that Gabriel could get closer.

"I don't know what you're talking about." He ground the words out between his teeth, and it may have been my imagination, but I thought his finger tightened on the trigger reflexively.

"No? You don't strike me as the kind of guy who would let some dickhead stiff you for a job you were hired to do."

"He paid me to do the job. And then you stole the money from me." Dane was starting to breathe hard, maybe panicked, maybe nervous.

My eyes widened. "Oh! I get it now. Karpov paid you to kill a guy, and then he photographed it to keep you on a leash. The million dollars was the hit money. "

Dane's skin had gone pale and sweaty, and I seriously wondered if the guy was going to have an aneurysm.

"You've seen them." Dane was alarmingly unfocused, and Gabriel needed to get his butt up to the lighthouse a little faster.

"I've seen what?" If twisty conversation kept me alive for thirty more seconds, I would be a master of it.

"Karpov's pictures, damn you!"

"They're not Karpov's anymore." Maybe he wouldn't be so quick to shoot me if there was a chance I had hidden the proof somewhere.

"Give them to me!" He lunged at me, which I wasn't expecting, and tried to grab me by the wetsuit. He couldn't get a grip on the tight neoprene though, and I ducked out of his reach.

Then I accidentally kicked him in the nuts. Whoops.

Gabriel hurled the empty thumb drive case up onto the porch and was sprinting the last twenty feet. "Here are the photos!" he yelled as my brain saw everything play out in one split-second slow-motion moment. Dane turned to fire at me, but Gabriel suddenly became the bigger target. The moment the gun had moved past me on its trajectory toward Gabriel, I lunged forward. Dane reflexively fired, but forward momentum carried my shoulder into his solar plexus, and I plowed into him so hard we both went down in a tangle of limbs.

Gabriel tore Dane away from me with some weird superhero strength and flung him into the lighthouse wall. The thunk of skull hitting wood vibrated through the deck, and a moment later, Gabriel had Dane's gun. I was down, stunned from the impact and mentally checking my whole body for gunshots. Gabriel's eyes were doing the same, and I wanted to yell at him to keep them on Dane so the slippery little bastard didn't run away. But I didn't have enough breath to make a sound, and all I could do was stare up at him.

Footsteps pounded on the deck. Someone else had arrived, but Gabriel blocked my view when he dropped down next to me. He used both hands to check me for holes, and I finally managed to gasp breath back into my lungs.

"I'm not shot."

"That was point blank." Gabriel's voice came out in a choked whisper, and I registered that the look in his eyes wasn't anger, it was fear. Cold, naked fear. I shivered, and he picked me up as if I were made of porcelain and cuddled me to his chest protectively.

My gaze landed on Van standing over an unconscious or maybe dead Dane with a gun pointed at his head.

"Van's here," I wheezed, stating the obvious. I shouldn't have, because Gabriel's expression darkened.

"Where the hell was he when Quimby got here?" He turned to glare at Van. "How could the bastard leave Chicago without you right on his tail?" Gabriel's voice was pitched to carry, and I pulled away to sit up.

"Don't—" I reached a hand out, but Gabriel was already on his feet.

"You had one bloody job! One job. Keep this knob away from her!"

Presumably Dane Quimby was the knob, and I was *her*, and with that word, I'd just been demoted from full partner to something considerably less qualified.

"Hey—" I began, but Gabriel interrupted me with his continued tirade.

"He's a bloody moron being tailed by the best in the business, and yet here he is with a gun." He took a menacing step toward Quimby, and I thought he was going to kick him, but instead, he spun to face me. "And you—" He seemed to struggle to find the words to fit the rage. "You threw yourself at a man with a gun. Of all the reckless ... careless ... *stupid* things to do!"

That was enough. I got to my feet and looked at Van, who was thin-lipped with his own anger. "He dead?" I indicated Quimby slumped on the ground.

Van shook his head grimly. "Knocked out."

Good thing, because the mood I was in, I might have bashed him over the head with something hard and spiked and maybe dipped in poison.

I turned to Gabriel. "I'm cold and I'm going to change." I didn't wait for a response, and he didn't give me one.

I squared my shoulders and walked away before the first tear fell.

[46]
GABRIEL

"Everything you want is on the other side of fear." – Miri Eze

---

Some part of my brain registered that Shane was angry, but it seemed a pale thing in comparison to the fear that still gripped me tightly in its fists. I was so relieved to see her get up and walk away – whole and undamaged, and away from the bastard who had *shot at her* – that I felt my knees go weak.

I had to stay upright and capable and strong. I needed to finish this and see Shane home safely, with no further threat to her from the man who had attempted to kill her. I should have felt the cold through my wetsuit, but nothing surpassed the chill of fear that remained in my blood at the sight of the gun aimed at the woman I loved.

Jesus. I loved her.

It was hard to breathe, and I must have looked as shaken as I felt, because Van's angry expression shifted into something less hostile.

"You alright, man?"

"I'll be better when this maggot is behind bars." I barely restrained myself from kicking the unconscious man at my feet, and I gripped the strap of the wet bag that was still slung across my chest as a gesture of control.

"Then we better do it right. Fiona called Quinn so he could get the feds out here. No point in risking another good-ol'-boy catch and release with this one. She's behind the lighthouse as back-up in case this one got past me again, but your girl did a good job taking him down."

"She almost got shot."

"Yeah, she did. And that's on me. The little prick ducked me on the L, and when I couldn't find him, we decided to put me on the two of you, just in case. Turns out you both did just fine on your own, but for what it's worth, I'll take the hit if you want to throw a punch."

I did, more than I cared to admit, but decided the cost to my hand would be greater than the satisfaction was worth.

"Boys are so strange," Fiona said as she came around the corner, holstering her gun behind her.

I nodded to her. "Thank you for your back-up."

She indicated Quimby's inert body. "Anyone check for a pulse?"

"He's breathing," Van said. "Although he hit the wall so hard I thought you might have broken his neck," he finished to me.

"A not-insubstantial part of me wishes I had," I groused. "I'm wet and cold, and I need to find Shane."

Fiona cocked an eyebrow at me. "She wanted to get home to her dog, so I gave her my keys, which means I'll need to ride with one of you. She said she'd come in to give her report in the morning."

I felt hollow at Fiona's words, and I wasn't sure if it was because of the words themselves or the expression of sympathy that accompanied them. I looked at Van to distract myself from the feeling of something lost.

"Do you need Fiona to ride in the car with you?" I asked him.

"Nah, I'll truss him up with zip ties and throw him in the back seat."

"Then I'll go with you," Fiona said to me.

I nodded my thanks. The hollowness was expanding rapidly, and it threatened to pull me under. "I'll just retrieve your husband's surfboard from the beach and change my clothes. Then I'll be back to help carry the trash out."

Van smirked. "Maybe we'll accidentally drop him a couple times on the way."

[47]

SHANE

"A lot of people make small mistakes. Why not go big and completely fuck it up?" – Dan O'Malley

---

I managed to get a couple hours of sleep in my own bed before my alarm woke me. I'd been too tired to change the sheets when I got home, so Gabriel's warm, spicy scent filled my nostrils every time I turned toward the pillow he'd slept on, and alternating waves of sadness and desire washed over me when I realized why my bed smelled so good.

The need to escape my bed made me drag my sorry carcass out of the sheets and into the shower, but that wasn't any better. Another wave of longing and lust hit me as I washed my hair, bracing myself against the walls by my elbows and wishing it were Gabriel's hands that held me up.

I didn't let myself go down that path, because frankly, I didn't have the energy to be objective. My heart hurt and my head ached, and the only cures that made sense were my dog and coffee, in that order. I finished the shower and went looking for Oscar, but only found a note by the coffee maker telling me that Jorge had taken my hound for a long run. I looked at the time and realized it was still early enough that if I was quick, I could give my report to the bosses at Cipher before the other agents on the team made it in.

To the casual observer, I was just some chick in jeans, boots, and a sport bike jacket, but I knew I'd armored up in "don't mess with me" clothes. No make-up, no coffee, wet hair tied back in a bun, and an all-black outfit. No one met my eyes on the L, and even the woman behind the desk at Cipher barely questioned the ID badge in my hand.

I went straight to Quinn Sullivan's office. The door was open, and I put my badge on his desk when he waved me in.

"The FBI is handling the capital case against Quimby," he said with barely a glance at my ID.

"Why? Murder is the state's jurisdiction."

"The victim was a federal judge," he said grimly.

Actually, everything about the owner of Cipher Security was grim and foreboding, so it was probably just normal speech for him.

I pulled the thumb drives out of my pocket and put them on the desk next to my badge. "These were in Karpov's safe with the photos."

"What's on them?" he asked as he grabbed one and inserted it into his laptop.

"I don't know."

He looked up at me, clearly surprised. I maintained a carefully neutral expression as I met his gaze, and the silence between us became a thing you could see hanging in the air.

Finally, he nodded – just once – as though I'd just confirmed something for him. He then reached into his desk drawer and pulled out a sealed envelope, which he placed next to my badge.

"You did good work, and there's an offer in there. It's a standing one."

I made no move to take it. "Thank you. Will you please thank the team for me? They were all true professionals, and I am honored to have worked with them."

The thumb drive menu popped up on Quinn's laptop, but he held my gaze for a long moment before he finally stood and held out his hand to shake mine.

"Stop by Alex's office on your way out, if you would?" I nodded wordlessly, and he sat and turned toward the computer as I left his office.

I fully intended to press the lobby button on the elevator, but my finger accidentally pressed the button for the fourth floor. I didn't work for Quinn Sullivan anymore, and I certainly didn't want to see anyone else I'd worked with at Cipher, but somehow my feet took me to Alex's office, and my hand knocked on the door.

"Come," a voice directed.

I opened the door to discover Alex at his desk working on three computers simultaneously while his wife, Sandra, sat on the edge of it flipping through a file. She looked up, and her megawatt smile fairly blinded me.

"Shane!" She hopped off the desk and threw her arms around me for the kind of hug that doesn't allow quick pats on the back. I surrendered to the inevitability of it and hugged her back. "You don't knit, do you?" she asked after she finally let me go.

I must have looked as baffled by her question as I felt, because she laughed. "It's either join my knitting group, or we're going to have to make a standing date for panty dance parties, because I have people you need to meet."

I stared at her and managed to get an incoherent sound out before I finally tore my gaze away to find Alex's eyes laughing at me. Not his mouth or any other part of his face, mind you, just his eyes.

"Quinn said you wanted to talk to me?" I asked him, mostly so I could think of something more than "um" to say to Sandra's outrageous invitation.

"I do?"

Sandra's gaze sharpened on me, and she leapt in before I could respond. "*I* do." She shot Alex an incomprehensible look, to which he just shrugged. She took me by the arm and walked me out of his office.

Sandra hooked her arm through mine, and I was vaguely uncomfortable to be so close to this woman, but she was a force of nature against whom I felt powerless.

"What happened?" she asked, when she finally directed me into an open conference room. "Wait," she said. She poured a mug of coffee from the pot that sat half-full on the sideboard, considered me for a second as she reached for the sugar, then shook her head and handed the black coffee to me. "You need this first."

"How did you know?" I took a sip of the slightly stale, still hot coffee, and almost sighed.

"That something happened, or that you needed coffee? Actually, the answer is the same. You look tired, fierce, and sad, in that order. Plus, Alex told me about what you and Gabriel and the team were up to last night, and I heard that you guys got your man. But you're not celebrating the victory, so something went wrong. Also, Alex didn't ask to see you, but Quinn knew I was here, which must be why he sent you up. So, spill. What happened?"

Sandra hadn't taken a visible breath through all of that, and it took me a moment to realize it was my turn to speak.

The problem was that I didn't know what to say.

She poured herself a cup of coffee and refilled mine, silent and watchful the whole time. Then she leaned against the conference table, and her silence shifted from something that allowed speech to something that invited and welcomed it. I had no idea what she'd done, but the dam on my words finally broke.

"Apparently I'm reckless, careless, and stupid. I'm not an equal partner, and I'm not capable enough to do the job." It was hard to force the words out past my constricted throat, but I managed somehow.

"Did someone say that out loud, or did you hear it in your head?" Sandra's tone was utterly devoid of judgment – a fact I found comforting.

"It was out loud, in front of other people." My own voice sounded flat in my ears.

"What happened the moment before the words were said?" Sandra didn't take her eyes off me, even though it was just a casual glance across a steamy coffee.

"I tackled Quimby as he shot at me."

One eyebrow arched up. "So, you're not incapable."

The anger that had warred with the emptiness in the pit of my stomach the whole drive home came back in a rush. "Clearly not."

"Was anyone hurt?" she asked with the same casualness that was in her gaze.

"Just the perp. Gabriel threw him into a wall and knocked him unconscious."

"As he was presumably calling you reckless and careless?"

"And stupid," I said, swallowing the rage that came up with the word.

"Are you stupid?" she asked, her eyebrow still raised.

"No."

"So," she said, "not stupid, and not incapable."

"No." I tried not to sound like a petulant child, but Sandra didn't seem to care if I did.

"In my experience, Shane, people tend to hurl words like this when they're either angry or afraid."

"Not always," I countered, and that eyebrow went right back up.

"Really? Someone rational said you were stupid?"

I mentally cringed away from the memory of that voice, and I must have flinched because Sandra put a hand on my arm. She searched my face with worried eyes, and I finally nodded.

"My mom."

"Oh, Shane," she exhaled, right before she pulled me into her arms for another hug. This one should have been much more awkward than it actually felt, but it wasn't, and I let myself relax a tiny bit.

She finally pulled back so she could look me in the eyes, but she continued to hold one of my hands. "We're taught that parents are the ones we're supposed to trust to protect us, and if they do their jobs right, we get to learn self-reliance in a safe and secure environment. But when they screw up – and boy, do they screw up – parental betrayal is possibly the worst thing a person can ever go through. When the person you trust most in the world tells you you're shit, you either believe them, or you break."

I couldn't find my words and could barely find my breath. It was stuttery and thin, and I felt like the glass coating I'd used to protect myself was splintering.

"You didn't break," Sandra said softly.

I shook my head.

"She lied to you, Shane. Your mother lied."

The sobs bunched up in my throat and got trapped there along with my voice, so I just nodded and looked down at my hands still clutching the coffee mug. They were good hands – strong, with long fingers and short nails. Capable hands that could find things other people overlooked. They were weapons and tools, and I pictured them running through my dog's fur, scratching his ears, making him go glassy-eyed with bliss.

And then I remembered them clutching Gabriel's shirt, running under it along the smooth skin of his back. I pictured my fingers caressing his jaw, smoothing the collar of his jacket, entwined with his, and I closed my eyes.

"Whatever words get said in the heat of anger, or cold fear, or even calm conversation, it is your choice to believe them, and your choice to give them meaning. Because you know what? They are just words, and the only power words have over us is the power we give them." Sandra's voice soothed the jagged edges of my heart, and her tone was comfortable and straightforward, like what she said was real and true and just common sense.

"Honestly, sometimes people are so strange," she continued. "We have trouble believing the good things people say – how smart, or interesting, or remarkable we are – but we have no trouble totally owning the bad stuff. If I'm going to give words any power at all, I'm going to make damn sure it's the ones that light me up like a sunrise, you know?"

That elicited a huff of laughter from me, and I could finally look up and meet her eyes. "How's this for sunshine? You're a kind and generous person, clearly excellent at your job, and you have the kind of presence that brightens any room you walk into. The only thing that makes you human at all is your questionable taste in husbands."

She laughed out loud and kissed my cheek. "He would be delighted that you agree with him. On all counts."

Sparky was bent over a circuit board when I stepped out of the freight elevator into his loft. He looked up at me and blinked. "How'd the dive leg work?"

"Like a dream. My favorite part was the waterproof container inside the shaft."

"Did you get your bad guy?"

"Yeah."

He wore an odd expression as he studied me. "You lost something," he finally said. "You're like Rocket after Groot died, like your spark dimmed."

I tried for a smirk that may have come out more like a grimace. "I've never been sparky – that's you."

"Not true," he said, focusing his eyes, but not his attention, back on the circuit board. "You spark like a fricking transformer around your hunky partner."

I scoffed. "He'd be flattered to know you think he's hunky."

Sparky's mouth quirked in a half-smile. "I wear hot pink Crocs and I cry at happy endings. I'm not afraid to admit when guys are hunky."

"Well, he's not my partner anymore, because it was a one-time consulting gig."

Sparky sat up and put down his tools. He regarded me for a long moment before he finally spoke. "You know how Gamora is all badass and shut down because Thanos tortured her and used his affection and attention as a weapon?"

"*Guardians of the Galaxy*?" I asked.

"Yeah. And you know how Star-Lord doesn't let her put him off – he just wears her down by sticking by her, no matter how thick her emotional walls are?"

"What's your point, Spark?"

"Dude, you're Gamora. And that hunky bastard is your Star-Lord, whether you admit it or not. And here's the deal. Star-Lord is the only one who can save Gamora from herself, because without him making her laugh and sticking by her no matter how tough and crusty she gets, she'd be a bitter assassin with no life and no fun."

"You're kind of a jerk, you know that?" I said, not really kidding.

"If by jerk you mean I love you enough to call you on your crap, then yeah, I'll own that."

He bent over his circuit board again, but then straightened to meet my eyes before I could turn to leave. "Here's the thing. Characters who don't change and grow with each life experience turn into caricatures. They're cardboard cutouts of people who eventually become boring because they're predictable. But to grow you need to take risks, and this thing with the hunkster was the first real risk I've seen you take in a long time. Gamora takes risks, no matter how scared she is, and that's what makes her interesting. Be Gamora, Shane. Take the risk."

It was a long time before I could lift my eyes to meet his, and thankfully, he'd gone back to work on the circuit board when I did.

"We're going to need to schedule a photo shoot for all the legs you want me to model. I didn't have time to take any shots while I was working," I finally said.

"You know I'm going to dress you up and put you in action poses like the Bionic Woman, right?" Sparky actually said that with a straight face.

"I'm told I look more like Jaclyn Smith than Lindsay Wagner," I said carefully.

At that, my friend looked up with a grin of pure glee. "Yes! I can totally see a whole photo series of you dressed as 1970s action heroines! All of Charlie's Angels, the Bionic Woman, and oh yeah, definitely Wonder Woman too." Sparky started posing with his hands on his hips, in a semi-crouch with an imaginary gun in the air, and in a slow-motion run, complete with a Bionic Woman sound effect.

The laughter inspired by my ridiculous friend splintered another fragment of the hard shell in which I'd encased myself, and I reminded myself how very lucky I was.

[48]
GABRIEL

"Behind every great man is a woman rolling her eyes." – Fiona Archer

---

The drive back to Chicago with Fiona was enlightening.

By the time I dropped her off at the apartment she shared with her husband and three kids, I felt like I'd just been adopted by an older sister. She invited me up to meet her husband, Greg, who was sprawled on the sofa watching YouTube videos about string theory with their toddler. The two older kids were at school, but evidence of their brilliance was all around the apartment, from the handwritten music on the piano to the drawings of fantastical weapons I was told were designed for the family's various D&D characters.

At his daughter's demand, Greg handed the little girl with dandelion hair to her mother, who promptly whisked her away for a hand and face wash.

"You're the blighter Fi found in Nigeria," he said in an accent that spoke of means, a good school, and lots of travel.

I smiled at that and held out my hand. "I'm that blighter. It's nice to finally meet you, Greg. You're a bit of a legend among the Cipher crew."

He winced. "I shudder to think." He hit the button on the electric tea kettle. "Coffee or tea?"

"Actually, I need to get in to the office."

"Why? They'll have called in a report." Greg spooned Earl Grey into an Alice in Wonderland teapot and arranged three mugs on a tray. He dropped two sugar cubes in one mug, four in another, and then looked up at me questioningly.

I shook my head. "I have unfinished business."

Fiona re-entered the kitchen. "There's groveling to be done." She kissed her husband with enthusiasm, and he held her tightly, uncaring that they had an audience.

Greg spoke between her kisses. "Whatever groveling must be done, my love, I'll do on my knees in front of you, worshipping your body as befits the goddess you are."

Fiona laughed. "I'm sure I'll find something for you to grovel about, but I was talking about Gabriel."

Greg shot me a scowl. "He's not allowed to grovel to you unless he does it from across the room."

Fiona poked him, and he leapt back in protest. She poured the boiling water into the teapot with a smirk. "Like many males of the species, his inner caveman has no concept of how condescending and infuriating his words may have sounded to the capable woman he loves."

Greg shot me a sympathetic look full of "uh oh," and I winced back.

"So," she continued, "I took it upon myself to translate his words into something he could understand."

"Something properly mortifying and painful, no doubt." Greg had clearly been on the receiving end of such a conversation.

"Shockingly so," I agreed. I still felt hollow with regret at the words I barely remembered saying, but which Fiona had recounted for me with horrifying detail.

"And did she also educate you in the finer points of a successful grovel?" Greg asked as he wrapped his arms around his wife's waist and nuzzled her hair.

"My mother and grandmother made sure my education in proper apologies was complete, though my sister would tell you I'm out of practice."

"You've been alone too long. Apologies are what inevitably happen when you allow people to matter to you." Greg nibbled Fiona's ear. "Consequently, I am masterful at them." He grinned and murmured into her neck. "Hmm, what transgression can I make up to you today?"

Fiona shook her head playfully. "I'm sure you'll think of something."

"Ah well, Gabriel had best get to work then," Greg said as he kissed her collarbones. She pulled away with a laugh.

"We're not sending him away without tea," she said, even as he drew her back into his arms.

"He doesn't want any. He's inspired by our perfect relationship to go repair his own," Greg murmured.

"Actually, he's not wrong. Fiona, thank you for setting me straight, and I look forward to working together again. Greg, it's good to finally meet the legend in person, and see that your reputation is totally undeserved."

Greg barked a laugh and sent me off with a wave. They were engaged in a tickle fight when I left the apartment, and it wasn't until I was back in my car that the smile on my face finally faded.

O'Malley informed me that Shane had come and gone, but suggested that I do a proper debrief with himself and Sullivan before they sent me home for the day. I did as he suggested, despite my every instinct demanding to see Shane as soon as possible, and it was lunchtime when I finally left the Cipher building.

I texted Shane's mobile several times and called twice, but I received no answer to any of my attempts to reach her. I even stopped at her apartment on my way to my own, but there was no answer to my knock and no barking dog to warn me away. I thought she might be out running, so the park was my next stop as soon as I changed my shoes.

I was surprised to find my apartment unlocked, and then delighted to find a giant hairy beast barreling toward me as I entered the sitting room.

I braced myself for impact and then dropped to one knee to ruffle Oscar's fur while looking around the room for his mistress. There was no sign of her.

I gave Oscar another enthusiastic scratch and then set off to find her. She was not in my bed, sadly, though that would likely have been far too easy. Instead, she was sitting on the sill of the open window that overlooked the central courtyard from the bedroom. Her eyes were closed as the sun shone on her face, and I was forcibly reminded that this was a California girl who transplanted herself to a city known more for its cold wind than warm sunshine.

Her eyes opened and found mine as I knelt by her knee and took her hand. "I am so sorry. I said unforgivable things to you, and I am appalled that those words came out of my mouth."

Her expression didn't change, but she touched my face gently. "I need to tell you a story," she said finally. My breath caught. Was this the part where she tells me she's finished, or was there a chance her natural instinct to leave difficult situations could be overridden?

She inhaled, as though bracing herself, and I tried not to expect the worst. "My name is Samantha Hane," she said quietly.

I could feel how much it cost her to say the name out loud, but I allowed myself a glimmer of hope. She wouldn't trust me with her real name if she were planning to leave me, would she? I settled myself next to her on the window sill, but I didn't relinquish her hand, and she let me trace the outline of her knuckles with a light touch.

"My dad used to call me Sam, which fit better than Samantha ever did. And after he died—" Her voice caught in her throat, and I lifted her hand to kiss the back of it. She inhaled, and her voice got stronger.

"I had just started dating Mitch when my dad and brother died, so he and I got pretty close in that way tragedies force people to. My mom was a wreck, and there were a lot of nights Mitch and I made dinner for her, did laundry, wrote checks for bills that she'd forgotten to pay, and things like that. I basically became a grown-up, and to his credit, Mitch stood next to me for a lot of that time."

Shane's voice had a faraway quality to it, as if she were outside herself watching the film version of her past. Her eyes had drifted back out to the view from the window.

"When I got into college in Santa Barbara, I wanted to leave everything behind me, including Mitch, and go back to being eighteen instead of the adult I'd had to be for my mom. I wanted to go to parties and dance clubs, and flirt with guys, and giggle with girlfriends, but Mitch didn't want to break up. He convinced me that we could stay together, even if we only saw each other on breaks and during the summer. I agreed because I didn't have a really compelling reason not to."

I studied Shane as she spoke. Her face was devoid of make-up, and her hair was tied back in some sort of messy knot. Freckles dotted the skin on her cheekbones and across her nose, and tiny gold hoop earrings glinted at her earlobes. Her eyes looked tired, and her posture almost seemed resigned, as though there was an inevitable outcome to the story.

Then her voice lost whatever spark it had held. "The summer after my freshman year in college, I was nineteen and full of plans to backpack around Europe with some friends from school. I went home for two weeks to earn a little traveling cash at my old waitressing job, and one night Mitch picked me up after work in a 1966 Mustang he'd bought to restore. He didn't want me to go on my trip and was trying to talk me into staying home and spending the summer with him. I was adamant that I was going, which pissed him off, so when the engine sputtered to a stop, he told me to get out and push while he steered it off the road to a dirt lot."

I was indignant on her behalf but didn't say so out loud because her voice sounded so flat, as if every word cost something to say. I was afraid to break the momentum.

"I heard the car come up behind us, but we were already heading down into the lot, and the Mustang was starting to pick up a little speed on the slope. I ran behind it and was just going to veer off to let it go when the other car rear-ended the Mustang and sandwiched me between the two bumpers. Mitch must have hit the brakes reflexively, because my right leg was crushed instantly. The other driver was drunk, and the cops had been right behind him. One of the officers was a trained medic, which is why I didn't bleed out on the trunk of Mitch's car, but all of them – the cops, the drunk, and Mitch – were so full of guilt about what happened ..." Her voice trailed off, and a shudder went up her spine at a memory she didn't want to relive.

"Guilt is why Mitch asked me to marry him when I was still in the hospital recovering. I didn't want to say yes, but he'd been so good to my mom, and she almost completely lost it when another drunk driver almost took out what was left of her family." Shane scoffed without humor, and she finally met my eyes.

"It took six months of really hard work before I could go back to college, and everything I've done since then has been about proving I am more than just a missing limb, which was all I could see in Mitch's eyes when he looked at me." She inhaled a shaky breath. "Worse, though, was the expression on his face whenever he saw the stump of my leg."

I wanted to kill the man for having made this extraordinary woman feel anything less than beautiful and whole. She must have seen something of my thoughts on my face, because she allowed a tiny smile. I kissed her knuckles and would have spoken, but she wasn't finished.

"I need to tell you all of it, so you understand."

My brain, which had foolishly begun to hope the revelations were a sign she had forgiven me, protested loudly. So I understood what? Why she was leaving me?

"The fact that I stayed with Mitch for six months after I walked in on him with another woman was partly because of something my mother said." Shane's voice shifted to parrot her mother. "Samantha, no one else will ever know what you were like before the accident. Mitch is the only man who will ever see you as the athletic girl in a bikini you used to be."

There was disappointment and perhaps scorn in the voice she used to recall her mother's words. No wonder she hated the name Samantha. Shane's grip had tightened on my hand, but she was still deep in her memories of her mother as she continued speaking.

"She said I was stupid to leave Mitch because there'd never be anyone else who would understand what I'd gone through." She met my appalled gaze. "I was stupid, she said. He said it too. Six months after I'd walked in on him with someone else, he accused me of having an affair with a guy I worked with. He said I was stupid if I thought the guy – his name was Todd, and he was a good friend of mine – would ever have sex with me with the lights on, because no guy could ever keep a hard-on with my stump staring him in the face."

"Christ," I whispered as I pulled Shane to my chest, as if I could shield her from the hateful words all those years ago.

I was shaking with the kind of protective rage that had gotten me in trouble with her in the first place. I took several deep breaths to calm down and order my thoughts. Shane let me hold her while I did so, and the feeling of her against my heartbeat grounded me.

I spoke into her hair. "If he were standing here right now, he'd be dead."

I could feel her smile. "I would have castrated him already, so he'd beg you to kill him."

I pulled back so I could see her face, and I searched her eyes for the depth of pain in them. "Why didn't you punish him then? Why did you take all those horrific words with you when you left?"

She inhaled deeply as she thought about her answer. "Sandra said something today that unpacked it for me. She said that when my mother called me stupid, I either had to believe her or break. I was always too strong to break – I didn't when my dad and brother died, and I didn't when I lost my leg. But believing her meant I couldn't write him off as an asshole, because by her words, he was my only shot at happiness."

I closed my eyes against the truth that hit me. "I used the word 'stupid,' didn't I?"

"Yeah." She looked away, and I cupped her face in my hands so she would meet my eyes.

"You are the smartest, bravest, strongest woman I know. The only stupidity in the room was mine at letting my fear for you overrule my experience of your calm, capable grace under pressure." I tried to smooth away the tightness around her eyes with my thumbs, and perhaps she believed me a little bit, because she continued to hold my gaze.

Shane spoke quietly, but with confidence. "You said you have to run things through a filter before you ask me certain questions, so I don't clam up or shut down. Last night I felt like I had to filter the words you said through my understanding of the things you've gone through so I didn't take them personally. That's a lot of second-guessing that I don't want either of us to have to do."

"Neither do I." I brushed a piece of hair back from her face and studied her eyes. I started to say something else, but she got there first.

"I've done a pretty big number on myself the last few years, and some of those things have become habits. They might take a little time to break, but if you're willing to hang in there for a bit—"

I kissed her. I should have waited until she finished speaking, but all I could see was her mouth saying "yes."

I finally stopped kissing her so I could see her eyes. "I like the name you chose for yourself. Shane. It's strong, and soft, and mysterious, and alive – just as you are."

She smiled, and I took a breath for courage.

"I want you." I said, meaning it to depths of my soul. "I want you to be the first person I speak to every morning, and the last one every night. I want to kiss you, and touch you, and make love to you, and I want to laugh, and dream, and plan with you. I'll probably make mistakes, I'll be afraid for your safety, and I'll be annoyed that I can't do anything better than you except pee standing up, but I'll grovel for all of it if only for the make-up sex and the chance to become a better person in your eyes."

She smiled at "make-up sex," and I exhaled.

We men are simple creatures.

She took my hands in hers and leaned back against the window frame. "In my head, you've had one foot out the door, and I've been protecting myself from that the whole time."

I scoffed. "In my head, something was going to happen to you that I couldn't prevent, and I've been protecting myself from that the entire time."

"I'll survive whatever happens to me, Gabriel."

"I don't leave the people I love, Shane."

[49]
GABRIEL

"Falling kisses are the ones that whisper like snowfall in a great forest, filling the silent spaces with perfection. They make you feel as though you are the only two people in the whole world who understand." – Miri Eze

---

Shane swallowed visibly and stared, as if waiting for me to take back the words. Instead, I kissed her hand, and then I stood.

"Wait here," I said. "I'll be right back."

I could feel her eyes on my back as I went into the sitting room and printed the e-mail I'd received from the university that morning.

I stopped to scratch Oscar behind the ears, then returned to the bedroom to find Shane still sitting on the window sill, again facing the sun with her eyes closed. "You miss California," I said with no question mark in my tone.

She nodded, eyes still closed. "I miss the sunshine. I miss the mountains and the ocean, and occasionally, very occasionally, I miss my mom." She turned to look at me. "Seeing you with your family makes me realize what I've missed."

"My mum has always been a firm believer in 'the more, the merrier' around her table."

She smiled, and it lit the dark places in my soul to see it. I held my hand out to her. "Come." I led her over to the bed I hadn't slept in for two days. "Lie down and close your eyes."

She raised an eyebrow with a smirk. "Moving pretty fast, aren't you, Eze?"

I grinned. "Not nearly as fast as I'd like. No, I want you to imagine something, but you need to close your eyes."

She didn't hesitate then – she kicked off her low boots and lay back on the coverlet. She ran her hand across the soft sateen. "Nice." It was a Moorish pattern in jewel tones I'd picked up when I got to Chicago.

"It suits my story."

"Now I'm curious." She settled herself on the side of the bed I'd already begun thinking of as hers and closed her eyes. I sat next to her and just barely resisted reaching a hand out to touch her – any part of her would have been fine, really. I just wanted the contact.

"Okay, now picture this. You're in prison—" Her eyes flew open and she scowled. "No, not you, sorry. A woman is in prison in St. Jago de la Vega, Jamaica. The year is 1720, and it's November."

Her scowl turned speculative as she looked at the printed paper in my hand, but I pulled it to my chest, out of view, so she settled back and closed her eyes. "Okay. Prison in Jamaica, 1720. Got it."

"The man she loves has just been sentenced to hang by the neck until dead, and she's furious at him for letting them get caught," I continued.

She cracked an eyelid to squint at me. "1720, Jamaica, sentenced to hang ... for piracy?"

I smiled. "You know your history."

"I used to play Pirates and Privateers with my brother and his friends. I was the Pirate Queen and they were her majesty's privateers. Due to my superior size and fighting skills, the pirates always won."

"Well, then, you'll find this story rather fascinating," I said, grinning as she sat up to face me. "Not going to pretend anymore?"

"I don't need to. My imagination is already fully engaged. Tell me the story." She pulled her left leg in front of her and then tugged the right leg of her trousers up to detach her prosthetic, which she dropped to the ground beside the bed. Then she sat cross-legged on the bed facing me with wide, intrigued eyes.

I continued. "The woman receives a letter from the man, presumably smuggled to her by a prison guard. It's all about how it wasn't supposed to go down like it did, and how they screwed him over when they captured him—"

She snorted, "In that language."

"In flowery eighteenth-century language that requires copious amounts of translation, yes."

"Okay, go on." She was grinning, and I loved that I could make her smile.

"Apparently, he had made a deal with the English when they captured his ship that he would go quietly if they gave her clemency."

"And yet she sat in prison." Shane was a step ahead of my story. "Which meant she was a pirate too!" She sat silent for a moment, calculating, and then turned her gaze back to me. "Anne Bonny and Mary Read were the only two female pirates I know of who were in the Caribbean in the 1700s, and Anne was either the lover or the wife of Captain Jack Rackham, who was captured and hung in Jamaica."

I was impressed. "Damn. You should have been the one to open the letter."

"What letter? What are you talking about?"

I grinned at her. "The letter you found in the secret compartment of my nana's antique secretary." I showed her the printed e-mail. "I got this from the head of the History Department at the University of Chicago."

She took the paper and scanned the contents before looking up at me in wonder. "They think the letter is from Rackham to Anne Bonny?"

I held my hand out for the paper. "May I?"

She handed it to me, and I found the passage I wanted to read out loud. *"I thought to give you the chance to have our child in freedom, where she'd grow capable and strong and beautiful like her mother.*

But in protecting you I failed you, for I know now that by your side I would have died with my love or escaped with you to spend our days together in freedom. I know your strength but trusted not my own to see you hurt or killed beside me, and for that I will pay with my life and your liberty. The cost of my fear was too high, my love. Forgive me my failings, and pray love our child in spite of her father's thin blood."

I looked up to see her eyes shining at me. "The historian who translated it took some liberties and modernized the language for me, since I'm not a scholar, but it landed a solid punch on me when I read it."

She exhaled softly and whispered, "Wow."

"It's dated November 16, 1720, and is addressed to 'Bonn' and signed by 'John.' A simple Google search on the date gave the historians their starting point, and from there, I gather it was fairly easy to put the pieces together. They'd like to study Nana's secretary, as there are no records of what happened to Anne Bonny after she was granted a stay of execution, but there are theories that she traveled to Cuba or to the Carolinas after her baby was born. In any case, she was likely aboard a ship at some point, and possibly hid the letter in the secretary herself."

"Can we see the letter?" Shane asked, a little breathlessly.

"It's still ours until we gift it."

She frowned. "Ours?"

"I've been opening that drawer for more than twenty years, and I never found it. It's as much your discovery as it is mine."

She got up on her knees and pushed me over so I lay back on the bed, then crawled over me until she was looking down at my face. "You're my discovery. It just took me a while to believe that what I found could be mine."

She kissed me then, with lips so soft and gentle they whispered against me. I felt the kiss settle on my skin and all around us like the softest, whitest snow, and the whispered promise of it filled me with a peace so pure and clear that I finally understood.

"A falling kiss," I murmured against her mouth, and I felt her lips smile next to mine.

After a delicious kiss that lasted several lifetimes, Shane sat back and regarded me. "I'm going to say this out loud, and it's really hard because my brain has been willing you to know exactly what I want without me saying it."

I sat up suddenly. "Say it. Because I want things that I'm holding back too."

She exhaled with a little nervous smile. "Okay," she closed her eyes with a wince, like she couldn't believe she was saying it. "You know what Mitch said about my leg."

I scowled. "And I want to beat the shit out of him for it."

She looked away. "I'm actually trying not to freak out about whether you think my stump is gross."

I must have been staring, open-mouthed, for an eternity, because she finally squared her shoulders and met my gaze. And when she saw the shock in my expression, something in her seemed to relax fractionally. I finally found words that made sense from among the jumble of outraged protestations in my brain.

"I understand that your confidence took a big hit from that asshole whose name need not be mentioned again unless it's to read his death notice. However –" I made sure she was looking right in my eyes as I said it, so she'd know I really meant it. "I think you're stunning, and amazing, and outrageously sexy, and I intend to worship every inch of you – with my mouth if possible, and certainly other parts." She giggled quietly, and I pulled her to me and kissed her hair.

"When I stepped into the shower with you up in Northport," I continued solemnly, "it took all the self-control I possessed not to roam every inch of your body with my hands, my lips, my tongue—" My voice sounded ragged in my own ears, and I throbbed with a primal need to be inside of her.

"I want you, Shane. I want to know every inch of you, and there isn't a part of you that doesn't turn me on. Your scars are beautiful because they mean you're alive, and when I kiss them it'll be in reverence for what you've survived and who you've become because of them."

She looked up at me and I kissed her hard, the way I'd been

needing to, and it fueled the hunger for her that had settled in and become part of me.

"What were you holding back?" she asked, when she could finally breathe.

"This," I said, kissing her fiercely again. "I can do soft and gentle – I'm actually a fairly gentle guy." She chuckled at that. "But I'm not feeling very gentle at the moment. I—" I struggled to find the word. "I crave you. You're like the air when I'm underwater, or like fire when I'm frostbitten. I need to smell your hair, taste your skin, feel the weight of your body on mine. I am so fucking *hungry* for you..." I groaned and rolled her under me. Her hands clutched at my back, and I reveled in the strength of her fingers. She wrapped her legs around my hips and pulled me in to press against her. I ground myself into her heat and was suddenly desperate to lose the layers of fabric between us.

I lifted myself off her and peeled my t-shirt over my head. Her hands went to my stomach, and her touch sent a lightning bolt of sensation straight through me. Then she pulled her own t-shirt off, and my eyes devoured every inch of her body as she revealed it. Her tiny bralette was simple cotton with thin straps, and I pulled it off over her head.

Shane's skin had the golden leftovers of sun, but no tan lines, and the image of her naked on a tropical beach filled my brain. She pulled me down to her so my chest met her breasts, and my stomach met her hip bones.

My hands roamed her body as we kissed, and I explored every plain, every hill, and every valley of the landscape that was this gorgeous woman.

She reached for the button on my jeans, and I helped her open them. I broke our kiss long enough to pull them off, and she tugged on the waistband of my boxer briefs. "Those too," she gasped, as my tongue found her nipple. She slid the briefs down, and then her hands trailed up my thighs and I moaned.

I needed to see all of her. I kissed down her ribcage to her stomach, and then opened her jeans while inhaling the vague scent of vanilla and amber from her skin. She arched up to help me when I tugged the jeans off over that perfect ass which had first caught my attention, and I caught a brief glimpse of hot pink cotton thong underwear before I hooked them with my thumbs and they were gone too.

The only thing she still wore was the neoprene sleeve on the end of her leg, and I could feel her go still as I reached for it. I looked up to find her watching me, so I smiled. "Does it roll off, or pull off?"

She reached down and began to roll it, but I pushed her hands away and continued what she'd begun. The skin beneath the sleeve was red from the constriction, and there was a line where the seam had pressed. I traced the line with gentle fingers. "Does this hurt?"

She shook her head, and I met her eyes. They were wary, and she looked so vulnerable. I ran my hands down her thigh, over her knee, and across the smooth scar at the end of her leg. She shuddered, and I kissed her as I indulged in my desire to explore every ... damn ... inch.

[50]

SHANE

"I have a dirty mind, and right now you're running through it naked." – Gabriel Eze

---

Gabriel's hands on my body were strong and careful and soothing and the most sensuous thing I'd ever felt. It had been years since anyone had touched me with more than clinical care, and I gave in to the indulgence of just being felt.

His mouth followed his hands, and then my own hands explored every plane of his spectacular body, which was strong, capable, and totally responsive to stimulus. I smiled to myself as he arched toward me in a wordless plea for *more* – more touching, more pressure, more kisses. I felt powerful and desirable with him, and stimulation of his body could easily become my specialty.

He finally groaned my name to stop me. He pulled a condom from the nightstand and rolled it on before pulling me on top of him to ease himself inside me. We fit together perfectly, and I ground myself against him until every nerve ending caught fire and I shattered into several thousand points of heat.

Afterwards, we rolled to face each other, and he tucked my head onto his arm and wrapped my leg over his hip. He smoothed the hair back from my cheek and kissed my fingertips when I touched his face.

"Somewhere along the way I fell in love with you," he said in the quiet voice he used to draw people in. My breath caught, and I let the words settle near my heart, testing them against my own reserve.

"I'm not sure I know what that feels like," I whispered.

He smiled as he traced my eyebrow and then my cheekbone with his fingertips. "It might be different for other people, but for me, it feels like a superpower."

My answering smile allowed his words to nestle in and make themselves comfortable. "And what does this superpower give you?"

"Well, right now I feel like I could fly, maybe take on a few villains and single-handedly battle them into submission. I also feel fairly combustible, which either makes me useful or dangerous, I haven't decided which."

He was grinning, and it made my heart thump wildly.

"Huh. I think loving you makes me identify with Anne Bonny a little bit."

His grin got even wider. "Really? How so?"

"When she met Jack, he was like a mirror for her true self – the person she hadn't dared to reveal until he stood next to her, supporting her, encouraging her, loving her. Their partnership made each of them much stronger than when they'd been alone."

I rolled back on top of him and kissed him deeply. "Also for the record, I have a peg leg, so there's that."

His laughter was so loud that Oscar came barreling into the room to save us, and we had to dive under the covers to save ourselves from his enthusiastic kisses.

And as I buried my face in his chest and he protected me from the Oscar beast, I let my own unspoken feelings find the place where his words had nestled in my heart, and I thought I could love this man for a long, long time.

EPILOGUE
GABRIEL

"Best friends don't care if your house is clean – they care if you have wine." – Sandra Greene

---

The security guard in the lobby of the condo building greeted Shane by name.

"I understand congratulations are in order, Miss Hane," the guard said. "Welcome to Cipher Security."

"Thank you," she said graciously. The fact that she didn't say his name was my cue.

I stuck my hand out to introduce myself, thereby completing the unspoken task of the couple – when one person doesn't remember a name, it's the other one's job to get it. "I don't know that we've met yet. I'm Gabriel Eze."

A compact man of Asian descent somewhere in his mid-thirties, the guard smiled in a way that told me he was very well-versed in the game. "Good to meet you, Gabriel. I'm Han, and yes, I shoot first."

I started in surprise, and Shane burst out laughing. "I told you that was his defining moment," she said to me. Then she turned back to Han. "Han Solo was the romantic lead of the original trilogy, right?"

The faint smile on Han's face was likely the equivalent of a full-blown grin on anyone else. "His journey was the greatest, so yes, I'd have to agree. Go on up," he said as he keyed the elevator and pushed the button for the fourth floor. "The Greenes are expecting you."

When the elevator door closed, Shane turned, flung her arms around my neck, and gave me the kind of kiss that's likely illegal in ten states. "Wow," I gasped, when she stepped back as the elevator doors opened. Shane smirked as she stepped out into the hall.

"Just in case you were nervous about tonight," she said mischievously.

I grabbed her hand and brought it to my lips, murmuring, "I wasn't, until I realized I'll be walking into the Hacker's flat with a raging hard-on. Thanks for that." I adjusted myself uncomfortably.

Shane turned her twinkling gaze to me. "It was my pleasure."

"It will be," I growled, wishing I could turn us right around and go back home. I hadn't quite convinced Shane to move in and make my apartment *our place* yet, but she'd spent every night of the past month there, and most of her clothes and all of her prosthetics had migrated upstairs. I had insisted on a fashion show of every leg, with a demonstration of all the gadgets, functions, and hidden caches in each, and was absurdly pleased to discover her penchant for leglessness at home. Even better was her habit of stripping down to panties and a t-shirt upon entry into the flat, and her predilection for working in bed.

Tonight, for the first time since I'd known her, Shane was wearing a skirt. It happened to be of the pencil variety that caressed every delectable curve and ended just above her knees. She had paired it with a simple linen t-shirt and red silk strappy shoes with three-inch heels. It had been with considerable effort that I dragged my gaze up to meet hers when she had emerged from the bedroom.

My lust must have been written on my face, because the nervous expression on hers had relaxed into a genuine smile. "I have to practice walking in these."

"You look amazing, but I think you should lose the clothes and keep the shoes – for practice, you know." I gave her my most suggestive leer, and she laughed.

Our invitation to Alex and Sandra Greene's place was a benchmark in our relationship for a couple of reasons. One, my gorgeous girlfriend was wearing a skirt in public, and she was absolutely rocking it. Two, the company for which we both worked had not only acknowledged our relationship but seemed to be embracing it. They'd given us several other cases on which to work together, and our continued successes were proof positive that we were an excellent fit.

I mentally smirked at the wordplay that descended into smut in my head. The male brain was terribly predictable that way.

I put my hand on the Greenes' front door and paused to look Shane in the eyes. "Are you sure I can't talk you into a night at home with a movie, a big dog, and a naked tickle fight?"

"Every instinct I have is screaming at me to run," she said. "There are women in there who apparently want to be friends with me, and I'm not even wearing my usual armor of boots and black clothes to face them. I put on a *skirt*, for Pete's sake!"

"Who is Pete, and when can I thank him for the skirt?" I said with a grin.

Rather than pinch me, which I was sure I deserved on principle, my lovely lady gave me the softest, sweetest kiss.

"Later," she whispered to my mouth, "when you take it off me."

And with that provocative statement, which guaranteed a tent in my trousers for the rest of the evening, the most fascinating woman in the world bit my lip, gave me a saucy grin, and walked through the door like she belonged there.

The End

ACKNOWLEDGMENTS

The year I published my first book, a time travel fantasy novel called *Marking Time*, I stumbled across a romantic comedy with an odd cover featuring a young woman holding a heart in front of her face. It was free that weekend, so I downloaded and inhaled it in a day. I laughed so often while I read that delightfully smart romance with the wonderfully ridiculous title, *Neanderthal Seeks Human*, that I tweeted my review to thank the author for writing it. She answered my tweet, and the official version is that I stalked her until we became friends. But that's creepy and not really true. I'm not entirely sure why Penny chose me, but I chose her because she's a bucket-filler of the highest order. Every time I see her, every exchange of messages, and every phone call with my friend leaves me feeling replenished, as though the kinetic energy of words between us recharges my brain, my heart, my sense of humor, and my creativity.

It's not a surprise, then, that her books do the same thing.

Penny's generosity is unparalleled, as evidenced by this Smarty-pants Romance adventure we're on. She has allowed me and several other authors the opportunity to write books in the worlds she created, and to let our characters interact with the people in her stories we've come to love. It is absurdly pleasurable to think like Dan the security man, and to be outrageous like Sandra, who makes men cry. My favorite voice to write in *Code of Conduct* was Alex, because his intellect and his love for his wife are as epic as his bafflement about common human interactions.

Penny's words, characters, and generosity inspired me to step outside my comfort zone of historical mystery, fantasy, paranormal, and time travel stories, and into a realm filled with so many incredible, funny, smart, fabulous readers. It is an honor to write in Penny's Knitting in the City world, it is a privilege to give voice to her characters, and it is the gift of a lifetime to be trusted to tell stories for the readers of her books.

Thank you, Penny Reid. You are extraordinary.

This book could not have happened without the stories and wisdom of my dear friend, Casey Pieretti, the care and precision of my exceptional editor, Angela Houle, and the wisdom and insight of the lovely Rose Dreadnaught. Nicole McCurdy, Rebecca Kimmel, and the ladies of Smartypants Romance, your encouragement and enthusiasm got me past the hard parts, and to my family – you are the laughter, the love, and the joy in my soul.

ABOUT THE AUTHOR

April White is the author of The Immortal Descendants series, which blends history, time travel, fantasy, and romance into a five-book adventure. Book one, *Marking Time*, is the 2016 Library Journal ebook award winner with more than a thousand five-star reviews on Amazon, and is currently free for e-readers on all platforms.

In *Marking Time*, Seventeen-year-old tagger Saira Elian can handle anything … a mother who mysteriously disappears, a stranger who stalks her around London, and even the noble English grandmother who kicked Saira and her mother out of the family. But when an old graffiti tag in a Tube station transports Saira to the nineteenth century and she comes face-to-face with Jack the Ripper, she realizes she needs help after all.

For more information about April's books, recommendations for her favorite reads, and to sign up for her monthly newsletter and her Facebook reader group, Kick-ass Heroines, go to https://aprilwhitebooks.com

* * *

Website: https://www.aprilwhitebooks.com/
Facebook: https://www.facebook.com/AprilWhiteBooks/
Goodreads:
https://www.goodreads.com/author/show/6570694.April_White
Twitter: @ahwhite
Instagram: @aprilwhitebooks

Find Smartypants Romance online:

Website: www.smartypantsromance.com

Facebook: www.facebook.com/smartypantsromance/

Goodreads: www.goodreads.com/smartypantsromance

Twitter: @smartypantsrom

Instagram: @smartypantsromance

Made in the USA
Columbia, SC
13 December 2021

51237074R00221